Praise for Chris Humphreys

'Wonderful characters and great world-building, in Humphreys' special brand of addictive storytelling'
Diana Gabaldon, author of the award-winning *Outlander* series

'Humphreys' plot, prose, and characters give this book a sense of quality and gravity without skimping on fun and readability' *Grimdark Magazine*

'Insanely gripping and thoroughly unusual'
Morning Star

'An intriguing premise . . . an intricate, fast-paced story . . . Humphreys packs gods, deicide, warring tribes and some impressive world-building into just over 300 pages' *Guardian*

'A brilliant epic fantasy debut from a master storyteller' Sebastien de Castell

'Chris Humphreys skilfully weaves together several different storylines without any feeling like they're rushed over and still manages to keep the momentum of the plot going throughout the book. It's an intriguing new look at immortality in a fantasy novel, and I highly recommend it' *The Book Bundle*

'Cleverly written, at times very funny, I thoroughly enjoyed this new book' *Rambling Mads*

By Chris Humphreys from Gollancz:

IMMORTAL'S BLOOD

Smoke in the Glass
The Coming of the Dark
The Wars of Gods and Men

THE WARS OF GODS AND MEN

Chris Humphreys

This edition first published in Great Britain in 2023

First published in Great Britain in 2022 by Gollancz
an imprint of The Orion Publishing Group Ltd
Carmelite House, 50 Victoria Embankment
London EC4Y 0DZ

An Hachette UK Company

1 3 5 7 9 10 8 6 4 2

A CIP catalogue record for this book
is available from the British Library.

ISBN (Mass Market Paperback) 978 1 473 22610 4
ISBN (eBook) 978 1 473 22611 1
ISBN (Audio Download) 978 1 473 22846 7

Typeset by Deltatype Ltd, Birkenhead, Merseyside

Printed in Great Britain by Clays Ltd, Elcograf S.p.A.

www.gollancz.co.uk

To Jim Skinner
Who helps me tell the shadow from the light

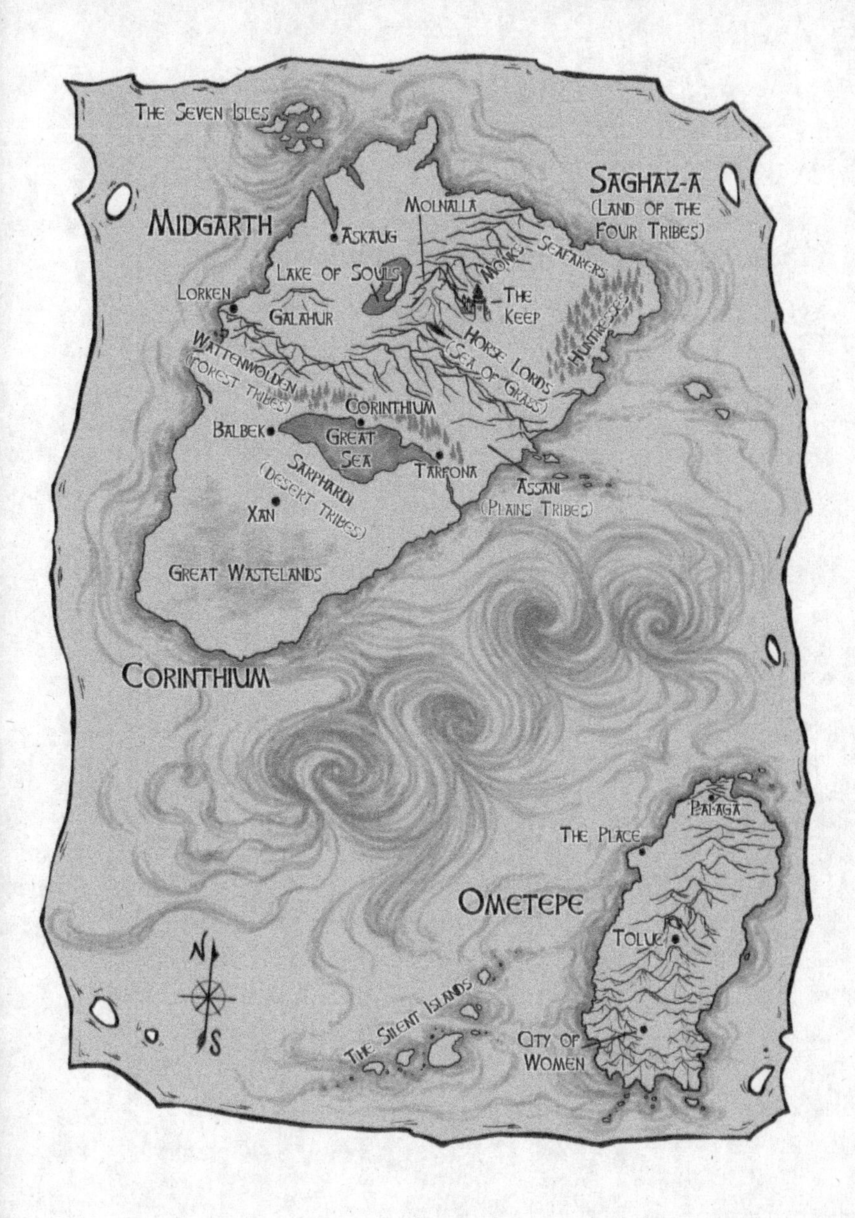

The Seven Isles
Midgarth
Saghaz-a
(Land of the Four Tribes)
Askaug
Molnalla
Monks
Seafarers
Lake of Souls
Lorken
Galahur
The Keep
Huntresses
Horse Lords
(Sea of Grass)
Wattenwolden
(Forest Tribes)
Corinthium
Balbek
Great Sea
Tarfona
Sarphardi
(Desert Tribes)
Assani
(Plains Tribes)
Xan
Great Wastelands
Corinthium
Pai-aga
The Place
Ometepe
Toluc
The Silent Islands
City of Women
N
S

Dramatis Personae

Corinthium:
Ferros, also known as Arcturien of the Wattenwolden
Lara
Roxanna
Makron
Zok, doorman
Severos, 'King' of Asprodon
Graco, drug dealer
Andronikos, legendary hero, mortal
Cosara, young lover
Fruka, Lara's mother
Brankos, Lara's father
Aisha, Lara's sister
Arak, caravan guide
Gan, Timian monk
Havlos, Balbek exile
Speros, City Guard Captain

Saghaz-a (Land of the Four Tribes):
Anazat, High Monk
Gistrane, Huntress
Korshak, Horse Lord
Karania, leader of the Huntresses

Baromolak, King of the Horse Lords
Framilor, captain of the Seafarers
Toparak, monk

Ometepe:
Intitepe
Sekantor the Savage, pirat
Besema
Sayel, Besema's lover
Toman, Intitepe's officer

Midgarth:
Luck
Atisha
Their children:
- Bjorn
- Freya

The dead gods:
- Freya
- Hovard
- Bjorn Swift-Sword
- Stromvar, Dragon Lord

Warkan, wolfhound
Marla
Gytta, Luck's dead wife
Ulrich the smith
Tiny Elric, Ulrich's son
Peki Asarko
Petr the Red
Brena

Wattenwolden:
Malvolen, High Chief

Domen, Wattenwolden warrior
Haldan, also known as Stauren of the Wattenwolden

Sirene
Melgayne

Poum

I am Sirene.

A name that will do, in this place where now we meet, which is no place. In a form that you can hear, which is no form. Sirene is the name I am known by in the world of four lands you set me to watch. There, I am the distillation of a plant, a way of seeing you gave to the world. Here I am thought, moving through your minds.

You wish to know what have been the results of your three gifts.

The first, immortality, an inheritance in the blood, passed on randomly to a few, differently in three of those lands.

The second, the ability for those immortals to possess another entity.

Finally, to another people, a different kind of gift: Hope. Hope in the prophecy of the One, come to save them all.

I can tell you much of it – but not everything. For I may only see each world when people in it use me, travelling within the smoke in the glass. I cannot tell you what transpires with those who do not travel, only what the traveller observes or learns. Yet enough do use me and so I can report most of what happens, what has happened, what may yet happen.

It has been nearly sixteen of their years since last you summoned me.

The largest of their lands is an empire and a city both known as Corinthium, though renamed by its conquerors *Saghaz-a-akana* – 'The Little Land of Joy'. Most who live there call it rather 'The Land of Little Joy' because many of their former pleasures are gone, replaced by a formal, restrictive worship of the One.

Of all the lands, I see that one most easily, for many there travel with Sirene. One man is the clearest, the monk known as Anazat, leader of the conquering Four Tribes of Saghaz-a. It was Anazat who travelled with me most to begin with, who used me and his belief in the One to change the whole world utterly. With a world so vast, so different in all its parts, its problems are vast as well and this requires Anazat to move constantly between lands. So he has left two immortals in charge of what was Corinthium, to rule it for him and for the One. Makron is one. He lets me see some things there, for he uses Sirene to communicate if not to travel, and so lets me in. His wife, the immortal Roxanna, does not use me. I glimpse her through him. This allows me to see their great ambition: to rule separate from Anazat. To restore, perhaps, the control of the Corinthian Immortals. *Their* control at least.

Their opportunity is fast approaching. For Anazat will be distracted by what has transpired in those other two realms – Midgarth and Ometepe.

In the north, since the battle known as 'The Coming of the Dark', in which the majority of the immortals there, whom they named gods, were killed, a man named Peki Asarko has ruled on behalf of Anazat. A sexually deviant tyrant, he has subdued most of the realm in the name of the One, putting down with great cruelty any brief flarings of rebellion. He is one of my most devoted followers and I see his desires clearly: to rule Midgarth alone and throw off any restraints of the sort Anazat puts upon him.

His problem, and his master's too, lies in the far west, on the island of Ometepe. For the only immortal male there, Intitepe, is finally poised to crush the revolution that exploded when he left his lands for the new world he'd discovered. When he does, he will want to return to Midgarth and claim what he was promised: its throne. He does not follow me but he has advisers from the Four Tribes who do, the monks. And they show me a god who does not think to stop at Midgarth.

For Intitepe, you will remember, is the father of the One. And though at first he tried to kill the child – fearing an ancient prophecy that, just as he killed his own father, so his son would kill him – he has now come to believe something quite different: that since the One is neither son nor daughter but both, so father and child are destined to jointly rule the whole world.

The whole world. From Toluc, the volcano that is his brother god in Ometepe, across the waters to Midgarth, and beyond that through the Lands of the Four Tribes, Saghaz-a. Finally to what was the empire of Corinthium itself. He has only seen that in visions told him by his advisers, those monks sent by Anazat. He sees it as his place of destiny. Where he will be emperor of … everything.

As you have realised, there is an element missing. Something on which everything else depends. Someone.

The One.

The child who is neither man nor woman but both. The child who is now nearly sixteen of their years old.

Poum.

If the child lives. For *they* – I have come to think of Poum in the plural – disappeared fifteen years ago. Vanished into the high mountains between Midgarth and Saghaz-a after that same Coming of the Dark. Only Peki Asarko knows in which direction they headed and he has told no one, not even Anazat, fearing that if the One was brought back and established as the God of All Worlds, his own power would end. Anazat has organised searches all over the world and has found not a trace.

The god known as Luck, and the child's mother, Atisha, have kept the child hidden all this time.

It is strange. Of all who ever journeyed with me, the one that roved the furthest, who revelled the deepest, was this same Luck of Midgarth. I believed that he was bound to me for ever in chains he could never break. But he has not journeyed with me once these fifteen years. He has a will as strong as anyone I have ever encountered, across the galaxies and throughout time.

Yet this I know – he plans to return to me one day. For just before he betrayed Anazat and vanished with the child, he asked for, and was given, not a supply of the distilled drug but the plant itself.

Somewhere at the top of the world, Luck is creating his own store of me.

I know you do not fear. Why would you, when you have lived so long, have the power to change worlds almost on a thought? Yet I will tell you – this Luck has come closer than anyone you have ever thought of to being able to *see* you. For he asked me, when last he travelled with me, something I'd never been asked before.

He asked me *why* I am.

I am Sirene. I do not lie, or evade questions. So I told him. Told him that I was the watcher. Told him that I watched for you. Told him of the gifts you gave to the world, two of which he had received – immortality, and the power to possess.

Then I answered his question. His *why*. Told him that you gave each of the peoples those gifts to see what they would do with them.

He was not pleased to hear that he was a part of what he called 'an experiment'.

Still, you are the only *true* immortals, are you not? He cannot threaten you.

However, this I believe – that if he has survived, he has been living with the answer to all mankind's hopes, the source of all its worship, and so many of its dreams.

He has been living with, and shaping the mind of, the One.

We cannot know what powers the One will have until Luck allows me to see. Until he travels with me again. And next time, I believe he will not travel alone.

I am Sirene. I have told all I know. Now I will return to learn the rest. When next we meet, I shall tell you more.

I
Hope of the World

'Where are they?'

Atisha turned to the doorway. To the angry man standing in it. 'They, Luck? Which *they* do you seek? Bjorn and Freya? They are picking daisies in the meadow.'

'Not them.'

'Oh, the sheep? Or do you mean the goats? You will find the one in that same meadow, competing for flowers. The goats are on the hillside.'

'Atisha, you know who I mean.' Luck marched into the centre of the hut. 'Where are *they*?'

'Oh, is it Poum you are referring to in that furious voice?' She put down the carrot and the knife she was using to chop it. 'No wonder I was confused. For Poum is no longer "they". Poum is "he".'

'What? Since when? Last week he was they!'

'And the week before, she.' Atisha wiped her hands on her smock, and came and stood before him. 'You have to accept that Poum is still discovering ... who he is.'

'It is what else they – *he* – is discovering that worries me.' He gestured to the door. 'Call him, wife. He will come for you, when he will not for me.'

'He certainly won't now he's heard the tone in which you call.'

She reached and pulled a wood shaving from his beard. 'You have been shouting for him with all that fury for a while now.'

'You heard?'

'Husband, they heard you over the mountains in Midgarth.'

Luck dropped heavily onto a stool by the table. Pushed one hand through his forelock, leaving more traces of wood there. 'I waited for him in the woodshed for an hour. Today was his carpentry lesson.'

'I thought it was the writing of *tolanpa-sen* that you taught him today?'

'That was this morning. Carpentry this afternoon.'

'All day at his studies? With the last of the summer sun on the land?' She glanced outside. 'He should be frolicking with his brother and sister and the sheep in the meadow.'

'They are children. It is different.'

'He – *they* – are different.' Atisha sat on the next stool. 'He has but fifteen summers. It is a life still caught between the child and the adult. And Poum is … such a special child. Turning into such a special adult.' She took Luck's hand, rubbed at the calluses on his palm for a moment, then spoke again. 'Husband, it is time to tell him.'

He frowned at her. 'Tell him what?'

'Everything. Everything you have not already told him.'

'They are not ready for that!' He pulled his hand from hers, looked away. 'Poum is disobedient, moody, quick to anger, holds a grudge. Can be cruel, mischievous—'

'Like every other near-sixteen-year-old you ever knew. Like you were then, I suspect.'

'I can't remember. That was …' He looked above her head, thinking. 'Four hundred and one years ago.' His eyes narrowed. 'No, I *can* remember. Because I killed a man when I was fifteen. For the first time. In my first battle.' He looked at her. 'Can you see Poum killing a man?'

'No. And I pray he never has to. For it is a horrible thing.'

'Atisha, you say he is like every other fifteen-year-old. But he is not. *They* are not. For no other fifteen-year-old is called "the One", and worshipped throughout the world.'

'The One? Ha!' she exclaimed. 'The One is just a title. A prophecy dreamed by men to serve their purposes.' She shook her head. 'My Poum is ... an excuse. A way to rule, to control. Poum isn't important to the world. Only the idea of him is.' She shuddered. 'You saw the terrible things done in the name of the One. You lost many whom you loved because of it. And you know, because you visited it five years ago, that the world has become even more terrible during our absence.'

'And worse since, no doubt.' Luck shuddered, as he remembered that trip he'd felt he had to take five years before. Midgarth in the hands of that perverted madman Peki Asarko. A land of terror, where the few remaining immortals were hunted down and killed, and mortals were slaves to whims of the tyrant. He'd learned all this when he'd managed to track down one of the few surviving gods, Petr the Red, he and a few others still trying to fight, living the squalid life of outlaws in caves. Petr had also told him what little he'd heard of the world beyond Midgarth. The Empire of Corinthium that was now the Empire of the One, governed by monks every bit as cruel as Peki Asarko. By one especially, Luck's former gaoler, Anazat. The black-eyed monk who had introduced Luck to Sirene – and who would never cease looking for the child that Luck had stolen, that his brother and sister gods had died for. Yet they had died for a small hope – and Luck would not betray their sacrifice by not believing in that hope still.

He took Atisha's hand now, to try to chase away the darkness that had come into her eyes. 'My love,' he said softly, 'ideas are what change the world. And think, if the idea of Poum brought the darkness, might not the actual Poum bring the light?'

'Oh, only that? He brought the dark and now he must bring back the light?' She laughed. 'And you wonder why he is moody!'

Luck gripped her tighter. 'You haven't told him?'

'Only as much as we agreed. Of the darkness across the mountains. Of his birth across the sea in Ometepe, where his father tried to kill him. Of the prophecy of the One, though not that he is it. But the omission is starting to feel more and more like lying.' She placed her other hand on top of Luck's, squeezed it, sought his eyes. 'Now we must tell him the rest. We must!'

Luck stared at her for a long moment, then nodded. 'You are right,' he said. 'Also, I think that is why I have been so angry with … them. Because I knew that we must tell them everything.'

'Really?' She grinned. 'Is that why you have been angry? Or is it … moody?'

'You knew?'

'Husband, your moods are like the words you teach from the books you stole. Easy to read.'

He smiled back, then sighed. 'But when we tell him, everything will change.' He looked to the open door, stared out at the autumn sunshine. 'I know it has not been easy here all this time. Those first years were hard, and to live in a land where winter lasts so long?' He broke off, turned back. 'But I have loved this life we have made. The children we have made.' He sighed, squeezed. 'I have never been so happy.'

'You have, my love,' she replied. 'With Gytta.'

He looked at her a long moment. 'Yes,' he said, 'with Gytta, for a short time, it is true.'

She lifted her hands, took his face in them. 'I do not mind, husband. We both have loved, been loved, before. Those we loved … left. But love, its memory, lasts for ever.' She leaned forward and kissed him, then sat back, looked where he'd looked, out the door. 'Love is one of the things that Poum must discover alone. Another of the reasons we must tell him the rest.'

'Where to begin? With immortality? With possession? He does not know that I am immortal. We do not know whether he is. It is rare, and so would be unlikely. Yet his father is. And he – they – are so different.' He ran his hand over his head, leaving more wood shavings there. 'But how to begin to tell? Where do we start?'

'Do you remember, love,' Atisha said, leaning forward and picking more chips from his red-brown locks, 'when you met Sirene on your last journey with her, the question you asked?'

Sirene. At the mention of her name, Luck looked across the room. The cuttings he'd brought across the mountain he'd grown into a plant, distilled its essence, then placed it into a pot; sealed that, then locked it away in the wooden chest he'd fashioned, asking Atisha to hide the key from him. Yet through clay and wood she still called to him. Every day, for fifteen years – hearing, yearning, refusing the call. The hunger as strong now as it had ever been. 'Remind me,' he replied, not looking at her, his voice suddenly thick, all other thoughts lost in desire.

'You asked her … not *who* she was, but *why* she was.' She leaned into his vision, brought his eyes back to hers. 'Now it is time to give Poum the answer to that same question. The one they have been asking all their life.' She smiled. '*Why* they are.'

Fingertips found the tiny ledges, toes the little cracks. With a final burst of lung power, muscle power, Poum surged up the last of the cliff face, powered over the lip, flopped onto the ledge. Only then, and for the first time in a while, did they look down. Gasped.

Poum had never climbed this peak. It had been hard enough

on its lower slopes, which were steep and rubble-strewn. It looked impossible from the base of the final cliff – which did not look any more feasible from its top. 'Did it!' they whooped, arms thrust high in triumph. Lowering them, Poum took in the view.

It was spectacular. The homestead was far below and to the left, its every detail clear in the cool, late afternoon, late summer mountain air. The turf roof, with its solitary sheep – an aggressive older male known as Bull. It attacked any other ram, many ewes and any human it caught on open ground with no provocation and no warning. It was not to be trusted with the rest of the flock grazing in the meadow above the steading. Poum suspected that before long Bull would mostly be appearing to them in the form of sausages.

Between the streams that threaded the valley were the fields where the last of the oat was waiting to be cropped, and the water meadows where the sheep grazed. Twenty of them, roaming free, and, roaming among them, Bjorn and Freya. The boy was nine years old, the girl seven. His siblings had been named for relatives of Luck, great warriors who had died in battle when Poum had less than a year. A battle that, as Luck never failed to add when he talked of it, had been fought to save Poum's life. Though he was always vague as to why.

Poum glowered, turned away. They had never asked anyone to die for them. *Him*, Poum thought, I am him this week, though that was more to annoy his parents than anything else. Mostly, Poum accepted that he and she were *they*. That the otherness at the core of them, so different from Bjorn and Freya and, yes, Luck and Atisha, and Bull, and any of the beasts, made them *them*. But of the three languages he spoke – Midgarth's, Ometepe's, even *tolanpa-sen*, the 'one word' of the Land of the Four Tribes – none of them produced a word that could sum *them* up. *He* would just have to accept that.

The Land of the Four Tribes. To glimpse it was the reason for climbing this peak, for its better view. Turning away from the steading, facing the opposite way, Poum now looked east.

While there were two lines of mountains between their farm and Midgarth, only one separated it from Saghaz-a. Luck had told him that it was from the west that killers might come for them, sent from his homeland; which was one reason, apart from its fertile siting, that he and Atisha had chosen this place to settle – to be further from that danger. It was less likely any would come from the east.

But the east was what Poum dreamed of. As soon as they had heard of Horse Lords, Seafarers and Huntresses, Poum had wanted to be one of them. Since they were different anyway, why be the same as the peoples their parents came from? But to sail the seas looking for fights and booty? To ride mighty steeds across the Sea of Grass seeking honour in battle? To hunt wild beasts by bow in the vast dark forests? Luck had made all of them out to be savages. But his own people of Midgarth did not sound so very different in their desires, and neither did the men and women of Ometepe.

The only tribe he wanted nothing to do with were the monks. To spend your life in prayer for a saviour called 'The One'? Though they were also meant to be extraordinary fighters, it still did not sound like the life of adventure that Poum craved.

And speaking of adventure ...

There was another reason they'd climbed up there. The week before, from the next peak over, and with their keen sight, they'd spotted an eagle's nest, and they wanted to confirm that what they'd discovered by chance one week before was true.

That they could dissolve into an animal.

It had happened like this. Once more avoiding Luck and his shouting – the man was obsessed with teaching his boring subjects, going on and on and on – Poum had fled to the waterfall.

It was a long way for Luck to limp in pursuit and the tumbling water drowned out his father's shouts. Ufda had come along, grandaughter of the first sheepdog that had accompanied them over the mountains. There was something strange about the dog – Luck said all the dogs were a little strange as their father was also their brother and that didn't make for sense. Luck had found wild sheep he'd been able to breed with the ones he'd brought, but there were no wild dogs. So confused Ufda would chase things only she could see, barking furiously at nothing. She was also on heat again, which made her doubly mad.

She'd behaved like that at the falls. And Poum was so bored, and the dog so excited by her nothing, that Poum called her over. 'What is it that you see, Ufda?' they'd said. Taking the hound by her head, they stared into her eyes, 'Show me!' they'd cried. 'Show me!'

Which was when it happened. Their body – *they* – were gone. Except they weren't. They were *her* – seeing through the dog's eyes, sniffing the world through her snout. They were Poum still ... but they were also Ufda. They could control – run down there, pick up that stick, bark at the waterfall. They'd discovered though that it felt better to let the dog do all that for herself. To feel the animal yield to her desires. To run, jump ... *howl* as her.

Until Ufda went to leap into the pond beneath the waterfall. Poum knew how freezing it was. Poum hated swimming. So Poum decided to leave Ufda – and discovered that it was as easy going out as going in. But it had also been too late and they'd fallen into the pond anyway.

They'd been right. It had been freezing. But the cold faded fast in the sunny patch they'd found – while the wonder about it, and the desire to try it again, only grew.

They hadn't, not once during the whole week since. They had too many questions about it. Was it only dogs they could become? It seemed limiting. They thought of trying Bull the ram. But what if you became trapped in a beast? And Bull had his rendezvous with the butcher's block. Could Poum die, even as the beast died?

They'd thought it through carefully. If they were going to be stuck in any animal it had to be something magnificent. Something with opportunities.

Something that could fly.

That was why, a week later, Poum was peering along the clifftop. No, they couldn't see the nest from here. But it was there, built into a hollow in the crags. They could hear the high, sharp-pitched shrieks of eagle-kind. When they'd observed it the week before, they'd seen the mother and two huge chicks, near full grown. They'd even observed her teaching her offspring to fly. From the cries there was another lesson going on now. I should be at my lesson learning how to build a chair, Poum thought, grinning as they rose. This is better. To learn how to fly?

But would it work again? Was a bird even possible to … possess? Possess. That would be the word. What if they leaped over the crag they were stealthily approaching, looked in the eagle's eyes – and nothing happened except the beast wanting to peck out theirs?

Poum reached and drew out their knife. The sounds ahead had changed; the eagle was now feeding its young. If it was the same as with Ufda, he would only need a moment.

Thrusting the knife out, Poum took a deep breath – and leaped over the crag.

The mother eagle saw them on the instant. Rising from the nest, wings spread wide over its two fledglings, she shrieked, lunged, black eyes fixed on Poum's …

Gone. In the gap between heartbeats. Possessed.

There was a moment, far more powerful than the one Poum

had felt with the dog, when the eagle tried to eject them. A moment when they felt … between. Half bird, half human. Yet though they had almost never done it, they knew what to do. It was like … like spreading out inside an old shirt, too small for them now, stretching their body to fit it all. Poum pushed … and the seams between them did not split.

Eagle and mortal were one.

To the shrieks of her offspring who did not understand why their meal had so suddenly ceased, the eagle flapped hard, rose straight up from the nest, and dived over the cliff edge. Poum discovered that they did not need to fly – the bird did that. Flapped its wings when it needed to, spread them to catch the warmer air rising from the heated rocks below, rising on that, tilting its body to change direction, at Poum's command. The methods were hers, the path through the sky theirs.

The eyes! Poum's were sharp but the eagle's? Extraordinary. Swooping towards the steading, they could make out its every detail. Bull, on the turf roof, aware of the bird of prey descending, eyes narrowing in challenge. The daisy crowns on Bjorn and Freya's heads, each flower distinct as they rose, pointed, cried out; those cries drawing Atisha fast from the hut, to see that the children were well, then follow the arms that pointed at the gliding bird. Ufda barking wildly, trained to scare off carrion birds who would sometimes try to kill the newborn lambs. Lastly Luck, stepping from the woodshed, where Poum was meant to be studying, a hand raised to shelter his eyes from the glare.

Waggling her wings as if waving hands, the bird soared over them all, on, up, climbing high. The world opened, they were above all the peaks now, could see east towards the range that gazed down on Saghaz-a. Tempted to fly there, to begin to explore that world they yearned to see. But in a glimpse the other way, towards Midgarth, they saw something glimmer.

Sunlight on water. There was a huge lake in that next valley. Every spring the whole family would make an expedition there, to camp for a few weeks on its shore, and fish for what Luck called, in the Midgarth tongue, the sorghan. To eat fresh flesh after the deprivations of one winter and to catch many more to smoke or salt for the next one. It was fun too, for the sorghan ran big, as big as the length of an arm, and were mighty fighters on the hook. Luck and Poum competed each year for who would catch most. Poum had won the last two years.

Poum liked fish, the cleanness of them, better than any meat with its ruddy taste. Yet they realised that the eagle liked it even more. Sorghan was its diet. Also it was hungry. Its chicks were hungry.

Letting the eagle take them, Poum passed over the crag, rose on its heat, glided again. Her sharp eyes looked in the water, saw the shapes at the surface, feeding on insects. Folding her wings, she dived.

Poum was good at taking fish. The eagle was brilliant. At the very last moment, just as she was about to crash into the lake, she shot her wings out, slowing in an instant. So it was her outstretched talons that hit the water and sank deep into a sorghan's back. Another surge, like leaping off a branch, and the eagle rose. The fish twisted and jerked, and the eagle shot its head down, driving its beak into the sorghan's head. It ceased moving, and the eagle turned back, climbing more slowly with the weight she carried towards the crags, depositing it on a rock shelf.

Something moved beyond the lake. There were wolves, bears, a type of ox sometimes too. But the glance showed something moving differently than any beast.

On two legs.

Poum had let the eagle carry them, revelling in its flying, its killing skills. But now they exerted their will. The eagle was reluctant, wanted to take the sorghan back to the nest, feed her young. Poum was in command though, and took off from the crag, gliding lower, closer.

Even without the eagle's sight, Poum would have been able to tell that it was a man walking along the western edge of the lake. He wore a wide-brimmed hat to keep off the sun, had a bow slung across his back, a quiver of arrows at one hip and a short sword at the other. At his heels trotted a dog so big it made Ufda and her kin look like stunted puppies.

Poum turned the eagle and flew fast over the crag and down to the base of the cliff they'd climbed only a little time before. The going out was again as easy as the going in. The eagle looked dazed for a moment, then furious. Shrieking at them, she rose in the air, and flew up the rockface.

Poum didn't watch her reach the crest. They began to sprint hard for the steading, their heart beating fast from the exertion, and from the fear. Luck had warned about this possibility for years, warned that they must always be on their guard. For this.

For the day a killer came from Midgarth.

'You are certain, Poum? Certain that it was not a bear, walking on its hind legs?'

'With a bow on its back, and a dog at its heels? It was no bear.'

'And you saw this where, love?'

Poum turned to Atisha. 'From the top of Hawk's Crag,' they replied, adding the lie, 'I climbed up there to hunt for plovers' eggs.'

'After I told you not to? It's too dangerous a cl—'

'It does not matter,' Luck interrupted. 'For once their disobedience has aided us.' He turned back to Poum. 'You are also certain there was just one killer? It would seem odd for Peki Asarko to send but one.' He did not say what he truly thought – that killing was intended for just him and Atisha. That the world still awaited the return of the One. And a single experienced killer should be able to accomplish both tasks easily enough, for neither he nor Atisha truly had the skills to protect themselves.

But what they did have was surprise and a little time. 'You have done well,' Luck said, reaching out to lay a hand behind Poum's neck. 'But next time, obey your mother, yes?'

He said it with a grin, and Poum grinned back. 'Maybe,' they replied.

Luck sat back, thought. He may not have been gifted in the art of killing but he had accomplished it when he absolutely needed to. As he did now. And his one advantage was that he had this warning. And something else, of course. Though he was quite sure Peki Asarko would have warned his killer about Luck's ability to possess an animal, being warned and being able to deal with it were different. In the difference lay a little hope.

He turned again to Atisha. 'Are you still good with that bow?'

Atisha glanced at the weapon, slack-stringed and held on hooks on the roof beam. 'My eye isn't what it was. But I still manage to beat my child most of the time.'

Luck continued over Poum's snort. 'Then our plan is the same. Bring everyone to the cave. Both take your bows. The goats will warn you of any approach and they've cropped the slope clear of any bushes that might hide someone sneaking up.'

'It will be dark soon. But aztapi is full this night, and the slope will be bright with blue light.' Atisha rose from the table, pulled the bow from the beam, laid it on the table. 'Fetch yours,' she told Poum, 'and a full quiver of arrows apiece. I'll get us some provisions which I hope we will not need.' She looked at Luck. 'And where will you be, husband?'

'Out there. Setting an ambush.'

'I should be with you,' Poum blurted. 'Not hiding in a cave with my mother.'

'No, you shouldn't. I work better on my own.'

'Truly?'

It was extraordinary how much contempt a fifteen-year-old could get into a single word, accompanied by a glance at their father's shorter right leg, which gave him his limp, and one nickname in Midgarth, 'Luck the Lame'. Luck was tempted to tell them that he ran a lot faster as a bear or a wolf. But now was not the time for that revelation. It was strange that he had in fact been about to reveal all that, after his talk with Atisha that morning. Now he could only hope he would get the chance. 'Do what your mother tells you,' he growled.

Poum slunk away, muttering. Atisha kneeled before Luck, placing her hands on his knees. 'You go as something else?'

'Yes. Something. I am not sure what yet. I—' He broke off, then reached and took her face between both his hands. 'Don't worry about me.'

'I never have,' she smiled, 'and I always will.' She kissed one of the hands, then stood. 'But if you cannot kill this killer, if all does not go well, get back to us. Get to the cave.' She picked up her bow. 'Remember when I killed that puma, fifteen years ago on the way up here? A man is a much easier shot.'

Luck stood. 'My warrior,' he said.

'Never that,' she replied. 'But I will always fight to save the ones I love.' She stared a moment, then moved away, began to gather the things she would need. 'Now go,' she said, 'and kill the killer who comes, so I won't have to.'

Luck went outside, closed the door behind him. Stared towards Hawk's Crag, over which the killer must come. I should catch him up there, he thought. Tired from his climb. But what should I be? One of my dogs? No, Poum said the one who comes has a dog the size of a wolf and it would know another of its kind too soon. There are eagles on the cliffs behind me, though to climb up and get one would tire me.

Then he heard it. A scratching, a snuffling, right above his head. He stepped out of the entrance, turned, looked up.

Wide white eyes glared down at him, their centres square and black. Huge horns curled in a majestic sweep, up and around the forehead. Cloven hooves dug at the roof turf. A series of angry snorts came from the cavernous black nostrils. Only the height of the building stopped the ram from leaping down and battering his captor to pieces.

Bull, Luck thought and, for the first time in a while, smiled.

With Poum dispatched with Ufda to herd the sheep into their pen, and fetch their brother and sister, Luck had looked into the ram's eyes from the ground, and gone into him on the roof. First he forewarned Atisha, who came and leaned planks to the eaves so Luck-as-Bull could slide down the steep slope of wood. Then, with a single grunt, he set out at a run for the far peak.

Where as himself he would have struggled up the steep, scree- and rock-strewn slope to Hawk's Crag, Bull ran and leaped, Luck yielding to the beast's urges. The ram had been confined to the turf roof for several weeks, ever since his last assaults on the rest of the flock. Luck had reckoned that since the animal was to provide much of the meat for the coming winter, he might as well be fattened up before slaughter – less running, more chewing. But Bull was bred to charge and run. Freed from that limiting patch of grass, he did both those things and Luck let him. Partly for the need to be up at the top well before the killer. Partly for the joy of it. Sprinting through life was not something he could do as himself.

He took over when they were still one hundred paces beneath the crest. Poum had spotted the killer on the lake's western side, maybe an hour before; so no matter how swiftly they climbed they would not yet be near its summit. But Luck assumed that any killer Peki Asarko dispatched, one who had made it all the way from Midgarth and across two mountain ranges, would be skilled at what he did. He would have a hunter's ears and nose – and a wolf-dog's ears and nose besides. Luck wanted to search the ground well for the best place to launch his ambush, and do so quietly.

Just as there was one main trail on the steading's side of Hawk's Crag, so there was one on the other. They used it when they made their yearly trek to the lake to fish. It was easy enough to spot from the lakeshore, for it had been widened over the years by their trips and the hooves of the pack animals – mules bred from the horse and donkeys they'd arrived with – which they used to bring back the filleted and smoked catch.

If the killer had kept coming, he could be halfway up that trail by now.

There was a kind of passage between the valleys – a steep-walled ravine. On his side of that there was a flat and open shelf of ground, about fifty paces in depth, with a screen of scrubby bushes just before the slope. Thick enough for some concealment – but not enough to obstruct a sudden, swift charge.

Luck took the ram down the passage to the other side. There was a shallower shelf beyond, about half the size of the other. He went close to the far edge, stopped just short of the plunge. Light was strongly in his eyes, the sun about to drop behind the distant western mountains beyond which Midgarth lay. Yet a ram's sight was not his strongest power. In the mountains he would listen for rivals or possible mates. And he would scent them.

The wind was blowing from those western mountains. Spreading the black nostrils wide, Luck caught the faintest scent of dog fur and then heard the slipping of a foot on stone.

Carefully he backed away, turned and walked back down the passage. It had grown darker on the shelf even in the time he'd been gone, with the sun slipping below the western ramparts. Anyone approaching would not see him in the shadows. With the wind coming from behind them, they would not scent him either. But he would scent them.

Though the ram still wanted to run, Luck settled him down to wait. And while he waited he considered how it was that someone had finally found them.

When he'd slipped over to Midgarth that one time five years before, by a combination of stealth and possessing animals, he'd managed finally to track down some of the handful of Midgarthians who still fought against the conquest of their land. In the northern forests of Palur, there were still a few places that Peki Asarko's soldiers had not found – even though they were guided by Huntresses, that tribe of women from Saghaz-a, the finest trackers in the world. There Luck had met Petr the Red, a fellow immortal who had, by a series of amazing strokes of fortune, survived the Coming of the Dark, that last battle that had killed almost all the gods.

Petr, with a dwindling band of mortals, fought on. There were other groups scattered through the land. Some on the western islands, some in the forests of the south, some in deep caves on the slopes of the eastern mountains. A few immortals here and there with them. All living the hard life of the fugitive. Pursued, starved, brutally tortured and killed when caught or, if not, enslaved. By the time Luck found Petr, his band had less than one hundred men and women. Many had left, more left every month, gone back to live in villages that, if they had none of the joy that they had enjoyed before, at least had food.

'If they do not feast in them any more, at least they do not starve,' Petr had said to him, ladling a bowl of thin gruel made from roots and grasses and handing it to him.

Petr could not go. There was no life for a god in Midgarth any more. Someone would betray him, for the price of a piece of meat. And then his head would be taken.

'How often do I wish I had died on that great day when the Dark came,' he'd said. 'Perhaps I'd be feasting now with my brothers and sisters in the great hall of the gods instead of ...' He took another sip from his bowl, made a face, put it down. 'But you look well fed, Luck of Askaug. Tell me how that is.'

That was when I must have told him, Luck realised. Told him enough of how I lived, in love with Atisha, with our ... children. With fresh meat, fish, the beer I brewed, the cheese Atisha made. Told him enough of the *where* of it too – over the two mountains to a third, with a lake before it. And he must have told another who told another ... who told a Monk, or a Huntress, or a Horse Lord, to spare himself the pain of torture, or for a loaf of bread for his family.

Petr had also said to him that the Four Tribes had never stopped looking for Luck the Lame and those who had fled with him, whom they did not speak about but whom they sought throughout Midgarth. The rewards offered were enormous. Some had sought over the first range of mountains and up to the slopes of the second. But no one had ever crossed the great plain to the third.

Until the killer who came now. One only, and that was a puzzle. The assassin would need to solve it, before Luck killed him.

It was the only way. Did this man – whose harsh breaths Luck could now hear along the darkened passage – come on whim and guesswork? Or was he eager for the reward, and came ahead of others who followed fast? If it was that, then their time in the steading was over and they would have to flee – though where he could not guess. He could kill this one. Maybe the next. But if killers came in a group his family was finished.

It was fully dark when the sound of breathing changed. Someone sighed; a dog growled. The wind was still coming from behind them, and bore the smells he'd smelled before, of man and beast.

They were starting down the passage. The first beams of the blue moon were lighting it. Luck brought the ram to his feet, sensed the animal look to those who came. An enemy to him too, for all who walked were. He would be better than Luck at the killing. As if he were riding a horse to jump a stone wall, Luck would let Bull have his head.

Shapes appeared in the entrance to the ravine. He might not be able to see them clearly. But he could smell human, smell dog. Bursting from the bushes, Luck-as-Bull charged at the dog.

A smaller, nimbler hound might have dodged out of the way, despite Luck's speed. But this was a wolfhound, stood as tall as the killer's hip. It had no fear, and had time to part its huge jaws in a snarl before the ram hit it, horn to chest. The dog flew backwards, and the momentum of the charge, the strike, carried Bull a few paces on. Swiftly, Luck turned him, bent his legs again, leaped ...

Pain, sharp and sudden in Bull's shoulder. It did not stop him but it slowed him, spun him a little, lowered his head, so he struck the killer hard on one thigh, not in the centre of his belly. Still, it was enough to launch him backwards, giving a sharp, high-pitched cry as he fell, the bow he'd managed to shoot snapping in half.

Luck tried to follow the mortal, butt him again as he struggled to get to his knees. He had the will to do it – yet he suddenly did not have the strength. Coughing, he tasted blood in Bull's mouth; spat some out, sank onto his forelegs. Luck-as-Bull felt where the arrow had gone. Through a lung. The beast was finished.

The killer gave up trying to rise, fell back with a groan. The dog was still down, though also trying to stand, unable to. Luck had a moment before they recovered. Seizing it, he left the dying ram.

In all the times he'd possessed an animal, he'd only been hurt in one thrice. Something of the pain carried over, and for a moment he bent down over his own legs, trying to get air into lungs one of which still felt like it had an arrow through it. The first breath was agony, the next less so. Three more and he was able to stand, and see.

The wolfhound was shaking its head as if to clear it, whimpering as it tried to get onto its paws. The killer was lying on his back, clutching his leg, moans emerging through the scarf that covered half his face. Drawing his knife, Luck lurched forward, kneeled, and seized the man by the front of his doublet. 'Tell me how you found me!' he shouted.

'Please! Please! Do not hurt me!'

The voice was high-pitched. The body he'd jerked off the ground light. Luck realised fully what he had seen and not noted before – the killer was small of stature, no taller than him. He released his grip, and as the man slumped back onto the ground, Luck reached and ripped off his mask.

No, not *his* mask. Hers.

He stared. A young woman, less than twenty, he thought. With the blue eyes and fair hair of West Midgarth. His own land. Her face was drawn, hunger-thin, but she was still pretty – which did not mean she was not a killer, so he did not lower his knife. 'Who are you?' he demanded.

'Marla,' she yelped, eyes on the blade. Then they shifted onto him. 'And you must be Luck of Askaug.'

'How do you know that?'

'Only a god can come out of a beast. I cannot think there is another in these mountains.'

'So you know me.' He leaned closer. 'Did Peki Asarko send you to kill me?'

'Peki Asarko? No.' She raised her hands beside her head in a gesture of surrender. 'I was sent to find you by Petr the Red.'

Luck lowered the knife and flopped back onto his haunches. His heart, that had been beating so fast – both as ram and god – he feared it might burst, began to slow. 'Petr sent you?' he mumbled.

'Yes.' She raised herself onto her elbows. 'There is news from Midgarth you must hear.' She looked behind him, her eyes widened and suddenly she was shouting. 'No! Sit, Warkan. Sit!'

Luck slowly turned. The wolfhound was on his feet, his eyes had cleared, and he was looking at Luck with pure fury. For a moment, the god feared Warkan was going to disobey and attack him anyway. Then, with a growl, he sat.

'Good dog,' the girl said to him, then continued, 'He does not like it that you hold a weapon near me. He has been trained to attack if anyone does.'

'Then I will stop.' Luck sheathed the knife, then rose slowly to his feet as the dog growled at him again. He looked down. 'Are you badly hurt?'

'I do not know. I think—' She grasped the hand that Luck offered her, and used it to pull herself off the ground. Groaned when she was standing, bent to rub her thigh. 'I think it is bruised, but not broken.' She walked a few steps, grimacing. 'It feels dead.' She rubbed it again.

'And your dog?'

She whistled and he came straight to her, though he did not take his eyes off Luck. She felt his chest. The dog whimpered. 'Bruised too, but he has hard bones, my Warkan.'

'So only my ram will not walk again.' Luck looked at Bull, the arrow in him. 'You are swift with the bow.'

'It was an early choice I made,' she replied softly. 'Be swift or die.'

Darkness swept into her eyes. Luck noted it, recognised it. 'Come then … Marla, is it? Let us go where we can sit, talk, eat.'

Light drove away the darkness. 'Eat?' she echoed. 'You mean something other than dried squirrel?'

He smiled. 'Something other, yes.' She smiled too, and it changed her face.

He looked down at Bull. 'I will send my children up with a mule to bring the ram down.'

'He was fierce.'

'And now he will be tasty. Come.'

Yet Bull was not the centre of the feast that night. Meat needed to be hung to achieve its fullest flavour and besides, Atisha was determined to honour the first visitor ever to come to the valley with the most sumptuous meal she could create. Marla was fed oat bread and soup on arrival at the steading, for she was close to starving. But she was more than happy to be fed again later that night, when Atisha and Poum had had the time to prepare properly. Smoked and pickled fish began it, while a leg from a lamb, recently slaughtered, properly aged, was the main course: boned, rolled and stuffed with herbs and wild garlic. There were root vegetables, mashed and softened with sheep's milk butter. There was a bean stew, made fiery by seeds from a mountain bush she had found which mimicked almost exactly the heat of the fruit of bushes she'd grown up with in Ometepe. Finally, there was a pie, the crust made from oat flour, the filling from sour berries rendered sweet by long soaking in the honey from her hive, the delight topped with whipped cream. Every course was washed down with mead, or Luck's sweet, rich oat ale.

Despite Luck's eagerness to hear Petr the Red's news, Atisha had forbidden all talk until after the feast. 'Good news or bad, joy or sadness will all ruin an appetite,' she'd said, studying Marla's gaunt features, 'and our visitor needs to eat.' So it was that they waited till the meal was done, the younger children finally fallen asleep after all the excitement, and they could gather before the hearth, which crackled with flame. The seasons changed swiftly in the high mountains. The last week's warmth had been an echo of summer only, autumn was fully there, they could smell snow on the wind, and the nights were already cold. The family watched Marla, and let her speak almost without interruption. Poum, indeed, had not said one word since she'd arrived. But *they* never, for a moment, took their intense gaze from her.

It did not take Marla long to tell the first part of what she'd been sent to tell. Of a different Midgarth than the one Luck had seen five years before – perhaps because, at last, there was some hope in it.

'You say that resistance has grown, not shrunk?'

'Yes. And especially in the last year, when the changes began.'

'What kind of changes?'

'Many of the most dangerous of our enemies began to leave the land.'

'Of whom do you speak?'

'The Four Tribes,' she replied. Poum started, and leaned forward, eyes wide, as she continued. 'The Huntresses who could discover us in our forest lairs, the Horse Lords who attacked when they did, the Seafarers who ruled the ports and stole what little the land produced ...' Marla leaned forward and held her hands out to the flames, 'many of them returned to their homelands.'

'Do you know the reason?'

'No, lady. No one is sure. But in a raid Petr made on the town of Kroken – his band has grown large enough for such actions – he stole some papers. He cannot read them of course but sent them with me because he knows that you can.'

She pulled out the papers from the satchel she'd brought. 'These have the stamp of the Eye upon it – the mark of the One.' She glanced at Poum when she said this. 'Petr thought they might be important.'

Atisha brought a tallow candle closer, and Luck read swiftly. 'Yes, yes, I see,' he muttered as he read. He put down the first letter, was about to start on the second, when Poum spoke.

'May I, Father?'

Luck looked at Poum, then up at Atisha, who nodded. 'Well, you were meant to be studying *tolanpa-sen* today anyway. Go ahead.'

They were not as swift a reader as Luck, but they got through the page soon enough. 'Father, you have told me of the sender, this Anazat. He is the leader of the Warrior Monks, is he not?'

'He is.'

'And he orders the governor of Kroken to send back five of every ten members of the other tribes to fight ... I do not know this name.' They held out the paper to Luck, forefinger on a word.

'Wattenwolden. They are a large tribe, dwelling in the vast forests north of the city of Corinthium.'

Poum looked down again. 'This Anazat says they are finally going to send an army north to conquer these last enemies.'

'Yes. The reason why they are bringing many of their strongest fighters back.'

'But, husband,' said Atisha, taking the paper from her child, looking at it, though her reading of *tolanpa-sen* was not strong, 'does that mean he is giving up on Peki Asarko? With Midgarth short of troops will not the rebels grow ever stronger?'

Luck, who'd glanced down at the second, shorter letter while Poum questioned, now lifted it. 'I think this may explain.' He read, '"From Anazat, leader of the Council of the Four Tribes, to Peki Asarko, supreme governor of the province of Midgarth, greetings. This is to inform you that after fifteen years of fighting, Intitepe has finally extinguished all rebellion in his land of Ometepe."' He glanced up at Atisha, who'd taken a loud, short breath, then continued, '"He will return soon to claim what was promised him: lordship of the province of Midgarth. You will, of course, honour the agreement. The Council thanks you for your good work. You may retire, with all the wealth you have accumulated in gold and slaves, to your home on the Lake of Souls. Signed this day ..."'

'He has dismissed Peki Asarko?' Marla gasped. 'But the tyrant will never give up his power!'

Luck shook his head. 'Anazat doesn't expect him to. This,' he raised the paper again, 'is designed to provoke.' He looked at his wife again. 'If Intitepe is on his way back to claim Midgarth, Anazat expects Peki to fight him. Hopes that the two enemies will destroy each other – three, if you consider Petr's and others' resistance – or so weaken each other that his forces, after dealing with the Wattenwolden, can return and finish off whoever is left – and then go on to conquer Ometepe too.' He shook the paper. 'If these plans succeed, there will be not a single people left in the world to oppose them. The One will rule them all.'

'The One is not there to rule them.' Atisha raised her eyebrows. 'But as I said to you this morning, husband, the time has come to tell ... everything.'

'You were right as ever, my love.' Luck looked from her to her child. 'I knew this day would come. I thought to begin tomorrow, continue through the winter, perhaps be ready to act on the knowledge by the spring.' He lifted the papers again. 'But the news Marla has brought means we have not got that time.' He shrugged. 'No, if I am to teach *everything* before the snows block all the passes to Midgarth and we are trapped here,' he carried on, overriding the gasps that the two younger people made, 'then tonight Poum must meet Sirene.'

*

Poum had always been aware that there was something special in the locked wooden chest. It sat in the corner of the outer shed that Luck used for what he called his experiments, the place where he brewed his beers, where he distilled plants and berries down to their liquid essence. Poum had always helped, knew nearly as much of the process as Luck. Except one time, five years before, when Luck had insisted on working alone and had emerged a week later, gaunt, exhausted – and angry. Ever after, when they laboured again in the shed, when they caught Luck staring too long at the chest, when they sensed his … terrible yearning, they'd learned to creep away. For if they did not, Luck would jerk his gaze away from the chest as if startled awake, growl and seek things for Poum to do that they had no desire to do, or punish them with tasks for some minor crime Luck would usually have ignored.

Whatever was in the chest had a grip on their father. Something powerful, magical, secret lay within. Poum had yearned to know what it was since they first became aware of the effect it had. So when Luck, later that same night of the meal, pulled out a small, stoppered clay jar, Poum was disappointed.

'That is all, Father?'

'Not quite,' Luck replied, and delved into the chest again. This time he brought out an old sack and placed it, its opening downwards, upon the table. Carefully, he pulled the cloth away from its contents.

'Ha!' Poum gasped. There were a few items of glass in the steading, brought from Midgarth. Two bottles. A cracked mirror. A large, strange-shaped flask that Luck used in his distilling. Nothing like this … globe, this … container. What was most startling – smoke swirled within it. 'May I touch it?'

'Gently.'

Poum stretched out a finger – then jerked it back. 'So cold! So cold it burns!'

'Yes.'

It was such a little word. Yet it carried a world of sorrow and of yearning in it, and Poum glanced up sharply. Luck's face was drawn, as if the skin had suddenly tightened, revealing the bones beneath. 'What is this, Father?' Poum whispered, curiosity driven away by sudden fear, as chill as the feeling on their finger, which they could not rub away.

'It is … everything.' Luck answered with that same intensity, then jerked his gaze away from the globe, focused on Poum. His next words were low, rapid. 'There is no way to prepare you for what must be. Each journey with Sirene is different for each person. She will show you what you most want to see, even if you do not know that yourself.'

So many questions flooded Poum's mind. One came first. 'She?'

'Sirene appears in the form of a woman. I think. It's … it's hard to tell.'

'Sirene lives within this glass?'

'Yes … and no. She is also in this.' Luck lifted the stoppered jar. 'Yet both are a … a doorway to another world. When the two are joined, you will travel to it.'

'Travel?'

'Into the smoke. Then out into that world.' He shook his head. 'Into every world.'

'Father, I … I don't understand.'

'No.' Luck swallowed, gazing at the globe. 'It cannot *be* understood. It can only be experienced.'

'I see.' Poum nodded, then frowned. 'Wait. You said, *you* will travel. You meant we, yes?'

Luck swallowed. 'I cannot come with you.'

'You can.'

'I can. But I must not.' Luck wiped a sleeve across his forehead, which Poum now noticed glistened with sweat despite the chill in the shed. 'It is my greatest desire. And I must not yield to it. There will come a time,' his voice cracked, 'but it is not now. Now you must go alone.' He leaned forward and gripped Poum's arm. 'Everything I have ever taught you was to prepare you for this moment.' Poum saw a tear glisten in reflected candlelight in Luck's eyes. 'I have never told you how proud I am of you, my son. You are ready for this. For things I cannot teach you, show you in a lifetime of lessons.' He released Poum's arm, leaned back. 'I am going to pour the contents of this jar onto the globe. When I do, lean forward and breathe in the smoke.'

'Father, I cannot do this!'

'You can. For listen to this. Listen to this last. It will shock you, but it is best you take this knowledge with you, so she does not surprise you with it.' He took a deep breath. 'We kept it from you, because ... because your mother and I felt that it was hard enough growing up alone on a mountain with your parents, without also knowing how ... special you were. How different.' Luck untied the scarf from around his neck, doubled it, and tied it over his lower face. His next words came muffled. 'I have taught you about the One. The saviour prophesied to the world, that the Four Tribes have used to conquer nearly all of it.'

'Yes.' Poum swallowed. 'A child born in a faraway land. A myth. A story only.'

'No myth. The child is real. The child is different from any other.'

'In what way?'

Luck finished his tying then looked straight into Poum's eyes. 'The child is neither man nor woman. The child is both.'

Poum flushed cold, colder than the touch of skin on smoking globe. 'You ... you m-mean,' they stammered, 'th-that I ... I—'

'Yes. *You* are the One.' As Poum gasped, he leaned in and whispered, 'I cannot come with you. But Sirene will remember me. So if you get a chance tell her this.' His eyes darkened. 'Tell her that I remember her as well, and *why she is*.' Then with a flick of his thumb, Luck popped the cork off the jar and leaned far back, before tipping the contents onto the globe. Smoke poured off it. 'Breathe!' he yelled.

Shocked, terrified ... yet exhilarated too, Poum leaned forward and obeyed.

There was darkness. They fell into it.

There was light.

A halo of it surrounded a figure that stood about ten paces ahead of Poum. It was as if the figure itself was the source of the light. It wore hooded, white robes that moved gently in a warm breeze Poum could now feel on their skin. There was a face, though Poum could only see the mouth.

'You are Sirene,' Poum said.

'And you are the One. I have been waiting for you.'

Though *they* were now in a world that was not a world, a darkness that had nothing to do with the absence of light, something of the world they had come from had come with them. And Poum realised that the shock of what Luck had said was somehow less shocking here. Here, in a way they were yet to understand, the revelation made some sort of sense.

There was something Luck had told them to tell Sirene. That could wait. But the memory of it prompted their own question. 'Tell me,' Poum said, stepping closer.

'Yes?'

'Why I am.'

There was a pause before Sirene spoke again. 'One you know once asked me that same question ... of myself. Luck of Midgarth was not happy with my answer.' Within the hood, lips shaped a smile. 'Will you be?'

Something of Poum's anger, their frustration at being denied the knowledge they wanted of the world came to them now. 'Answer me,' they said.

'I cannot. But I can show you.' Raising her arm, Sirene took Poum into that place that was the opposite of the dark, and was not light.

Two days later . . .

She had said her goodbyes, in a dozen different ways. The new scarf she'd knitted, the favourite pastries she'd made, the treats at every meal. Held her child for so long they had become embarrassed, looking over their mother's shoulder at Marla, shrugging. Finally, Atisha had let Poum go, to lead the two mules with their loads down the ravine that led to the next valley. A wave, without turning back, the slope taking Poum from her sight. It took all Atisha's will not to rush down the ravine, seize them again. No more crying, she urged herself. Enough tears.

'Are you sure, wife?'

She took a deep breath before turning. She must not let his last sight of her be tears either. 'I am sure, husband,' she replied.

'I hate to leave you alone here. Hate it!'

'I know. But I will not be alone.' She nodded ahead, to Bjorn and Freya who'd followed Poum and Marla down the ravine and were now standing on the cliff's edge waving and calling farewells. 'And you know that you cannot do what you must, while trying to protect us all.' She looked back, down the valley to the steading. 'Besides, I have duties here.'

Luck looked where she did, and she saw tears come into his eyes. 'I have been so happy here, Atisha. I would not leave now except . . .'

'Except you must. Because the people you loved gave their lives so you could have this time. Hovard and Freya. Bjorn and Stromvar. Many others. They let the Dark come, only because they knew that when it was time you would return with the light.'

'I know. Yet ...' He shoved the heels of his hands into his eyes, rubbed. 'Can I do this? There is so much evil out there. And I feel old ...'

She smiled, took one hand. 'Old? That is not how you appeared to me last night.'

He caught her smile. 'Well, you have always had ways of making a god feel young again.'

'Ways, eh?' She pulled the hand she held, then placed it against her belly. 'Perhaps Ufda will not be the only one who has a litter within.' She glanced across to the sheepdog, straining against the rope that held her, whining to be free and to follow her recent lover, Warkan, all the way to Midgarth.

He gasped. 'You think it possible?'

'Of course it is possible.'

'All the more reason for me to stay.'

'No.' She felt the tears rise, forced them down. 'Though it is a good reason to return with the spring.'

'Then that is what I will do,' he said, his voice firmer, as he raised both his hands and held her face. 'Believe that, wife. I will be back and we will have our life here again.'

'Our life here was good. But it is so cold here, and winter so long.' She stared above him for a moment. 'I dream of a beach in Ometepe. Warm air, warm ocean, warm life. All year.' She placed her hands over his. 'When you have done what you must, perhaps we shall go there?'

'When *I* have done it? I think it is more what others will do. What Poum will do.' He took her hands, lowered them. 'Did they tell you much of what Sirene showed them?'

'Not much. We talked of the prophecy of their birth, of Intitepe—'

'What did you tell them of their father?'

'That he is a cruel and merciless tyrant.' She sighed. 'And how I loved him once, utterly.'

'It is a good lesson to learn. How even tyrants seek love. And how love can change to hate in moments.' Luck nodded. 'Now, according to Anazat, Intitepe returns to Midgarth.'

'Yes.' Her eyes narrowed. 'That does make me wish I was coming – to look at him over an arrow I've nocked – before I put that arrow through his heart.'

Luck smiled. 'Which makes me fear for you less, my love. Because you are fierce. Poum will have that fierceness too. That gives me hope.'

'We also have another hope, don't we?' She held his face as he held hers. 'Do you remember that fierce couple you freed from the Keep?'

'Ferros and Lara. I think of them often.' Luck looked down into the valley, to the hut she spoke of. 'Yes. We are not alone in this fight.'

They held each other in silence for a short time more. Until Ufda started barking again, because Bjorn and Freya were running back down the ravine. 'There are hawks, Mother. Hawks, on a nest,' her daughter shouted. 'Can we go steal their eggs?'

Luck stooped, swept the two children into his arms, lifted them, kissed them both hard, at which they protested loudly because of the prickliness of his beard. He put them down and they ran off to comfort Ufda. He stood again. 'Wife,' he said.

'Husband,' she replied, stepped close, kissed him.

There was nothing left to say. All final words were in the kiss. It went on a while, and ended too soon when Atisha broke away, marched to her children, loosed the dog from the rock and, with the leash in one hand, and Bjorn and Freya fighting for her other, went to the path, and began her descent. Like her firstborn, headed the other way, she did not look back.

Luck watched his family till they vanished between boulders, then looked again at the steading, this place he'd helped build, this place he loved. I will return, he vowed, with the spring. Then, putting his carry sack on his back, lifting his staff, he followed Poum down the trail.

2
City of Despair

Corinthium. Twelve days later.

As soon as the head of the column reached the summit, Malvolen reined in. The old chieftain did not need to give a further command. All knew what to do. They had done it on this same day – Midwinter's Day – every year. The anniversary of that day fifteen years before when the treaty was signed and the Wattenwolden, after three months of looting and pillage, finally quit Corinthium.

The horsemen switched from column to line, and spread out along the ridge to either side of him. Eighty men, the number agreed that the High Chief would bring each year to the Day of Tribute.

Vapour rose from the horses because the air was crisp, and they had galloped up the steep slope to this viewpoint from which the entirety of the city could be seen. Some previous years rain clouds had obscured the walls; on others driven sleet or snow had made lingering on the ridge uncomfortable. Not today though. Today was glorious, the bluest of skies unblemished by cloud. Below them the city glittered in the afternoon sun.

Gasps and curses of wonder exploded all along the line.

For forty men it was the first time they'd seen the sight. Each year half who came needed to be young enough to never have come before. So that they could experience the wonder of a city and an empire that their forebears had defeated in battle. These young warriors had earned the right to come by winning the fierce competitions that took place in the weeks leading up to the departure. Races were run, javelins and axes thrown, bows shot, limbs broken in duels fought with wooden staves. For a people who dwelt in forests, where the largest town had but two thousand houses, a city of more than one hundred thousand structures, with towers taller than their tallest trees, was overwhelming.

Ferros remembered how he too had gasped when he first saw it, though he'd arrived by sea. He and Lara, clutching each other like stunned children, as they marvelled at those towers, as they sailed under the conjoined arms of the Twins, those statues of Wisdom and Strength that had stood sentinel for three hundred years over the city's harbour. Gone now, of course. The prophecy which foretold that the day they fell so would Corinthium had been proved right.

For a moment, he was back there, on that day of fire and slaughter nearly sixteen years before. Fighting his way back into the city. Fighting to save it. Fighting his way out when its doom was clear, with Lara dead before him on his horse's neck, and the remnant of the Ninth Balbek Riders following. To escape he'd had to fight his way past some of the men who sat their mounts beside him now on the ridge. But once he'd broken clear and, weeks later, led his troop to his recent enemies' native forests, and deep into them, he did what so many who'd fled Corinthium over the centuries had done – rode to the timbered hall, laid his sword on the ground before him, and kissed the High Chief's feet.

There was something everyone in the empire knew of the

Wattenwolden. They were the most savage race in war – and the most hospitable in peace. The story was that their gods decreed the whole world theirs, and therefore all its other peoples were merely cattle that had strayed and so would be welcomed back. Return to the land of forests, swear to abide by the Law, make obeisance to the High Chief and you would be given shelter from any storm you fled, with no questions asked or price demanded. If you wanted to truly become one of the tribe, though, to go with them to war and help shape any peace, then rites had to be undertaken. Over two years, a warrior was initiated. Once he'd survived the ordeals of fire, water and earth, once he'd slain his aurens, one of the fierce wild oxen who roamed the deep forests, once he'd hung upon an ash tree for a day and a night, died to his old self, been reborn to his new, then he was fully accepted. Then he was given his name.

Thus Ferros had become Arcturien. And yet, looking down at the city he'd fought so long for, he knew he was still Ferros too.

'Did you miss it, Arcturien? Does your first sight of it in all these years make you yearn for its former glory that you were part of?'

Ferros looked at the man who'd asked the question – Malvolen, the High Chief whose Spear and Shield he had lately become. Under the exploded bushes of his grey-streaked eyebrows, the old man's blue eyes were bright and keen. 'No, lord,' he replied. 'If there was any glory, it was in the deserts of the Sarphardi, when I was young and foolish enough to believe in the empire. But that changed when I arrived here, and saw the corruption at its heart.' He looked the older man straight in his eyes. 'Do you ask because you fear that the moment I ride through its gate I will recall old loyalties and abandon recent ones?'

'I do not. For you undertook the rites. You have your name. The gods consider you Wattenwolden, as much as any man here.' Malvolen reached down and patted the neck of his stallion, who was restive, throwing his head up and down. 'And you would not have become my Spear and Shield two years ago if there was any question as to that.'

'Truly? There was I thinking I got that title only because I defeated three of your hairiest-arsed champions in single combat.'

The blue eyes crinkled in a smile. 'There was that. But you still would not have been so appointed were it not for your other skills.'

Ferros shrugged. 'I didn't think any others were required.'

'You know that is not true.' Malvolen glanced each way down the lines, where men were still pointing, and exclaiming loudly. 'No High Chief survives long if their Spear and Shield can only fight. For his true worth is not in how he uses this,' he tapped his own spear, sheath-slung along his horse's flank, 'but this.' He patted the side of his grizzled head. 'To keep ten tribes united, to watch for lesser chieftains who think it might be their turn to sit in the High Chair of the Aurens, to balance ever our need to fight with our need to nurture and grow?' He nodded. 'That takes more than a fighter's skill. Though you are gifted in that, Arcturien, your true worth to me is in your mind. Also in your history … down there.' He jerked his chin at the distant city, then shivered. 'Indeed there may never have been a time when a High Chief has needed it more.'

'Yet you did not take my advice, lord.' Ferros pushed his mount closer to the other's so he could lower his voice. 'That this year we should make the Corinthians meet us outside the city, in pavilions in an open field, in case of treachery.'

'It is true. Our priests have read the signs in the entrails of beasts, in the movement within fire, in the cry of birds come too early to the forests.' He sniffed. 'All speak of betrayal. Yet I fear it more from some of those who stayed behind.'

'That turd Barallingen for one.'

'That turd Barallingen for most. His sudden sickness so

that he could not accompany us seemed … convenient, did it not?'

'It did.' Ferros reached up and ran his hand over his beard. 'Though my men watch him closely. Try to move the people against you in your absence and he'll find he has a new arsehole.' He turned and spat. 'If you feared the signs of birds and entrails did you not think to feign sickness too? To not come at all? Like last year, when there was plague in the city?'

'I did not even consider it.' Malvolen jerked his head along the line of men. 'If I showed my fear, my own would fall on me like hounds on a spear-struck deer.' He shook his head. 'If we did not come, we would again not collect the tribute they pay us for the treaty's renewal. Two years without it? Our people have grown too used to the gold, the fancy weapons and the fancy wines it buys to give them up for my fears. And this time, of course, we will have last year's as well as this year's to take back. Besides,' he lifted his fingers to his nose and leaned over to void its contents onto the ground, 'our spies do not speak of an empire powerful enough to strike back yet. I know that they are planning to. But it will not be this year.'

'Yet many of our spies have fallen silent lately.'

'Which is another reason to go. To see for ourselves. Another reason you are the Spear and Shield and not one of those … hairy-arsed champions you *defeated*.'

There was an emphasis on the word that Ferros didn't care for. 'Are you saying, lord, that they let me win?'

'That would be an outrage to our gods, Arcturien.' Malvolen grinned. 'Let us just say that, in this case, the gods decided on behalf of the wise as well as the sword-skilled.'

Ferros grunted but decided not to press the point. It was true that none of those he'd defeated were proficient in much more than weaponry – and not perhaps the very best with those. And if the High Chief was right in his estimate about what lay ahead, a man who knew Corinthium's customs and people would indeed be very useful.

He was staring at the city, when Malvolen spoke again. 'What was your name there? Before you were born to your new life?'

'I was called Ferros.'

'Is there anything you fear in your return? Anyone? Sixteen years is not so long for *some* wounds to heal.'

The old chief was shrewd. Most leaders did not survive the diminishment of their fighting skills. He had ruled longer than any chief in memory. 'There is someone,' Ferros replied softly, 'who I would not see again. Yet if she lives, she will be at the heart of all that happens.'

'Roxanna.'

Malvolen whispered the name he'd got from Ferros at the feast where he'd been given the spear and shield of his new office. Ferros drank little, and never to excess. But there were a series of ritual toasts to be observed that he could not shirk and, for once, his caution had slipped. Which was probably the secondary purpose of the feast. 'Roxanna,' he confirmed.

Malvolen studied him for a moment, then nodded. 'She will not know you now, Arcturien. Your face, that was the bronze of my shield boss when you came to us, is now as pale as goat's milk. Your beard and hair are as long, and as styled, as befits our warriors – though I marvel that they still have no grey.' He sighed, running his fingers over the braids of his own beard, which retained no colour *but* grey. 'Besides, you will keep to the shadows, doing the work we discussed. Making contact with those spies that remain. For my part,' he turned to the side and spat, 'I look forward to seeing that bitch again. For she is ever a pleasure to the eye, is she not?' When Ferros didn't reply, he took up his reins. 'Now come. Let us warm our bones at Corinthium's fires, fill our bellies with their food and drink. That ice wine they serve – what is it called?'

'Tinderos.'

Malvolen nodded. 'That I am looking forward to. I prefer it to our own ales, these days. Must be getting old. Come.'

He heeled his horse, and the stallion set off down the slope. All down the line the collectors of the tribute followed. Only Ferros lingered, continuing to stare down. Though now he was thinking not of one woman, but of two.

Both were in the city ahead. When last he'd seen them together, fifteen years before, the one had killed the other. Though, of course, neither of them could die.

'Lara.' He breathed her name, and it emerged like smoke in the chill air.

Lara had not done so well with their new way of life. Unlike in parts of the empire – and, Ferros knew, in the land of the Four Tribes – women were never warriors in the Wattenwold. They were accepted, treated well, even respected – but only as hearth-tenders, bread-makers, child-bearers. Which was never going to suit Lara. It would not have suited for long the spirited girl Ferros had first known and loved back in Balbek. It certainly did not suit the immortal she'd become. Especially since she loved the aspect of immortality that he still truly did not.

Possession.

They had agreed that they must never use that power among the Wattenwolden. That it would be a betrayal of hospitality – and mean death if discovered. Lara had accepted that, accepted her new role – wife, cook, hearth-tender. She had borne no children though. Whether it was nature, or her decision, he did not know – and never asked. She said she had forgiven him for his straying with Roxanna. She also said that she had things she still needed to accomplish back in the world they'd come from. For her, their exile was only a pause. Mostly, he knew that what she craved was vengeance on the woman who'd killed her.

For a third time, her name disturbed the air in vapour. 'Roxanna,' he breathed.

Even saying her name still provoked him. He remembered the different ways he'd said it. With fury, with hurt. With, perhaps most of all, a near overwhelming lust. He knew that the night she'd seduced him, at the feast of Simbala, she had used a drug in his wine to lower his resistance. With other drugs he'd had to take – like the essence of poppy to cope with the agony of being reborn – or even with strong beer or Tinderos wine, memory was a blur, shadows dancing in a mist. Yet he remembered every moment of making love with Roxanna. Every touch and caress. Every slap, kiss, bite ... rake of nails. He remembered laying her on her belly over the balustrade on her balcony, his hands around her throat. Hours of it, a dream unspooling – and every image still vivid and clear.

She had killed the woman he truly loved – not once, but twice. She'd used her beauty, her wits, the power of possession, to bend the world to her will. He had hated her. Yet he had discovered that hate and desire sometimes had everything to do with each other.

While he'd been reminiscing, the Wattenwolden, in column again, had made it halfway to the city walls. It had been decided that he would not ride in beside Malvolen, as his Spear and Shield should. For just as they had spies in Corinthium, so the city had spies in the forests. They would have told of Arcturien's appointment, and the powers in the city would be keen to see him. So Haldan – one of those who'd fled with Ferros and Lara fifteen years before, one of the final three surviving members of the Ninth Balbek Riders, who, like Ferros, was a full Wattenwolden now – would deputise at Malvolen's shoulder. Ferros would follow, near the end of the column.

As he heeled his horse down the slope, Ferros thought of those 'powers in the city'. Roxanna and Makron ruled – but they did so in the name of Corinthium's true conquerors: the people of the Four Tribes. The people of the One. Spies had reported how they'd changed the city, from one that lived for profit and pleasure to one of pious worship. Enforced with ceremony and harsh punishments.

Spies, he thought, thinking of one in particular, his heart quickening as he did.

Taking his horse to canter, he caught up with the column, forced his way into it so he was about ten riders from its end. They were now only three hundred paces from what had been the northern wall of the city. This was now a low ruin – kept so because part of the treaty decreed that should it be broken by either party, the Wattenwolden could sweep down from their forests and reclaim the two northern hills of the city they'd held for three months before they were paid to leave. The buildings on those hills had been largely destroyed in the pillage and burning that followed the conquest. Ferros could see that not much had been rebuilt. But on the charred wasteland a tent city had been erected, as he'd heard it was every year, to house the tribute collectors.

They rode through all that remained of the gate – twin posts, one leaning away from the two half-tumbled towers. On a rough square of open ground that could hold them, the Wattenwolden halted, spread out. The perimeter of the square was filled with gawking townsfolk, held back by guards in the uniform of the city's militia. In a line before them, on a raised dais, stood representatives of Corinthium and of the Four Tribes, one of each – a Seafarer, a Huntress, a Horse Lord, and a Warrior Monk. Ferros had fought all four tribes on the grasslands of Cuerdocia, and again on the walls and in the streets of the city.

Roxanna and Makron were not there. He wondered at that – until he heard the Seafarer declare, in a tedious speech of welcome, that the two had been taken by a sweating sickness but were early recovered and would see them at the feast in three days' time.

It was easy to spot a lie, and he knew Malvolen would note it. There would be a reason for their absence, something that Ferros would find out. As the man droned on, Ferros looked along the ranks of watching townsfolk. They looked dull, resentful … gaunt, as if they did not get enough food. And whereas when he'd been in the city before he'd been struck by its varied colours and styles of dress, for people from all parts of the empire had come there, now most wore either dull working smocks or brown, hooded monkish robes. He was sure that had to do with the worship of the One, which dominated all life.

Then he saw it. A flash of colour, there a moment, gone, then there again before finally vanishing – an emerald scarf. The first time it had drawn his eyes, the second flash focused them. And he saw her.

He took a sharp breath. His horse, reacting to his sudden tension, started jerking its head up and down. When he'd settled him, and looked once more, the scarf waver was gone. But he knew her. Because he'd bought her that scarf at a market on the Feast of the Two Moons one year before.

He scanned the crowd but knew he wouldn't spot her. Just as he knew where he would find her later. That rendezvous had been arranged when she first went into the city to spy, six months before.

'Lara,' he whispered.

Sevrapol was a shadow of the place Lara had first visited fifteen years before. Then the city's fourth and central hill had also been the centre of all entertainment – and of all sin. Elegant theatres had lined the Stradun – the city's spine and main street – visited by the elites. Behind those palaces of higher culture, though, lower forms of recreation had been offered. In the dark and narrow alleys that twisted away on either side could be found … *anything* that men – usually men – desired and would pay for. Cock fights, dog fights, dice dens. Brothels. When she'd first come here she'd been an innocent provincial girl and, newly arrived, she'd been shocked by what she'd seen. Later, not so innocent after being murdered then reborn, she'd been less shocked by what went on, which got worse the deeper into the alleys she penetrated. Now, she never raised an eyebrow at what some men sought, and did.

The theatres were long gone, for the elites who would buy tickets were mainly gone too, swept away by the conquest. The immortals were no longer paying for anything, of course, being dead. Besides, frivolous entertainments were discouraged in the sombre new world of the worship of the One. As was sin. Though discouraging it and stopping it were entirely different things. Where there was hunger, men must feed – with others always there to provide the meal.

Which was why she was now standing in front of the door of the finest whorehouse in Sevrapol. Though that single term did not sum up what lay beyond the door, which was almost another city: Asprodon. Three levels of sin named for the Assani God of Mayhem and Lust.

She did not knock yet. There were things she must do within this day that would take all her courage and guile and she wanted a few breaths of the better air that was found outside sin city to steady herself. Fortunately, she no longer needed to spend most of her time on her back pleasuring customers as she had three months before. Even though she'd done that in the form of a young whore she'd borrowed for the purpose, it was not an experience she wished to repeat. While you picked up certain skills from those you possessed, you also lived their loves and, perhaps more acutely, their disgusts and hates. But she'd learned enough that one day to make herself useful in another way – as a courier for the main supplier of a narcotic leaf many there liked to chew. A male courier, Laro by name. Saved all the groping and fondling that would have occurred had she remained Lara. Well, she reminded herself, most of the groping.

Kefa came all the way from the far south of the empire, from the province of Xan, brought by camel across the deserts to the port of Balbek, and then across the Great Sea to the city itself. Since Balbek was her home town, she'd found it easy enough to ingratiate herself with the fellow townsman who ran the operation in the port of Corinthium. Graco didn't even demand the slim Laro sleep with him, preferring large and beefy sailors as he did. But when drunk, which was often, he was sentimental, and her accent reminded him of home. Besides, the skills she'd acquired with a knife from one of her early possessions had proved useful when, at their first meeting, a rival tried to steal his latest shipment. She had dealt with one assailant, Graco the other, and they'd been comrades of the blade ever since.

She patted the package beneath her clothing which gave her a pot-bellied look, Kefa was her passage into the underground world. Gave her an excuse to linger too, for Severos, the 'king' of Asprodon, would need to chew a few leaves to make sure he wasn't being cheated. The full effect required a bit of time, so after delivery she could hang around in Zarel's, one of Asprodon's several taverns, to wait for Graco's payment.

But really to wait for Ferros.

She knew he'd seen her. With his hunter's eye, he had caught the flash of the scarf he'd given her. She felt the softness of that, binding her breasts – she looked forward to Ferros untying it later. Six months since she'd last seen him, and she was hungry for him again. Even in the time of her anger with him, at his betrayal of her with Roxanna, she had never truly ceased being hungry for him.

Roxanna! The image of that ebony face, that magnificent body, those cruel eyes came vividly to her again. The bitch had killed her … twice! One day, she thought, I will have my revenge for that. Perhaps one day soon.

Back down the alley, she heard footsteps. This entrance to Asprodon was for suppliers only. At least she wouldn't meet one of her former clients there. But neither did she want delays. Raising her hand, she rapped three times.

'Laro,' the doorman said as he unbolted and swung the heavy door open. 'Bring something nice for us, did ya?'

She had discovered on several occasions that making friends with a doorman was a good thing. So now she slipped a small package of kefa from beneath her shirt into his hands. 'Something for your dreams, Zok,' she said, and he grunted his thanks. 'Where's Severos?'

'Field of Dreams,' he replied, then turned to the still open door where a man had appeared. 'No, no, no,' he said loudly, 'I told you last time. Not this way.'

She left them arguing. The Field of Dreams was the next level down. It was neither a field, nor especially dreamy. The name came from one of those fancy Stradun theatres, now a ruin. This area was also where a type of performance went on, though from what she'd observed there was little poetry in it.

She heard him before she saw him. 'By the giant balls of Mavros, you stupid whore. You only cry when they pay you to cry. You don't cry when you're dancing!'

She entered the room. Severos was sitting on a barrel, gazing up at a sort of platform on which five half-dressed women were shuffling back and forth to the music of a bored-looking man plucking at a torba while another, equally dull-eyed, banged a hollow wooden box. One of the whores, the youngest, was weeping as she moved.

Whenever she saw him, she always thought of an expression

her father often used: 'Every man's disaster is another man's triumph.' Severos had risen from being just another brothel keeper to almost the only one in Sevrapol, because nearly all the others had been put out of action by the invasion. He used to be Severos the Pander. Now he was the King of Asprodon.

Though that's not the reason I'm going to be nice to him, she thought. The reason was what she remembered seeing in Severos's small brothel fifteen years before. She'd followed the immortal Streone into the building and witnessed him pouring a black liquid onto a glass globe – and then talking through it to a man on the other side of the world, whose prisoner she later became: Makron, now co-regent of Corinthium.

She'd learned more about the liquid – the drug, Sirene – since she'd returned to be a Wattenwolden spy in the city half a year before. How it not only allowed people to communicate, but gave them visions too, even as it blackened their eyes and teeth – like it had done to the man who'd held them prisoner in the Keep, the leader of the Four Tribes whose name was Anazat. It was there that she'd seen a globe for the second time; shown it by the man who'd helped them escape – Luck of Midgarth. As they'd parted, he'd brought out a globe, and a vial of the liquid. Though they didn't really speak each other's language he'd communicated that it could be a way for friends to speak as well as enemies. She and Ferros had often spoken about the strange little man who protected the mother and child who had so changed the world. How they shared an enemy, and so a fight.

She'd desired a globe ever since ... like the one she'd seen in Severos' old brothel. And last time they'd talked she felt he'd been hinting that he still possessed it.

The torba player tipped his head towards her, where she stood at the edge of the room. Severos turned. 'Laro,' he cried. 'Just the person I want to see!' He swivelled back to the stage. 'You,' he pointed at the bored musician. 'Try to get some life into them, for fuck's sake. And you,' he jabbed a finger at the young whore. 'Stop crying or I'll give you something to really cry about.'

He swung back round to face Lara. She averted her eyes from his vast and black-haired belly, protruding from his unbuttoned shirt. It was damp, like the rest of him. 'It's hard work, getting whores to do anything other than fuck. You'd think they would welcome a chance to get off their knees and onto their feet.' He wiped a hand across his sweaty brow. 'Let's get a drink.'

In his office, a few doors down from the Field of Dreams, he poured them both wine. He grunted thanks for the package she handed over, extracted a few leaves and shoved them into his mouth, forming a pouch of them in one cheek, which bulged out. He looked like a sweaty squirrel. 'Good. Good. I can tell already. Always like doing business with Graco. He has quality goods. You tell him that.'

'He likes doing business with you as well, master. Especially when he gets paid promptly.'

Severos surprised her by taking the hint, reaching into a satchel on the floor, pulling out a small, clinking leather purse. He usually waited for half an hour until the full effect of the kefa was clear. Now, he played with the purse for a little, as if he didn't want to part with it, then sighed and threw it across. 'You don't need to count it.'

'Oh, but I do. My skin if you've made a ... little mistake.'

She tipped the bag out, began stacking the silver coins in piles of ten. 'Beat you, does he, Graco?' He tsked. 'You should come work for me. I can always use a bright lad. And I won't pester you for nothing else. I don't like boys that way.' He beamed. 'Have some more wine.'

He reached, poured. Lara-as-Laro was quite happy for Severos to think she was Graco's male lover. And his talk didn't put her off her count. 'Two centanos short,' she said.

'Oh yeah? Silly me.' He flicked two coins across the table. 'Bright lad,' he said again. 'Now I wonder ... wonder if you are even brighter.' He ran a finger around the cavern of his belly button, pulled something out, studied it, then wiped it away on his shirt. 'Remember I mentioned that I was in the market for ... something stronger than kefa?' He wiped some drool from his mouth. 'This *is* good, by the way.'

'You said.' Lara scooped all the coins back into the pouch, tucked it under her shirt, then reached, sipped the wine. It was good too. '*Is* there anything stronger than kefa?'

'Oh yes. Stronger – and much rarer too. Much higher cost means much bigger profits.' He ran his tongue over his lips. His eyes were brighter with the kefa – and with greed.

'Oh yeah?' Lara feigned a weariness, looking away to the wall.

Severos leaned across the table, lowering his voice. 'It's called Sirene. Or some people say, "*She* is called Sirene." Because apparently you use it and you ... see her. She takes you travelling.'

'Travelling where?'

'Dunno. Away from your shit world anyway.' He scratched his nose. 'You hear any whispers about it at the port?'

She looked back at him. A line of brown liquid was running from his mouth into his stubble and he didn't bother to wipe it away. 'You know what? I did hear some traders talking. They were from ... where was it?'

Severos's eyes narrowed. 'Omersh?'

'Yes.'

'Traders? That's a laugh. Fucking pirates, everyone from that island.'

Lara had not heard anyone talking. But it was a good idea to feed the man's hunger to get information. 'Could have been. Dunno. Anyway, one of them was drunk in a tavern and mentioned some lady who took you travelling ... without leaving the room, he said.' She looked above him, took a risk on the greed and the kefa. 'Though this person said that you needed something else. Something that she … worked on.'

Severos's eyes narrowed for a moment, suspicion in them. Then he leaned back, wiped his mouth, slapped the table. 'You know, years ago, even before the conquest, ships would come from Omersh. And then certain of my clients were especially happy. I put aside a room for one …' He broke off, looked around as if they might be overheard, then leaned closer. 'You want to see something special?' he asked softly.

'So long as it's not a dancing whore.'

Severos laughed, stood up. 'No, no,' he said, 'much better.' Behind him, in the centre of the wall, was a tapestry, some ancient scene of lust being enacted. Pushing it aside revealed a large metal box built into, and flush with, the wall. He unclipped the large set of keys he kept at his hip, found one, inserted it, opened the box's side, and pulled a velvet bag out. Setting it carefully down on the table, he arranged it so the opening was downwards, then jerked the bag off.

Lara couldn't help the cry. It was a globe. Smoke swirled within it. She swallowed, took a breath, steadied her voice. 'So that's Sirene?'

'No. Sirene is the drug. It comes in vials like this.' He held one up. It had no stopper and, when he held it upside down, nothing came out. 'See? There are still people – immortals who survived the massacre, mostly – who would pay a fortune if this was full.' He tapped the glass. 'They say that you see paradise in here.'

'Whose paradise? Simbala's garden? The Assani's war palace? The fields of flowing Amber …'

'From what I gather, it's your own paradise you see. However you've dreamed it.'

He looked down again and, for a brief moment, Lara wondered if she should pull her knife, seize the globe, run for the world. Severos was fat, slow and drugged, while Zok the doorman owed her one, after all. But she didn't move. Without Sirene it was just a glass filled with smoke. 'I can …' she coughed. 'I can make some enquiries, if you like.'

'I do like. And so will you.' He pointed at her belly. 'There's five times what's in that purse for you for a single vial.' His eyes gleamed. 'Yours to keep, if you don't involve Graco. 'Cos he's a bit too greedy, don't you think?'

Lara drained her wine, stood. 'I'll think about it,' she said. 'Meantime, someone to see.'

'I've got to get back too. Work, always work.' He sighed. 'I wonder if that bitch has stopped crying yet.' He folded the bag over the globe, tucked it back in the metal box, locked it, let the tapestry fall. Ushering her out into the corridor he locked the door behind him. 'I'll be hearing from you?'

'You will.'

'Good lad.' Severos patted his shoulder then walked off down the corridor. Lara stood outside his door for a moment longer, then went the opposite way, passing other doors from which emerged sighs, groans, drunken laughter. She descended a level, and walked through the doors of Zarel's tavern.

The air was fetid, too far from the surface, rank with sweat and the smoke of the cheap incense they burned to try to take the stench away. Crowded too. Off-duty whores, their recent or future customers. Most tables were occupied. But in an alcove at the back she spotted him, the huge Wattenwolden warrior. Despite the crowds, there was a space cleared all around him, people avoiding one of those who'd brought so much horror to the city fifteen years before, and now visited it once a year. For three days, the young men of the tribes were allowed to go anywhere in the city and the citizens had learned to leave them alone, having witnessed the lingering deaths of those who didn't.

Eyes followed her as she crossed to him, sat down. 'Hello, Ferros,' she said softly.

'Hello … Laro,' he replied, eyeing her male attire. 'Want a drink?'

'Sure.' She lifted the tankard he poured her, held it without drinking.

'A toast?' he queried.

'Yes. Because I think I may have found what we have been seeking. Half of it anyway.'

'I see.' Ferros looked around the tavern. 'And the other things we sought? The information?' He ran a tongue over his lips. 'Will there be treachery at the Feast of Tribute in three days?'

'No.' She lowered her voice still further. 'But they are massing forces in Balbek and in Cuerdocia. By the time the Wattenwolden have returned to sleep through the rest of winter, the fleets will have sailed here – and the Four Tribes will invade immediately.'

Ferros nodded, sipped. People were muttering at them, but keeping their distance. Perhaps it was the glare he gave them. 'So. You have found this Sirene?'

'Not exactly. But I have found one part of her. A seeing globe – like the one that Luck of Midgarth showed us at the Keep. That I saw Streone use when we first came to the city.'

'The missing part is the liquid, yes? The drug?'

'Yes. The man who is the king of this kingdom,' she glanced around, 'the man with the globe, has just asked me to find … *her*.'

'Why does he think you could do that?'

'Because I work for Graco, the biggest dealer in drugs in Corinthium.'

'Do you?' Ferros's question sounded slightly weary, as he sometimes did when Lara revealed yet another new thing that she had done, or become. 'And will this Graco have Sirene?'

'I do not think so. I have heard nothing and I probably would have if it is as valuable as Severos says.'

Ferros took another gulp of ale. 'You know who will certainly have it?'

'Who?'

'Our former gaoler. Makron. Remember, he uses it to speak to Anazat.'

'Makron will have it, yes.' Lara smiled. 'So all we need do is get into the Sanctum, and steal some.'

Ferros didn't reply for a moment, as he stared at the ceiling. Then he looked at her again. 'No, we don't. We don't need to go to them.' Ferros drained his mug, then put it down. 'Because they will be coming to us. To the feast.'

Lara had raised her own mug to finish it because the ale, together with Severos's wine, had flushed her whole body and she really needed to get Ferros to her room at the port and have him. But she paused with the vessel at her lips, didn't drink. Was there something in the way he'd said *they*? Perhaps. But even if he hadn't emphasised the word, it was there. *She* was there. Someone who would be coming to the Feast of Tribute. And even if her name was not in his mind, as Lara swallowed the last of her ale it was in hers.

Roxanna.

3
Feast of Blood

Three days later ...

It is not every dawn you wake up and know that by sunset you will have murdered your husband.

It was Roxanna's first thought, even before she opened her eyes. She did not need to see him. She could hear him, that snuffling snore of his: two grunts, a whistling inhale, a snort-snort-snort as the air went out. On and on. Those sounds had driven her close to madness these last fifteen years. Probably had when they'd been married before. Another of the details she'd forgotten about him, in the fifty years of their estrangement.

She looked forward to never hearing it again. Wondered how high on the list of things she looked forward to today it was. Near the top, anyway. Probably just below the joy she'd take when he realised what she had done. All that she had done. She would tell him, when he was powerless to affect it. The horror in his eyes would still be pleasing her, long after the memory of his snoring had faded.

Thrusting the noise aside, she focused inward behind her closed eyelids. There were risks to this day still, the one she had been planning for so long. Because she had to depend on others to execute much of the plan. She hated that. Especially as all of them were men.

Three men. Two of them especially she had bound to her with the strongest of ties – lust, in all its forms. For power, wealth. For her.

She thought first of the one who was in the city. Korshak, the Horse Lord. He'd been her lover for just a few months: long enough to bind him tight in the first flushes of fleshly desire which he called love. He was besotted by her, had been easy to persuade of the rightness of what she proposed. It suited his sense of loyalty as well, to his people, and the cause he'd always fought for: the One. It had been ridiculously easy, in the fading glow of their exertions, to feign her own growing passion for the child that was neither man nor woman. The child that this Korshak had actually fetched from the savage land across the sea. This child who had vanished in that same reshaping of the wide world fifteen years before. Yet belief in the One had not faded with absence. Rather the reverse. It was easy to control people who had suffered so much – conquest, famine, a plague – with the belief that an innocent child would return and save them all. Korshak believed that she now believed – and if ever a moment came when he suspected that she didn't, she distracted him.

The second man was not in the city. His part of the plan was to arrive later, with an army. The obese Barallingen was one of the more disgusting men she'd ever slept with. Perhaps her distaste had showed, because he was less bound to her by lust. What tied him to her was his ambition. She had not only offered him the throne of his people by eliminating all who stood between him and it. She had also offered him glory, which his people prized above all things. To sweep down from the forests and avenge the slaying of their old High Chief, Malvolen. Killed not by their old enemies of Corinthium, who were beaten and abject still fifteen years after the conquest. No. Killed by their new enemies, the true power in the empire: the Four Tribes, who next were coming for them.

She laughed – and there was a hitch in the snuffling of Makron beside her. He would wake soon, and they must be about the day. Yet perhaps a few moments first to consider the last man, the one she no longer controlled but hoped to again.

She'd learned something over the years from the prostitutes she'd possessed. That no matter how many men they fucked, there was usually one person who they loved. Often another woman. Sometimes a man. He, or she, was the one they thought of when suffering their work. There was one for her. Just one, in her hundreds of years of seductions, that her mind went to when she was suffering hers.

Ferros.

She did not know why. It annoyed her, truly, that any man could hold even a small piece of her. But when, at the Feast of Tribute two years before, Barallingen had answered the question that had plagued her these fifteen years, where Ferros had been, by telling her that he was the new Shield and Spear of the High Chief, her breath had caught. And caught again when, from the shadows of a ruined doorway, she'd watched him ride in at the end of the column of Wattenwolden. Recognising him instantly, despite his thick plaited beard and long hair.

On that night when the empire fell, after she had killed – for the second time! – his little bitch of a wife, she had told him that they would meet again one day. Today was that day and it was the one part of her plan that worried her. For it was not controllable. *He* was not controllable. Yet she knew that if she felt this about him, there would be a part of him that felt the same for her. She would just have to find it.

Makron gave a last huge snuffle. He was awake now, she knew, but lying there considering this momentous day as she had done. 'Did you sleep well?' she said, opening her eyes.

'I did. You?'

'Terribly. You snored all night.'

He laughed, threw back the sheet, stood and stretched. 'I don't snore. You know that.' He rang a bell on the bedside table to summon food. It would come fast, for slaves did not like to be beaten. 'It is nearly time, isn't it, wife?'

'Time?' she said, startled. Could he see anything else in her eyes? He'd known her a long time after all. Over one hundred years.

'To speak to Anazat. He said he would contact us soon after sunrise.'

'Ah yes. You eat. I'll bathe.' She rose, crossed to a door, opened it. A female slave waiting on the stair jumped up, bowed and called down. Three big men carried a large wooden bath up and into the room, placing it behind screens that sheltered a corner. More slaves came, staggering under the weight of jugs of hot water which they poured into the tub.

She would wash any trace of Makron from her skin. Korshak would be too busy to visit her and taint her again. There was only one man's scent she wanted on her this night. This night of triumph.

As she lowered herself into the warm water and slaves began to scrub her, she closed her eyes again, enjoying the touch. It was one of the better things the Four Tribes had brought to Corinthium, slavery. There had been none before in the empire which, in retrospect, was an error. When she ruled alone, she would keep some of the improvements that had come with conquest.

It was when she was being dried with soft blankets that she heard her husband speak. 'Anazat,' Makron said. 'How good it is to see you. I trust you are enjoying fresh winds upon the water.'

'I am not,' came the reply, that steely voice she'd come to

know well. More often than not used to give her and Makron commands. They ruled Corinthium, but only as regents for the One.

Obedience, she thought. This night would also see the beginning of its end.

Roxanna came back quietly through the silken cloths into the room. Makron glanced at her and she shook her head. Unless she was ordered to be present, she preferred to listen out of sight. Anazat could sometimes be indiscreet about her when he did not think she was there. It was always useful to know a little more of what went on within those black, black eyes.

'Where is your lady?'

'At the stables. Would you like me to send someone to fetch her?'

'No need. I must be brief anyway. I am on my way to Midgarth.'

'Midgarth?' Makron frowned. 'When we spoke three weeks ago you were in Tarfona, about to embark with the fleet and bring the army to Corinthium for the execution of our plan.'

'Our plan has not changed in respect of the Wattenwolden. The army still sails to help you defeat them, though storms were delaying departure when I left.'

'Where are you now?'

'I arrived at the Keep yesterday.'

'The Keep?'

'Yes. And I cross the mountain to Midgarth today.'

'Why?'

Anazat leaned closer in. There was an extra brightness in the darkness of his eyes. 'The One has returned,' he whispered.

'The One?' Both Makron and Roxanna jumped. 'When? Where are ... *they*?'

'We are not certain. When I said returned I meant reappeared.'

Anazat rubbed his eyes and Roxanna, who at the news had

come nearer so she could see him but still not be seen, noted how tired he looked. To go from Tarfona through the tunnel in the mountains and all the way to the Keep in three weeks meant moving fast, and never resting.

The monk continued. 'You know that I am always aware of when the seeing globes are used. Have a sense of where they are. It is a second sight that comes from all my years with Sirene.' He knuckled his eyes again, sat back. 'The globe that Luck stole when he fled the Keep with the One and the mother has been silent since. Three weeks ago, somewhere in the high mountains between Saghaz-a and Midgarth, it was used for the first time in fifteen years.'

'By Luck?'

'That I cannot tell. I do not know who travels with Sirene, only that someone does.' He ran a tongue over chapped lips. 'But Luck was with the One. And he was clever. Strong too, to have resisted Sirene's near irresistible call these several years. That he succumbs now must mean that he is ready ... to do something.'

'To do what?'

'He was the only one of their so-called gods that I ever feared. I got to know him well. Now, I think he is getting ready to strike back.'

'To retake Midgarth?'

'That would be where I would start, if I were him. My regent there, Peki Asarko, has largely subjugated the land with,' he shuddered slightly, 'deviant cruelties. Our recent plan for the northlands was to withdraw many of our forces, weakening him just enough to ensure that when that savage from the west, Intitepe, returned to claim the throne of Midgarth that we offered him – as my monks in Ometepe inform me he is about to do – then the two of them would tear each other apart. We would destroy whoever remained.'

Makron smiled. 'Your mastery of manipulation is a lesson to us all, lord.'

Anazat shrugged the compliment away. 'But the plan has changed with this new development. Accelerated, rather. Now I need Peki Asarko again. For if we have the One in our possession, with the devotion *they* inspire,' the eyes gleamed again, 'we will sweep the world up in months not years. As we should have done all those years ago.'

'Praise her! Praise him!'

'Praise *them*.' Anazat looked away, to someone who had entered. 'I'm coming,' he said, before turning back. 'I must leave. It is necessary to get over Molnalla before the first promised snow falls on its summit.'

'What would you have us do?'

'Your part of the plan has not changed. The Wattenwolden still need to be defeated. The storms on the Great Sea should have abated and the fleet sailed. There will be no problem. Your plans should only be delayed by a week.'

'Each week deeper into a Wattenwold winter is a problem, Anazat. Your army won't wish to be caught in the pass of Kristun if the snows come early. They would pray for the delights of a sea storm then.'

'You shall just set out earlier. You planned to muster for a week? Halve that. Are your city brigades ready?'

'Ready and keen. Your Horse Lords and Huntresses have been working them hard.'

'And the monks too?' Roxanna could hear the extra sharpness in the question. 'Weapons are nothing compared to faith in the One. Especially now.'

'Praise her. Praise him,' Makron intoned again. Out of sight, Roxanna rolled her eyes, which her husband must have noticed because he coughed and went on hastily, 'But do these changes not indicate another? Perhaps we should ... *deal* with the

Wattenwolden at the feast tonight? We could kill their High Chief, and many of their best fighters.'

'All Wattenwolden are good fighters. And since they have many spies in the city, and a system of pigeons and messengers that bring back word almost daily, they would hear of the treachery and prepare for what followed it. Then the forces we bring might truly suffer in the pass at Kristun. Surprise is what we need.' Anazat cleared his throat. 'No, follow the plan. Feast them well, then let them return slowly to their homes, burdened with tribute. We will be close behind and finish what we could not fifteen years ago.'

'We only thought—'

'*We?*' The interruption was fast and low. 'So your wife has been disagreeing? Again?'

'No, Anazat. She obeys me totally. And she is as devoted to the One.'

The mutter came. 'Somehow I doubt both those things.' He glanced away again. 'Yes, yes!' he snapped. Turning briefly back, he said, 'I go. Do all that I have commanded. I will be there in early spring. And perhaps I will not be alone.'

A last gleam and he was gone. Roxanna came forward. 'He doesn't like me, does he?'

'He doesn't like either of us. Never has. Necessity alone forced him to make us regents here.' Makron wrapped the globe in a shroud of velvet. 'So I believe that once he has dealt with the Wattenwolden he will use his returning forces to deal with us. Look how casually he throws away his servant in the north.' He picked up the vial of Sirene and fingered it, before stoppering it and slipping it into a drawer. 'Those brigades of the city he has trained for us. Korshak tells me that now only two go north with the invasion. Four are to remain to quiet our restive people. If the Wattenwolden fight as well as they can, and take a toll, when the Four Tribes return, well ...' he smiled, 'more than one people can make use of surprise.' He rose, came behind his wife, wrapped his arms around her. 'Did I not promise you a city to rule?'

'Actually, husband, you promised me the world.'

'Well, one step at a time. And the first is to make sure our guests feast well, and leave the city not suspecting a thing, no?' He bent, kissed her neck. 'You have your things to take care of, and I mine, eh?'

'I do indeed.'

'Then I shall see you at the feast.' He studied her body, its shape pressing out the sheet wrapped around her. 'I trust you will look magnificent?'

'Do you doubt it?'

He left and she looked around, wrinkling her nose at the signs that she had to share this space that had for so long been hers alone. Still, it would be hers again, and soon.

She clapped her hands. More slaves came, took away the bath, while the one who was her personal body servant stood before her, hands crossed, eyes lowered. Roxanna considered what clothes to order the girl to fetch from her dressing room below. She would make a show this night at the feast. After all, it wasn't every day you murdered a husband ... and took the first step towards ruling the world.

There were several reasons that could account for Ferros's edginess.

The ceremony that had just concluded was one. There were elaborate rituals to be performed, a token re-enactment of the fall of the city, with five players dressed as city militia briefly fighting and being defeated by Wattenwolden warriors. Wearing a mask, for he still thought it best to conceal himself in case anyone should penetrate the layers of hair and recognise him, he was one. Then Malvolen gave a speech, glorifying the fallen, denigrating Corinthium, telling the tale of how the mighty empire had been forced to submit. Finally, the tribute was carried into the pavilion – double the normal amount since they had not collected last year due to plague. A mound of silver and gold, bags of coins and stacks of fresh-forged armour and weapons occupied one side of the large tent, and an equal sized hoard was outside. When the slaves who had borne it had withdrawn on their knees – slaves in Corinthium, a sight that made his stomach turn – the feasting began.

Another reason for his concern.

It was meant to be decorous, a meal made up of successive courses. That was the Corinthian way – but not that of the Wattenwolden. So it had degenerated quite quickly into a combination of drinking contest and trough guzzling. Ferros didn't drink and barely ate. Indeed he was too on edge to sit long, preferring to walk the perimeter of the pavilion, both inside and out.

He knew that the High Chief had dismissed his fears of betrayal. Of Corinthians killing the gathered tribesmen to avenge both the defeat and the humiliations heaped on them every year since at this Feast of Tribute. He knew the arguments against – that the treaty stipulated that the forces in the city be kept small; that those who trained them, of the Four Tribes, must be few in number too. That betrayal and murder would be reported swiftly, and the Wattenwolden would return to overrun walls that had not been rebuilt, bringing death by sword and fire. But he also knew that those who governed the city did not bear restrictions or humiliations well.

And perhaps that was the biggest reason for his edginess. Because one of those governors had not come.

She had not come.

Ferros came to a halt outside the pavilion. He had been shutting the noise out with thoughts but it now exploded again behind him. He was close to the top table, could hear Malvolen, through his translator, haranguing the Horse Lord who sat near him about boar spears. One representative of each of the Four Tribes was there. Makron was there, at the far end of the table from where Ferros had been seated and so unlikely to recognise Ferros under all his hair. But the chair next to him was vacant. 'My wife apologises for her tardiness,' Makron had explained when taking his seat. 'She says that for this occasion she must strive to look even more special.'

That is the main reason I am so jumpy, he realised. How do I just sit there and watch her enter like a player in a spectacle at a theatre on the Stradun? How do I not leap up, cry her name? Take her in my arms? Fuck her? Stab her?

He felt the length of tempered steel against his calf muscle. The only weapons allowed in the pavilion were those of the tribute, and the antler-handled knives used to cut meat. But edginess had made him arm himself, if only that much.

He turned around the corner of the tent, planning on re-entering. Malvolen would be missing him, especially as it sounded as though the dispute over spears was getting heated. But then he stopped when he saw movement ahead, figures emerging between the two ruined buildings that marked the wide street that led to the seventh hill of Agueros, and the Sanctum upon it.

It was a palanquin, a silk tent on a moving platform. Three hefty, bare-chested men were at each of the four poles. As they marched closer, he noticed that two of the tent sides were pinned up. When they turned to face the entrance, he saw the figure he'd known would be the sole occupant.

Roxanna.

He could not help his gasp. Fifteen years since he'd seen her and, of course, she had not aged. She had never been shy about her charms, wore clothes designed to reveal, to provoke. Now he could see that she was wearing ... scarcely anything at all.

The palanquin entered through the wide entrance of the pavilion. The roar inside dwindled to a hum and thence to silence. Ferros moved around and watched as the vehicle was lowered, and the two biggest guards went to its front and offered hands. Two black ones emerged and took one each. Then Roxanna stepped out.

Like Ferros, all gasped. The nothing she wore was a golden, thin-hooped chain that ran from her neck to her waist, a tail of it dropping to dangle between her thighs. Her breasts, her magnificent, full, rose-nippled breasts stood bare. Her hair, woven with smaller chains of silver, rose high and Ferros saw that the column of it was held at a single point – by a slim silver dagger.

He did not think that anyone would question Roxanna bringing a weapon to the feast.

She stepped away from the men who'd helped her descend, and halted where the lamplight was strongest, reflecting on ebony skin that was lightly dusted in gold powder. In a clear, sultry voice she purred, 'Welcome, lords of the Wattenwold, to Corinthium.'

The silence was filled, suddenly, completely. Men roared, and banged tankards on the table. Ferros watched until Makron descended, took her hand, led her to the dais, before he turned away. That first sight of her had confirmed the worst of his fears. He hated her. He had never wanted anyone – *anything* – so badly.

He walked fast to the same ruined entranceway she'd come through. It was a clear night, the two moons – Blue Revlas, Horned Saipha, both waning – between them shedding enough light to show him the next hill of Agueros, the buildings of the Sanctum black shadows upon it. From this angle he could also see, rising from that dark, the tall tower where she lived. If he squinted hard he might even be able to make out the balustrade he'd laid her across.

Stop it, Ferros! He cursed himself in the three languages he spoke. He was a soldier, had never allowed emotions to take him except when they helped him in a fight. And yet the sight of a woman he'd fucked once – once! – fifteen years before had weakened his knees.

He looked at the tower again. Perhaps he should go there right now because, as he had said to Lara, it was where Sirene was likely to be. It was his task to get it, as it was hers to steal the globe. Perhaps it was the time, while everyone was so distracted. By a feast. By a naked woman.

He was in the moon shadows of the ruined buildings. He was about to step from them when he heard a noise, a stone falling. It would have been nothing, a further crumbling of the house he sheltered beside, if it had not been accompanied by the harsh whisper of a single word. A word in *tolanpa-sen*, language of the Four Tribes.

'Quiet!'

Ferros slipped fully back into the dark. He listened, and for a while could only hear the noise from the pavilion behind him. But he'd been a hunter all his life, had learned to shut out everything that was not prey and soon enough he heard it – the soft breathing of men trying not to be heard.

Eventually he was focused enough to tell the different breaths. Six men – if they were all men – no more than ten paces from him, crouching in the ruin of what had once been the cellar of the other house. He supposed they could be soldiers sharing a bottle, away from their superiors. But if so, why the silence? Perhaps they'd bedded down for the night? Except all were awake, yet none spoke. It was a mystery and he'd have to solve it. There was a window, glassless and with half its frame gone, an opening in a broken wall. He began to move to it, step after noiseless step, as if he was about to raid an enemy camp at night. Perhaps he was.

And then he didn't need to be quiet any longer. Because, from the pavilion, all the voices hushed and one came clear. Hers. Roxanna was singing, quite beautifully, which surprised him because he hadn't known that she could. It was an old sailor's song of Corinthium, a woman's ballad for a love lost to the sea.

I kissed him hard upon the dock,
As a southerly filled his sails.
A kiss to take to a distant shore
And keep him safe in gales.

However, he wasn't surprised by the word that came from in front of him, as the first verse ended. 'Now,' the man said, and stepped out of the cellar.

The Horse Lord was the one surprised – by the figure in the moonlight before him. And though he had a sword, and Ferros only a knife, the one was drawn and the other wasn't. And though no one had declared any intentions, Ferros could smell treachery as clearly as he would shit on a battlefield. Hear it too in the voice of the near naked woman who sang and summoned killers with her song. So Ferros lunged, putting his dagger through the Horse Lord's throat. He gurgled, wrapped his fingers around the blade, that were cut off as Ferros jerked the knife back. But he did not think to kill more, even though the soldiers rising from the cellar shouted and reached for him. He just turned and sprinted away.

As he ran he realised he was far from the only one running. The pavilion had been sited in the centre of a much larger area of waste ground, where the food and drink could be prepared. From the ruined buildings that ringed it, men were emerging, and moonlight glimmered on helmet and spear, in a thousand points of light.

The second verse was just beginning up ahead. 'Treachery!' he screamed. 'To arms! To arms! Wattenwolden, to arms!'

An arrow passed through the sleeve of his tunic. He stumbled, kept his feet, ran on.

> He took the kiss to that distant shore,
> Though faithless did he prove.
> My—

The cry interrupted her song. 'To arms! To arms! Wattenwolden, to arms!' and she was disappointed, not so much because she wouldn't get to finish something she'd been practising for a while but because her elaborate planning was already unravelling. The end of the first verse was meant to bring her soldiers to their feet and moving, the end of the second was to see them rush into the tent to slaughter the startled guests within. Who were less startled now, and reacting with the instinct of warriors. On the dais beside her men leaped up, meat knives in hand. On the floor, many others were already rushing to the tribute pile and the weapons stacked there. They reached it, as the shouter ran through the entrance, and she recognised him as the one she'd sought already with her eyes and had not found till now.

'We are betrayed!' Ferros cried, bending and snatching up a long sword. 'To arms and on me!'

He spun round, and the first Horse Lords who came through the entrance died on his swirling sword. It gave those who'd heeded his call time to arm and join him, and though the next wave was larger, it crashed onto the rock of the Wattenwolden. It bought Ferros a moment, to step away, look about the pavilion for other dangers, and finally look straight at her.

'Is this your doing?' Makron had risen beside her. Now he

grabbed her wrist, and swung her hard around. 'Tell me,' he shouted, 'did you do this?'

'I did.'

'It is too soon, you stupid bitch.' He looked wildly around. 'Anazat will come and kill us for this.'

Roxanna pulled her arm from his grasp. 'Not if I kill him first.'

He looked back at her, his eyes narrowing with fury. 'Later for this. We must leave here now. Now!' he screamed.

He grabbed again for her arm. She jerked it beyond his reach. 'I must,' she said, reaching up into her hair, 'but you won't.'

Maybe it was the cascade of hair tumbling down that blinded him to it. To the silver blade that had held it all up, descending now. She drove it into his neck, where his artery pulsed. It had stood out in his fury. Now, it shot blood into her face.

She kept it in him, holding him by it as his knees gave. Thrust her face close. 'And you do snore,' she said, jerking the dagger out.

As Makron collapsed, she heard a shout from behind her, a chair being thrown back. She turned and saw, a dozen paces away, the High Chief, Malvolen. She was close enough to see in his eyes that he knew. Knew who had betrayed them. With a bellow, he started across towards her. He had a knife in his hand, as did she. But he was old, and even if she was far older, she was younger too. She smiled as he threw aside more chairs to get to her, and dropped into the knife fighter's stance.

But then another part of her plan did work. For killers did not need to enter a tent only by its entrance. Swords slashed through the canvas behind the table and a dozen Horse Lords burst in. Korshak was leading them. Malvolen, seeing the odds, and with an agility that belied his age, leaped off the dais and ran towards the place where his tribe was fighting.

'Woman!' Korshak cried, seizing her about the waist. His

eyes were bright with combat and lust. He bent to kiss her.

She slapped him away. 'Not now, fool. Do what I told you. Find *him*. Bring him.'

She stepped off the dais at the back, and out through the slit Korshak's warriors had made. There was no need to stay and witness the fight. The Wattenwolden might be great warriors but they were outnumbered here five to one. She'd urged the Horse Lords to take prisoners if they could. There was always a call for slaves and hostages.

But there was only one person she truly needed to see. She'd pointed Ferros out to Korshak when the Wattenwolden had ridden into the city. She had impressed upon the Horse Lord how vital the man was to all their futures. I need him alive, she'd said. Ferros was, of course, immortal, but she didn't want the Horse Lord to know that.

As she walked swiftly away towards Agueros, the clash of arms, the shrieks and the death cries faded. She found herself thinking of Makron. He was dead, but could be reborn. She'd been tempted to allow it, so that she could savour a more prolonged death. But no. The look in his eyes had been enough to sate her, so she'd ordered Korshak to lop off his head.

Besides, she thought, enjoying the cool breeze on her naked body, I hope to be busy later. Very busy.

Ferros had known one thing all his life: loyalty. Once it had been to the empire, an empire he now knew to be corrupt and cruel. Now he had another, had sworn deep oaths to it only recently.

Here, he was Arcturien. He was the High Chief's Spear and Shield. He had neither of those in his hands, but he had a long sword and he had always been good with that.

The enemy – mainly Horse Lords, but there were Seafarers among them in their gaudy attire, some Huntresses, some men in the uniform of the City Guard – had streamed in from all sides of the pavilion, and cut down many men armed with only the knives they'd been using to cut meat. But enough Wattenwolden had heeded his cry and grabbed the weapons meant for tribute from the stacks. A body of them, perhaps fifty, were clustered in the tent's middle, behind tables overturned to form a kind of fort. In their midst, roaring orders, he could see Malvolen, his chief, the man he'd sworn his oaths to.

A guardsman lunged for him with his pike. Ferros swivelled, let the point pass his chest, cocked his sword to the side, ran the length of wood to the man, and took his head. A Horse Lord swung his huge curved sword down, seeking to split him from scalp to groin. Lunging hard to the side, Ferros made his sword a slope of steel crossways above his head. The curved sword slid down it, and Ferros brought his back leg up, spun, stood tall and, two-handed, flicked his weapon over and down to sever his enemy's hand at the wrist. It cleared a space, a sort of passage bounded by clashing swords and fighting men. He ran down it, and vaulted over a table.

Men turned to him as he landed; recognised him, turned back to the fray. Ferros did not stop, but ran to the centre of the rough square. 'High Chief,' he cried, 'it is time to go.'

'Go? When there are enemies to kill?' Malvolen roared. He was leaning on a spear someone must have brought him, its butt to the floor. He spun it up into the air, caught it, bent and threw. A Horse Lord, a leader perhaps, foolish enough to have leaped onto a table's side to urge his men over the barrier, tumbled back, steel-tipped wood through his chest.

'Too many enemies. And they win if they take us.' Ferros was looking around as he spoke. Fewer of the enemy had come through the rear-side of the pavilion. That way lay the ruined walls – and a few hundred paces beyond them the camp where the Wattenwolden servants were keeping the horses.

He turned. The enemy were pressing from all sides – and massing in the centre for what was shaping to be a final assault. There were just too many of them – yet not as many behind.

One of the many things he'd needed to learn to become the Spear and Shield was in one way the simplest, yet in another the hardest – he'd learned to whistle. It was how the warriors communicated on the battlefield, to switch tactics; to form a shield wall for defence, a spear wedge for assault ... or to retreat in order and rally again. He had wasted spit and wind for weeks struggling to get it, until one day he simply did.

Putting his thumb and forefinger tip to tip he placed them in his mouth and blew a single note that pierced even the battle tumult. And every Wattenwolden who could turn away without getting a blade in the back did, looking to the High Chief and the man standing beside him. As he felt their attention, Ferros blew a different, four-note song. Trained to obey on the instant, the tribesmen turned as one and followed the High Chief and his Spear and Shield. Sweeping aside the few who sought to hold them, they poured from the back of the tent.

The tactic had obviously shocked the enemy for they did not start to follow till the Wattenwolden were halfway to the tumbled walls. Then arrows began to fly, the Huntresses at last able to loose. A few men fell, were gathered up, most dodged and swerved, running on.

They gained the shelter of the ruins – and the enemy appeared to halt when they did, though arrows still bounced and clattered on the stones. Ducking, Ferros grabbed the arm of a young warrior. His name was Domen, and he'd won all the footraces in the contest, which was why he was there. 'Run to the camp. Get the horses saddled. The High Chief comes. Ride back immediately on one, and bring another with as many bows, sheaves of arrows, shields and javelins you can load onto it in the space of fifty breaths. Go!' Domen ran, and Ferros looked again at the enemy. He saw horses there. The Horse Lords had sent for theirs too. No cavalryman liked to fight on foot if he had the choice. But it was taking time. Time he could use.

He dropped down beside Malvolen. The old chief, though he had fought well, was now puffing hard beside him. Ferros sought and spotted Haldan, one of the Ninth Balbek he'd led in the deserts and then away from the fall of Corinthium; like him, now a bearded tribesman of the Wattenwold – though Ferros suddenly could not remember his tribal name. 'Haldan,' he called, and the man, crouching low to avoid the arrows that still flew, slid across. 'Pick me twenty of the best men that survive here and tell them they stay. Then take three men and help the High Chief with the rest as fast as you can back to the camp.'

'Help me? Help yourself!' Malvolen threw off the reaching arm, came onto his knees. 'We go. We all go now.'

'No, lord. They have horsemen now and they'd catch us on open ground halfway to the camp. But if they delay a little longer and I get those bows—' He broke off, confirmed what he'd noted before. 'This is good ground for a stand. The broken walls each side are still too high to ride over. They have to come through this gap here.' He slapped a stone in front of him. 'With twenty men I can hold it.'

'You are right. And we will mount and ride back to fight with you.'

'Do not, lord!' He shouted it, then lowered his voice. 'That is a fight for another day. You must use the time we win you to outdistance those who will pursue you, and get back to the Wattenwold.'

Malvolen sighed. 'That is the second time you have contradicted me. You know that the Spear and Shield's duty is to advise and then obey.'

'I thought his duty was to preserve the life of his lord?' He grinned. 'Besides, it looks like I may be one of the shortest-ever-lived holders of that post.'

'Not if I can help it.' With a grunt, Malvolen forced himself to his feet. 'Live, Arcturien, by whatever means you can.' He stared out at the gathering enemy, steel in his eyes. 'I will return with an army in weeks and revenge those who died this day.'

'Now that I agree with, lord.' Ferros bowed, then turned to Haldan who had returned. 'See him safe.'

They and the rest went without another word, crouching low so the enemy did not see them go. The twenty selected remained and Ferros saw that Haldan had done well. They were all young, those warriors who had won the right to come by their prowess in arms. He swiftly whistled them close. 'These rocks,' he said, pointing to jagged remnants, most about the size of a man's head and chest. 'Throw them over the gap here to slow their horses.'

As they obeyed, he looked to the front again. There were many more men mounted now, and other bodies forming into columns. It would not be long and Ferros found himself doing an unaccustomed thing for him. He prayed – for the swift return of the young man he'd sent. He didn't discriminate. Gods of the desert, city and forest, of the Sarphardi, the Wattenwolden and Corinthium were all solicited. Then, just as it looked as though the enemy was about to charge, one of those gods answered him – for Domen rode into camp with two other young men, and three laden packhorses.

'You've done well, lad,' Ferros said, as his men ran and grabbed bows, spears, javelins and shields. 'Now back off with you to the Chief.'

'Oh no, Arcturien.' He grinned. 'Malvolen told us to stay with you. For we three,' he jerked his head at the youths beside him, 'are the best archers in the tribe.'

It may or may not have been true, but there was no time to

argue, not with the enemies' horns now sounding the attack. At his nod, Domen and the other two seized a bow and quiver apiece and scrambled, agile as squirrels, up the ruined tower of the gatehouse. When they reached its apex, a trumpet blew a clear single note – and the enemy came.

First they sent a shower of arrows that fell like winter rain. Soon the Wattenwolden shields were studded like quills on a hedgehog. When this hail slackened the trumpet came again – and the enemy charged.

The city militia came first. And though the Horse Lords had been training them, and they had courage, they were not as skilled as their masters. Rubble tripped them, a shield lowered for a moment presented a gap to hurl a javelin through, shoot an arrow, jab a spear. Their own dying made their passage even harder and, when he saw the moment, Ferros put his fingers in his mouth and blew two notes. His twenty were over the lip and among them in a heartbeat and he the instant after. There was a brief skirmish, screams of terror seeming to blend into one anguished howl . . . and then the attackers broke.

'Hold! Hold!' yelled Ferros because he remembered how when a young man was battle-crazed it was so tempting to follow and stab at the fleeing backs. His young men did hold, and followed him back to the shelter of scattered stone.

More arrows came then, many more, falling again onto rock and upraised shield. He didn't dare look. 'Domen,' he called up to the runner in the tower, 'do they come?'

The young man used his glance to step around a jut of rock and loose his own arrow. He stepped back. 'Those mad bitches are leading, shooting their bows. The horsemen follow.'

'How many of them?'

'Many.' He grinned. 'I am glad I am up here and not down there.'

Ferros couldn't help grinning back. 'How many, you whelp?'

Domen's grin faded. 'A hundred at least.'

Ferros nodded. The enemy did not know how many they faced. For all they knew, all the survivors of the tent were awaiting them, hence the cautious approach. They would charge and retreat, charge again when they realised how few opposed them, and no matter how many his men killed, in the end they would be swept away. Before that, though, they might have done enough to help Malvolen get to the forests north of the walls. Among trees, the Wattenwolden were the best warriors in the world, and the Horse Lords would be struck down like deer.

Still, they could do more. He looked at his men. He had lost none in the militia's attack. Twenty faces looked back at him. 'Ten men with bows, ten with shields to cover them.' As they swiftly scrambled to obey, he hefted his own bow, nocked and said, 'Shoot past the Huntresses to the horses. They haven't had time to armour them. Kill as many as you can.' He looked. They were ready. 'Now,' he shouted.

He stepped up. He had no shelter of shield so he sighted, loosed, saw his arrow pierce a great roan chest, dropped behind the lip again. As arrows thunked into the shields beside him, he heard more than one high-pitched shriek of terror and agony. He loved horses, hated killing them. Hated even more having them killed under him. Any cavalryman did. He thought it might provoke the Horse Lords to come more swiftly, before they were quite prepared.

It did. The horns changed their blare, a command like his whistling upon a battlefield. Hooves pounded the turf. 'Javelins, then spears, then swords.' He raised his own spear high. 'For the Wattenwold! Gods and Soil!'

'Gods and Soil!' came the echo as twenty young men followed him up the slope.

The first wave of the enemy had arrived. But their horses were shying at the rubble he'd had thrown out onto that slope, and they were a close and easy target for javelins, and arrows from the tower. But the second wave came hard behind, its riders forcing their mounts through the fallen and up the slight slope with hard jabs of their spurred heels. Too close for javelins. His men seized spears, lunged at horses' chests and riders' bellies. Ferros didn't count how many he'd killed of either. Lost to the fight, no need to command, only to kill if he could, live if he could. He'd swapped spear for sword and shield without noticing when. So had his men. They fought from the crest, and the slope was churned by hooves, bodies and blood.

There was a moment, a giving, and the wave drew off. Wiping blood from his eyes – he didn't think it was his own – Ferros saw another wave building, leaders bringing their mounts up onto their rear legs, shrieking the command for the last assault, for the finish. He looked at his men – only eight were on their feet now, and only Domen in the tower. But five times that number lay dead or dying at the slope's base. Nine men left of his first command of the Wattenwolden in battle. He had never fought with better. And I commanded the Ninth Balbek, he thought, and smiled.

Now it was time to save as many as he could. So once again he put fingers to lips, and gave a different, three-note call.

His men looked at him, in exhaustion, in wonder. But they were trained to obey and, as one, they turned and ran into the night. When Domen was down from the tower, Ferros grabbed his arm and the two of them ran too.

He heard the blare of horns, the commanders' last urging cries, the pounding of hooves. These slowed as the Horse Lords reached the bloodied slope, as they braced for javelin and arrow. None came, and the next thing Ferros heard as he ran were the clearer cries as the enemy crested the slope. Then the hoof-falls started again.

He ran with Domen a little further then touched his arm, pointed. The youth nodded and split away. The remains of his command were now scattered over the open, moonlit ground, offering choices of pursuit. Some might make it, he thought, his breaths coming in great heaves. The first trees, and these shadows, are not that far away, surely?

Too far for him. He heard the hoof-falls, felt a flung spear, lurched to the side and it passed him. He turned, tried to draw his sword . . .

The horse's chest drove into him, flinging him back. He landed hard, all his air gone, and he could only lie there and wait for the lance blows that would pierce him, as they had the first time he'd fought these men, at the Battle of the Ridge in Cuerdocia. If they cut off his head he would not be born again to the agony of healing wounds. As his breath did not come, and his sight faded, he almost wished they would.

Yet just before he slipped away, he heard footsteps, felt someone kneeling by him, anticipated the knife thrust that would end it all. Someone took his chin in their hand. He heard a voice, a man ask, 'Is this him, Korshak?'

'It is him.' Ferros heard the reply and then it all went dark.

It was still dark when he awoke. But that, he swiftly realised, was not because he was dead, but because of the sack on his head. The other thing he noticed was that though he ached all over, especially in the chest where the horse had ridden him down, the pain was not the pain of rebirth. He had not died.

They had spared him. Why, he could not know. But before he had the answer to that he needed other answers first. Such as where he was. Why he was lying not on the ground or a gaol cell's stone floor but on something soft. And why his hands were untied.

He used his other senses. Listened, but there was no sound

nearby; nothing save for a faint chirping of birds, which sounded like a morning greeting to him. He could smell no trace of battle, except the sweat of it upon himself. Its taints of blood and shit were gone. If anything he smelled almost the opposite through the sacking that covered his head – a floral fragrance that seemed to him, suddenly, strangely familiar.

He stretched out his fingers, rubbed. He was lying on silk!

'Is anyone there?' he called.

Silence. Carefully he raised his hands and slipped the sack off his head.

It took him but a moment to recognise the room though he had only been in it once, near sixteen years before. It's not the time you spend there but what happens to you that matters, he thought, sitting up, wincing as he did.

He was in the room at the top of the tower. The place where he'd lost his mind, and a part of his heart, to Roxanna. It was her scent, something of forest flowers and honey, that lingered in the air. He had a feeling that she had just been there, watching him.

He stood, rubbed at the ache of his chest through his tunic, all he still wore, and looked around. The style of the room had changed, it was less opulent. Yet it was undoubtedly the same room. The balcony where he'd taken her – *taken* her! – over the balustrade was revealed and concealed as a silk curtain blew in on a slight morning breeze. The bed was different, in a different place, and octagonal now like the room. The table had not been there, nor the wooden tub filled with steaming water …

The table. He looked back at it. Because what he'd seen and not noticed drew him back again. He could not help his gasp.

Sitting in the middle of the table was a seeing globe.

In the distance, beyond the door and so at the bottom of the tower's spiral stair, he heard voices. Groaning as he did so, he shuffled over to the table. Smoke swirled within the glass. In the open drawer of the table was a small glass vial, half filled with dark liquid

He had told Lara that he thought he might find some of this Sirene in the Sanctum. With that, and the globe, they hoped to speak to the man who'd freed them at the Keep. The enemy of their enemy and so their friend. He had urged them to do so.

The voices were getting closer. A man and a woman, arguing. They seemed to stop a level below, volume and intensity rising. His tunic didn't have a pocket so he left the vial where it was and closed the drawer. He would take it when he left. Which he planned on doing soon.

He was sitting on the bed again when the door opened. He was not surprised to see her walk through it.

'You are awake,' Roxanna said.

'I am.'

She closed the door, leaned against it, smiled, spoke.

'Welcome back, my love.'

4
God of the Skies

Intitepe raised his hand – and kept it there. Those who could see him watched intently – none more than the two archers, one either side of him, who held their bowstrings taut and their flammable arrows above some burning logs. When he dropped his hand, they would set the arrowheads alight and shoot them into the sky for those who could *not* see him: the signal to commence the final assault of the last battle of the fifteen-year war.

Intitepe peered ahead. At the City of Women. It felt right that the war should end here, where it had begun. Once this had been a place of peace, where those who had lived their time and loved him in his marana went when their twelve years were up, together with other women who, for whatever reason, sought refuge away from the world of men. A haven – until it had become the spark to the fires of rebellion, their focus and symbol. He had besieged it right at the beginning, was about to storm it and kill the child that threatened him, his child with Atisha … when something extraordinary had happened. The two of them had escaped.

The memory of how was what kept his arm up in the air now.

He had thought that on his return from Midgarth he would extinguish those flames in a few months. He was the Fire King, after all. But he'd discovered something new about fire.

That though you could put it out in one place – brutally, as an example to all – it would smoulder underground then flare up a few months later somewhere else entirely. Up and down his realm he'd trekked, from the ice mountains of Palaga in the north, to the white sands of Volpaio in the far south, stamping out every new flame. It had taken fifteen years – only to end up back here, where that woman had again seized this citadel on a rock he'd left too poorly defended, and launched yet another revolt. Today, at last, it ended. Yet in its ending something else began. Something wonderful.

If...

The thought, the sudden doubt in it, surprised him. He looked at his two archers, tense with readiness. All knew that instant obedience was what he required. He looked past them, left and right, to the warriors he could see. Veterans all now, as were those beyond them. It was the benefit of continuous conflict, for now he had an army hardened by constant war, fit for any purpose he would put it to. A fleet too, for rebels had set up bases on offshore islands and he'd had to fight them there. Though much of the fighting was small-scale, ambush and raid, there'd been sieges as well, and two pitched battles. So he had made sure that the advisers the black-eyed one had sent with him, and kept sending – Horse Lords, Seafarers and munke – trained his troops in all ways of fighting.

It was another way of preparing for the wonderful thing to come.

Still he did not drop his arm. He looked back to the fortress. It was an island of rock, a plug thrust up from the earth. Before, when he'd taken it, he'd built just one bridge across the gorge. Now he had six. And although this time there were a lot more fighters in the city – not just women – even if all were hardened as well, they were too few to stop an assault from six positions simultaneously.

Intitepe's arm began to shake. When he'd raised it, he'd thought to hold it up only a few moments, before sending his forces in. Yet he'd started thinking of the beginning after this end; started thinking again of that woman who opposed him. The one who, more than any other, had kept the revolt burning in his realm all this time. Who waited again for him this day, up ahead.

Besema.

How he wanted her alive! It was the one part of his plan that was flawed. Not because she, like Atisha, had once been his 'One', his favourite from those years in the marana seventy years before, and so should be punished for this ultimate betrayal. No. He wanted her alive because of what she could make him.

He wanted a floating globe.

He thought back to the first time he'd seen one, rising from the city ahead, Atisha and their child escaping in it. Remembered other times he'd seen it. Floating above battlefields. Gliding over his encampments at night, dropping death in bottles of flaming, burning liquid, destroying his supplies, terrifying his troops. And however crude that first one might have been, Besema had improved them since. Was able to steer them. Only when he'd copied the huge bows that the Seafarers fought with from their ships, built dozens, adapted them to shoot into the sky, had he been able to lessen their influence, forcing them to fly high. Still, they'd floated above his armies, had warned of his approach, allowed for ambush or escape. They had dragged out this war. Their immense power was clear to him.

He wanted that power. For what he planned after this battle, for his new beginning, he wanted it very much. To have it, he needed the inventor alive.

Yet why would Besema remain so? She would know how Intitepe would treat the woman who had betrayed their love. She knew him well, after all.

He thought of the three women he had in the city, whose families he held hostage. When the arrows lit the sky, they were meant to seize Besema, barricade themselves in a room, keep her safe until his troops arrived. Yet now, looking into the eyes of his warriors either side of him, seeing their hunger for this final slaughter, he was suddenly certain that no one would be safe in the City of Women. There were some things even he could not control.

Intitepe was not used to doubts, or a change of mind. But sixteen years earlier he had thought he ruled the whole world as its only god. Now he knew differently.

No, he thought. There has to be a better way. 'Hold! Hold!' he called out along the lines. With a glare at the archers, so they eased the tension on their bowstrings, he slowly lowered his arm.

Though the war had been notable for its savagery – on both sides – there had been occasions when they'd had to parley – to save the slaughter of children perhaps, or to collect wounded. Intitepe had not wanted to parley here, had not sent out a herald urging surrender in exchange for life. A final massacre needed no parley. Now that had changed. But he would send no herald. He would do it himself.

He snapped his fingers at Toman, the commander of his forces. The much-scarred veteran came and kneeled. 'Bring me trumpeters,' he said.

The man's eyes narrowed. He was perplexed enough to question. 'No attack, lord?'

'Later. First—' Intitepe broke off, and looked again at the city. 'Trumpeters.'

Besema sat in the window arch, looking out at the enemy. She'd watched from the moment they began to muster soon after dawn, then as each of the units moved into position.

Looked for any weakness, any area where some of the troops might be newer recruits, less well trained, less committed. Over the years she'd looked out on many such situations and found ways to exploit them. A sudden assault at a weak point. Spies in the night persuading new recruits to mutiny. Launching an air globe to rain flame from the sky.

Not today, though, she thought. Intitepe has left nothing to chance here.

All his troops were veterans, and he had gathered many of his allies, those fearsome Horse Lords, the Seafarers. He had mustered a dozen of those vast bows, all angled skywards. When the enemy did not know where her globes were coming from, or when, they always had a chance. However, there was nowhere in the City of Women where she could gain height swiftly enough to avoid those huge arrows.

She looked down at her own troops, waiting behind barricades that faced each one of those six bridges. Too few, far too few. Yet every man and woman there would fight and die this day. It was that or surrender – which Intitepe had not even offered. He'd realised that there would be no point. As did her people. To die in battle was a better option than to die slowly under the torturer's caress, or on the pyres where the Fire King burned his enemies alive. Or even in chains on benches, as slavs rowing his fleet.

Slavs. Another cruel innovation from the world across the seas.

At least it was only her soldiers that would die. They'd taken all their children out the day before the last valley was blocked. Children who had grown up in freedom and with their parents' cause. So perhaps, even if the rebellion ended this day, a small spark would be kept glowing in the hearts of the next generation. A spark of defiance, to burst into flame again.

Not for me, she thought, stood, groaned, instant ache in all her bones. For me, this end will be almost a relief. What am I? Eighty-six? Eighty-eight? Too old to remember. And too old to still be the leader of an army, that was for sure.

She glanced out again, searching for anything she'd missed … *anything*. Hope is stubborn, and resistance a habit hard to break. All she saw were Intitepe's last troops moving into place.

Nearly sixteen years since that first spark of rebellion, and that first flight, today it was finally over, in the place where it had begun.

She often thought of that day. How when she was already old, and had thought her life almost finished, she'd discovered that, in so many, many ways, it had yet to begin. When Atisha and her child – her miraculous, prophesied child – arrived.

She breathed the name out now. 'Poum.'

When she'd seen the child's differences, Besema had known that something had altered in the world. She didn't know how much until, during a raid, they'd captured one of Intitepe's advisers, a man with a shaven head and blackening eyes who called himself a munke. He had revealed a world too vast to truly grasp, filled with extraordinary people so different from those of Ometepe. He'd also told how Atisha's child was prophesied in that other vast world too. Not as the slayer-son of a king-father. As a saviour.

The last thing he'd told – for he died the next day in a counter raid when Intitepe's troops tried to take him back – was that Atisha and Poum had been carried there, across the water … and then, after a time, had vanished. That had made Besema smile for she knew how fierce Atisha was. The news had given her hope, sustained her in the fight.

She took the stairs down to the main hall carefully. Not very glorious to die an old woman's death by falling and breaking her neck. Halfway down, she paused to look at her warriors, whispering in groups. Should she make a speech, urging great acts of courage? She'd made a few over the years. But today, at the last? Truly, all that could be said had been. Perhaps she should save what little remained of her strength to see if she could end the life of one last enemy.

Still, they expected something. 'Brothers and sisters,' she began, and they all looked up.

Which was when the trumpets sounded. All knew the enemy's various calls. This was not the one they were expecting, for attack. Startled by the sudden sound, Besema swayed and immediately Sayel was there, taking her arm. Sayel, who'd replaced Norvara at her side when her old friend had been killed. Replaced her in her bed too, for those few moments when there was time for love as well as war. Some years ago now, for Besema had found that she had grown as tired of lovemaking as she had of war.

Still, she loved her, and leaned on her, gazing into the younger woman's brown eyes. 'So the Fire King does wish to parley, after all.'

'He wishes to take the city without losing a man, Mother,' Sayel replied, helping her down the last few steps. 'To give his word and then break it, as he has done so often before.'

Mother! They all called her that. It always seemed odd to her, especially coming from someone who'd been her lover not so many years before. She stopped on the level, and looked up at all the men and women clutching their weapons. 'A delay helps us, not them,' she said. 'Sayel, go and listen to what the bastard has to say.'

A chair was brought and she lowered herself into it. People murmured about her, but she kept silent, studying a long crack in one of the hall's flagstones until she heard running feet and Sayel burst back into the hall. 'The herald does not ask for our surrender,' she blurted.

'What does he want then, child?'

'He asked—' She broke off, looked around at everyone. 'He said that Intitepe commands … no, wait, that Intitepe *requests* …' she swallowed, and looked back at Besema, 'that you meet him, Mother. In a tent in the middle of the centre bridge. And that you meet him … alone.' There were gasps at that, and everyone began to talk at once. Sayel crouched so that she could be heard. 'But you will not do this.'

'Why not?'

'Because … because it will be a trick. He will kill you.'

'Kill me?' Besema couldn't help her laugh. 'Child, he's here to kill us all. Why would he lure an old woman to a tent to kill me first?'

'But—'

'Enough. Send word back that I will come … in one hour.'

'He wants to see you now.'

'He doesn't give the orders here. Not yet.' Besema looked down at her tattered, grimy dress, ran her hand through her straggly white hair, then laughed. 'Besides, if I am going to meet my old lover, I am going to look my best.'

The tent was not large: square and perhaps five man's strides across. It had two entrances, facing either way along the bridge. The end on the city side had not yet been quite completed, would only be so when the enemy threw down the last of it to attack. So her people laid a narrower bridge of planks to span the gap. Despite the stick she used, Besema was still wobbly, and so took Sayel's arm to help her across. Once she reached the more solid planking she sent her back, though the young woman went only as far as the bridge end, flung herself down there, clutching the dagger at her waist, unhappy and watchful.

Besema placed a hand on the entrance seam of the canvas and took a deep breath. Exhaling, she parted it and stepped through.

The day outside was dull and cold. Inside the tent it was

bright, light coming from an oil lamp hanging on the central pole, and from a brazier resting by a small table, its heat taking away any chill. Chairs faced each other either side of the table and steam rose from a flagon upon it.

He stood across from her, near his own entrance. Since the lamp was on her side of the pole, there was shadow on his face, so she could not see him properly. His voice came from the shadow. 'Welcome, Besema,' he said. 'Will you sit?'

'Gladly,' she replied, and moved across to the chair. But as she reached it he stepped into the light and she had to hold on to the back to stop herself falling. Because the face she saw looked exactly as it had the day he'd sent her from his marana … seventy years before.

They studied each other. 'You have changed, Besema,' he said softly.

She took a deep breath, centring herself, before she spoke again. 'It's what happens to mortals,' she said, lowering herself carefully, resting her stick against the table's edge. 'But you, Fire King? You have not.'

'Do you not think so?' He sat too. 'Come, you were my One. For twelve years I loved you best of all. So you would know this face better than most. Can you truly see no difference?' He leaned further into the light. 'Unless you can't remember?'

'I remember … everything,' she said, and leaned closer too, until their faces were but a hand's breadth apart. 'Ha. Yes. Yes,' she said, studying. 'Your face does not show the years. But your eyes do.'

'My eyes? What do you see in them?'

'What I always did. Power. Intelligence. Five hundred years of experience.'

'So what is different now?'

She studied him a moment longer, then sat back, looked away. 'You have let hate back into them,' she said softly.

'Hate?' She could tell he was surprised. 'Why do you say that? And why *back* into them?'

She looked at him again. 'When I was ... when we had our time, you'd vanquished the last of your enemies three hundred years before. You were safe, settled, your whole life was about love, ease, contemplation. The hate you'd needed to fuel your fight was a memory. You had no need of it any more. Now, something has brought it back.'

'*Something* has? You know what has.' Anger was also in his eyes then, and in his voice. 'Ometepe was peaceful, people lived easy lives, with enough food, with order, at one with the land. And then it was invaded by ... *outsiders* who spurred my own peaceful people to revolt ...'

He broke off, breathing hard.

'No, Intitepe,' she said, 'you did that.'

'When?'

'When?' She licked her dry lips. 'Well, for all the peace you talk of, you killed any who opposed you. But you did it finally,' she leaned closer so she could be certain to see his eyes, 'when you tried to murder an innocent child.'

'You dare ...' He stood, looking as if he was about to shout, to call for soldiers, have her thrown into the gorge, or reach for her and throw her in himself. But then something changed in those eyes she was watching so closely. Hate and anger went and were replaced by ... amusement. 'You say my memory is good,' he said, sitting again, 'but I tell you this – I had forgotten the very thing that made you special to me. Why I chose you as my One. You were never the prettiest ...'

'Why, thank you.'

'... and you had the temper of a cornered puma.'

'My thanks again.'

'But you also had more wit and intelligence than any ... who came before you. You were never afraid to tell me exactly what you thought, even when you knew it would anger me. Perhaps especially then.' He stared a moment longer then gestured to the jug which steamed in front of him. 'Would you like some wine?'

'I was wondering how long it would take you to offer. And whether I would get to drink before you killed me.'

'You are here under parley, Besema. Did you think I would break that truce?'

'You are Intitepe. You plan to slaughter everyone in the City of Women within the hour. What is breaking a truce compared to that?'

'Yet still you came.'

'Yet still I came.' She leaned in. 'Because I wouldn't have traded looking into your eyes one last time for ten more years of life.'

'Ha!' He grunted, picked up the jug, poured wine into two goblets. He lifted them both, handed one to her, looked at her over the rim. 'To . . . truth,' he said, pledging her, then drinking.

'Truth?' she queried in her echo, sipped, then wrapped her fingers around the fired clay, warming herself. 'Well then, in the spirit of truth, tell me this.' She looked into his eyes again. 'You said that, of all the Ones in your marana, I had a greater wit than any who came before me.'

'Yes.'

'But you did not say, "the greatest wit ever". Meaning someone since had a greater one?'

'Yes,' he said again, differently.

'Who?'

'You know,' he said, putting down his goblet.

'I do.' She put down hers. 'Atisha.'

He stared at her a long moment, then swallowed. 'Yes.' He leaned suddenly forward. 'She betrayed me, Besema.'

'She had your child.'

'She knew the prophecy.'

'That as you killed your father, so a son of yours would slay you.'

'Yes! All she had to do was not get with child ...'

'Or if she did, not give birth to a boy?'

'Yes!'

'She didn't. Poum is neither boy nor girl. And both.'

'I know that ... now!' Intitepe's voice rose to a shout again, and he banged the table with his fist. 'And if I could go back, I would do things ... differently.'

'Kill the child yourself in the birthing pool?'

'No!' he shouted. But then he slumped back. 'No,' he muttered, passing a hand over his eyes.

She watched him for a long moment, before picking up her goblet and taking another sip of wine. Finally spoke. 'Why have you asked me here, lord?'

He dropped his hand and stared back at her before replying. 'How much do you know of the world, Besema?' he asked at last.

She knew he did not mean Ometepe. 'Little enough. Yet enough to know it is vaster than I could ever hope to comprehend.'

'It is almost beyond the comprehension of a god. And yet I have studied hard to understand it.' His eyes, which she was still studying closely, were clear of pain, of hate, burned now only with passion. 'I crossed the ocean, Besema. I saw ... wonders! Peoples you could scarcely imagine. Whereas we in Ometepe are nearly all the same, they are as different ... as different as fish in the sea.' He ran his tongue along his upper teeth's edge. 'Yet if I was shocked by them, they were in awe of me. I made a kind of peace. When I returned,' he flushed, 'to deal with you, I brought advisers back with me. You have seen them. Men who fight from huge beasts called horses and sweep all before them. Seafarers who are masters of the seas in ways I have studied hard to equal. Munke who can show me places I haven't visited yet in a glass the size of my two hands joined.' He slapped them together. 'In that I have seen more of their worlds – and two empires of power that make Ometepe look ... look like a fishing village on our coast.' His eyes gleamed. 'Yet do you know what all those mighty kingdoms, all those hordes of different people want more than anything else?'

'What?'

'They want my child!' He slapped his chest. '*My* child!'

'Atisha's child,' she said.

'Yes. Mine and Atisha's. What we made.' He ran his hands over his head. 'They call our child the One. That one who will unite the whole world in worship. Who will rule them all.'

'Yet I heard the child has disappeared.'

'You heard that? Oh yes, the munke you captured.'

'So perhaps the child is dead.'

'I do not think so.' Intitepe smiled. 'This is Atisha we are talking about. She is hiding our child. Waiting.'

Besema frowned. 'For what?'

He leaned close again, fire back in his eyes. 'For me.'

'For you?' Besema leaned close too, disbelieving. 'Why would she wait for you?'

'To conquer that vast world. To become the new god, my child will need help from the old one.' His smile went wider, his eyes brighter. 'The God-Father!'

Now, she could not hold in her gasp. For years ... centuries, perhaps, after he took Ometepe for himself, Intitepe had never had any more ambition. Why would he, when there was nowhere left to conquer? Now he did. But was it ambition? Was that what she saw in his eyes now or was it ... insanity? Careful, she thought. 'Why did you summon me here, lord? To tell me this?'

He sat back, grabbed his goblet, drank. When he spoke, his

voice was calm again. 'No, Besema, I called you here to make you an offer.'

'Of surrender? We will not do it.'

'No. An offer of partnership. To do what I hope to do sounds impossible, does it not? Tiny Ometepe against those vast empires? I can see it in your eyes – you think me mad, don't you?' He smiled. 'Perhaps I am. Perhaps I need to be. But listen.' He sat straight, his voice dropping. 'Boldness and madness are twin cubs born from the same puma. If I find Atisha and our child, if I take them with me, then ...' He ran his tongue over his teeth and his eyes gleamed. 'Then I can storm those empires and bring them down. I have a small, fierce army; a small, tough navy. All I need is surprise. That ... and one other advantage. One that you can give me.'

'Which is?'

He took a long pause before he answered, lamplight gleaming in his eyes. 'I need your floating globes.'

She cried out then. It was not anything she'd thought that he would ask.

He went on immediately. 'In return ... I will spare all the people in the City of Women. I will allow everyone in it to return safe to their villages.'

'And if they rebel again? As they will.'

He stared at her for a while before he replied. 'Then they can have Ometepe,' he whispered. 'For my child and I will have ... the world.' He sat back, his smile wide now. 'Come. What do you say, Besema? You have fought me for years. You are a great leader, a great strategist. Be that again, at Intitepe's side. Be it for your lost friend, Atisha. Be it for the child she and I made, foretold to save the world.'

He lifted his goblet again, a pledge in the gesture. She did not lift hers. It was so much to take in. She'd thought that, at best, she was coming to receive an offer for the city's total surrender. Death for many, escape in slavery for the rest. She never would have thought she'd be offered a share in the saving of the whole world.

That was far away though. She had seen hate in Intitepe's eyes. She'd seen ambition brushing insanity. But what that meant, right now, was that all her people would live. They could rejoin their families. Could even keep that flame of revolution burning in the land. Or perhaps, with Intitepe gone, revolution, true change, would consume Ometepe? While in exchange all she needed to do, right then, was offer to share something that she loved. To soar above the world like a bird.

Yes, Besema thought, I can do that.

She raised her goblet, looked at him over its rim, made the pledge. 'To truth,' she said, and drank.

5

Voyages in the Dark

The black-eyed killer tumbled off the back of the cart. When his head struck the ground, it snapped off.

'Fool!' Peki Asarko shrieked, running over and starting to slap and kick the servant, who fell onto her knees, hands raised to protect herself, begging for forgiveness. But Peki tired easily, and any blows that connected were hurting his hands probably more than the wretched girl's head. He thought of finding a stick – then remembered he had no time for this. *That* satisfaction would have to wait till later. Besides ...

'Oh, my dear, precious child,' he moaned, crouching down to pick up the broken-off head. One of the wooden eyes had popped out and he couldn't see it anywhere. The other one stared blackly back. He felt like weeping. He had been so proud of this work, one of the finest of his creations. The seam at the neck, where he'd separated the head from the body to extract the brains then rejoined it, had been almost invisible, the paint he'd applied making it look like a natural neck wrinkle. 'I'll fix you, I'll fix you,' he crooned, rocking the head back and forth in his lap. Then he looked up, to see all his servants staring at him, and at the weeping girl who'd shuffled away, and remembered he didn't have time for weeping either. 'Take more care, you idiots. Get them away. Get them to the shed.'

He rose, placed the head beside the body that the others had lifted back onto the cart, before they ran to the front of the vehicle and dragged it away. He stood and watched his silent friends depart. It was his entire collection of skilfully, artistically preserved bodies, who usually stood proud and separate in his hall. Now they were all jumbled every which way, bodies on bodies, fingers pressed into noses or tangled into hair. There would be more damage to repair. They looked as if they were in a grave pit, like the one he'd had dug the year before near Lorken, throwing into it all the inhabitants of the village of rebels he'd destroyed. Well, some were undoubtedly rebels, the rest were rebels' families, or friends or ... anyway, they were an example to be made.

The cart was dragged slowly off. Peki looked down – and a black eye looked back. He bent and snatched it up. He would have time to make repairs later, during the coming winter. Add to his collection perhaps – a far better punishment for that clumsy girl than a beating. Unless the man who was even now being rowed across the Lake of Souls had other plans for him, and for Midgarth.

That man had caused all the panic. Was as responsible as the girl for the accident in some ways. Sixteen years before, the only time he had visited the island, he hadn't been delighted when Peki had shown him his collection. He'd been revolted. Despised him as had all his fellow gods in Midgarth, which is what had exiled Peki to the Lake of Souls in the first place. Immediately he had forbidden Peki the practice of his art. Of course, he had never returned, and this was his first time back in the land since the Coming of the Dark. He hadn't asked too many questions, in the times they talked in the smoke in the glass. About art, anyway. All he wanted to talk about was the subjugation of the land to the cause of the One; and the search for Luck, a god like Peki, who had survived that last battle.

Who had vanished after it with the One, that baby who had caused all the excitement in the first place.

Now the man was back, had sent word in the smoke – only a few hours before, dammit! – that he would be arriving shortly, that there had been developments which he needed to discuss. Which was why Peki had been forced to so hastily hide his beauties. He may have hated the man who ruled him, when no one else in Midgarth did. But the man controlled him with *his* control of the supply of Sirene, whom Peki loved even more than he loved his art. So he could not be seen to disobey him.

He realised he was still holding something. He opened his palm, and gazed into the black wooden eye that rested there. It was, as all his work was, exquisite. But even he could not capture the depth of blackness in the eye of the man who was coming.

'A boat, lord,' came the cry from one of his sentries on the cliff.

'Anazat,' he muttered, tucking the eye away into a pocket of the huge smock he wore. Why was he coming? Only a few months before the black-eyed monk had sent him a letter allowing him to retire, to give up the burden of his tasks. Tasks he was so bored with. The land was largely subjugated, only a few bands holding out, living in caves like animals, causing minor trouble. It had been a relief to realise he could stop making plans, ordering executions, burning towns. Anyone could do that work, and as long as he was still acknowledged as King of Midgarth – he'd had himself crowned on Galahur, telling Anazat it was a necessary step in controlling a sullen people – and as long as he still received his tributes, he could let lesser men get on with the little details. The savage in the west, Intitepe, who'd been promised Midgarth for his help in finishing off Peki's brother gods at the Coming of the Dark, had been sucked into never-ending wars in his own country, it appeared. So they would never see him again. All of which meant that Peki was free to focus on something only he could do: his art!

Anazat's coming changed that, though, in a way he could not yet know. Something must have happened. What it also meant was that Anazat would be bringing more Sirene. That was the good news in all of this. Though he had managed to lessen his dependence, only venturing with her once a month ... twice ... well, three times in a longer month ... he had run dangerously low of the liquid.

As he descended the path to greet his master on the beach, Peki was both excited and nervous. He reached into the pocket of his smock, rolled the eyeball between his fingers. Soon, he thought, I will live once again only for my art. For now – he sighed on the thought – I suppose I will still have to be the King of Midgarth.

Anazat coughed, then spat something foul over the side of the boat. He drew his black cloak about him, and shivered, though it was strangely warm on the water, not like on Molnalla, the mountain he'd just descended. When he'd visited the Lake of Souls that one time before, it had taken him more than a month to get over the infection of the chest he'd picked up. The surrounding marshland exuded foul gases that, on some days, moved over the water's surface like smoke snakes. He could see many now, feel the burn as some trace reached his lungs. Only ahead, on the tall island at the lake's centre, was there any relief from the poisons, which was why the people built their houses there. He could see many of those, clustered on the clifftops. Below, on a beach at the cliff's base, stood the large, lumpen figure of the man he'd come to see.

He detested him. Anazat knew that he himself was called cruel by some. But the difference between his actions and those of the man who waited ahead was that the Monk was cruel only when necessity demanded it, to set an example. He never hurt people for pleasure – unlike Peki Asarko. Anazat knew he himself had a purpose – the freeing of the whole world in the cause of the One. If some harsh methods needed to be practised in that cause, they would be forgotten fast in a glorious future. Cruelty gone, slavery gone, peace restored … *love* restored. He knew that he had known little of love since his unknown Huntress mother had given him up soon after birth to the order of Warrior Monks of which he'd risen to be the head. In the world to come, though, in the redemption to be found in it, even he would find love, for the very first time and then for as long as he lived.

Which will not be long, he thought, as he hawked and spat again, if I linger here. One night should be enough. One night … if she will show me where they are.

They. The One.

They. Poum the Child and Luck the God.

She. Sirene.

He knew that there were several in the world who used her only to communicate, fearing a deeper fall, like the scheming Makron in Corinthium. Others used her only for delight, to travel across the stars, through time that is, was, or had never been. He had done that, when he was first introduced to her, seduced by her as he had never been by any man or woman on the planet. But soon he'd seen – been given to see, by her – that Sirene was far greater than that. That if there was a god other than the One in the world, she was it, for she was the revealer of all truths.

Only one other that he knew saw her as he did. Used her to answer questions he had not even known existed. Luck of Askaug had been his prisoner for a time. But Anazat knew that the question he'd asked the Midgarthian the very first time they'd met was the question that would be haunting him still.

Are you happy?

He knew Luck had resisted her all these years. That only recently had he opened that door again. Now he had, he would be powerless to resist going through it. Especially now, when the answer to the monk's question glimmered in the dark.

The answer to be provided by the One.

How he looked forward to seeing them both again.

Even as the boat was grounding onto pebbles, and the two paddlers leaped out to steady it, Peki Asarko was grovelling. 'Lord, master, it is so good to see you again. Welcome to the island. My only wish is to make your stay fulfilling and happy, tell me what I can do to please you. Anything I have is yours. Anything—'

Anazat took the outstretched hand, using it to take a long step from boat to shore without putting his feet in the water. 'Help me get out of this foul air, fast.' He spat something solid onto the stones. 'How you can live here astonishes me.'

'We adapt, lord, we adapt. And up there the air is sweet.'

He gestured with his head to the path, and beckoned Anazat to follow. He climbed the steps cut into the cliff face and emerged, breathing painfully, onto a large flat area in front of the first of the straw-roofed houses. Many of Peki's followers had gathered there, men and women to the back, a line of children to the fore – all dressed alike in a simple tunic that fell to their knees, bare arms and legs painted in alternating stripes of black and white; their faces too, though the stripes there were thinner.

'The children will sing our song of greeting for you, lord,' Peki cried, and waved at the boys and girls who started immediately. To Anazat, used to the harmonious chants of his monk brothers at the Keep, this sounded like a dozen cats fighting in a bag.

He stood it for as long as he could, which was about four of his tortured breaths, before he cried out, 'Enough!' Peki shouted too, something in the guttural tongue of the lake, and the voices ceased instantly. 'Take me to food and shelter,' Anazat growled.

'Immediately, master.' Peki clapped his hands, the people scattered, and the large man led him to the longhouse which he'd visited once when he'd come to conquer Midgarth all those years before.

It was actually two longhouses joined into one. At the end they entered there was a hearth, a dais with a huge chair upon it below which two smaller chairs faced each other over a table. There was food on that, jugs of liquid too. At the far end, where the two longhouses joined, Anazat could see through a doorway into the next one. It was a place he remembered well, a place of abomination – for Peki Asarko delighted in the dismembering, preserving and reassembling of human bodies for display. He had ordered him to cease on the instant. Such disgusting acts had no place in the world of the One that was coming. Of course, he had no way of knowing if he had been obeyed, though the emptiness of the hall, its bare floors and lack of any signs of living, made him think that it had lately been occupied.

It did not matter. Nothing did except the reason he had come. Peki Asarko's time in the world was going to be short anyway. For now, though, Anazat needed him.

'Eat, master?' Peki waved at the table.

'Later. First, dismiss these men.'

Two servants had followed them in and stood by with heads lowered.

'They are to serve us food, lord.'

'In a while. There's something we must do first.'

Peki grunted a word at the men, who bowed and left, closing the door behind them. Peki turned back. His eyes, small and bulging in that huge fleshy face, were now filled with excitement. 'Do we travel first, lord?' he asked, his voice quavering.

Anazat did not answer him directly. 'Fetch the globe. Set it on a table in the doorway between the houses.'

Having dismissed his servants, Peki rushed into that other longhouse himself, coming back first and fast with a small wooden table, and then much more slowly, holding carefully something that was wrapped in black velvet. He placed it on the table and gently pulled off the covering.

In the glass globe, smoke moved.

'I have very little Sirene left, lord,' Peki said, rubbing his hands back and forth over his mouth. 'I hope you have brought some.'

'I have brought plenty,' Anazat replied. 'But we do not travel yet.'

'Soon, though, I hope?' Peki whined.

'Soon, and with a special purpose.' He sat at the first table, and beckoned the other man. 'Come, eat, and I will tell you what that is, and your part in it.'

With a lingering look back at the globe, Peki joined him. 'I will do anything, lord,' he said as he sat.

'I know you will.' Anazat stared at the obese man opposite him for a moment, concealing his distaste. The man – they called him a god in Midgarth! – was a tool, no more. To be used and discarded soon. Very soon, Anazat hoped.

After one more glance at the smoke in the glass, which swirled placidly, he began to eat. The food surprised him by being excellent – smoked fish and deer sausages, creamy sheep's milk cheeses, crusty breads, with wine to drink that would not have disgraced the cellar in the Keep. But of course Peki Asarko had ruled this land for fifteen years. He would have made sure that he was always well stocked with the things he craved.

Peki nibbled, distracted by the object between the houses. His hunger for Sirene would be great, and his supply low. Kept so deliberatedly, for Anazat knew exactly how much each of his servants had and therefore how … manageable they would be. It was different for him. His supply was limitless, of course, and he had voyaged more with Sirene than any other man in the world. Indeed, more than most of them combined. But all those years of use had not created the dependency that it did with every other man. Indeed, the opposite was true. He was the one in control, with powers as a voyager most could only dream of. Which is what he needed to discuss now.

He did not speak while he ate, despite the yearning he felt from the man on the other side of the table. Only when he was sated did he sit back and fold his hands into his lap. 'Peki Asarko,' he whispered.

The man, who'd been staring at the globe again, jerked his head back. 'Lord?'

'The One has returned.'

'Truly? Oh glory! Praise her! Praise him!'

The big man's face quivered in an ecstasy as false as the fervour in his voice. Anazat knew that immortals anywhere, since they considered themselves gods, did not seek salvation in any other. It was as true in Corinthium, with Makron and Roxanna, as he'd witnessed with Luck of Midgarth, or with this Peki Asarko. No doubt that savage across the water, Intitepe, felt the same. Though he had even more cause since the One was born of his union with the child's mother.

Their belief did not matter. It was enough that all mortals believed. The One was not sent to save gods but to save the world *from* them. At the final triumph they would all be gone – killed, as most had been at the fall of Corinthium. As those of Midgarth had been at what they called the Coming of the Dark. 'Praise him, praise her, indeed.'

'Has she … have *they* returned to you?'

'Not yet. But they are close. Your fellow god who stole them, Luck of Askaug …'

'Curse him …'

'… who you lost …'

'Lord,' Peki whined. 'I explained. The mountain, the fog, that woman with her arrows—'

Anazat raised his hand, halting the excuses. 'It does not matter. Since we are about to get them back. Both of them.'

'How, lord?' Peki leaned across the table. 'How can I help?'

'In a way I think you will enjoy.' Anazat steepled his fingers under his chin. 'You are going to come with me into the smoke.'

'With you?' The disappointment in the other man's voice was clear. 'But I have only ever travelled alone.'

And I am sure you did unspeakable things when you did, Anazat thought, didn't say. Sirene knew a traveller's deepest yearnings and guided him to them. The embalmed humans no longer standing in the other longhouse gave some clue to what Peki's would be. Again it was not something he needed to say. 'I will leave you plenty of the liquid. After I have gone you will be able to … travel wherever you like. Do whatever—' He broke off, then continued. 'This time, though, you will accompany me.'

'To do what?' Peki grumbled. 'Besides, I do not have any control when I am there. She takes me where she will. How can I help you?'

'She does when you are alone. When you are with someone it is different. That person can show you things. Share things. Help you to do things.' His lips parted in a smile, revealing his black teeth. 'Especially when that someone is as experienced as me.'

'What will you show me?'

'Whatever Luck wishes to see.'

'Luck?' Peki threw himself back in his seat. 'We will meet *him* there?'

'We will. Him, and them. For the One will be with him.'

'How do you know this, lord?'

'I know. Because I know Luck. He was my prisoner and I travelled with him in the smoke. You get to know someone quite well then. And as I told you, I also know Sirene.' He glanced again at the globe, its gently swirling clouds. 'Your brother god of Askaug has resisted her for fifteen years. That is an accomplishment that very few could ever achieve. But I know when a globe is used, and by whom. It is ...' He stared up for a moment into the rafters, at the cobwebs there. 'Like a spider's web, when a trapped fly vibrates along a far-off strand and the spider finds him. I felt his vibration.' He picked up his goblet, held it out, and Peki quickly refilled it from the jug. Anazat sipped, and continued. 'I also know how ... *hungry* Luck will be now, having tasted Sirene again. I will feel his vibration soon, very soon. Maybe even this night.'

'This night?' Peki glanced at the globe again, then licked his lips. 'But how do you know the One will be with him?'

'Because if Luck is at last bringing *them* from their hiding place, it must be because he thinks he has a chance of taking Midgarth back. A chance of defeating me – and you. To do that he will need the One.' He sipped again. 'Luck will have recognised that the One is the real power in the world. But to use it, he will have to show the One that vast world – just as I showed it to Luck when he and I first met.'

'So we will meet them in the smoke?'

'We will.'

'So we go into it? Now?' Peki's voice throbbed with eagerness again.

'No. We wait till they do. Then, we follow.'

'How will we know?'

'There are signs. The first is when the smoke swirls faster.'

'I will not sleep! I will watch it till it does, lord!'

'No. It will not help us if we are exhausted. And it may not happen for a day, several, a week. No, no.' He drained his goblet, set it down, stood. 'You will prepare me a bed on one side of the globe. You will sleep on the other. We do not leave it for anything. Anything! And while we sleep, you set men to watch. Do you have those who will stay awake and do that?'

'If they wish to keep their skins they will.'

'Good. Make the arrangements.' Anazat rose, yawned, stretched, then leaned down and fixed Peki with his black, black eyes. 'Do not fail me in this, Peki Asarko. You will not be happy if you do. But when we succeed,' the eyes gleamed, 'you will have helped me win the world.'

It was hard for Luck, for his short, uneven legs, that final steep descent back into Midgarth, retracing the route he'd taken from it all those years before. That day mists had mostly blocked his view of the vale of Galahur. On this day, the sun shining from the clearest of blue early winter skies gilded the valley in golden light and as soon as he crested the last ridge he could see it clearly, the high-lipped bowl where his people, both mortals and immortals, used to gather for their moot and agree how to proceed in their world.

Perhaps it was not his legs that dragged so much as his heart. For when he came over that last ridge and his feet touched Midgarth itself, it wasn't shale and scree under his boots, it was his country, the entirety of it, there again. The place where he'd been born, where he'd lived, loved – and where he'd seen those he loved die. From these eastern mountains to the western shores, from the vast forests of the north to the southern fjords, for four hundred years he had limped along its every path, studied its varied peoples, its birds, beasts, trees and flowers, the colours and the scents of each of its seasons. The death of winter, the rebirth of spring, the short, vibrant summer. He loved every part of it – though it was the west he held deepest within him. 'Askaug,' he murmured, shielding his eyes from a sun just beginning its descent, to look beyond what he could actually see to what he had dreamed of all these years of exile. 'Askaug,' he said again, then took his next stumbly step after the others, Marla and Poum leading the two mules, Marla's dog Warkan at her heels.

He knew he could have borrowed one of the small birds who hovered around them, and flown down. When one settled on a rock, he was tempted, to relieve his aching knees. Yet he did not. He had not yet revealed his special ability to his child. They had enough to deal with, learning of the world, without learning that the man Poum called father could possess a beast! That revelation would come soon enough, along with many others.

It was dusk by the time they reached the valley floor, forded the river and climbed the slopes of Galahur. The bowl's inner sides and bottom, which in the old days were kept trimmed by the priests who tended the gathering place, now were covered in dying, knee-high grass, making it harder to reach the centre, the turf-roofed barrow there, because of the concealed things that caused them to trip: rusting helmets, pots, a shovel without a shaft.

At least there were no bones. Marla, at the various camps they'd made in the two-week trek from the steading, had told of what had happened in Midgarth since Luck had left it. In the tyranny that had ensued, supported by the forces of the Four Tribes, every village and town had its garrison, every place could testify to the cruelty of the conquerors, and especially the hideous practices of the tyrant Peki Asarko.

She'd also spoken of the aftermath of the Coming of the Dark. The victorious enemy had buried their own dead but left the Midgarthian gods to rot, heads separated from their bodies, as a symbol of the land's defeat. Yet, though it was forbidden, over the years men and women had slipped back to house their fallen in unmarked graves. It comforted Luck a little to know that those he'd known so long and loved – Bjorn Swift-Sword, Hovard and Freya – especially Freya! – slept the long sleep now under holy soil. They had earned their rest, for their sacrifice had allowed Luck, Atisha and Poum, and all the mortals to escape.

They climbed the barrow – revered as the grave of the first king of Midgarth, who'd united gods and men, Haakon the Great – and then stood looking down into the grassy bowl. Luck turned to the others, wiping away tears he hadn't noticed fall. 'Ah, you should have seen this place when it was crowded. Deputations came from everywhere in Midgarth. Gods and mortals. Oh, the arguments!' He laughed. 'Oh, the drinking!'

'We shall see those times again, Father. Have no fear of that.'

Luck looked at Poum. *They* had looked different from the time they took their solo voyage with Sirene. What had happened had not been much discussed, though it would need to be soon. Luck could guess at some. He remembered his own first time alone, every moment of it as clear now as it had been when he'd experienced it. But of course, he had seen Gytta, his dead wife restored to him. From the very little they had said, Luck knew that Poum had seen – been guided to see – what *they* were. How they were the focus of so much ... *prophecy* across the wide world.

He'd expected Poum to writhe under the burden; be shattered by revelations and expectations. The moody child Luck had known lately, the sulker and the snapper, certainly would have. But they had not. There were other changes in Poum's eyes, beyond the faintest darkening that the drug had bestowed with that first use. Within them they didn't look daunted. They looked ... excited.

Luck looked into those eyes again now, then away to the sunlight fading across the grasses. 'There is a place close to the river, just over there,' he waved over the bowl's lip, 'beneath a huge willow where those of Askaug would pitch their tents. We should make camp, before we have to do it in the dark.'

They all descended from the barrow, climbed back up the slope. At its lip they paused, gazing out over the valley. 'And after dark, Father? We voyage with her together?'

Luck had told Poum that when they reached Midgarth they would need to use Sirene again. There was so much to learn, to help them in deciding what must be done next. His pulse immediately quickened at the thought but he took a deep breath, slowed it down. 'No, tonight we rest, maybe tomorrow too. We need to wait, to—'

'No.' Poum's interruption was loud, and sharp. 'There is no point in resting. Nothing to wait for. We have come to take Midgarth back from its invaders. Let us begin.'

Luck looked at Poum. They'd been loud – but not petulant. They were certain – and as stubborn as their mother once she'd made up her mind. Looking into their eyes, taking of that certainty, the dam of restraint and caution Luck had built over the years to hold desire back shattered in the instant, flooding him. 'You are right,' he said, licking his lips. 'Let us begin.'

As soon as the tent they all shared was set up, Luck went into it alone to rest a little. It was the same wherever they'd camped, and Poum would have been outraged at the injustice of having to do all the other work ... were it not that it gave them exactly what they wanted.

They got to be alone with Marla.

Having grown up alone with aged parents – one of them over four hundred years old! – and then suddenly forced to share their attention with an annoying brother and soon after an equally annoying sister, Poum found Marla fascinating. She'd grown up in a town, Kroken. And even if that was ruled by the enemy with their harsh laws, there was, in so many ways, more freedom there than on a freezing mountain. Mostly the freedom to be with someone their own age. Each time Luck rested, while they searched for firewood, or prepared the evening meals, they would talk. Or rather Poum would listen, excited – and sometimes horrified – by the way someone like them, but one who'd grown up in the world, observed it, and the people in it.

Mostly they'd been excited – and sometimes horrified – by how they behaved with others of their age.

Poum had grown up on a farm. They knew how nature worked. But what seemed easy for a ram, or a dog, was, in Marla's tales, much more complex. It seemed it wasn't based simply on an animal's need to create another like them. There were different desires involved, different attractions. It confused them – but not as much as their attraction to Marla.

They watched her now, busy about the fireplace. Until she stopped and looked at Poum. 'Are you going to help?' she asked, tossing her head so that her long brown hair fell from one side of her face to the other. Something she often did, and usually accompanied by the same challenging smile she gave now. 'Or are you just going to sit and stare?'

'Help. Of course.'

They got up, went to where the mules were tethered. Led them down to a meadow, then put halters on their front legs, so the beasts could roam and crop the rich grass without going far. When Poum returned, they did so quietly, standing beneath an oak at the edge of the clearing to watch Marla again, unobserved. She had the metal frame erected and the pot of stew already hanging over the flames. She was stirring it, softly crooning some tune. Then, without looking up she asked, 'Aren't you going to join me?'

Poum ambled over, trying to look casual. Yet when they

sat beside her, close to her, the casualness dissolved and they stared. Marla, still singing, gave the pot a final stir then pulled the wooden spoon out, licked it, set it down … and leaned into Poum. 'Tell me another story,' she said.

The first time they had done this was at the third camp. When Luck had been resting, and the camp was ready, she'd flipped her hair, looked Poum in the eyes, and asked, 'Tell me. Are you a boy or a girl?'

It was a question they'd expected but had prepared no answer. So they'd replied, 'Does it matter?'

'Not to me,' she'd said. Then she'd settled against them and said, 'Tell me a story.'

They had done the same thing at every camp since. Poum found that they were gifted in the telling of stories and that Marla leaning against them, laughing or gasping, was the thing they most looked forward to in life.

The stories came only from their imagination, never from their own life. They did not know if Marla knew their secret. That they were 'the One'. If she did, she didn't show it. She certainly didn't treat them as they assumed the 'saviour of the world' would be treated. There was no worship. But of course, she was of Midgarth and had her own gods. No matter how the conquerors had tried to change that and impose their own, Midgarthians were a stubborn people. *They* might be received differently, elsewhere.

Whether it was the scent of the stew, flavoured with the fresh-picked local herbs she knew, the warmth of the fire against the cold of nightfall, or the relief of finally arriving back in her own land, Marla enjoyed this tale more than any other. And Poum strove to please her, the shambling one-eyed giant bemused by the smart farm girl in a plot of increasing complexity whose climax had her shaking with laughter.

'Excellent! The best ever!'

'You say that every time.'

'It is true every time. You keep getting better and better.' She pulled away from them, spun to look at them. They stared at each other for a moment. Then she leaned in and kissed Poum.

It was as if they'd been picked up and flung against a tree. Or a lightning blast had sizzled through the ground, and flashed through to the tip of every individual hair. Their eyes shot wide, taking in each part of the face that had pulled back only a very little. Marla smiled and tipped her head, the cascade of hair tumbling. 'Again?' she whispered.

'Again. Oh yes, again.'

Which was when the voice came from the tent, just out of sight through the trees. 'Are you going to torment me with the smells of home much longer, or is that stew ready?' Luck called.

Marla leaped back, while Poum fell forward into the place where she'd been. 'Ready!' she called, and in another moment Luck was there.

'What?' he said, puzzled, looking between the two of them, Poum still on their hands and knees, Marla stirring, humming.

'What, what?' Marla shrugged and bent for a bowl. 'Let's eat.'

Poum tried. But they found that their appetite had suddenly vanished.

When Luck had licked his bowl clean, he placed it on the ground. 'Marla,' he said. 'There is something Poum and I must do tonight. Alone in the tent. It is something very important. We will be there, but we will also,' he glanced at Poum, 'be gone. For a few hours at least we … journey. To you it will seem that we are asleep.'

'I cannot come on this … journey?'

'You cannot.'

Instead of questioning further, she simply nodded and began tidying up. 'Will you be all right?' he asked.

'Of course. I have the fire, and Warkan.' The dog, head on paws, growled at his naming. 'You'll be colder in the tent.'

'We will not feel the cold.'

'So I will keep guard?'

'Please. But only wake us for the utmost urgency.' He turned to Poum. 'Come,' he said.

The tent was only ever a place to sleep, with their blankets laid out side by side. But these were now piled one atop the other, making a base for what sat in their centre.

The globe.

They sat either side of it. Poum took a sharp breath. They had not seen it since that time back at the steading – though they had looked at it every day where it swayed in a sack on the rump of one of the mules. Looked at it hungrily, for the experience they'd had when Sirene opened the world to them had caused a craving within they'd never known before. They'd seen wonders – and horrors. Witnessed how they themselves were the focus of so much hope – and fear. Felt a purpose in the smoke they had never had tending animals on a mountaintop. All they'd wanted to do since was to journey again.

They licked their lips, looked up – and saw the exact same hunger mirrored in Luck's blue eyes. He was staring into the swirling smoke. Poum coughed, and the eyes rose to look at them, briefly startled, as if he had forgotten they were there. 'Do we go, Father?' Poum said, trying not to sound too excited. 'Do we take Sirene's hand?'

Luck swallowed. 'No,' he rasped, then cleared his throat. 'When we travel together, as I did with Anazat the priest the very first time, we use a smaller dose. We can choose to see the world but not lose ourselves in it. To go where we will but not where she wills. It is different from when you travel alone.'

'But ...' Poum chewed at their lip, remembering vividly that time before, the loss of control, the joy of that. 'But I want to lose myself, Father. I do not know the questions I need to ask. Let her be the guide. We will learn quicker.'

Luck gave a great sigh, then shook his head. 'You do not know how much I wish to lose myself as well.'

'Then let us!'

'I must not. Nor must you. Believe me, Poum. The dangers of losing yourself are too great. For what we must accomplish here in Midgarth, we must be in control, not Sirene.'

Poum started to protest, then stopped. They had learned over the years that when Luck made up his mind, argument would never make him change it. They had also learned other ways of getting what they wanted. 'Do it then,' they grumbled. 'Guide me to what you want me to see.'

Luck nodded, then reached beneath an edge of blanket and pulled out a small glass vial. 'As before,' he said, putting a thumb under the stopper that was attached to the vessel's neck by a small metal chain, 'breathe deep then lie back.' He flicked the stopper off, reached forward, carefully tipped it. Three drops fell, sizzling on impact. The smoke within the globe began to whirl faster, coalescing into a column. Shapes began to appear.

But Poum did not focus on them. Instead, shooting their arm forward, they put their hand under Luck's elbow and pushed it up.

Black liquid poured out, down. Vapour burst up from the surface of the glass. Poum inhaled deep, fell in, lost. Yet as they fell they heard, as if from far away and fading fast, a single word, cried out in despair.

'No!' wailed Luck.

They were in a forest. Yet it was so different from the one they'd just come from. The trees surrounding Galahur were towering columns, their thin branches laden with needles. The trees here were smaller but wider, thick branches stretching out like arms, bearing leaves the size of platters. These swayed in a hot breeze – hot, when the place they'd come from was cold. At Galahur, only crows called, ravens barked, eagles or kites gave out their high-pitched hunting cries as they circled above, black-feathered against the sky. Here, brightly coloured birds, yellow of wing and chest, smaller than the breadth of a hand, swooped and flitted between perches, to pause and let out melodious runs of notes.

Dazzled, Poum gazed about. The vibrancy of the world assaulted all senses. For there was scent too, flowers lining the path as diverse in fragrance as they were in colours. Heavy-bodied bees hummed among them, settling to suck nectar on stamens that looked like the eyes of other giant insects. Poum kneeled, shoving their hand into the thick grass, snatching up one tall stem. Snapping it near its base, they put it in their mouth, sucked. Sweetness came, far exceeding any they had ever tasted at home, as if the honey the bees would make was already in the plant.

They sighed, sat, turned their face to the hot sun, closed their eyes, revelling in drone, hum, breeze and birdsong. Then they remembered again where they'd come from. Why they'd come. It was not to succumb to pleasures. Luck had said that they must only observe, that they must not lose control if they wished to learn all they needed to. Poum laughed, and the birds changed their songs to laugh as well. I will show him, Poum said, and without opening their eyes called, 'Come to me.'

Nothing changed. Birds, bees, wafting smells. Poum opened one eye. The cowled figure was not there. 'Sirene?' they commanded.

Nothing happened … until they heard, faintly, someone singing. It sounded like Marla, which was wrong because she could not be there. Rising, they followed the sound, along the path, threading through the trees. The voice got clearer. It was another Midgarth song, one for bedtime. Luck had sung it to them when they were a young child.

The path dipped, Poum glimpsed sunlight on water. One moment they were pushing through tall reeds, the next they were standing on a grassy bank, a small pond before them. It was about a dozen paces long and wide. White-barked trees drooped their leaf-laden branches to its surface.

On the opposite bank sat a girl.

She was about Marla's age, a similar height and build. But this girl's hair was white-blonde, not brown, and fell in waves beyond her shoulders halfway down her back. Instead of dark winter clothes, a tunic and breeches, she was in a dress that hung from bare shoulders and ended at her thighs. The skin revealed was golden, the sun hitting her arms and legs, where tiny hairs glowed like filaments of fire.

She was staring at her reflection in the pond's surface. But when they took a loud breath, she looked up. 'Welcome, Poum,' she said.

'You know me.'

'I have been waiting for you.'

'Are you Sirene?'

She laughed, her voice throaty and rich. 'I am not. Except of course, here,' she shook her head, and blonde waves cascaded around it, 'everything is. Even you.'

Poum frowned. 'I am not.'

She laughed again. 'Are you sure?' She stood, stretched out a hand towards them. 'My name is Kipé,' she said. 'Come, let's swim.'

'I . . . I cannot swim.'

She smiled. 'You can here.' Then, crossing her hands at her hips, she pulled the dress over her head.

Poum could not breathe, could only stare at her body glowing golden in the sun. Her breasts were small and shapely, her waist narrow, her legs long and slim. Where they met, at her core, was the only darkness. 'Come,' she called again and stepped into the water.

They wanted to, more than anything they'd ever wanted. But they were *they*? What would she say, when she saw what lay at *their* core? The darkness there?

And then they felt something different there. Something single. One, where there had always been two.

Boots were fumbled off feet, shirt jerked over head, hands going to the buttons that fastened the garments at the waist. Hesitation there, only for the moment before looking up again at Kipé, swimming now, getting closer, her eyes a startling azure against the light green of the water.

Poum slipped off his breeches, looked down. There *he* was. He, for the first time ever and fully. Smiling, he slipped into the water and found that she'd been right.

He could swim, after all.

Both Luck's fury and his worry for Poum followed him as he inhaled more and fell into the darkness; then vanished when he emerged into the light. Because he recognised the place immediately, this place where he'd once again found his love. The path he stood on led to Gytta's garden and though he knew he should not follow it, knew he was there for other reasons, he also knew he could not help himself. Poum, their rashness, had seen to that.

I must remember to thank them next time we meet, Luck thought as he set off, smiling.

Once again, Sirene healed all in him. He walked without a limp, his legs of even length. Without a lurch, now his shoulders matched each other too. It was the wonder of the place, this healing. One of the wonders, he thought, as he broke into a run. She was up there, just ahead. The slight slope took him.

Then, just before he stepped into her garden, he heard a splash not too far away, someone laughing. He turned to the sound, even took a step – and then she spoke.

'Come, my love,' Gytta said. 'I have waited for you so long.'

Fear and worry, gone again. Caressed away by her voice. He turned back, and stooped below the bloom-laden branch of an elm.

She sat where she had before, in a bower made of strands of woven willow, threaded through with roses in every shade from deepest crimson to the yellow of the sun. On her lap she had wool, knitting needles in it. 'I was making you a scarf,' she said. 'Wanted to finish it for when next you returned. But you have been gone so long so ... look.' She gathered the multi-hued garment, and Luck saw that it ran from her lap, out along the path, to disappear into a flower bed.

He laughed. 'It is no longer just a scarf, love. It is a blanket I will wind about myself each night to keep out the cold.'

She laughed too, then patted the bench beside her. He sat. 'Why *were* you gone so long?' she asked.

From the moment he saw where Sirene had taken him, he knew he would have to tell her. Needed to tell her, she to whom he had always told everything.

So he did. Told of his imprisonment in the land of Saghaz-a. Told of how one day he realised his purpose there, when two special people arrived. And though he feared to see hurt in her eyes when he told the last of it, he spoke of the love he'd found with Atisha.

There was no hurt in her eyes, which shone. Nor in her voice when she spoke. 'But, my heart,' she said, 'I wanted nothing more for you when I died. I told you, on my death bed, that the worst thing you could do to me was to live without love, and only in memories of us.' She squeezed the hand she'd taken. 'I think you did that for too long. Now you have found love again, I feel free. You have let me go.'

'I will never love you less, Gytta. You know that.'

'Why would you?' She raised his hand, kissed it. 'For love doesn't die. It is boundless. It lasts for ever.'

He knew she was right. Any doubt or guilt he'd had was swept away. Suddenly, he missed Atisha keenly. Though that did not detract in any way from the joy he felt sitting there, holding Gytta's hand.

Time passed, in drowsy rest. He felt at ease, no need to be up and doing, such a rare feeling for him. But eventually it was Gytta who stirred, spoke, questioned again. And so he told her of Poum, of what the two of them had crossed back over the mountains to do.

'And where does that begin?'

'I do not know. I will journey to Petr the Red, in the north. He leads the resistance there. The fire of revolt glows. A few breaths, perhaps we can turn it into flame.'

'The north? But you are not of the north. You are a westerner. You are Luck of Askaug.'

The name struck him like a blow. He'd thought of Askaug every day of his exile, at the Keep, on the mountain; dreamed of it every night. That very morning, when he'd climbed the last crest and come again into Midgarth, it was to the west he looked. More than anything, he yearned to go home.

'Yes, Luck,' she said, reaching up and taking his face in both her hands. 'Home.'

He shivered. Suddenly, there was a cloud over the sun, the air cooled. Something didn't feel quite right. He looked at her again. 'Is that you speaking, Gytta? Or is it Sirene?'

Her lips did not move in the reply that came. 'Everything here is Sirene,' she said.

He turned. Across the garden, under the petal-rich bough,

she stood. As always, a white robe moved in the wind about her. As before, he could not see her eyes, only her mouth. Which moved again with words. 'You know that, Luck. Everything here is a reflection of your desires. This garden. Its maker.'

'Gytta's urging?' He stood. 'Do you wish me to go to Askaug?'

'I wish nothing. Only you make the wishes here.'

Luck nodded. He had found so many answers in dreams and visions he was not surprised to find one here. 'I will go there,' he said. 'And now I wish that you go, and leave me again to my dreams.'

'You do not have the time,' Sirene said. 'This dream is over.'

Even as the words were spoken, Luck felt the world shimmer, begin to dissolve. He looked down. Gytta, the scarf she knitted, both were gone.

'You are summoned.'

Luck heard it then, beyond Sirene's words. The faintest of cries, as if shouted from beyond the next hill. Felt the slightest of tugs at his chest, as if a hand pulled him by the shirt. He took one step towards the figure and even that one step showed him that his limp had returned. 'Wait,' he said. 'One thing more. When last we met you told me that there were others who watched us, who ... *experimented* with us.'

'That was your word, not mine. But yes, I watch for others. I tell them what men and gods do here.'

'Then tell them this.' He limped towards Sirene, part pulled by the tug in his chest, part drawn by the shouting getting louder somewhere beyond the garden. Beyond the world. When he drew level, he leaned in so he could look under the shroud. White eyes, no centre or colour to them, looked back. 'When I have taken back my world, I am going to come and ask them about theirs.'

If a blank whiteness could reflect surprise it did then. But

Luck had only a moment to note it, before he was gone, tumbling once more into the dark.

Luck was back, on the floor of the tent. Someone's hand was on his mouth. He struggled, and the someone hissed for quiet. The lamp was out, but by starlight he now could see that the hand that gagged him belonged to Marla – and that her other one was clamped over Poum's mouth.

'Seafarers!' she whispered. 'A patrol of them, coming in a boat along the river. We must go. Now!'

'No! No!' Poum escaped her hand, was rolling on the ground, reaching for the vial. 'I must go back. I must!'

Luck took their wrist in one hand, the vial in the other. Shoving Poum back, he corked the vial. Yet though he was still angry at what Poum had done, he remembered his bliss in Gytta's garden, and her message to him. Besides, now there was no time for anger, only a danger to be faced. Over Marla's shoulder, he could see a light moving through the reeds – the enemy's boat, approaching. 'You two, get the mules,' he whispered. 'I'll pack up here.' He placed the bottle in the pack then began rolling the blankets. 'Go,' he said, and shoved Poum.

The child was weeping as they stumbled from the tent. They moaned something that sounded like 'complete' but Luck was too busy to think about it.

When he joined them at the river, the patrol's craft was just pulling into the dock about a hundred paces distant. Luck jerked his head, and led the first mule away, its hoofs muffled on the meadow grass.

When they'd crested the first ridge out of the valley, Marla came up beside him. 'What happened to Poum? They can't stop crying.'

'I do not know,' answered Luck. 'No time to ask now.'

'Sir,' she said. 'We should stop soon, now we are beyond

hearing. Wait till they have gone. My home – Kroken – is the other way.'

'The plan has changed. We do not go north. We go west.'

Her eyebrows rose. 'West? Where?'

'Askaug.'

6

Changes of the Heart

Ferros stared at Roxanna. In the near sixteen years since they'd first come together she had not lost a hair of her allure. Rather . . .

She closed the door behind her, leaned against it, stared back. They stayed like that for ten slow breaths. 'Are you recovered, Ferros?' she finally asked.

He'd been knocked unconscious when the horse clattered into him. When he'd woken, his chest had still hurt. He could barely feel that blow now, such were the healing powers of immortals. And despite the flung spears and clashing swords, he had not been cut even once. So he nodded.

'Good,' she said, and left the door, crossed the room to the table on which stood an array of bottles. 'I would have been displeased if I had been disobeyed.' She lifted a bottle, looked at him, raised an eyebrow. 'Tinderos wine? I can send for ale if you prefer?'

'Wine.' He watched her pour the clear, almost blue liquid into two thin, tall crystal glasses. When she came to him and held one out, he didn't take it. 'Are you saying you told them to bring me to you alive?'

'I did. I did not want to wait for you to be reborn, to heal.'

'Why?'

'You ask why? Here, in this room?'

She smiled, looked around the room; at the bed, the chairs, the table, out to the balcony, letting her gaze rest on each. And though he did not look with her he saw, in her eyes, his memory of every place they'd had each other. His own eyes dropped. She was wearing a gown, the colour a deep scarlet, its neckline plunging, her breasts thrusting up, ebony skin gleaming in the lamplight. He ran his tongue over his lips, took the glass, looked away. 'I am with Lara,' he said, his voice hoarse.

'Still? I did wonder. So she eventually forgave you your,' again her eyes travelled the room, though more swiftly this time, 'indiscretions?'

It was not anything he wished to discuss. He raised his glass, but she tsked as it came to his lips and he paused there. 'Is it not customary to toast at a reunion?' she said.

'And what toast would you make, Roxanna? To Simbala? To Mavros? The Wattenwolden toast the father god, Varinger.' He looked her in the eyes. 'Or do you only toast the One these days in Corinthium?'

'Many do. I don't. Nor any other god.'

'Then what?'

'I toast ...' She lifted her glass. 'Unlimited possibilities.'

'Now *that* I can toast.'

She pledged him with her eyes. He pledged her back. Then they both sipped, and raised their glasses again in acknowledgement. 'Would you sit?' she said.

There was a chair either side of the table with the bottles. They both sat, and stared again into each other's eyes. Ferros could see a question in hers and was about to ask what it was, when she spoke. 'Lara,' she said. 'You say you are *with* her again. But you did not answer me when I asked if she'd forgiven you. Forgiven you ... *me*. Did you regain your former love?'

He considered. Was it worth a lie? He decided not. Whatever

was happening in this room, there could be no evasions. So he replied, 'No. Love does not stay still. It changes, as people change.'

'And there can be no bigger change than the discovery that you are immortal, eh?' She shook her head. 'Though I have lived three hundred years, I don't think I have ever been more shocked than when your Lara revealed herself to me from the mouth of a sailor on that boat from Tarfona.'

She laughed, and he couldn't help his smile. 'You should have seen my face in the caves of Cuerdocia. She ... emerged suddenly out of a dying comrade.'

'Truly?' She tipped back her head, her long black hair dancing with further laughter on her shoulders. 'Ah, possession eh? Perhaps that should be the toast.' She raised her glass. He lowered his. 'What? Do you still hate that gift?'

'You do not understand.' He lifted his glass, watched light play in the wine. 'I loved it too much. And a love for something like that, like too great a love for wine, would make my life not my own.' He sipped, and put the glass down. 'So I refrain.'

'And does Lara feel the same?'

He hesitated. 'We made a pact that we would not ... while we lived among the Wattenwolden.'

'I see.' Roxanna nodded to the night. 'But now she is out there, isn't she? Free of the pact.'

He shrugged. 'Perhaps.'

'I see,' she said again, as she picked up the bottle, topped up both their glasses. 'You know,' she said, setting the bottle back down, 'I admired you from the first time I met you. Your determination. Your sense of honour. Your loyalty. That was as rare as dragons' eggs in Corinthium.' She dipped her finger in the wine, ran it around the rim of her glass. A note sounded, faint, high-pitched. 'But do you know what I have always wondered? What would it be like if you discovered a loyalty ... to yourself?'

He frowned. 'What do you mean?'

She bent towards him. 'This. First you were loyal to an empire. Only to discover rot at its heart. Now you are loyal to the Wattenwolden. A barbaric tribe. Helping them to conquer, pillage, rape, murder innocents—'

'I do none of those things.'

'What *do* you do then?'

He shrugged. 'My duty.'

'Yet your duty leads you to use your skills in war that enable others to do those things that you do not.'

It was not as if he'd never thought about it. But he took refuge in what he'd always believed. 'I am an orphan. The army raised me. I am trained to obey.'

'So what if you obeyed something else? Some*one* else?'

'You?'

'No, Ferros. Yourself. Yourself!' She sat back. 'What would it be like to have loyalty only to the cause of *you*?' The high, sustained note she was drawing from her crystal had an intensity almost painful to his ears. Suddenly she lifted her finger, dipped it in the wine again, put it in her mouth. Her eyes never left his. 'What would you choose to do then?'

'For my life?'

'Well, as we know, that is an endless thing. No. I am speaking of now. Right here and now. Where you are the only loyalty, the only cause. What would you choose?'

It was as if a dam had burst. 'You know what,' he growled.

'Tell me.'

'I'd choose you.'

'You want me?'

'You know I do. You have been playing with that want ever since you came into the room.'

'Oh no, Ferros. I do not play. This can no longer be a game between you and me.'

'So you don't want me?'

'More than anyone I have ever wanted. And I have lived through three hundred years of desire.'

He grunted. It was beyond words for him now. Beyond … restraint. The room. His memories of it. Of her. He put the glass down.

She did not. She said, 'Before anything else, I need to know why you want me.'

'You want compliments first? Sweet words?'

'No. I know you desire me …'

'More than desire.'

'Yes. You wish to consume me. I wish to consume you back.'

'Then there is no problem.'

'But there is.' She raised her hand, palm out, preventing his rise. 'We would get pleasure from our … consumption. Now. All this night, in many of the nights to come. But what did you say, about you and Lara? How love does not stay still? How it changes, as people change?'

'So?'

'We would change. We would need something more than desire.'

Now he was certain, he was impatient to get to it. 'What?' he said, his voice a rasp.

'What I said before. Loyalty to yourself. Duty only to yourself. Your great skills, your determination, used only for you. And for me.' She smiled. 'Oh, I have dreamed of it, Ferros, these years without you. Waiting to see you free. To be everything you ever wanted to be, not at the service of others. Only at the service of yourself.'

It paused him. His hunger for her still gnawed at him, working through his body. But her words stirred in his body too.

'Listen to me, my lover,' she continued, her voice low. She reached across the table, took his hand. 'When the Four Tribes conquered us, we thought we would be slaves to their mad vision of the "One". But what they also brought was nothing less than a vision of the entire world, vaster than anything we could ever have dreamed. And in that world there were others like us, like you and me, Ferros, immortals ... but different from us. Greater than us in some ways. Because they understood – in Midgarth, in Ometepe – that they were not just longer lived than mortals, with a power to be used for pleasure, which was the way we regarded ourselves in Corinthium. They accepted that they were gods!' Her eyes glowed and she squeezed his hand hard. 'Gods, Ferros! You and me! So why would you return to being a general for the empire, or the Spear and Shield for a barbarian tribe when, if you but choose it, you could be a god?'

Her grip, her eyes, but most of all the fervour of her words were taking the energy he felt inside and focusing it elsewhere. From the moment he'd discovered he was immortal he had all but denied it. Failed to live it. Failed to recognise that his destiny had changed entirely. But she had understood it, he saw that now. Fifteen years before she'd thought only to serve her kind and her city. Now she had embraced what she was encouraging him to understand.

'And once we accept that we are gods?' he said, his voice quavering. 'What then? Do we rule the world?'

'If you wanted to. But I have discovered in controlling this city the last fifteen years that ruling is boring!' She threw back her head and laughed. 'Boring petty details, all day, every day, on and on. Why would gods want to do that? When gods can do ... anything?'

He saw it then. Suddenly, completely. This had been there from the moment an arrow entered his eye in the desert near Balbek and took his first life. Waiting for him to recognise ... himself. Who he was.

He'd been looking above her. Now he stared again into her

burning eyes – and saw her see what he now knew. 'Yes,' she said, putting down the glass at last. Rising. Reaching.

'Yes,' he echoed, moving to her.

His lips found hers. She shoved him back. His knees hit the edge of the bed, he fell onto it. She fell onto him, bent, put her mouth to his ear. 'Don't fuck me like a man,' she whispered. 'Fuck me like a god.'

He reached to her dress, pulled it off her shoulders, bent and took one huge, hard nipple in his mouth. She moaned, reached a hand back …

The pounding was sudden, loud, before the door burst open.

A Horse Lord was standing there. Korshak. Ferros remembered his name from the welcome of the Wattenwolden. His eyes, wide in shock, changed straight to fury. 'I thought so,' he cried, and seized the grip of the sword at his waist. 'You are mine, woman. So you must die.'

Roxanna had left him as soon as the door burst in. And even if Ferros had been about to fuck like a god, he was both an animal interrupted, and a warrior. So though Korshak's sword had just cleared its sheath, he hadn't had time to raise it before Ferros smashed the bottle of Tinderos wine across his face. Then he went for the sword. But Korshak was bigger, at least as strong, and a warrior too. He wrenched his arm back, and Ferros fell onto him, the two of them plunging to the floor, rolling back and forth, smashing furniture. Then the Horse Lord whipped an elbow into Ferros's face, knocked him onto his back. He saw the sword jerked to the side, the cutting edge pulled hard in. Seizing a broken chair leg he parried the blow, though the leg snapped in two. The sword went back again …

The knife passed between them, and embedded itself in Korshak's cheek. He bellowed, tried to brush it away with his other hand. Ferros seized the moment, and drove the splintered end of the chair leg into the man's left eye. He cried out again – but he loosened his grip on the sword. Ferros swung his legs, kicked the sword hand hard; the weapon flew – and Ferros dived after it. Korshak tried to hold him but Ferros wrenched clear, grabbed the sword, flipped onto his back, cut down. The hand the Horse Lord raised couldn't catch the falling steel.

Lurching to his feet Ferros stumbled, dropping the weapon as he fell back. Through eyes still blurred by the elbow blow, he tried to get up again – then saw that he did not need to.

The blade was buried in Korshak's forehead. The Horse Lord stared either side of it, eyes bright with death.

Ferros lurched to his feet. Roxanna bent and drew her dagger from the dead man's cheek.

Ferros dropped onto the bed. 'His woman?' he asked, rubbing where he'd been hit.

'No more,' she said, and slipped the blade into a sheath strapped to her left calf. Then she straightened, looked at him. 'Jealous?'

Maybe it was the blow to the head. Maybe the realisation he'd had before. Or perhaps it was simply the relief of not being the man with the sword splitting his skull. But he laughed. 'No, Roxanna,' he said, 'I think I am learning that none of the common emotions can ever be felt with you.'

She smiled, then stepped over the body, bent and ran a finger down his cheek. 'Good god,' she said, as she would to a dog. Then she bent and kissed him. His mouth opened to her, and she fell onto him, straddling him on the blood-spattered bed.

As Lara walked up the Stradun, the spine of the city that ran from the port over the seven hills all the way to the last one, Agueros, she looked at the people lining it, the market traders and customers, marvelling again at their will to survive.

When she'd returned to the city to spy for the Wattenwolden, she'd heard tales of the devastation after the conquest, so much of the city burned, pillaged by the conquerors from south and north. There'd been famine, sickness. More had died in the aftermath of Corinthium's fall than had been killed in the fall itself. Now, fifteen years later, there were few traces of those horrors. Once they had made the treaty with the Wattenwolden that saw them leave the city, its conquerors' leaders had recognised that the city was the source of huge wealth and power. They imposed the worship of the One, persecuted other faiths, made people dress more soberly, closed the places of sin – which only sent them underground, as she knew well, her destination this day once again being Asprodon, the place beneath the stones. But the Four Tribes decided that profit was more important than persecution. The city gradually reopened, and soon ships were docking again, bringing the wealth of the former empire.

Bringing many things, she thought, and patted the glass vial wrapped in bandages tight against her spine.

There was another reason Lara looked at people. Sometimes she would see one of those she'd possessed. In the half year that she'd been back there had been many, since she'd made up for the time of abstinence among the Wattenwolden by perhaps over indulging her delight on her return. And if she saw one? Well, it was like meeting a dear friend, one who you'd once known so much about, their most intimate secrets, but had lost touch with. She'd follow them for a bit, seeing how their life had gone on. Most had not changed: same aches, wants, hates. Same loves. Although some ...

She stopped sharply by a stall of beads and trinkets, seeing a woman shopping at it, wearing a shawl that was of a colour and a pattern that she recognised, worn in a style she knew. The woman glanced up as if feeling her attention. But Lara was already turning away. She'd known, before glimpsing a face that was wrinkled, careworn, that it wasn't Cosara. Because Cosara was dead.

Because Lara had helped to kill her.

As she walked on, she remembered possessing the young seamstress. Remembered why she had. Because something had changed in her, the more she took over a life. Before it had been about the exhilaration of experience, feeling all that a person was. Yet she'd come to focus more and more on a person's sorrows, less on their joys. Most people, she discovered, lived lives of hidden desperation. Struggling to earn enough in a day to survive, to help those close to them survive, people entered the world each day with more fear than hope. Fear that someone cleverer than they were would outwit them, take the little they had. Yet the greatest abundance of fear centred around love – a word whose meaning was so different for so many people.

It had been halfway through her time among the Wattenwolden that she'd realised that for her, in her relationship with Ferros, love had become custom, routine, something unsatisfying which was grasped tightly for fear that anything else would be dangerous, uncontrollable. It was one of the two hidden reasons why she'd forced them to let her return to Corinthium as a spy. The other, of course, was possession.

She'd thought that only she felt the way she did, yet again and again she witnessed lives – shared lives – where people were always uncertain in love. Impoverished by love. Weary of love, of its repetitiveness, its blandness.

But discovering all she had about the sorrows of love had one day made her wish for its opposite: for the joys she'd felt in the early years together with Ferros, in Balbek, before either of them knew they were immortal. The touch of the lover like lightning hitting the skin. The flush of desire as they glimpsed each other across a room. The ache when they left, the ache assuaged when they returned. So she'd sought out someone who felt that kind of love. Sought the joy.

Discovered the sorrow.

She'd observed Cosara first walking the streets near the port with a smile that lit the day. Followed that smile to a rendezvous with a very handsome, slightly older but still young man, of a different class, well dressed, a lawyer. Possessed her as they climbed the stairs to a simple, clean room he rented above an inn. Possessed her but in a way she'd discovered she could – let the one she'd taken do all she wanted, be all she needed to be, do what she wished. Lay within and revelled in passions she'd almost forgotten. That could not truly be remembered in the mind because they were experiences *beyond* the mind.

It made her believe in love again, for those hours. In the lovemaking and its aftermath, when Cosara told her lover her dreams and he promised to make them all come true. It had made Lara think that when Ferros came for the paying of the tribute she would take him away, to a room above an inn, and see if she could find again what they had lost. To dream again, as these lovers did.

Then, the next day, she'd seen the lawyer at a market, with a well-dressed woman his own age on his arm. She'd followed the pair, into a more affluent district, to a well-appointed house standing separate from its neighbours. And there, in its rich garden, two children played, and a third, a babe, was held to the breast of a wet nurse while the man and woman, proud parents, fussed.

She'd thought to leave it there, another sad, common lesson in love learned. But then later she saw the maid walking again by the port, no smile now, a greyness in her eyes that matched the sky, and tears to match the rain. Lara could not help it – she possessed her, to learn that the man had missed the next four rendezvous. Had sent a cold message that it was over, without explaining why. Angry, Lara took the maid to the house, feeling she should know of her betrayal. Left her at the gate as the man came out, dragged her a little way down the street, shook her, mocked her, laughed at her tears. Stopped laughing when Cosara pulled a knife from beneath her dress and stabbed him in the throat. Then, before Lara could get across the road, she'd stabbed herself in the heart.

Neither of them were born again.

'You just goin' to stand there, Laro, staring like a fuckin' fool, or you comin' in?'

Lara looked down to the cellar below the street to see Zok the doorman frowning up at her. She'd walked the rest of the way to Asprodon without seeing anything but Cosara's face. She shook herself. 'Coming,' she said, and stepped under the arch. As usual, she slipped Zok a small packet of kefa.

'Obliged,' he said, and pushed the door open.

The underground city seemed subdued – or perhaps that was just her mood. Few cries of faked pleasure came from behind the curtained doorways. The Field of Dreams, where certain performances took place, was dark. Only a little further down was there some noise – Severos, in his office, hurling abuse at some underling. Lara paused to listen. And it was soon clear that the underling being yelled at had failed to get coin up front from three Wattenwolden clients the week before.

'Now they are either dead, or fucked off back to their own country!' the self-styled King of Asprodon continued. 'So how do you intend to get the money from them that you owe me, huh?'

The other man mumbled something that Lara didn't catch, didn't try. She was back with thoughts she'd had every day since the slaughter at the tribute feast two days before. The rumours spoke of drunk tribesmen running mad, of the guardians of the city needing to contain them, how it had all exploded. Knowing the Wattenwolden as she did, it was possible but unlikely. Why would they riot when they were being given all that gold? They'd been betrayed, that was pretty certain. Since some escaped – including, she'd heard, the chief Malvolen – she was fairly certain that he would return soon with an army. What she had not heard was if his Spear and Shield had escaped as well. Was Ferros riding hard now for the Wattenwold? Or was he dead, and thus reborn, in the city? If so, where was he? She'd sent pigeons asking that question. None had come back with an answer. If she did not hear soon, she'd have to possess someone and try to enter the Sanctum. Because if he was still there he was probably there with … her.

Thoughts of Roxanna, and the instant hatred they conjured, were disturbed by the door flying open – and a man flying out. 'Go on!' yelled Severos, lowering his foot from the kick he'd obviously just planted on the underling's backside, 'and don't come back without my money!'

The man ran down the corridor and Severos's snarl changed to a grin. 'Laro, my friend,' he cried. 'I hope you're here to make me happy. Unlike that idiot.'

'Depends on what you mean by happy,' said Lara, following him back into the room.

'Well, your usual big bag of kefa will be a good start,' Severos said, going behind his desk, picking up a bottle of wine, pouring two mugfuls.

'Sorry, but that big storm has delayed the fleet from Balbek. Kefa is in short supply.'

'Fuck,' Severos grunted, waving Lara into the seat opposite him, then tipping his own back on its rear legs to more easily scratch at his large, hairy belly. His eyes narrowed. 'But your answer implied that there was some good news.'

'There is.' Lara picked up the mug, took a gulp. Severos only served rotgut in his taverns, keeping the good stuff for himself. This didn't disappoint. 'Last time I was here you implied that you'd be very generous if I could get you a, uh, certain rare liquid.'

Severos brought his chair onto all four legs. 'You haven't?'

'I may have. Remind me how generous you were going to be?'

'What quantity are we talking here?'

Lara raised her mug. 'Enough to fill this.'

Severos whistled. 'When I watched that fat bastard Streone use it, a spoonful would send him to paradise. So that …' He took his lower lip between his teeth. 'I think I said I'd give you five hundred centanos.'

'I think you said ten.'

'You know, I'm feeling generous. I'm not even going to argue.' He clicked his tongue. 'Do you have it with you?'

'I do. Some of it.' Lara put down her mug, stood, and reached to the small of her back. She pulled out the vial, and set it down on the table.

'Where'd you get it?'

'Like you said – the pirates of Omersh. One of their ships made it through the storm.'

Severos leaned in, studying. 'How do you know that's not prune juice?'

'Because the pirate in question … demonstrated. On a glass globe,' she nodded over his shoulder, 'like the one you keep in the wall there.'

Severos whistled. 'Streone would be gone for hours, drooling and laughing. Is that what happened to the pirate?'

'No. He only used a very little. Two drops.'

'So how do you know it works?'

'A man appeared. His face in the glass.' She grinned. 'A very angry man, with very black eyes.'

'Yeah, Streone would do that too. See someone. Well, well.' Severos rubbed at his black stubble, the sound a rasp, and looked from the bottle to Lara. 'If I am going to pay you that sort of money, I think I need to, uh, sample the goods, don't you?'

Lara stiffened, though she was careful not to let hope show on her face. She didn't know if Ferros was even alive, let alone still in the city. But his part of their plan was to get hold of Sirene. Hers was to get a globe. Now it appeared that she might be able to do both. 'You go ahead,' she said. 'Since you are paying for it.'

'No, no, Laro. What sort of host would I be if I didn't offer you some, eh?'

Lara raised her hands, palms out. 'I'm fine,' she said.

He smiled – but just with his mouth. 'But I insist. Otherwise, no deal. No offence, but how do I know you won't let me ... slip away, and then rob me?' He shook his head. 'Besides, I think we are in this together, don't you? Remember what I told you? How those who use it talk about paradise? Your own paradise, not anyone else's. Aren't you curious?'

She was about to argue, refuse – but then she thought about what this could bring. If Ferros was in the Sanctum, especially if he was with *her*, there was a globe there too, and Sirene. She didn't know how the drug worked – but people communicated through it and the globe. That was why they wanted it, to speak to the man who'd freed them from the Keep, Luck of Midgarth. Or maybe, since Severos was about to bring out the globe, now would be a chance to do what he said – then steal it. Also, he was right. She was curious. 'Very well,' she said.

'Now you're talking.'

He stood, went to the wall behind him, drew back the velvet cloth there, inserted a key into the metal box in the wall, opened the door, drew out the globe, pulled off its covering, and set it on the table. She stood up too, and they faced each other over it as he picked up the bottle and, with a bit of effort, prised out the cork.

'Now, remember,' she said, 'only two drops.'

'Of course,' said the King of Asprodon. Then he grabbed

her by her back collar, pulled her over the globe and poured a mouthful onto the glass.

She opened her mouth, took a breath to shout.

She didn't remember sitting. Nor the departure of the light. But she *was* sitting in the dark now, on what, she couldn't see, though she was off the ground. She reached down and her hand touched stone under her legs, rough on her fingers as if unfinished. All around her, and to an arm's length, there was nothing. 'Hello?' she called.

'Hello? Hello? Hello? Hello?'

The echo went far before fading. A cave? she wondered, peering into the dark before her. Though now she contemplated it, it didn't feel like the absence of light so much as something ... something only defined by itself. As though the dark had weight and texture.

She shook her head. Why was she here? Severos had tricked her, forced her to inhale. Perhaps visions only came to those who undertook the journey willingly? Where was Severos? Perhaps she would just sit there until he returned. As if this was the room outside the Pantheon in the Sanctum where the servants waited while their masters debated within the chamber.

As her heartbeat settled, that thought irked her. She was no servant. 'What, not worthy to see?' she demanded aloud.

Her words brought change. At first, just a tiny light she thought might simply be her eyes playing tricks in the total darkness, until she accepted that the light was growing from far away, slowly at first, then quicker and quicker, until she could see that she sat upon a stone plinth, a thrust of smoothed grey rock. It was the only object in a space that had become the presence of light, not the absence of dark. Nothing else to shine upon, no walls, no ceiling, no boundaries at all. Yet no sense of infinity either. Contained and boundless.

'Is that better?'

It was a woman's voice, though deep as many men's, speaking out of nowhere.

Lara found that she could stand, even if she was still not sure what on. 'Where are you?'

'Here,' the voice came again and where there had been nothing now stood … someone. A figure of medium height, shrouded from head to foot in robes of white. Only a part of a face showed, half a cheek, a hint of nose, a mouth.

'Who are you?'

'I am Sirene.'

'You are the drug?' There was no reply. Lara looked around. 'I was told you would take me to paradise?'

'Paradise?' Within the shroud, Sirene smiled. 'Whoever told you that?'

Lara shuddered. Something … passed through her. And she recognised the feeling, for it was the same one she often had, only this time it was reversed.

She felt … possessed. It lasted a heartbeat before it was gone, the infinity of light gone, Sirene gone and she was standing in a room she'd never seen before. A small room, with walls made from mud the colour of red sand and scarcely four paces across. Not much in it, a table, three chairs, a shelf of pots, a hearth with a small cauldron dangling from a metal frame over it. Cots pressed against three of the walls, a door opened in the fourth from which a rectangle of sharp, bright sunlight angled to the toe of her left foot – sandalled, she saw now, not booted as she had been. She looked at the rest of herself, saw and felt the lightness of her clothes: trousers, a shirt, both flowing gossamer cotton, not the heavy woollen weaves she'd been wearing against the cold.

A dry hot wind came with the light through the door and she felt her skin prickle with instant sweat. She crossed to the doorway, throwing up a hand to protect her eyes from a harsh sun so she could see.

Houses, like the one she stood in, stretched to the limits of vision. They were jammed together, with narrow passageways dividing them. Clothes like tattered flags stirred in the hot breeze on lines that passed between houses. Small children ran down the lanes, some chasing, some trying to provoke dogs who lay in whatever shade they could find, tongues lolling. Men and women with shrouded heads stood about singly, or in pairs, immobile, not speaking.

She saw them when they were still quite far away, because they were some of the very few people actually moving. And though they were different from when she'd last seen them, stooped and aged by years and suffering, they were still, undoubtedly, her parents. Following them was a young woman, bent beneath the weight of a large earthen jar.

It was her mother, Fruka, who saw her first. Her eyes had been fixed on the ground, folded over as she was by the scraps of wood and snapped branches that she carried. But a dozen paces away she looked up, gave a cry, halted so suddenly that Lara's father, Brankos, knocked into her, and the young woman into him. The three tottered, gaping, lowering their loads to the ground.

'Who are you? Fruka cried, her own hand raised like Lara's against the glare of sun on packed earth. 'What do you want? We've done nothing wrong!'

Lara couldn't speak. Her throat had swollen, at the sight – and with memories. For the last time she'd seen her parents was back in Balbek when they'd forbidden her to follow the man she loved to Corinthium. Told her that if she dishonoured her family so, she was forever dead to them. Sixteen years before, and a world so changed since. She knew that Balbek had fallen to the Four Tribes, that thousands were killed or had fled. She'd wanted to go there anyway, seek for those she loved. But Ferros would not go and, once again, she'd followed him.

All this in her mind now, stopping her speech.

It was Fruka who spoke again. A change in her face now, wonder replacing fear. She raised a hand, moved it before her, as if tracing the shape of a face in the air. 'La … Lara?' she murmured.

Lara found words. One, anyway. 'Mother.'

With cries like birds her parents rushed at her, forcing her out of the hot sun, into the hot room. And even though a voice in her head told her that this was a dream, a vision of Sirene only, their caresses all over her, their words in her ears, their tears mingling with hers on faces pressed together, all felt as real as anything she'd ever felt. So she pushed aside the voice. Touched, murmured, wept.

After a while she saw, through the mist in her eyes, a figure in the doorway: the young woman with the huge jar on her back. She'd been a girl of nine when Lara had last seen her. She'd been crying then, begging Lara not to go, not to abandon her.

There were no tears on her sister's face now. Now Aisha looked simply furious.

There'd been few words, only whispers of wonder, of joy. Now her mother spoke. Turning, she said, 'Aisha, water! Give your sister some water.' She turned back, running hands up and down Lara's arms. 'It is cold, from the well. Delicious! Aisha, bring your sister water.'

The voice was cold too. 'Let her get her own.'

There was a thump as the jar hit the ground. 'Aisha,' Lara called, but the young woman glared, and was gone.

'Aisha!' Lara cried again, trying to step past her parents.

But they held her. 'Let her be,' her father said, gripping her. 'She … she suffered more than any before we came here.'

Questions overwhelmed Lara. She groped for one. 'Where is here?'

Her mother pushed her down into a chair, then went and fetched the water jug. As her father sat beside her, Fruka poured them both water. It wasn't that cold, it wasn't that clean, but Lara smiled anyway as she drank it, as her parents watched her anxiously.

Brankos frowned. In her memories and dreams he'd remained young, with his chubby cheeks, skin as smooth as a baby's, hair dark and thick. Now a thin face slipped into deep grooves beneath a few wisps of grey hair. 'But you know where we are, Lara. You found us here,' he said.

'Tell me anyway,' she said.

It was Fruka who took her hand, spoke. 'It is a place for those who fled the invasion,' she said, squeezing. 'From towns all along the coast of the Great Sea, from Tarfona to Balbek, people sought to escape,' she swallowed, 'the slaughter. Thousands crossed the desert and those who survived settled here, outside Xan.'

Xan, Lara thought. She remembered it vaguely, from lessons she'd been taught. Far to the south of the Great Sea, a city built around a string of oases. The tutor who'd accompanied her and Ferros when they'd gone to Corinthium was from here. A flash came, of a very tall man, with skin the colour of midnight, in white robes. 'There are ... holy men here, yes?'

'The Timian Monks,' Brankos replied. 'They gave us this land, helped us build these houses from mud, help us grow food, raise chickens, goats.' His eyes darkened. 'We work for it though. In the kefa fields.'

'Kefa?' She shook her head. It was too big a question for now. 'How many of us are here?'

'Too many. Thousands,' Brankos answered. 'And more keep coming. Keep ... breeding.' He hawked, looked as if he was about to spit onto the floor. But a look from his wife stopped him. He rose, went to the door, spat over the threshold.

Lara looked at him, silhouetted against the glare. 'And Aisha?' she asked softly.

Fruka lifted one hand from her daughter's arm to rub away the tears that fell again, fast and sudden. 'She ... in the deserts, some Sarphardi tribesmen caught us. They ...'

Lara flushed cold. 'She was a girl,' she whispered.

'Not after that day,' her father muttered without turning around.

They all cried then. Yet even as she wept, Lara questioned. If this is a dream, she wondered, however horrible it is, it is not made from my very worst fears. Those had my family slaughtered when the Four Tribes and their allies swept into Balbek. In this dream, my family live. Poorly, sadly. But they live.

Then the thought struck her: could this be a vision of what is, instead of a dream of what is not?

She stood on her thought. 'I must go,' she said.

Her father turned, her mother clung to her arm, tried to pull her back down. 'Go? Where?' Fruka wailed. 'There is nowhere to go.'

'There is. And I must return there.' She looked down, laid a hand to her mother's tear-stained face. 'But I promise you this: I will be back.'

It was gone on the instant. The feel of tears on her palm. Heat. Tainted water in her mouth. She was in the void of light and dark ... and then she was back in the room in Asprodon.

She sat up. She was still in her chair and, across the table, Severos sprawled in his. His head was thrown back, his eyes part open, and he was making little grunts of pleasure in his throat. In the lamp, the light flickered as it burned the very last of the oil. Between them, smoke swirled in the globe. Beside it lay the glass vial she'd brought, a dark stain on the wood beneath its neck.

She picked it up. It was empty. It did not matter. She'd only brought him half of what she'd obtained from the pirate of Omersh. She'd lied about the kefa not arriving. She'd used all of Graco's kefa money to buy Sirene.

She stood, went to the metal box in the wall behind the table. Severos kept his silver there, and Lara swept all the coins that were on the shelf into a bag. Tying that swiftly to her belt, she turned back to the table, picked up the velvet sack, and dropped it over the globe.

'What? What?'

Severos sat up. His eyes rolled, trying to focus. As they did, Lara picked up the sack and ran for the door.

His office was the third level down in Asprodon. She sprinted up the slopes and stairs, pursued by his voice. 'Stop him!' Severos bellowed. 'Stop Laro.'

She reached the door. Zok, the huge gatekeeper, loomed there. 'Leaving, Laro?' he asked. Then he looked past her, to the stairwell, and the sounds of feet and shouting.

'How's that kefa I brought you, Zok?' she said.

He looked back to her, as her name was yelled again. 'Lovely,' he said, shifting the bulge in his mouth to his other cheek as he unbolted the door.

She was through it fast, down the alley, down another, finally out into the crowds on the Stradun. Shouting followed her for a while, then faded. She paused only to tuck the purses she'd tied to her belt beneath her blouse. You couldn't be too careful in Sevrapol. There were thieves about.

As she made for the port and her lodgings – the first place Severos would look for her, so she would only stop by to grab a few essentials – she thought about what she needed to do.

There was Ferros. But she had the globe now, a way of seeing across the world. She'd find him in it, somehow. And if she did not, for now? Well, she had time to change her mind. So much time to fall out of love and perhaps back into it? Being immortal gave her that, when mortals did not have that choice. As Cosara the seamstress, and her lover, had learned.

Whatever. Those were questions for another day. There were only two that she needed answers to now.

When does the next ship sail for Balbek? And, once there, how does one cross the desert to Xan?

7
Home and Hearth

No one knew the forests near Askaug better than Luck. Over the hundreds of years since his birth there, whereas his brother and sister gods went off to fight each summer as was the custom, Luck had realised after his first campaign that he was neither shaped for, nor interested in, war. He remained behind – and got to know his world. The land, its every feature, every bird and beast in it. Knew under which bushes the ptarmigan nested, which trees housed the owl or the hawk; where, in a scoop of land hollowed out by a river long since diverted to bring water into the town, families of mink lived, had lived for generations. Always alert, with sharp eyes, sensitive nose, acute hearing, a mink could slide into places many others could not, had teeth and claws to defend itself from the surprise of dog, cat or rat, moved fast and silently.

It was the perfect creature for spying.

Luck had used it for that purpose scores of times over his life. He would use it again now. 'I am sorry you cannot have a fire,' he said, looking down at Marla and Poum, both shivering on the ground in the small glade. 'But until we know what is happening in the town, it is best that no one knows we are here. There are men in Askaug who will smell smoke and come seeking its source.'

'I still do not understand why we do not all go,' Poum grumbled. 'We can come close and observe with you.'

'Three of us, three times the chance of being caught,' Luck replied. 'I must use stealth to get close, to see.'

'Stealth is needed?' Poum shook their head. 'Then, Father, I should be the one to go. I am more agile than you—' Poum broke off, though their look at Luck's lame leg added what they did not say.

'True,' said Luck, 'if I was going as myself.'

He had only told Poum of the power of the gods of Midgarth to possess other creatures the night after they left Galahur. Had not included it in their lessons over the years. For it was not just in Midgarth that he'd needed to spy. That he was able to observe Poum unseen was a secret he'd kept. Despite his love for the child, the truth was that they were 'the One'. The focus of so much of the wider world's hopes and passions. They were ... foretold to change the entire world. And Luck, for all his years and acquired wisdom, had never raised a child himself before he'd met Atisha. With Poum the focus of so much ... *prophecy*, how was he to know if the child would grow up loving or cruel?

Loving, he'd decided long before. Still, he had not told. Had observed, in case. And when he finally did tell, that night a week before, Poum had only grunted and looked away, in that way a young person of their years had, of displaying that anything their parents said was the dullest thing possible.

Just as well, Luck thought, rising from his crouch. 'Stay here. If I do not return by dawn tomorrow, do not try to follow me.' He turned to the girl. 'Take Poum north, Marla. To your home. To Petr the Red and the rebels there.'

'I will, sir.'

Luck turned back to Poum. 'Will you wish me fortune?'

The child didn't even look up, just drew the cloak tighter

around themselves. 'Why would you need fortune, Luck, when you are so clever?' they grunted.

Luck sighed. 'I will see you long before dawn,' he said. 'And with fortune,' he glanced at Poum again, 'I will return with the news we learned in Sirene's smoke – that Askaug is ready to be the first spark of the fire of rebellion that will set all Midgarth alight.'

He set out down the slope that led to the old riverbed.

When his limping footsteps had faded, Poum turned to Marla and asked, 'How long do we give him?'

'Until night is fully come,' she said, 'and a little after.' She looked up, at a clear sky. 'The Blue Moon is full tonight.' She grinned. 'We should be able to see a lot.'

The mink he took was still young but full grown and strong. As he ran through the woods towards the top of the town, Luck within felt the exhilaration of possession, as well as excitement at what lay ahead. Home, he thought.

His old house was on the edge of town, near to where the forests began, away from the sea. A slight detour took him to it. Heartache took him there, mostly. Almost sixteen years before he'd set out from there to climb the mountains, and discover what threatened his world. That he had certainly learned, yet he had been unable to do anything to prevent it. Most of those he'd known and loved were dead, killed in the Coming of the Dark. Hovard and Bjorn – and Freya whom he'd loved best of all. Almost all the gods of Midgarth had died that day; finally died, never to be reborn. Yet there were mortals in the town he'd also been fond of. He wondered if they lived. How they lived.

From the base of the elm he used to sit in often as a bird and herald the dawn, he studied his old house. It was shuttered against the night, but the light that marked the edges of window hole and door frame showed that it was occupied. Was an Askaug family within? So many had fled the invasion, when the Four Tribes and their ally from the far west, Intitepe, had taken the town. But in night camps on the journey here Marla, who'd come to fetch him, had told him of the history he'd missed. How residents had returned gradually, having truly nowhere else to go, to accept the rule of the conquerors.

He loped towards the house. This was the third dwelling he'd built on his land over the centuries. Only a quarter-century old, because when Gytta died he'd torn down the house they'd shared so he wouldn't look for her in every corner. He knew its every gap and entry. Slipping under the porch, he frightened off a rat who was gnawing something there, then, pushing his nose to a hole in a floorboard, he sniffed. Six mortals, he thought. He listened to the clink and drag of spoon on bowl. Some stewed deer was being consumed directly above him.

He ran to the edge of the house. There was a gap between the floor and the outer wall he'd always meant to plug. No one had since, it had only widened. Thrusting his head in, he saw that some box or trunk had been placed against the wall there. There was a space between it and the wall and he slipped silently into it. Waited a moment. When no dog barked, or cat came to investigate, he peered around the trunk's edge.

No Askaugians were in the room. Nevertheless he recognised the five men who were. Their type anyway. Horse Lords. The conquerors of Midgarth sat at his table and ate.

Luck felt fury flush him and he shivered from nose to tip of tail.

One of the men called out something and, a moment later, a woman appeared from the alcove where he'd kept his cooking stove. Her, he recognised immediately, even though she was so changed. It was the Widow Agnetha, dyer of cloths. All those years ago, at the last Oblivion's Feast they'd celebrated in

Askaug, Luck had predicted that should she make love with a god that night, she would have three sons who would help her with her trade. She'd taken the visiting god, Einar the Black, to her bed. But the black-eyed assassin had interrupted the tryst, tried to kill Einar. Luck, with Freya's help, had stopped him. Bjorn had killed him – and his appearance had begun the journey that had taken Luck away from this house, and hastened all the sorrows of the world.

Mortals aged when gods did not. But Agnetha looked as if far more than fifteen years had passed. Her fair, thick hair was grey and wispy now, her former fine, full figure shrunken. She stooped when she used to stride. She held a larger pot, and went to the five lords, ladling stew into their bowls. At the last, the man who'd called, she missed the bowl a little, caught its rim. Stew landed on the table edge, and fell into the Horse Lord's lap. He bellowed and backhanded her across the face.

It took all of Luck's willpower not to burst from the mink and shove the bowl down the man's throat. But he slid under the house again, heart beating faster. He was no fighter. But he knew people in the town who were, or had been. And if Gytta – or her vision – had been right back in her garden to send him there, those people would be ready to rise and kill the men who so oppressed them. Begin the revolt that would free not just their town, but the whole land.

He ran along the edges of Askaug's main thoroughfare, dodging from porch to porch, only stopped when he reached the rough centre. There the mead hall, where the inhabitants would gather to celebrate life, used to stand – but no more. Another wooden structure had taken its place and instead of the vast elk antlers that had hung over the great double doors, something else did: a cloth on which was emblazoned, on a white background, a single black eye. The sign of the One.

As he watched, three cowled figures came down the street

and entered the building. Through the now open door, Luck could see that they joined a dozen others already there. When they did, everyone began to chant. He had heard it often enough at the Keep. The night rituals for their god were starting.

He stared. The chanting of course made him think of Anazat. Of all his enemies, the black-eyed monk was the most formidable. Yet no doubt he was on the other side of the world, at this city of Corinthium. Compared to that, Midgarth was but a rock pool beside the ocean. The monk would not be one of those lifting his voice in prayer right now.

Still, he stared at their backs a few moments longer. Then, shaking himself, he set out at a mink's swift scamper climbing the slope towards the eastern gate, hoping that the place he next sought would still be there.

It was. The forge's doors were open to the night: here, rather than shut out the night cold, it was welcomed, for the fires within burned white hot, while the men he'd hoped were still alive were standing in the glow of forge fire, hammering metal.

Luck rose on his hind legs and watched them work. Ulrich the Smith was still a huge man, though Luck could see that, like Agnetha, he was leaner than he'd been. His son, Tiny Elric, was even bigger, and did not appear much diminished by the years. Bare chested, both men took turns to draw sparks from the anvil, bringing their smelting hammers down hard again and again, then thrusting the beaten metal into troughs of water that hissed and steamed, before returning it to the coals. There was a pause, as the metal strips heated again. Elric used a cloth to wipe his face, then took the mug his father had drunk from and drank as much.

Luck dropped back onto his forepaws, ran into the forge, halting to the side of the doors.

Elric saw him straight away. 'Rat,' he yelled, reaching for a wooden stave.

'Mink, and bold with it,' his father corrected, grasping his son's arm, restraining his rush forward, adding, 'What are you doing here, little hunter?'

As usual, it took but a thought. 'Looking for you,' said Luck, as he stepped from the beast's body.

Tiny Elric gasped and dropped the stave. The mink hissed at them all then ran off. Ulrich, who'd once been on a longship rammed by a whale and had been heard to say, when he stepped into the water, 'Last one to shore is a donkey,' merely raised an eyebrow and said, 'I wondered when you'd be back.'

'Good to see you too, Ulrich,' Luck replied. 'Is that Askaug ale you are drinking?'

The smith nodded, and his son, his eyes still wide with surprise, brought Luck a mugful. 'Close the doors,' his father called to him, and Elric did. Filling his own mug with ale, he lifted it to Luck. 'To the gods,' he toasted, 'the living and the dead.'

Luck pledged, 'The gods!' then drank. Sighed. More than the sight of the town, the taste of it was in that first sip. 'Oh, I have missed that,' he said, smacking his lips. 'Couldn't grow barley in the mountains. And oat beer is ... not as good.'

'In the mountains, were you?' Ulrich gestured first to Elric to deal with the heating metals, and then over to two stools. Luck mounted one with difficulty; designed to suit the smiths, it left his feet dangling off the ground.

'I was.'

'For what reason have you returned now?'

'Revolt.'

Again, Ulrich showed no surprise – though a little extra light came into his eyes. 'I'll toast that,' he said, raising his mug, draining it, refilling both of theirs. 'And may I say, about bloody time.'

'Is it, though? You toasted the gods, living and dead. How many live?'

'Hard to say. They don't declare themselves very often, since the Four Tribes placed such a high bounty on their heads.' He nodded. 'Some escaped the Coming of the Dark, of course, the younger ones. Some more will be new, having died and been reborn for the first time.' The smith pulled at his beard. 'News is very restricted, along with many other things. Travel between different parts of Midgarth is only allowed under rare circumstances. But a year back I did hear that Petr the Red still lives near Kroken—'

'He does. It was he who got a message to me. That this might be the time.' Luck licked at the froth around the mug's lip. 'But there's one other immortal who does not need to hide, and travels where he wishes, is there not?'

'Peki Asarko.' Ulrich leaned away and spat onto the earth floor. 'That bastard does indeed parade himself all around the land. Especially if there is any opposition to his tyranny. Even the slightest hint of it, he descends on a town, rounds up people innocent or guilty, kills many on the spot, sends others to be slaves across the mountains or to his base on the Lake of Souls.' He shook his head. 'No one knows what happens to them there.'

Luck shuddered, because he did know. For a brief moment he saw again the flayed, displayed, preserved bodies in Peki Asarko's longhouse. It was nothing he need share, save to say, 'All who suffered will be avenged, Ulrich, trust me.'

'It's what we've been waiting for,' grunted the smith. 'Hard to plot rebellion across the land when we know so little of other places. But the people of Askaug are ready at least.'

'It begins here,' said Luck, leaning forward. 'Which is why I have returned. I need to find out more, where their forces are grouped, how strong they are—'

'Not as strong as they've been.' It was Elric who spoke, calling from the forge. 'Each town's garrison has been halved in the last few months. We can take those who remain. All our weapons were confiscated but some we managed to hide and others,' he lifted the single long piece of metal, glowing, from the flames, 'well, in the night, when the occupiers are less vigilant, we have been turning farm equipment into swords and spears, against the day.'

He began to hammer out the metal again. Luck raised his voice over the noise. 'Where are they strongest? The Lake of Souls, I suppose. We'll need to kill Peki Asarko first and fast. Cut off his head, and we cut off the head of their power.'

For the first time, a touch of emotion showed on the smith's placid face. 'Then I look forward to doing that myself, and soon. For he is here.'

Luck started. 'In Askaug?'

'Arrived a week ago. Brought more of his guards, of course. Still, we can deal with them.' He reached and tapped Luck's knee. 'Just give the command.'

Luck sipped again, and considered. He had thought to visit Petr the Red before launching the revolt, coordinating the action across the land. But this was a rare stroke of fortune indeed because he knew he was right. Kill the Lord of the Lake of Souls and resistance would be much weaker.

'Then let us not hesitate,' he said. 'How many men can you muster tonight? To be ready to act at dawn?'

'Dawn, hmm? There are men on the outlying farms we'll need. It's where most of the weapons, new and old, are hidden too.' The smith scratched his head. 'We would not have as many as I'd like by dawn.'

'But would we have enough?'

Ulrich sucked at his lower lip. At last, he nodded. 'With surprise and some luck, yes. Especially as the Horse Lords will be sleeping off all that they've drunk. The monks will be more of a problem as they don't drink and they are up early to pray. They are better fighters too.'

'How many monks are there?'

'Only a dozen. At least we know where they will be at dawn. Chanting in their damn chapel.'

Luck thought back to seeing the monks earlier. The fear of Anazat their black backs had recalled for him. Then he shook it off.

'Are there any Huntresses?'

'Aye. About five came with Peki Asarko. But they were obviously happy to be free once they delivered him here. They went off to hunt in the forest.'

Luck considered. It was another piece of good fortune that they were gone, for the women warriors were every bit as fierce as any Horse Lord or Monk. Another reason to move fast. 'Send the word, Ulrich. Peki Asarko's visit here is too good a chance to pass up.'

'I will.' He turned. 'Elric, stop that now.' When his son had put down his hammer, he continued, 'Go and fetch Arne, Tove and Sven. We need to send them—' He broke off, his brow creasing. 'What is that noise?'

Luck had also become aware of it, when the hammer blows ceased falling. Distant, angry shouting from several voices. He didn't know why he suddenly flushed cold. How he knew. But he did.

'Poum,' he said, slipping off the stool, his beer mug falling to the ground.

A few minutes earlier . . .

Though Marla was from the north, she had visited Askaug before, spending one summer in the town because an aunt lived there. Poum only knew it from their father's stories. So she led and they were happy to follow. The two of them had agreed that all they were going to do was look. At the slightest sign of danger they would flee back to the cold forest.

Marla had led them to the highest point of the town, a low hill just inside its broken front walls – torn down, she said, by the conquerors and never rebuilt. Lying belly down and concealed within the ruins of a wooden tower that must once have stood there, they were able to see much of Askaug from its summit because Havfor, the blue moon, was at its fullest. It was a delight to Poum, for whom a crowd was the family gathered around the steading's table. Here, though it was early evening and already dark, people moved about, gathered sometimes in groups to talk – though whenever a Horse Lord or Monk appeared they dispersed quickly.

'What is that building?' Poum asked, pointing. Easily the largest structure, the house was three storeys tall, the frames of many window openings etched by the lights within. 'It does not look like the other houses.'

'It is not. It was only built five years ago, the summer I was here. Peki Asarko was due to visit again and he'd complained before that the only place for him to stay was a fisherman's hovel. He sent a design ahead and the headman here built him ... that.'

'Peki Asarko, eh?' Poum scratched their head. They had heard of the ruler of Midgarth. The traitor to his people. Luck had taught them everything he could about the land, and spared no details of the god's depravity. Yet rather than being revolted, Poum had been fascinated. All the monsters in their parents' tales, from Ometepe or Midgarth, could not compare to the sheer sickness of the Lord of the Lake of Souls. 'Do you know that he kills people, flays the skin from them, and then preserves their bodies with special fluids?' they said.

'Yes, I did know.' Marla shook her head. 'Disgusting.'

'Completely,' Poum agreed. 'Did you hear how once he captured—'

'Shh!' Marla exclaimed. 'Who are they? At the big house's door?'

Poum peered. 'They are not of Askaug, are they?'

'No, I see them now.' Marla spat between the broken slats in front of her. 'They are members of the Four Tribes. The bare-chested ones are Horse Lords, the black-cowled one is a Monk, the others, with the feathers in their hats, are—'

'Seafarers,' Poum hissed, as delighted by them as they had been with thoughts of Peki Asarko. 'It is said they sail the world in search of adventure and plunder. Always fighting, stealing, competing for booty.'

'You sound as if you admire them, Poum.'

'Certainly not,' Poum replied. 'They are, of course, evil swine who—' They broke off. Someone else had joined the crowd. Smaller, and lost for the moment among the big men. Then some of these stepped aside. A brighter light came through the open doorway and shone on … her. Poum gasped. 'But that's … that's impossible. It can't be her. It can't!'

'Who? Who is it, Poum?' Marla leaned in, alarm on her face. 'What's the matter? You've gone white.'

'It's … h-h-her,' they stuttered. 'Kipé!'

They thought their eyes were playing tricks; stared and kept staring. But the young woman, dwarfed by the Horse Lords she stood among, was definitely the same young woman they had seen when they travelled with Sirene.

Poum flopped onto their back, breathing hard. Marla crouched over them, concern on her face. And she had reason, Poum thought. Because they liked Marla, had enjoyed the company of someone their own age. She'd kissed them once and it had been … nice. Then they had gone into the smoke, met Kipé. And they *loved* Kipé.

Was it love, though? They knew nothing of her, aside from that she was beautiful and … open in a way they had never experienced before. She had taken off her clothes, urged them to do the same. They'd hesitated, knowing how *different* they were, not knowing how another person who saw that difference would react. And then they'd realised that they weren't different there, in Sirene's visions. Or at least only in the normal difference between boy and girl.

He had taken off his clothes. He had slipped into the cool, delicious water. He had swum, which they could never do. Swum to her. Chased her around the pool. Caught her finally and she had laughed, then stopped laughing, then kissed him. And if Marla's kiss, their first, had been powerful, Kipé's was extraordinary. He felt the changes at his core, a hardening. She felt it too, and led him to a grassy bank. Lay beside him there, their bodies drying in the sun. Ran her hands over his body, all over his body, as he ran his over hers, exploring, wondering. Then she'd said, 'It is time,' and pulled him close.

Poum jerked upright. For that moment of remembering it was almost as if they were back there, on that grassy bank, that beautiful girl offering them something they'd feared, because of their difference, they could never have. But then he'd been wrenched away, torn away, back through smoke, back to the forest, back as *they* not *he*, with Luck beside them. Weeping, begging to go back. But they couldn't. Luck had explained that anything seen within the smoke was not real. Was only a manifestation of desire.

Then how was it that the young woman they'd swum with in that pond was in Askaug? Real, not fashioned from their desires by the smoke within the glass?

'We have to go,' Poum said, rising.

'Yes,' said Marla, getting up too. 'Luck may be coming back to the camp soon. He mustn't find us gone. Come.'

She took a step away. 'You don't understand,' Poum said, not moving. 'We have to go down there.'

'No! Poum, Luck will—'

'I don't care about Luck!' Poum's voice rose, and she hissed at them to lower it. 'You can come with me or not. But I am going to that house.'

'Why?'

'Someone I must see. Find out—' Poum broke off, turned, slid down the slope of the hill. Marla followed, muttering curses. When they reached level ground, Poum took a step forward to the road that led to Askaug's centre but Marla grabbed his arm. 'If you have to do this, let us try not to be caught. This way.'

She pulled them into the broken shadows of another burned and ruined house, led them through its overgrown garden and into a lane of knee-high grass that ran parallel to the road. Through gaps between structures, some occupied, some not, they caught glimpses of Peki Asarko's house. Those who had been standing in front of it had gone back inside.

'Close enough,' Marla said, pulling them into the lee of a wagon with only three wheels. A cat hissed at them from a dark corner, and they saw her, and five kittens suckling. 'You can see what you need from here.'

But the door of Peki's house was only part open, and all the window shutters were closed. Shadows moved, any one of which could be ... hers. 'I have to get closer,' Poum said.

'No! Poum, if we are caught ...'

'I won't be.' They took Marla by the shoulders. 'Because there is something I can do. I can ... transform into an animal.'

She stared back. 'You mean ... like a god? Like Luck?'

'Yes. I suppose ...' They shrugged. 'I suppose I am a god.'

She stared more, then finally shook her head. Said nothing.

It was the cat they chose. Harder to go into than Ufda the dog, not as hard as the eagle. Poum slipped inside. They felt the pull, as the mother sought to remain with her brood. But they were in control, and on padded feet they ran across to the open doorway. Cautiously, they thrust the cat's head into the gap.

It was a large room, a dozen paces across, a wide hearth to the side, on which a fire crackled. Men sat around it, the type they now knew to be called Horse Lords. Big men, with long hair tied in a braid down their backs, and eyes of bright blue in pale faces. No women, no Kipé … until Poum saw her, coming through a doorway at the back. She brought jugs, which were acclaimed by the men. A servant then, they thought, and if she did not have the sheer beauty of their memory of her at the pond, she still stopped their breath – that white-blonde hair, that golden skin. One of the Horse Lords liked her too, grabbing her by the wrist, pulling her close. She sloshed some beer on to his lap, the other men laughed, and she jerked her hand away, put the jugs down, and went back out by the door she'd come through.

A kitchen, Poum thought, retreating from the doorway. I will find her there.

They ran around the side of the house to the back. At the top of three steps, a door was ajar. Through the gap, they could hear a tune being softly hummed. They climbed the steps, pushed nose and whiskers in. She was standing with her back to the door, slicing bread.

I'd just like to hear her voice, Poum thought. See if she is at all like my memory of her.

Halting just inside the doorway, they gave a little mew. Kipé heard, turned. Smiled. 'Hello, sweets,' she said. Her voice was … different. Not as husky, and accented, a girl from the eastern ranges. She continued, 'Would you like some milk, little one?'

There was kindness in the voice. They couldn't help themselves. They went in, crossed to her, rubbed their cat's face against her ankles. She lifted a jug, poured some milk onto a small platter, set it down, then ran her fingers along the cat's spine. Poum arched it to her touch, thrilled by it, then bent to the milk.

The voice came inside their head. *My,* it said, *but you're a pretty one.*

Poum looked up, confused. Had Kipé spoken? But she wasn't looking at them, she was looking at the door, where Poum now looked too. Looked, and shrank back, all their hackles rising.

Another cat stood there, a big grey tom, old and much scarred from battle, with one ear missing and the other not much more than a nub. Yellow eyes gleamed, as the voice came again. *You know, it is strange to think this, but you and I have mated. I don't think you were very pleased by it though.*

Poum knew only one thing, to flee. She made a dart for the open door. But the tom was faster, pouncing, pinning. Poum's possession squealed, tried to get its own claws out, to scratch back, couldn't move. The thought-voice came again.

I think it is time you showed me who you really are, don't you?

It hit Poum, suddenly, hard. *How ... how do you know what I am?*

The tom's mouth widened into what could only be a smile.

Takes one to know one.

Poum lost control. Terror drove them out. They were there, sprawling on the floor. The cat was there too, though she swiftly ran shrieking out the door. This time the tom made no attempt to stop her. Nor did the man now standing there as well. He was wearing a kind of long dress, his huge body pushing out against the fabric. 'Peki Asarko,' he said, tipping his head. 'And you must be Poum.' He waved a hand. 'This lovely young lady is Brena.'

Poum got slowly to their feet. Everything was wrong, so wrong. 'Kipé. Her name is Kipé!'

Peki Asarko laughed. 'Oh now. That was just my little joke. My joke in the smoke.' He giggled. 'I took her image because my servant truly is so lovely. With such soft skin.' He reached out and pinched her cheek. She grimaced, though he did not see it, turning back. 'But the name? I didn't tell Anazat, he wouldn't have let me, but I knew you'd be too distracted to see,' he bent closer, till his face was but a hand's breadth away, 'what Kipé would spell if you rearranged the letters.'

It took a moment. Their gasp showed that they'd understood. And Peki, seeing that, threw back his head and laughed.

It was a moment only, the slightest of distractions. Poum seized it. There was no way past that bulk in the doorway. So they turned and ran into the main room.

The yelp of 'Stop him!' came too late. Poum was across the room and out of the door before the first Horse Lord had leaped up. They shouted, pursued. But they wouldn't have caught Poum, if they hadn't stopped dead at the sight before them …

… Marla, kneeling before five women dressed all in leather, with bows drawn.

The shouting Lords came, saw, seized. Poum too was forced to their knees.

And then a new voice came. One they had never heard before. One that chilled their heart.

'Let them up.'

Poum looked up at the speaker – a black-cowled monk with eyes of impenetrable black. Who stepped forward now and continued, 'For do you not know who this is?' He raised his arms, palms to the sky, and cried out, 'The One has returned to us. Praise her! Praise him!'

Then everyone was crying it.

'Praise her! Praise him! Praise the One!'

It was the angry shouting that had made him leap down from the stool flush cold, sensing that something had happened to Poum. But the distant, ecstatic cry confirmed it.

'Praise her! Praise him! Praise the One!'

Luck limped three steps towards the noise, stopped. It would take him too long to get down there as himself. And he had too recently possessed a creature to be able to do so again immediately. 'Elric,' he called.

'Here.' The young smith came and stood beside him.

'Run down there fast. Find out what is happening. Come as quickly back.'

Elric sprinted off. His father came and stood beside Luck. 'What has happened?' he asked.

'I don't know, for certain, but I fear—' Luck broke off. He hadn't told Ulrich about Poum. It was too big a subject to broach casually, especially when the priority was to gather forces for the revolt. Now he did not know if that was still possible. Not if what he feared had come to pass.

Elric returned soon after and as fast as he'd left. 'It's a bees' nest stirred,' he said, puffing only a little. 'The whole garrison, and half the town, are at Peki Asarko's house, cheering.'

'Cheering what?' his father asked.

'Well,' Elric reached up to scratch at his thick hedge of hair, 'they say that the One has come to Askaug.'

'The One? That ... myth?' Ulrich shrugged. 'How many times has this child been "sighted"? He doesn't exist. He's just a way to control credulous fools.'

'He ... *they* do exist.'

'How do you know, Luck?'

'Because I brought them here.' The two smiths gasped, and both opened their mouths to question. But Luck knew he had no time. 'Listen, it is all the more urgent that we get your men here as soon as possible. We have to fight now. We have to get the One back.'

'More urgent than you think,' Elric said. 'Atle told me that yesterday he'd been ordered to bring supplies to the port to a ship that sails with the morning tide for the land of the Four Tribes. He said the black-eyed one commanded him in person to—'

Luck grabbed his arm. 'What black-eyed one? One of the monks?'

'Not just any one,' Ulrich said. 'The way the others treat him means he is above them. Even Peki Asarko grovels to him.'

Anazat! It had to be him. But if he was here? Luck cursed under his breath. The news confirmed something he'd been fearing ever since he'd heard the cry acclaiming the One.

This wasn't chance. This was a trap, sprung. How, he had no idea. And there was no time to worry about it now. 'That ship must not sail,' he hissed. 'Gather as many of our fighters as you can. No matter how many you get, we must attack with the dawn.'

Elric ran one way, Ulrich another. Luck raised his arms, then dropped them again and sighed. There was nothing more he could do except rest, try to get back the strength he'd need for another possession.

Luck stared down towards the main part of the town. Noise still came from there, a faint, excited buzz. *Anazat*, he thought. The black-eyed monk had somehow lured him there. And though he could not be certain, he felt that it must have something to do with the last time he had voyaged with Sirene.

Gytta? He shook his head. Sirene would always be a mystery. When he'd first voyaged with her, Anazat had said that the drug was in control. The voyage not the voyager. Was this something to do with what he'd forced out of her that time? The Why of Sirene? That she … *watched*, was that what she'd said, for others? But Luck had always felt that watching was never a neutral thing. That observation changed the observed.

He swallowed. Again he realised that these were thoughts for another day. There was no point in wondering more, not now. All that mattered was Poum, getting them back. The Four Tribes had been fired up enough by the myth and by Poum's brief visitation before Luck stole them away fifteen years before. If Anazat succeeded in getting the One back to Saghaz-a, the reality of the One would make their myth inconsequential. All hope would be gone, not only in Midgarth but across the wide world. So it was not just for Midgarth that the men and women of Askaug must rise up and fight at dawn, no matter the odds. It was for the freedom of the whole world. That woman Atisha talked about back in Ometepe who held out against Anazat's ally, Intitepe. Those two he'd freed the same night he'd rescued Poum at the Keep, Ferros and Lara. Doomed like everyone … if he could not do what he must on the morrow.

8

Alliance

Roxanna was not sure how they'd ended up in the cellar.

They were always blurred afterwards, those choices that began their latest bout of lovemaking. And bouts they were, for they were like wrestlers moving within a circle drawn in the sand. Unlike those fighters though, with Ferros there were no rules, no limitations. For the first week or so, she was the one who mostly led, he who followed. She had lived a lot longer than him, after all. Yet gradually that had changed, the power shifting. She, who had never liked to be dominated, nor to be subject to any man's desires, discovered a new joy … in surrender. In seeing how a man who'd put all his thought into serving the empire, and finding better ways to kill for it, now bent his mind and his body to serving her, but, as importantly, serving himself. *His* delight and pleasures, seeking ever better ways of increasing them. And all the while something in her began to grow, a feeling that she dimly remembered having once before, just once, when she was still so young she had not even known she was immortal. She fought it, dismissed it, ridiculed herself for it. Yet here, in this cellar, her hands tied above her to hooks, her cries matching his, just as her body's movements did his, she accepted what it was.

Love.

For the first time in three hundred years, Roxanna was in love.

It wasn't the quality and variety of the lovemaking. She was experienced enough to recognise the madness of the new, how the mind was led astray through the sensations of the body. She couldn't pin it to any one of Ferros's charms, of which there were many. His warrior's magnificent, much-scarred physique. Even the striking sword-blue of his eyes. She'd wondered if it might be what went on behind them – for she watched him come alive in them, own who he was in a way he never had when she'd first known him fifteen years before. He'd seen immortality as a curse then. Now he'd become aware of all its ... possibilities.

Still hard, he withdrew from her slowly, deliberately, both of them shuddering in the aftershocks as he did. Then he immediately reached up and untied her. They had both discovered that if some pain thrilled for the duration of the bout, it simply hurt after it.

There was a straw palliasse on the floor, presumably the bed of the cellarman who they'd driven out with their shouts. They flopped onto it now, her beneath, drawing his head to her breasts. She stroked his hair, stared at the hooks she'd hung from, wondered if it was the right time to tell him of another change within her. It would be her only chance, for he was leaving later that same day for the Wattenwold to execute his side of their plan. They would bathe together a final time and he would go.

He shifted, took a deep breath, the kind you took before you spoke. She smiled. It had always amused her, how swiftly most men moved from the delirium of passion to the practical. Even Ferros, more lost than most, would rapidly begin to think of what he must do next. She knew he felt guilty about it, tried to remain for longer in the aftermath. But she had never required him to be a courtier, versed, as so many in the Sanctum were, in studied politeness. Indeed, she thought, perhaps that is one of the things that makes me love him. Part of his self-owning had been his discovery of an ambition that matched hers. An ambition that was no longer to do with serving others but with serving himself; serving himself – and her. Though their plan would, of course, also serve his former loyalties, which were split, and thus complicated.

'Will they listen to you?'

'Who's they?' Ferros raised his head to look at her.

It was charming how he pretended. She sometimes forgot that though he was an immortal, he was also, and forever, the age when he'd become one: twenty-three years old. She laughed. 'The ones I see in your eyes now, Ferros. The Wattenwolden.'

For a moment he looked as if he might protest that all he was considering was her beauty. Then he shrugged, smiled and replied, 'I think they will. Malvolen trusts me.'

'Of course, since you are his Spear and Shield.' She ran a finger along the faintest of jagged scars on his shoulder. Though an immortal healed entirely from wounds, some trace of them was always left. 'And since you bring him the news of his betrayer.'

'The news, and then the man's head.'

Roxanna shuddered, as she remembered that head. The man Ferros referred to was Barallingen, the Wattenwolden she'd seduced at the last Tribute Day two years before. An obese lump, he had succumbed less to her charms than to what she'd promised: to massacre this year's tribute party, slay Malvolen, allow Barallingen to take the high chair. The Four Tribes would be blamed, not the city, and he would then lead the army down from the forests and destroy the force the Four Tribes were sending to destroy them. Her hope had been that they would destroy each other, leaving the weakened victor easy prey for the city army she'd been gradually rebuilding. It had always been a plan of thin margins, fraught with risk. That risk considerably lessened by the man on top of her now.

She squeezed him tightly. The talk of heads had made her think of another. Another man she'd held in her arms, only three weeks before.

Makron.

She'd killed him at the Tribute feast. But of course that was only the first death. The second, more permanent one was in the removal of his head. Something her other lover, Korshak, had been ordered to accomplish that night. Unfortunately they'd been forced to kill the Horse Lord ... before he'd told her whether her former husband was finally and forever dead. She hoped his trunk and separated head were feeding worms in the mass grave that had been dug. Korshak had been like all her other love slaves, keen to please. But it irritated her that she could not be entirely sure.

She sighed. The penalty of immortality – too many lovers, too many complications. She was glad that was all behind her. That she had the man she wanted now ... for ever.

Ferros mistook her sigh. He rolled to the side, raised himself on an elbow. 'Do not fear, my love,' he said, pushing his fingers up into her long, curly hair, combing them through. 'Malvolen will believe me. And will see the wisdom of the plan. Of fighting and destroying the first of the enemy's armies here. Of setting up Corinthium again, not as an empire to be feared, but as a city to ally with, to face the Four Tribes when they come again.'

'And you believe you can return here in three weeks?'

'I will ride there fast, in less than a week. Kill Barallingen. Persuade fast. It will take a little time to rally the forces we will need. But if we set out a week later then yes, I will return in three weeks.'

'The last report had the Four Tribes army still stuck in the southern ports of the Great Sea. First adverse winds and then an outbreak of the sweating sickness. Simbala has been kind to us.'

Ferros smiled. 'I thought you didn't believe in any of the gods.'

'Old habit of speech. But if the sickness and the winds both die, the Four Tribes army may be here before you return.'

'We can only pray to all the gods we no longer believe in that they are not. Yet even if they are, I am sure you will find a way to delay them, my love.'

His love. Roxanna bent her head, laid it in his palm. He was her love as well – but there was much that he did not need to know. Of past actions. Of ambitions. Not yet. Not till he was bound to her still further. Which thought reminded her.

She sat up, took his caressing hand, and placed it on her belly. He made to move it down – lovemaking for them did not always end at a fixed moment but could go on and on. But she stopped him, and splayed his fingers out. 'Do you feel?' she whispered.

'Feel what?'

'A heartbeat.'

His eyes went wide. 'What?' he gasped. 'How … how can you know?'

'I know. After three hundred years, trust me, I know.'

'You have … have carried children before?'

'I have. But I have seen to it that I have never kept them.'

'Why?'

'Because …' She placed her other hand on his face, and his eyes rose to hers. 'Because I have met no man that I ever wanted to have a child with. Until now.'

He looked down, pressed his fingers into her belly very gently. 'I don't feel a heartbeat.'

Roxanna laughed. 'Ah, my soldier! I was teasing. You won't yet, and won't for a while. Trust me, it is there.'

He raised eyes filled with wonder again. 'A son or a daughter, do you think?'

'Now *that* we will just have to wait and see.'

She was startled then, because tears came into his eyes. He sat up, turned away. 'Ferros?' she asked, rising too. 'You are unhappy with the news?'

'No, no, it is not that.' He turned and took her hand, kissed the palm. 'It is only that ... my parents died when I was so young I cannot remember them. So I have always been alone. Now,' he looked down and a tear ran from his eye, down his nose, dropped onto her belly, 'now somehow I feel I will not be.'

Roxanna felt her eyes prickle too. Tears? For her? She tried to force them back, found she couldn't. Found she didn't want to. This man, what they'd made! 'You will not. There is you, and me, and ...' She pressed their conjoined hands down into her belly. Held them there, with all her ready words gone.

She came to say her last farewell at the stables. It was a place of memories for them. The first time they'd ridden together, soon after he'd come to the city, they'd returned there, the heat between them raging – but Lara had surprised them, interrupted them. Later, on the day the city had fallen to the Four Tribes and the Wattenwolden, Ferros had discovered Roxanna and Lara there in a knife fight. Roxanna had slain Lara, to his horror. She had been reborn, of course. When he'd left the stables that day, Ferros had thought that he would hate Roxanna for ever, love Lara.

How life can change in fifteen years.

A last, long kiss, his hand placed a final time on her belly, then she turned and walked back into the Sanctum. He waited for a while, till he was certain she would not reappear, before urging his horse out of the yard. But then, instead of turning north for the forests, he faced south. There was one last thing he needed to do before he left Corinthium.

He needed to say goodbye to Lara.

He had not tried to contact her in the three weeks since the massacre. He'd told himself that it was because she was a spy, that he must keep her safe. But he'd known it was a poor excuse. He did not because he could not leave Roxanna ... and because he would not have known what to say. He and Lara, all they'd been to each other over the years, had been changed utterly by what had happened to them both, separate and together. The curse and the blessing of immortality. During the years they'd been reunited since her rebirth, through the fall of Corinthium and on into their time with the Wattenwolden, they had moved further and further apart. He'd thought that perhaps if they'd had children things might have been different. But she had not wanted to and had prevented it, in ways he did not understand nor ask about.

And now he was to have a child with someone else. The person Lara hated most in the world. The person he'd been startled to discover that he didn't simply desire, but whom he loved.

Ferros rode down to the the sixth hill, Perilinos, to its platform of the Heaven Road, and left his horse at the stables there. He climbed into a basket, then watched the houses slipping past beneath him. Though there remained charred gaps in every part of the city, much had healed over already. The Heaven Road itself had been repaired five years previously when the leaders of the Four Tribes realised how useful it was to speed messengers with their commands from the port to the Sanctum. He was sharing the basket with one of them, a flamboyantly dressed Seafarer whose attempts at conversation Ferros ignored. Although he'd had his long hair and beard trimmed and was dressed again in the tunic of the city, beneath that Ferros was still Wattenwolden too. Twin loyalties – and this man was the enemy of both of them.

He left the basket at the platform in Sevrapol, and the glowering Seafarer went on. Descending the stairs, Ferros reached the cobbles and looked about. This district had changed perhaps more than any other since the conquest. Before that, hordes would come here, seeking their varied pleasures – the elites, both mortal and immortal, to the marble-fronted theatres, the merchants to the taverns, cockpits and dice houses, the lustful of all classes to the brothels. But there were no elites any more, not in the old way. All were just servants of the One, and the monks put forward a new faith that was to do with worship and restraint, not self-delight. Yet sin was something some could not do without. So if people had money, other people would take it from them and provide what they desired.

The underground 'city' of Asprodon was where he'd met Lara before. It had several entrances, all inconspicuous. It might be the most ill-kept secret in Corinthium but the authorities of the One could only pretend it didn't exist if the centre of sin did not flaunt itself.

He tapped on a plain wooden door. A wooden slat behind a grille was pulled back and he was surveyed. Then the door opened, and a large doorman gestured him in with a grunt.

Ferros descended to the lower level and the tavern, Zarel's, where he'd met Lara before. He did not expect her to be there – but he thought someone there might know her, know where she lived. Her lodgings were at the port, she'd told him. Yet in that rat's nest of tenements, he would have no chance of finding her.

He sat in the alcove where he'd sat with her before, the tavern's sour ale largely untouched before him. It didn't take long for his casual mention of the name 'Laro' to the server to bear fruit – fruit in the form of two large men looming over his table.

One of the men, excessively hairy, with a forested belly thrusting out from his ill-buttoned shirt, demanded bluntly, 'Who are you?'

Ferros studied them. The one who'd asked was soft of body and voice. If it came to trouble it was the other who would bring it, hefty and strong-looking with a dagger easily accessible at his hip. Laying his hand over his own dagger which he'd placed on the bench beside him, Ferros said, 'Who's asking?'

'I am Severos. I am the King of Asprodon.' He didn't introduce the other man, obviously his muscle.

'I am Hanos,' Ferros replied, adding, 'Your Majesty.'

'You asked about Laro. Why?'

Ferros could tell from the way the name was emphasised that this man was not pleased with Laro. 'He owes me money,' he replied.

'Does he? Much?'

Ferros shrugged, the gesture enough. 'Well,' Severos continued, 'he owes me money too. Money and something else besides.' His small eyes narrowed further. 'Maybe we can help each other find him?'

Ferros had hoped someone here would know where she was. He didn't have much time to search. 'Maybe. Where did you last see him?'

'Here. Three weeks ago,' Severos scratched his unshaven chin, the sound a rasp, 'when he stole from me. I've enquired at the harbour. But even his boss, who he also stole from, doesn't know where he is. Or perhaps he does, but isn't saying.'

'His boss?'

'The man he worked for. Kefa, and ... other stuff.'

'What's this boss's name?'

Severos didn't answer. Instead he made a show of studying Ferros' clothes. 'You're from the Sanctum, aren't you?' Ferros nodded, and the man continued, 'Why is the Sanctum interested in a petty thief and kefa dealer?'

If Severos wanted to believe Ferros represented the power in the city – the power that looked away so Asprodon could exist – that was fine by him. Half-truths sometimes helped. 'We believe Laro might also be a spy for the Wattenwolden.'

The tall man bent now and whispered in Severos's ear. He nodded. 'Zok says that Laro met a Wattenwolden right here three weeks ago. Just before the massacre. In fact, right where you are sitting. So you could be right.' He placed his hands on the table, leaned down, lowered his voice. 'The Sanctum has informants in the port who may know even more than I do. Or Laro's boss might tell you things he wouldn't tell me. We all like to keep the Sanctum happy, don't we?' He licked his lips. 'How about you go down there with Zok here, and, uh, ask a few questions? Then share the answers, eh?'

Ferros studied the man. Now it was believed he represented the Sanctum, it put him in a better position. Also, since time pressed him, someone who knew the port could be useful. 'I might.' He answered as if it would be a great favour if he did. 'Who's the boss there?'

'Graco,' Severos replied. 'Zok knows where to find him. And if you do find Laro I'd be keen to have Zok have a, uh, conversation with him too. Ask a few questions. Get something returned that Laro took.' He reached into his shirt, and pulled out a small cloth bag. It clinked when he put it on the table. 'And I'd be delighted to contribute to the Sanctum for the privilege.'

Ferros nodded, took up the bag, tucked it away. Silver was silver and a soldier never knew when he'd see it next. Besides, in the character Severos had given him, it would have looked odd to refuse. Sheathing the dagger beside him, keeping it out of sight, he stood. 'The Sanctum accepts your tribute. And will share such information as we receive.'

Despite being such a large and capable-looking man, Zok became a small, scared child in the basket on the Heaven Road. He glanced over its rim once as it left the Sevrapol platform, sank into a corner, and remained there for the entire journey, eyes shut, moaning with every sway. It took him a while to recover when they reached the port but once he had his legs back they set out at a brisk pace for the Inn of the Lascaro.

The doormen knew Zok and they were swiftly admitted. Graco turned out to be as small, smooth and shaven as Severos had been large and hairy. They had one thing in common, though – a desire to see Laro. 'Little bastard never came back with my last kefa payments,' he said. But though he'd had spies out all over the port, he had found not a trace of the one who everyone now sought. All he had was the address of Laro's lodgings, though they had been abandoned since the disappearance.

Glumly, Ferros let Zok lead him there anyway. If the networks of the biggest criminals in Corinthium could not find her in three weeks, he knew he had little chance in the afternoon that was left to him. He would have to set out for the Wattenwold not knowing what had become of her, and unable to tell her what had happened to him. He owed her a farewell, for all they'd been to each other. And, of course, a part of him loved her still. Was concerned about her. All this thievery? What was she up to? Where could she have gone?

The woman who kept the house where Laro had a room was frightened by the two large men looming over her. 'I told them before, all who came,' she bleated. 'I didn't see him again. He never came back.'

'I'll see his room,' Ferros said.

The woman squeezed her hands together. 'But it's already

been searched, twice now. I've just tidied it up from last time. Please, I am trying to rent it out again. I need the money—'

'We will be careful,' Ferros said. 'I only wish to look.'

The small room still showed the signs of hard searching – some broken wall slats, a stoved-in chest, one of its drawers cracked and poorly repaired. There was almost nothing to show that Lara had ever been there. She had not come from the Wattenwold with much. There was an old carry sack with its contents emptied on the floor beside it, which the woman said she hadn't bothered to put back in as it would only be tipped out by the next searchers. There were some clothes, a strike-light, two small cooking pots. The largest object, about the length and girth of half Ferros's forearm, was a wooden carving of a horse. Someone had snapped off one of its legs, and it lay on its side, a broken thing, though it was well made, in the style of the carvers of their old hometown of Balbek, with a long curving neck and detailed mane and tail.

It made his breath catch as he looked at it. He had taught Lara to ride in those days of innocence and it had been their shared passion. Perhaps she had recently bought this to remind herself of those simpler times, of her home. It certainly reminded him – and the full force of what he was giving up, *who* he was giving up, hit him. Shaking his head, he stooped and picked up the horse. Though it was carved from aliantha, a hardwood, it did not weigh as much as he expected. Hollow, he thought, which was unusual with aliantha. Turning it over in his hand, he saw scratches on one haunch. Rough usage or ... he peered closer. The scratches were letters.

For F.

She had meant him to find this. A parting gift?

He turned it over and saw it. The carving was hollow because it wasn't one piece of wood but two. Joined in the belly. The join had been concealed in intricately carved hair, but it was definitely there.

His breath came faster. He put his thumbs into the join, tried to prise the halves apart but the seal was too strong. So he lifted the carving above the chest of drawers and brought it crashing down. Only the woman's cry and Zok's grunt reminded him that he was not alone.

The two halves parted – and a scroll, tied with a strip of linen, fell to the floor. He picked it up, parted the tie.

He had taught Lara to ride, and also to write. It was not customary for the daughter of a Balbek weaver to learn her letters, but once she'd mastered the horse, she had insisted that she wanted to master writing too. If she was not as good with a pen as she was with a rein, she was precise, unfancy. Plain letters were before him. The message was plain too.

My love,

This will be the last time I address you as such, even though you know I will always love you, just as I know you will always love me. For the time we had, when we were young and mortal. I will never forget those days as long as I live.

Which may be long indeed – and the reason I do what I must now alone. We never found a way to reconcile our new lives with our old. I realise now that you knew this, as soon as you were born again. Which is why you tried to leave me behind in Balbek when you were summoned to the Sanctum. I forced you to take me with you, because I could not understand how utterly immortality had changed you. I only truly understood that when I became immortal too.

I was hurt when you betrayed me with Roxanna. I let that hurt remain between us in the years since, when we fought the Four Tribes and afterwards when we lived in the

Wattenwold. I could not find a way to keep you in my heart but I was too frightened to finally let you leave it.

Now, I must. For I have seen a vision, in smoke in the glass – a sight of the family I thought were lost for ever. Now I must find out if that vision is true. Maybe when you read this – if you do – I will already be in Balbek. Maybe beyond.

Though we can never see where destiny leads us, yet I feel that we will meet again some day. After all, unless we lose our heads, we both have many days before us. Many lives to live.

Be well, Ferros, on whatever paths you follow. I will be well on mine.

Lara.

'What is that?'

It was Zok's voice that brought Ferros back to himself, and the room. He looked up, seeing the other man through a mist. He wiped his eyes. 'Nothing,' he said, folding the letter, and tucking it inside his shirt.

'But it's Laro's, isn't it? It might tell us where he's gone.' Zok stepped forward, one hand out. 'If it is nothing then let me see it.'

'No.' Ferros untied the pouch that Severos had given him and turned to the woman. 'Here,' he said, holding it out. 'This is for the damage and for any money Lara ... Laro ... may have owed you. I think he would want—'

'Oy!' Zok shouted, and grabbed Ferros's arm. 'I told you to give me that paper.' He drew his dagger. 'Or do I have to take it from you?'

Ferros dropped the purse, then jerked his arm back. Unwisely, Zok held on to it, and was pulled forward. 'Oy,' he said again, not angry now. Puzzled. He let go of Ferros's arm, looked down at his own, at the red line at his wrist which, even as he stared, swelled with blood.

Ferros stepped away, his own drawn dagger in front of him. 'Enough,' he said. 'Go—'

Zok roared, stepped close, whipping his knife fast towards Ferros's face. Ferros didn't move his feet, just leaned back, let the blade pass before his eyes. The man was angry now as well as bleeding. Neither would help him in a knife fight. Ferros tried, a final time. 'Stop now, so you may live,' he said.

Zok stared at him a moment, incredulous. Then he bellowed and came again, as the woman screamed.

His attacker had switched his grip to overhand, and drove the point down at Ferros's head. Where it had just been. Swivelling the top half of his body, Ferros let the point pass beside him. Now, using the twist of his body to swivel hard back, he buried his own knife deep in the man's side.

He was moving past, pulling out his knife, even as Zok fell. The woman's screams accompanied him for a short while down the street but were soon lost in the hubbub of the port.

Two weeks later …

Roxanna leaned on a crenel of the sea wall's central tower, facing the water. She still felt as if she might vomit again, as she had most of that morning, and every morning for the last ten days. Though she'd heard that some women could be so sick when carrying a baby, she had never experienced it. She did not like it, the weakness it brought. She'd much rather have been back in her bed in the Sanctum. Would have been, were it not for the news the messenger had brought the night before. He had arrived on a small, fast ship to announce that the rest of the fleet would come with the next morning's tide.

Simbala had not favoured Roxanna and Ferros. The winds

had reversed and blown the army of the Four Tribes fast to Corinthium.

She looked to either side of her. The city's occupiers were lined up along the sea wall – five hundred or so Seafarers, Horse Lords, Huntresses. There were even a few Warrior Monks, distinguished by their black robes, there to greet their compatriots. Her own City Guard waited in the streets behind the walls, their low status relegating them to the job of controlling the crowds that had been gathering all morning to see the arriving army; these men and women who were going to ride north and destroy the Wattenwolden once and for all.

Roxanna turned back. The distant ships had come appreciably closer, that same strong wind bellying their huge sails. She would have to do two things now. Master her stomach for the greeting formalities to come. And find a way to delay the army's marching north by a week. By then, Ferros should have returned with his tribesmen. Their plan required a battle in the streets, where her guards and those citizens of the city who still resented the conquerors could rise up. Only then would they have the numbers to take the city back.

Her stomach rose up into her mouth. She quelled it again. On the water she could now see one of those faster, smaller boats preceding the fleet. No doubt it would carry some functionary, sent ahead to check that the reception prepared was suitably grand. They were obsessed by ceremony, the Four Tribes. Everything had to be just so.

The boat docked at the pier fronting the tower. To her surprise it was not monks who disembarked, usually charged with dealing with all formalities, but a party of Huntresses. Five of them, dressed as they always were in green leather that fitted them like another skin. Roxanna was fond of leather too, especially when she fought. Yet their similar taste in clothing was almost all she shared with these fierce forest warriors. The Seafarers and the Horse Lords she could more easily control, for they were men and often governed by their groins rather than their heads. The monks were men too, though they showed no interest in women, and she'd been unable to persuade any otherwise. They remained a black-eyed mystery to her. And although she was never averse to using her sexual wiles on women – indeed, had often discovered that the delights to be had with them were of a greater variety than she enjoyed with most men she seduced – her few attempts to gain insight and power with a Huntress had all failed. They liked each other and no one else. She only knew of them what everyone knew: that they were fighters every bit as good as any man; and that they were as fanatical in their devotion to the cause of the One as any Monk.

The Huntresses walked the short distance to the gates, followed by a few male slaves, cloaked and cowled. As they entered the tower and left her sight, Roxanna released her hold on the crenel, took a deep breath, and turned. A small belch escaped her, carrying the taint of what she'd expelled before – bile, truly, for she was unable to keep much food down. She would do as much as she must, to greet the arrivals, then excuse herself as soon as possible from the ceremonies to follow. She needed her bed again.

Four of the Huntresses arrived, split, two going each side of the entrance. A moment later the fifth Huntress arrived, followed by one of the hooded slaves. He immediately crossed to the side of the platform. Roxanna studied the Huntress, who'd moved a few steps in then halted. She was obviously the leader. Though she also wore the same skin-tight leather, she was older than the others, her body heavier, her long hair grey.

Roxanna waited for the other to bow. She was, after all, the governor of the city – sole governor, since Makron, alas, had been killed in the Wattenwolden riot on the day of Tribute. Though the Four Tribes were the conquerors, she was still in charge.

The Huntress did not bow. Instead she looked Roxanna up and down with contempt. Roxanna was wearing a long and lavish green gown. She only liked leather when she fought, and sometimes when she seduced. In her present state, it was too … constricting.

The silence of stares extended. Finally, Roxanna would brook it no more. 'And you are?' she said.

'Gistrane,' came the curt reply. 'And you are … under arrest.'

Maybe she might have done something, reacted more swiftly; possessed someone, and escaped. But a rush of nausea held her back, and then hands did. One grabbed and twisted an arm behind her, making her yelp in pain, the other was at the back of her neck, forcing her head sharply down.

She cried out, tried to twist from the grasp. But it was as if she was held in steel manacles. And the voice that came – the familiar voice that came – had steel in it too.

'You are going nowhere, Roxanna. Neither as someone else nor as yourself.'

The grip did relax a little then. Only enough to allow her to twist around, look up.

Within his hood, Makron gazed back. The husband she'd killed three weeks before.

She stared a moment, and then her sight was taken. Some rough, foul-smelling sack was pulled over her head. The smell, the closeness, made her retch but fortunately she had nothing to bring up. The Huntress, Gistrane, spoke again, loudly, addressing many people.

'Behold, a traitor,' she cried. 'This woman has been plotting against the peace of the world and the glory of the One. Her guilt is undeniable. For her crimes she is condemned. For her crimes … we will take her head!'

Roxanna was forced to her knees, mind and body reeling. She was powerless, held in more than one unbreakable grip now.

They would take her head. She would die, finally die. Never to see Ferros again. Never to see ... their baby.

Then Gistrane spoke again. 'Tomorrow, in a ceremony at the northern walls, just before our glorious combined army of the City and the Four Tribes marches out to finish the Wattenwolden, this traitor will die.'

Relief came, then something else did – a blow to the back of the head. Roxanna fell, lost to the dark before her body reached the ground.

He came for her at noon. Just Makron, so he did not wear a hood and mask as her three guards had. She had only been released from her own evil-smelling sack late the evening before. Not from any kindness. Between the blow she'd taken, and her stomach still surging with child, it had looked as if she might drown in her own vomit. Though all knew she would be reborn later, it would not be soon enough to make a good show at her execution.

The hood's removal was the only improvement in her circumstances. She'd been left in the foul cell, soiled by its previous occupants, with nothing to lie on, nothing to puke into, except the floor. No food or water was brought, though she'd found some moss on one wall. When her thirst became unbearable, she sucked on that.

Now Makron was there. But he'd brought her nothing more than his smirk. 'So, wife,' he said, coming in, sitting on a stool he carried, 'your last day has come.'

Roxanna pulled herself up to sitting, put her back against the wall. 'You would let them kill me, husband?'

'Let them? I offered to do the work myself. But it turns out that the removal of a head with a sword requires experience and aptitude, both of which I lack.' He grinned. 'Your death will be the climax of a long day's ceremony which has already been going on for some time. They want the finale to be,' he reached up and scratched his own neck, 'one perfect stroke.'

'Is there not to be justice? Even a common murderer is allowed to plead his cause before a court.'

'Not an uncommon one, though.' He studied her for a long moment. 'How many is it you have killed over the centuries, Roxanna?' When she made no reply, he answered for her. 'Perhaps as many as one hundred, would you estimate? Must be difficult to remember. With me the last? Or have you managed a few more in the month since?'

'I only killed you to get you out of the way for the night, Makron. You'd disagreed with my plan.'

'To take on the Four Tribes too soon, by massacring the Wattenwolden at the Tribute? I did.'

Roxanna shrugged. 'But I knew you'd be born again, soon afterwards, husband. Born again to realise the wisdom of my plan. I left orders to keep your body safe.'

'I know what orders you left, bitch,' Makron snarled. 'I heard your pet Horse Lord Korshak repeat them when he came back to look for me in the pavilion, after the Wattenwolden had fled.' He laughed. 'Yet despite all your experience in killing, you failed with me. Badly wounded me, yes. But I had enough life to crawl under the platform on which the main table was set. Then I crawled under the canvas—' He shook his head. 'I realised what you'd done. All you'd done. Looking for you was purposeless. You were too strong for me. So once I'd healed enough, I took ship for Tarfona – and met the fleet just setting out.'

There came a sudden loud knocking on the door. Makron called, 'We come,' as he rose from the stool. 'One thing I am curious about. Korshak, the Horse Lord? You killed him, I suppose.' When she didn't reply, he nodded. 'Of course you did. To make room for young Ferros.' Again, she said nothing.

Again, he shook his head. 'I knew he was the one for you. There was something about the way you—' He broke off. 'Ach, it matters not. Up!' When she didn't move, he stepped closer. 'Oh yes, please do make this harder for me,' he hissed. 'I have so little time left with you.'

There was one last thing she could try. 'Husband, the reason you will help me escape – just show me one of those guards unmasked – is that . . .' She swallowed. 'That I am with child.'

He smiled. 'Really, Roxanna? What a lie to come up with at the end!'

'No lie. You can already tell. I can show you my belly if you don't believe me.'

'Why would this matter?'

'Because, Makron, you are the baby's father.'

He stared at her for a long, long moment, and then he burst out laughing. 'Oh, my wife! How long were we married? Fifty years before? These last fifteen? You have given me so much over the years. But never a child. I do not think you would begin now. Besides,' he bent, grabbed her arm, jerked her to her feet, 'even if you are pregnant, that child could be anyone's . . . you whore!'

He spat the word into her face, then threw her across the cell. She stumbled, then stood upright. 'Guards!' Makron called, and two men came through the door. Both had full face hoods, with eye slits. For one mad moment Roxanna thought to leap, rip a mask off, possess, kill the other guard, kill Makron – truly kill him this time – flee. But that same foul sack was over her head in an instant, and even those poor choices were gone. Her hands manacled again, she was dragged from the cell.

The wind was frigid with the deepening winter, her soiled dress no protection. Outside the gaol the noise also came immediately – the beat of drums, the call of trumpets, an ululation of voices, many voices, in many different tongues. A few of these she spoke herself and understood those she didn't by the others. It was a single word anyway, simple in any language.

'One! One!'

All the voices cried it, getting louder as she got nearer. At first the sound had come to her funnelled: they had to be leading her down some sort of passage. Then it suddenly grew in volume, spread wider, as the cold wind whipped into her.

'Anazat has possession of the child, did you know?' His voice came from just ahead, so neither of the hands that gripped her were his. 'No, why would you? I only heard myself yesterday in the smoke. He's caught the One in that same land of Midgarth where the infant disappeared. A young man now. No, a young woman. Neither. Both.' He halted, and her captors did too. 'He'll set out from that land in the next couple of days. Then once the One reaches Saghaz-a—' He broke off, as someone came and said something to him softly which she couldn't catch, only his reply of, 'We await her summons.' Then he spoke to her again. 'Well, wife, we thought we might beat them, you and I. Perhaps we still could have, if you had not betrayed me, one more time. One last time. Though really, I doubt it.' His voice lowered to a whisper. 'Listen to that, Roxanna. That belief in a word. I cannot fight that any longer. I can only ... find myself a place in the new order.'

Suddenly, the voices that had been building, building, ended on a single, drawn-out shout.

'One!'

The echoes had not even faded when Makron took her arm. 'Your turn,' he said, and jerked her forward. She stumbled, he pulled her, there were some steps, he dragged her up them. There had been so much noise, and now there was only silence – the silence of many people watching, listening. Yearning.

Thousands, she saw, the instant her hood was ripped off, the moment before Makron again shoved her to her knees, his hand staying hard against her neck, forcing her head down. She could see a little – the first few ranks of swaying, ecstatic people, townsfolk and Four Tribes intermingled, though with her head kept down she could not see any faces; the boots of others on what she saw was a platform, some with leather rising above them, others with flesh below metal-lined kirtles – Huntresses and Horse Lords, with here and there the long black robes of a Monk.

A single voice was speaking now, a woman's. Gistrane's, she realised, though she had only heard it once before, the day before, at the port. She was speaking the universal language of Saghaz-a, which was called *tolanpa-sen*. Roxanna hardly understood any of that. But simultaneously, from the other three sides of the platform, men were repeating the speech in the language of Corinthium. Proclaiming her every kind of sinner, each word drawing cries of hate and revulsion – whore, murderer, oppressor. Though the worst was saved for last, the ultimate sin.

'She is an immortal,' Gistrane yelled out, and the crowd booed and booed.

The pressure on her neck was suddenly released. The hand moved to her hair, yanking it, pulling her head up. Roxanna cried out then. But there was nothing else she could do. She glanced left, and there was a man in swirling brown robes, resting the flat of a short, heavy-bladed sword on his shoulder. She wouldn't have had the strength to possess anyway. She was too terrified, and finally too tired. She had lived so many lives in one life – and now she accepted that it was over. Even if he had not been wearing a mask she would not have tried to possess him.

She went limp, looked straight ahead. Makron stepped away to the side but stayed in her vision. It was clear he wished to look into her eyes, right at the very end of it all. His showed nothing but triumph.

It was the last thing she noted in them as the executioner bent at the knees, raised his sword ... and cut Makron's head off.

The sword was as good as its promise. Though he had never wielded an executioner's blade before, it was not so very different from others he had used over the years. The best ones had their own heft, their special purpose, some area in the blade where all the power and balance of the weapon had been focused in the forge. Here it was a hand's span of sharpest steel a little over halfway to the tip. It was that part Ferros put through Makron's neck.

It was the first distraction. The second came hard upon it, because his old comrade from the Ninth Balbek, Haldan – who had become Stauren the day Ferros had taken the name Arcturien – was watching for his signal from the same tower they'd defended six weeks before after the betrayal at the Feast of Tribute. The simplest of signals. The taking of the head. Makron's body had not even reached the ground before the next signal came: Stauren dropping his arm. On the instant, five war trumpets blared, and a thousand fiery arrows fell from the sky, bearing flame and death into the crowds.

Instant mayhem. Ferros didn't see it, as he'd fallen to protect Roxanna's body with the executioner's. An arrow glanced along his shoulder and he felt the man's pain. Felt it, left him, was in his own body again, shoving the man away, though snatching back his sword. It might have been designed for one task but it did adequately for another as the two Horse Lords on the platform rushed at him while drawing their weapons. Should have done that the other way round, Ferros thought, killing one man before his curved blade had cleared its sheath, the other when his weapon was out but drawn back for neither cut nor parry.

He looked about, sword raised before him – just as well, as an arrow struck and spun off the upright blade. The Huntress who'd shot it – their leader, Gistrane – cursed and drew out another arrow but had not got it nocked before Ferros ran at her, swirling his sword through the air. With a cry she turned and leaped with three others from the platform, dragging a fourth with them, a Wattenwolden arrow in her arm.

For a moment he and Roxanna, and the still stunned executioner, were the only people left on the platform. Alive, anyway. Below them the screaming crowd surged, away from the dead and the dying and the burning, pushing for the perimeter of the waste ground that had held buildings before the conquest, and the Tribute pavilion only a month before, their panic and desperation doubled when one thousand mounted tribesmen charged through the broken walls.

Ferros was back across to Roxanna in a moment. 'Come, my love,' he said, offering an arm.

She pulled herself up on it, fell into him, squeezed him tight. 'Ferros,' she murmured.

He could see that she was exhausted, dirty, sick. He bent, struck the manacles off her, then swept her up in his arms. He looked over and Haldan was there, in his saddle with the reins of Ferros's horse held behind him. Ferros laid Roxanna down, mounted his horse, reached and pulled her up before him. 'I will get you somewhere safe. And then—'

'No.' She leaned away to look him in the eye. 'This is the beginning of the battle we planned, Ferros. You must call off your men. There's no point massacring citizens. They must save themselves for the fight.'

Yet even as she spoke, trumpets sounded. 'Done,' he said. 'Their orders were clear. But where is the main enemy force?'

'They were allowed to get drunk this night in Sevrapol as long as they were fit to ride with the dawn.'

'And the four squadrons of the City Guard?'

'They were confined to their barracks on Perilinos. Awaiting my command.'

'Then we will collect them on our way to Sevrapol.' Ferros grinned. 'Killing the Four Tribes in Sevrapol sounds better than facing them in the open field. Are you strong enough to come with us?'

Roxanna smiled. 'Take me to the Sanctum, Ferros. Let me change my clothes, collect my sword and horse. Then I'll show you who is strong enough.'

Ferros nodded, then turned to Haldan. 'Use the crowds. Drive them towards Sevrapol. We will meet you there in one hour. Kill any of the enemy you can find in the taverns.'

'Sir!' Haldan turned around.

'Haldan?'

'Sir?'

'Don't get drunk.'

'As if I would.' With a grin, Haldan dug in his spurs and galloped to where the Wattenwolden had rallied to the trumpets.

'Let's to the Sanctum, love.' He sniffed. 'You could do with a bath as well.'

'You are no rose bower yourself, Ferros, my love.'

Ferros grinned. 'Well, we came fast when a pigeon arrived bearing news of the fleet's coming.'

He was just turning his horse's head when a low voice came from behind him. 'Sir,' the executioner said, 'can I have my sword back?' The man bobbed his head. 'It's how I make my living.'

'Thank you for its use,' Ferros laughed, as he laid it on the platform. 'Tell me, though, would you like to use it to kill some of your late employers?'

'The Horse Lords?' The big man spat off the platform. 'I hate those bastards.'

'Then join us, my friend ... in Sevrapol!'

9
God

As the face in the globe dissolved into whirling smoke, Anazat slumped back in his chair. It was the second one he'd seen there that evening and even if communicating using Sirene was not as exhausting as travelling with her, it still took a toll on mind and body. For a moment, he thumbed the cork on the vial of the liquid, tempted. He knew he could lose himself in visions for a time. Escape this world and all its demands. It had been many years since he had used Sirene thus. Surrender control to her, let her spirit him to a place without cares. He, alone of any in the world, had mastered her. Had even used her to lure Luck into this trap. But it did not mean that he did not sometimes yearn for his early days of exploration, of visions, of delight.

He leaned in, pressed with his thumb, felt the pliant material give. One flick, and he would be gone.

He laid the bottle on the table and sat back again. He must not. Not after what he'd heard in the glass. Everything depended on what he did next. How he handled the setback, just when he was on the verge of completing the great victory that the world had been waiting for ever since the prophecy of the One had first been spoken.

What had happened might change everything if he let it. He would not, so his plan still held, to sail for Saghaz-a with the morning tide. Speed was all the more necessary after the news in the globe. Not the word from his monk in Ometepe: that their Fire God, Intitepe, had finally ended the rebellion and was once again upon the sea. He and Peki Asarko would now wrestle for the kingship of Midgarth. Whoever survived would be dealt with later.

It was the other news that meant there would be no peace for Anazat.

Corinthium had thrown off his power. It was once again in the hands of immortals there. Worse, it had done so in alliance with its oldest enemy, the Wattenwolden. Together they had destroyed the army sent to destroy them. So now he must journey throughout Saghaz-a, showing the One to all, binding together again the Four Tribes who had begun to fracture. United, they were a force that no one in the world could stop. Corinthians and Wattenwolden had been enemies since the founding of the city. Even if they somehow remained together, they would be outnumbered five to one.

He stood. As he'd always known it would, it all came down to the One. The child that was neither man nor woman. The belief in *them*, bringing together four peoples who had slaughtered each other for centuries. Promising to bring together the whole world, vaster than anyone could have imagined. In love, not hate.

The One. Waiting for him in the next room in Peki Asarko's house in Askaug.

He moved to the door. Knocked.

There was silence. And then a voice.

'Come.'

Anazat lifted the latch

The door opened, and Poum looked at the man who entered. He was familiar, from all Luck's stories. Yet Poum did not see the monster, the tyrant who had taken over nearly all the world and had imposed his law upon it. Poum saw a man with a circlet of white hair around his otherwise shaven head. A stooped man, walking slowly, as if he carried a heavy load. What made him so different were his black eyes. Yet even if their darkness meant that nothing usual could be read in them, Poum still saw there what he'd seen in the eyes of all those who'd captured him.

Rapture. He'd learned it was how one looked at God.

'May I sit?'

Poum was at a table. Food was upon it, a sumptuous feast that they had barely touched. They still felt nauseous from the nature of their capture. The revelation of how they had been lured to Askaug; of 'Kipé's' part in it. Peki Asarko was a true monster, that they knew, and it still sickened them knowing how close the two of them had got within the vision of Sirene. At that cool pond, where they had swum, touched . . .

They shook their head to clear it. 'Sit,' they said. *Commanded*, they thought. For that is what I have just done. I command, he obeys, he sits. Yet for all that I am his God, I am also his prisoner. For this I know: it is not me they all worship. It is the *idea* of me. Already they have conquered the known world on the strength of that idea. What remains for them to do, now they have me as well?

It is what I must find out.

The two of them, young and old, stared at each other. Finally Anazat spoke. 'It is strange for me, to be sitting here with you. You who I have served for so many years, from long before your birth.'

'I can imagine.' Poum leaned a little more into the lamplight. 'Tell me what you see.'

'I see—' Anazat ran his tongue over cracked lips, and Poum glimpsed teeth as black as the eyes. 'I see your father in you.

And your mother. You have his bones, his brow, his nose. But you have her eyes.'

It startled Poum. They had never been told they had any resemblance to Intitepe. Atisha almost never talked about him. Luck had only taught Poum what he felt they needed to know. 'Tell me of him,' they said.

'There are several other things to discuss—'

'Tell me.'

It was interesting. Poum could see how the command annoyed. There was probably no one in the world who could order Anazat to do anything. But I can, they thought. And for the first time in their life, they felt a flush of power.

'He is … I only met him once. But I saw the strength that four hundred years of ruling alone had given him.'

'A strong man then? What else?'

Anazat shrugged. 'Cruel, inflexible, tyrannical. He …'

Poum interrupted. 'Just like your servant, Peki Asarko?'

'No. For the Lord of the Lake of Souls is cruel and tyrannical because he enjoys being those things. Your father …' He hesitated, then continued. 'Your father does them because he believes he is a god.'

But that *is* like Peki, like Luck, like all the immortals in Midgarth, Poum thought, didn't say. Also it is what you believe of me.

Perhaps Anazat sensed their thought. 'The only true god, of course, is you.'

'Why do you believe that?' Poum shook their head. 'Because of how I am, neither man nor woman? An accident of birth.'

'No accident.' It was Anazat who leaned forward now. 'The prophecy alone changed everything. Brought peace to a land where there had only been war and weeping.'

'Saghaz-a.'

'Saghaz-a.' Anazat nodded. 'You speak our language well, by the way. A little formally but—'

'I was … well taught.' Poum thought back to the steading, to Luck's lessons in *tolanpa-sen*. Their father knew some from before. Then, from the books Luck had brought, he had first taught himself better, and then taught Poum. Thinking of their tutor, they wondered where he was now. He had gone ahead to lead a revolt. But he would not have time to raise one now. The servant who had brought their food had said that Poum would be gone with the morning tide.

'Do you not see your power?' Anazat said. 'If a prophecy of you can bring peace to a land like Saghaz-a, in person you will bring peace to the world.'

'How?' Poum thought back to what they'd surmised before. 'I am only an idea.'

'Oh, my lord, you are far more than that.' Anazat smiled, a strange sight, with all those blackened teeth. 'You bring a philosophy of peace, of love—'

'How can I bring that?' Poum's voice took heat. 'I am fifteen years old. I am still a child, not yet a … whatever it is you call me in this world. Not fully grown.' They growled. 'I have no philosophy! I have no opinion about peace, and know very little about love.'

'Oh, but you do!' Anazat reached into the folds of his cloak, and pulled out an object just larger than the size of his hand. Poum could see that between two boards were held pieces of the same material that Luck's scrolls, which he taught from back on the mountain, were made from. 'Your opinions are written down in here.' He raised it. 'We call this a book. In it, your philosophy has already been gathered.'

'My philosophy?' Poum gasped. 'How is that even possible?'

'You will see, my lord.' Anazat laid this book on the table, pushed it a little across. 'Of course, we monks have worked hard for years to … distill the principles of how the best of all possible worlds would be. Read, and you will see how everything you could ever have wished to bring joy to the world is already here.' He tapped the cover, once for every word he next spoke. 'Law. Justice. Fairness. A way to live.'

'A way to rule,' Poum said softly, not colouring the phrase at all.

And Anazat took it the way he wished to hear it. 'Yes. Most people, whatever land they were born in, need ruling. Guiding to the light contained herein.' He tapped again. 'Read, lord. If anything displeases you, of course we can discuss it. Discuss anything you wish on the boat to Billandah, the journey through Saghaz-a. The journeys beyond.'

It had been hard to read much of anything in the blackness of the monk's eyes. But suddenly Poum could see something quite clearly in them – fanaticism. Again, not something to discuss now. They reached and pulled the book closer. It was going to be interesting to read what it was they had already given to the world without even knowing. Then they realised what the man had said. 'Journeys beyond where?'

'Through the mountains, to what was the empire of Corinthium. There is … an issue there. All to be solved by the arrival of the One.'

From outside the house came sudden shouting. Anazat frowned. 'Excuse me, my lord,' he said. 'I must see what that is about.'

He started to rise, but Poum reached suddenly, took his hand. 'First you must tell me something. I have been lied to so often in my life.' Anazat sat again, Poum still holding him. 'What you say delights me. That I can bring these,' they glanced down at the book their joined hands rested upon, 'joys, to everyone.' They looked up again. 'But I need you to swear that what you say is written here is true. That I will be the bringer of joy, not sorrow. Peace, not war. Love.' They squeezed the other's hand. 'Look me in the eyes and swear that to me.'

Anazat squeezed back. 'I swear it. An oath on the only thing I truly believe in. I swear it on you. On the One.'

It was hard to read a man's truths in that deep darkness. There was only one way to fully know them. Also to know if they truly were the god everyone called them.

So, on the thought, Poum possessed Anazat.

A few minutes earlier . . .

They weren't going to be enough, Luck thought, looking at the twenty men and five women gathered in Ulrich's forge. The enemy had at least their number. Peki's painted tribesmen from the Lake of Souls; Horse Lords, Seafarers, those Huntresses; trained warriors all. Whereas those of Midgarth lacked any formal training in war. Only Ulrich and his son, Tiny Elric, had ever stood in a shield wall. The others were too young to have known one, for after the Coming of the Dark fifteen years before, war, which had been the basis of their society for centuries, was banned. And even though Luck had always hated the constant battling that was the Midgarth way – gods fighting gods, mortals mortals, both seeking glory and booty – he wished now that these farm boys and girls had been trained in the way of it. A few belonged to groups who opposed the occupation of their land, and Peki Asarko's rule. Yet if a few had perhaps killed a sentry in the night, or Elric had taught them a few blows, that was the extent of their experience. Tonight they would have to gain it fast or die.

And he? He had fought in one battle, when he was fifteen years old. His brother gods, especially Bjorn, had told him that he must. 'The girls won't look at you, else,' Bjorn had said, and

Luck had believed him. So he had fought, though he'd mainly cowered and had scarce picked up a weapon since. He was gifted only with the sling, had killed enough animals for his pot with it. Strangely he had never used it to kill a man. This night he would try. All looked to him as the leader. He must lead in that too.

He watched Ulrich, dressed again in the chain-mail coat, wearing his steel helm, both hidden for years, as he walked along the line of recruits, checking sword, axe, long dagger. Any not sharp enough he sent to Elric at the grindstone, for at least all their edges would be honed. Now I regret the mink, he thought. For if I hadn't possessed that beast earlier I would have the strength to possess another – larger, fiercer. Marla had told him the tale of that last battle of the gods. At its beginning, Stromvar Dragon Lord had possessed a bear and charged alone into the ranks of the enemy, causing chaos that day.

Marla, he thought. Captured with Poum. He had ceased being angry with both of them. There was no point. There was only this attempt to get them back. It had to be tonight. They would be gone with the tide, beyond all hope. For Luck. For Atisha. For the world.

A last screech of a blade. Ulrich came to him, handed him the last weapon honed – a short battleaxe that Luck felt he could wield. 'We are ready.'

Luck looked past the huge smith, to the warriors. So young, he thought, but said, 'No more have come?'

'The furthest farms are too far,' Ulrich replied. 'I've sent boys to them, but no more warriors will get here till midday.' He raised an eyebrow. 'Do you wish to delay till they come?'

Yes, Luck thought, looking at the young men and women who would die this night. Though perhaps one among them was immortal, which they would only know with their first death. It could give him some hope in what was to come, he supposed.

Though he had little doubt that this too could be his last night. If Anazat took him alive, he would not stay so long. He had served the man's purpose. He had allowed himself to be lured into this trap. He didn't know exactly how Anazat had done it. But his experience with Sirene had given the black-eyed monk the victory. Forcing Luck to this desperate venture.

'Well?' Ulrich said.

Luck realised he'd left a silence too long. 'We fight.'

'Good. You had me worried there for a moment.' The smith grinned. 'I've been waiting for this day since I had to leave your brothers Bjorn and Hovard to fight without me. And Freya,' the big man's voice caught, 'especially Freya.'

Ulrich had been Freya's ship captain and her bodyguard. *Freya*, Luck thought. He had loved her too. For centuries. They had even *loved* once so she could pass on the gift of far-speaking, the ability to talk to each other though far apart. Only those who'd come together in love could communicate so. *How I wish I could speak to her now.*

Yet the thought of her didn't make him sad. The opposite. He knew how she would have gone to her final death: with a smile, and a singing sword. Though he did not have her skill with a weapon, he had her will. Life is risks, he thought. You lived longer, you just took more. 'Let us go,' he said.

They moved quietly down the main street of Askaug. Well short of their destination, they met one of Ulrich's scouts, a young woman, Teva. 'They have not stood down,' she said, slipping her bow over her head, taking the water flask held out. She drank and continued, 'They take turns, but the Huntresses are on guard now, spread around the house, bows drawn. Within it, the Horse Lords drink and shout. The Seafarers left for the port. Arne, who followed them, says they make the boat ready.'

It was a little good news. Five men less to fight. 'And Peki Asarko's warriors?'

'They have made a small camp to the side of the house, are gathered around a fire there.'

'Here's how it should go,' Ulrich said. 'We'll kill the women guards first, and silently. Then charge in and kill the painted ones by their fire. That only leaves the Horse Lords who we will take one by one as they emerge.'

Luck thought for a moment. Ulrich, though mortal, was far more experienced in raid and battle than he. But from his deep studies of his enemies he knew this: the Huntresses were the most skilled forest warriors living. Askaug's warriors might kill two with surprise but never five. And the warning the others would give would be enough. The enemy would barricade themselves in the house and, with the dawn, discover how few they faced. 'No,' he said, 'there is only one way for this. Straight in the front door.'

Ulrich looked at him a long moment, then laughed. 'Very well, my little war lord,' he said. 'But stay under my shield when those bitches start shooting.'

They moved closer. Now, through the last of the trees, they could see the house, hear the men inside. They were singing and thumping the table. Beside the house, around the fire, Peki's painted warriors were chanting and swaying to some prayer. Ulrich, crouching low, pointed to a tree halfway between them and the house. It took Luck a moment to see the deeper dark beside it. Ulrich mimed the shape of a woman.

Luck nodded, and pulled the sling from his neck. It was a long shot, perhaps fifty paces, but he had done this often over the centuries, by both day and night. There were two trees between him and the target, a space between them. Fitting the stone, standing, whirling, he had the leather sack going as fast as it ever would with five swings of his arm. It made that slight noise, like bees around a hive. The Huntress, alert, stepped slightly away from the trunk to seek the noise's source. Luck released, and his stone took her in the head.

Her fall made more noise than the stone's flight. Immediately a woman called, 'Karane?' and stepped from her own tree. A dozen arrows flew her way. One at least must have hit for her voice, when it came, was a pained shriek.

'Attack! Attack!'

'Now,' said Luck, and the young warriors of Askaug charged.

They outdistanced him fast. Immediately came much more shouting, screams of warning and of pain. Wrapping his sling again around his neck, clutching his battleaxe, Luck limped forward. But he did not head for the front of the house and the fight that had already begun there. There was a rear door, and it had been agreed that he would try that. If he could reach Poum, if they could escape, the fight would be over, and young lives saved.

He didn't make it. Stepping from the treeline, he was crossing to that door but could still see into the yard and the chaos there, a melding of bodies in motion. Then, something gave, someone cried out and broke away, back into the trees. The youth of Askaug fled. He saw Ulrich and Tiny Elric roaring at them to return. But there were bodies on the ground and, when they did not, the smiths fled too.

Luck could not blame the young. He'd have fled his first battle if he could have – and he could not die, not finally. Perhaps, though, they had been enough of a distraction to let him into the house? He crossed to the door, put his hand on the handle.

But didn't turn it. The voice stopped him. He had not heard it in fifteen years except in some very bad dreams. But it was not one he would ever forget.

'Luck of Askaug,' Anazat called. 'You cannot win here. It is over. Join us. Join … the One.'

Luck tried the door. It was locked. He had his axe, could

smash the lock. For what purpose? He'd be caught just across the threshold. He was no warrior. His strength was in his mind. Anazat was right. It was over. No more young men and women of his town need die this day. All he could do now was hope to see Poum again. If it was the last time, if the black-eyed priest decided to end his threat for ever? Well, he had lived a long, long life.

He moved to the corner of the house. 'If I come,' he called around it, 'will your men kill me?'

His voice drew them immediately. Two Horse Lords seized him, pulled his arms high behind him, dragged him out. Bent as he was, he could still look up and see his enemy – his gaoler, his conqueror – torchlight reflecting in the blackness of his eyes. Behind him he glimpsed the bulk of Peki Asarko. The Lord of the Lake of Souls was giggling.

'Bring him,' Anazat said, and went back into the house.

Luck was dragged up the steps, through some large room, following Anazat and Peki down a corridor to another door. The monk pushed it open. There was a table, a lamp on it, casting light upon a scroll, curiously bound in leather. 'Put him there,' Anazat ordered, and once his guards had shoved Luck down into a chair, added, 'and fetch that girl here.'

Luck looked around the room. 'Where is Poum?' he asked.

'Yes,' said Peki, 'where are they?'

'You will see them soon enough,' growled Anazat.

The guards returned. One of them was gripping Marla by an arm. She had a bruise on one cheek, some hay in her hair. 'Are you all right?' Luck asked.

She nodded. 'Sit on the floor,' Anazat ordered, and she did, putting her back against the wall. 'Out,' he told the guards, and they left. 'You as well,' he said, to Peki Asarko.

'Oh please, please may I stay?' Peki Asarko begged. 'There are *so* many questions I'd like to ask my brother god.'

The monk looked at him for a moment, then nodded. 'You may stay. As long as you keep quiet.' With a contented sigh, Peki stepped back. Anazat turned again. 'So we meet again, Luck. It has been some time.'

'It has. You have grown old.'

'The cares of the world.' He sighed. 'So many things to control. So many people not liking that. But that will all change now. Now I have the One.'

'Will it? You might find Poum will not like to be controlled either.'

'Oh, do you think so? I disagree.' Anazat sat, and fingered the book on the table. 'They and I had such a nice talk before you interrupted us with your pathetic attempt at rescue.' He lifted the book. 'They were so pleased to discover that their beliefs had already been written down. They were so looking forward to reading of the joys they are bringing to the world. To being treated like the god they are. They told me you did not revere them at all. That you treated them like … a child.'

'Their mother and I raised them to be responsible. To think for themselves. Which is why I think they will not obey you without question. What will you do then, monk?' Luck ran his tongue over his lips. 'When your god disagrees with you?'

'Can you not guess?' The monk smiled, black teeth gleaming. 'I will have them killed, of course.'

The three others in the room all gasped. Anazat, still smiling, continued. 'Though killed is not quite the right word. They will be sacrificed. Yes, *sacrificed* is so much more appropriate. Very publicly. They will be *martyred*. Another fine word. And their sacrifice, their martydom will finally bind together all the peoples of the world.' He shrugged. 'So you see, it does not really matter if they disagree with me or not. Because they are not actually that important. Only what they mean is.' He tapped the book again. 'What they say.'

Luck went to speak. Couldn't find any words. Here, finally, he had none. Suddenly he felt so weary. The Four Tribes had won – and the world had lost. He slumped back, stared at the table before him.

Anazat was watching him keenly. 'So interesting to find out what goes on deep inside someone's mind, don't you think? To discover all their plans? That would be hidden, totally hidden, from someone else. Of course, you understand some of that, don't you? When you possess an animal, you learn their depths, do you not?'

'What?' Luck looked up. He hadn't really been listening, lost to gloom as he was. 'What are you talking about?'

'Animals. The mink you possessed before? Did it reveal secrets to you? Or Bull? You possessed the ram, didn't you? Shared its life for a while. Still didn't stop you turning it into sausages, did it?'

Luck froze. How could Anazat have known about Bull the Ram? Would Poum have discussed it with him, in the short time they'd been together? It seemed unlikely ... yet far more likely than the other thought that sprang and clanged into his head then. The black eyes loomed closer, staring deep into Luck's. 'Yes, my father,' Anazat continued, 'you've guessed it.'

'What has he guessed?' Peki came forward, his brows creased in puzzlement. 'Why do you call him your father?'

'Because that is what he is,' Poum said, within Anazat, then stood up and put a dagger into Peki Asarko's heart.

Luck leaped up. In centuries of shocks, he had never had a greater one. 'Poum!' he cried.

The voice that replied was Anazat's. The words, his child's. 'He won't stay dead for long, will he?' they said, gesturing as the Lord of the Lake of Souls spluttered into death. 'And I can't hold this one for long either.' They slapped their chest. 'What do we do? Cut off both their heads?'

Luck shook his own head. It was tempting, to do both those things. But he understood so little of what had just happened, and he needed time to understand more. Anazat had told him at the Keep that the immortals of Corinthium could possess another human. He had scarcely believed it. He had also said that possession did not occur in Ometepe. But that was not true. It had simply not been discovered – before this day. 'No. We must go while we can.' He looked down at Marla, who had thrust herself into the corner as soon as Peki fell. He reached a hand to her, pulled her up, turned back. 'Can you hold a little longer? Enough to get us out of here?'

'I . . . I will try. How he fights!'

'Check the door there,' Luck said.

Poum opened it. The two Horse Lords were outside. 'Go. Join your brothers,' Poum said.

It was Anazat they obeyed. As soon as they'd left the corridor, Luck took Marla and Poum by the arm and led them the opposite way, to the back of the house where he'd tried to get in before. Unlocked the door, threw it open. 'Hurry,' the black-eyed monk gasped, his body convulsing.

They made it down the rear steps, and halfway across the yard. Then the black-cloaked figure lurched to a stop. 'Aiyee!' Poum screamed, in Anazat's voice . . . then in their own.

Two bodies lay on the ground. Luck seized one. 'Fast now,' he hissed and, pulling Poum to their feet, the three of them ran into the forest.

They were about twenty paces in when the screaming began. But since Anazat was only making sounds, terrible agonised sounds, and no words, no one pursued them till they were deep into the forest.

They began searching after dawn, but by then it was too late. The men from the outlying farms had begun to arrive. Soon the rebels were as many in number as the searchers from the Four Tribes. Shortly after, they had more, with more arriving. When there were enough armed men and women, all the rest of the people of Askaug found their courage and burst from their houses. Young or old, they began to take back their town.

Ulrich and Tiny Elric led. The Huntresses were tracked and then trapped in the woods. The Horse Lords barricaded themselves into Peki Asarko's house, but fire drove them out and blades finished them. Just before the roof collapsed, the men from the Lake of Souls charged out, were cut down. On their heels, rats fled the fire too, scattering into the woods. Though the men and women of Askaug searched the burning building for the tyrant, Peki Asarko's body was not found.

The Seafarers had come from their ships on Anazat's command to aid in the search. The half that survived managed to fight their way back, and cast off one of their two ships, the one that was due to leave with the dawn, the only one ready. In their midst, strangely silent, was Anazat. He sat on the deck, and stared at Askaug till it was out of sight.

At noon the next day, Luck and Poum came aboard the second of the Seafarers' vessels. It was smaller than the one that had gone – a *caraca*, this type was called, with sails only, no oars, and so no benches of slaves. A boat for coastal trading and only tied up at the dock still because it had been under repair, its damaged rudder dismantled. Ulrich and a crew had worked the rest of the day and night to repair that, since Luck had ordered it so. The vessel had been kept stocked for a voyage. Now it would take one.

'You are not both coming,' Luck said, eyeing the smiths, father and son. 'One should remain and organise the town. Peki Asarko may return.'

'There are plenty of greybeards in Askaug wise enough to set up our defences,' Ulrich replied, stroking his own grey beard.

'Besides, that bastard will be busy all over the land, not just here. Messengers have been sent to every town: Midgarth rises. They are the words every man, woman and remaining god has been waiting for these fifteen years.' He looked at the sails, furled but shifting in a strong offshore breeze. 'And who did you expect to sail this for you, Luck? Not one of your skills, I seem to remember? Too busy chopping up animals to learn shipcraft, am I right?'

'You are.' Luck grinned. 'I am glad to have you.'

'Just need a bearing from you now. You've told us you need to go, but not where.'

Luck looked at Poum. It was they who had determined the course. Their time within Anazat had been well spent. 'South,' he said.

'To Lorken? Good. And then you'll make along the river Tanas for Galahur and the moot?' One had been called, a month from then. With Midgarth risen there would be much to discuss.

It was the obvious reason. But Luck shook his head. 'South from Lorken,' he said.

'South from Lorken. There is nothing south from Lorken, except open sea and—' He broke off, squinted. 'You don't mean to sail into seas that have never been charted?'

'I do.'

'But they are … impossible. Hidden reefs. Storms of overpowering strength.'

'Sounds like the Maelstrom to the north. Yet you sailed through that, didn't you?'

'True.' Ulrich ran his hand over his head. 'But we knew the land of the Four Tribes lay that way. That's why we raided them. Do you know what lies south?'

'I do. Another mighty world. Where all our fates are to be decided.'

'Oh, is that all?' It was Tiny Elric who spoke. 'In that case, I'd better stow a few more barrels of beer, don't you think, Father?'

'I do.' He looked at the sacks that Luck and Poum carried. 'While you'd better get those below. You may be gods, but you are still going to have to share a cabin. The only one on this vessel.' He shuddered. 'Though why anyone would wish to sleep below a deck when the sky is so beautiful above ...'

He shook his head, turned and walked away, bellowing orders. Luck looked at Poum. 'You are sure of what you saw?'

'I am sure. It's different with animals. They focus on few things. Anazat thought of so many.' They took a deep breath. 'But I know he believed this: that all would be resolved in this place called Corinthium.'

Luck nodded. 'Somehow, I always knew that would be true. Fortunately, we have friends there.' He picked up one of the bags. Within it, a glass vial clinked against a glass globe. 'Now we just have to hope that we can find them in time.'

10

Xan

From her vantage on the dune, staring down at the lights scattered over the valley below like the fireflies that had visited their camp every night in the desert, Lara reflected on how much harder it had been to reach Xan the second time.

The first, she had journeyed there in a moment, using smoke in the glass. But she had resisted its further call, strong though it always was, for she could not trust that the visions it brought were true, rather than what Sirene wanted her to see. To know the truth, she had to go. Take the second journey.

So she had. By ship from Corinthium to Balbek. Two weeks there, while she waited to join one of the camel caravans that crossed the great southern desert every month, learning what had become of her home town, the devastation wrought by conquest and occupation. The crossing had taken two more weeks. The caravans rarely took passengers, for every beast was loaded with the trade goods of empire: metals, textiles, and wines in the main. They would return to Balbek with what they'd traded these for: dates and spices, and in many of the sacks on the camel's backs something quite different: kefa, the intoxicant so desired by many across the empire. Illegal, of course, and therefore much more valuable than any other goods. Kefa also meant she was not merely a passenger but an envoy ... of the largest dealer in Corinthium. Her story was that *he*, Laro – she'd kept the name and disguise – had been sent by Graco to learn of the trade that provided him with so much of his wealth. At least that was what she'd told Arak.

He joined her now by the fire she'd made, sat cross-legged beside her on the sheep's wool blanket, stretched out his hands to warm them, then leaned over the crest and spat into the dark. Kefa leaves needed a lot of spit to break them down – together with a fingernail's worth of dried bird shit. Lara had only tried it once, and had vomited for an hour afterwards. So she did not envy the man she looked at now, and the bulge in his black cheek, despite the gleam of pleasure in his eyes.

'Tomorrow I take you to where it is grown,' Arak said, picking up a conversation they'd had the night before as if no time had passed. 'You think the desert we crossed was desolate? Wait till you glimpse the Great Wastelands.'

'If they are so desolate, how does anything grow?'

Arak shrugged. 'It is the secret as well as the gift of Sadrak.' He danced his fingers down his face, the gesture all made when the supreme god of the Xan was mentioned. 'There is no water for them that we can find. Burning days, freezing nights. Yet the plant thrives, Laro, as long as it is tended.'

'And the tenders? Tell me again of them.'

Arak spat again, this time not just for the drug. 'The Exiles. They fled the fall of the cities on the Great Sea – Balbek, Tarfona, and every town between them. Scavengers, asking us to feed them, shelter them. Then complaining when we made them work in payment for our hospitality.' He looked up at Lara, and firelight lit his teeth as he grinned. 'Still, in some ways their coming was the blessing of Sadrak,' he made the same finger-fluttering gesture, 'for less and less Xanians wanted to work on the edge of the Great Wastelands. The plants were not well tended, were choking as they spread. The Exiles halted that, increased production.' He tapped Lara's knee. 'Better-quality kefa and more profit for Graco, eh?'

'These Exiles? Do they not complain?'

'At first they did. Then they didn't get fed, so they stopped.' He rubbed his hands for warmth, and for glee. 'Many die, of course. But since they breed like rats there is always another child to replace a father or mother in the fields.'

Father and mother, Lara thought, turning back to stare again into the valley below. Were hers sitting by one of those dancing lights? Or had they died in the kefa fields and now her sister Aisha worked them alone to live? The sight she'd had of them only a pleasing illusion of Sirene?

They were questions for the morrow. The answers to them would tell her what she would do next. For if her family was not alive …

She sighed. She did not truly know her course, even if they were. Would she just stay, work with them, suffer with them? Watch them die eventually, while she lived on? Perhaps. Yet she also knew that the world might not leave her even that option.

She gazed at the lights – but did not see them. Instead she was looking inwards, remembering the night before they set out from Balbek, after she'd secured her passage with Arak. The tavern where she ate a last meal, in the same street where her family home had been. The house itself was now occupied by some of the town's garrison of Horse Lords and Seafarers, who also swaggered around the tavern. Like every other Balbek resident, she kept her eyes lowered, and silently hated the conquerors.

A Horse Lord had come bursting into the room, shouting news to his comrades. Most there did not understand him, but she spoke *tolanpa-sen* and did. Keeping her head down, she'd listened.

'There's rebellion in Corinthium,' the man had yelled. 'Our brothers have been betrayed, and murdered in the streets. Not just by those dogs of the city. They have allied with their old enemy, the Wattenwolden.'

It was a shock to her, to hear that. But a bigger one came next.

'Who leads them?' asked another man.

'That black whore who governed the city for us. She fucks a Wattenwolden warrior now.'

It hit her hard. She'd left that letter for Ferros in the wooden horse. She did not know if he would find it. In it, she had let him go, urged him to do the same with her. But that did not mean that it did not hurt that he had obeyed her so quickly. Gone to *her*. The woman who had killed Lara twice. She knew that she would mourn for the ending of her and Ferros all her life. If what the Horse Lord shouted was true, Ferros had mourned for her ... not at all.

She'd stopped listening. Now she did again, when something else was shouted .

'... take it back. And this time we will destroy it. Not a stone of that cursed city will stand when we are done.'

'How do you know this?'

'I was with our lord, Baromolak, when the news came. It was what he vowed. He has already sent messengers to every garrison between here and Tarfona, and through the mountains to Saghaz-a. The Four Tribes will rally here in Balbek, assembling the greatest fleet ever seen. And then we will cross the sea and crush the rebels.'

Cheers came, and the Horse Lords began to sing a song of triumph in their ancient tongue, which Lara did not speak. She had heard enough anyway.

Now she focused again on the lights below. Somehow she had to reconcile the call of her family with her call to a world's destiny. For she had no doubt that was what was being shaped. That a final confrontation between the forces of the One and all who opposed them was about to occur.

She had accepted that it was not just immortality that had been given her when she died and was born again. It was destiny. Hers, her family's and the world's, all entwined. Destiny had a path that led to it. And the first step began tomorrow, when she went to the kefa fields of Xan, to see if those she loved still lived.

She spent the day with Arak, letting him show Graco's envoy, 'Laro', everything to do with the production of kefa.

They visited the warehouse to which the vines were brought, and examined for rot or pest, to both of which the plant was prone. Masked workers stripped the approved leaves and small buds off and carried them to a second building, where they spread them out on racks to dry. Some – the best – were then taken to a third, smaller building, and placed on metal sieves above smouldering fires that gave off smoke scented with various herbs. Lara had thought that the drug was simply one thing, one plant, and only chewed for its effect, and said so.

'No, no,' Arak assured her. 'As with wine, you have those who appreciate different flavours. Some enjoy the coolness of manala, others the robustness of kefa when it is toasted over aliantha chips. I myself enjoy some hints of the robara pod.' He pushed his tongue into his cheek, bulging further what was already distended, and she caught a whiff of that plant's peppery aroma. 'People pay more for the quality product. But most does not make the roasting floor here, for most people can't afford more than the basic leaf.'

He waved his hand and she looked again, this time studying not the work, but the workers. Most of the people she'd seen in Xan were black-skinned, of varying shades. All in the warehouses were as brown-skinned as herself, and all were women. They bent to their tasks, barely glancing at her, as supervisors exhorted them to greater effort. 'These are the exiles you talked about?'

'Yes. The ones who fled their homes on the coast after the invasion.'

Lara studied eyes above the masks, seeking her mother, her sister. Did not find them. 'The men?'

'They work the fields. It is ... harder.'

'And what did you do before you had slaves, Arak?'

His eyes went wide. 'Slaves? There is no slavery in Xan. These people are paid – in the food that keeps them alive. In roofs over their heads, clothes for their bodies.'

'Just as slaves are *paid*.'

'They are free to leave at any time.' Arak shrugged. 'They are just happy to be alive,' he said, then led her from the warehouse.

I wonder, she thought, and followed.

He showed her some of the town, though it was really a series of villages, spread among five oases, linked by shallow streams lined with houses. In the largest oasis they drank cooling fruit juices in the second biggest structure in Xan, the central marketplace. It was a columned hall beside the biggest building of all, the walled palace. From there, she was informed, the town's council ruled the city, and the surrounding land. Though Xan had been conquered by Corinthium two centuries before, and was the southernmost province of the empire, it was largely left alone as long as tributes were paid, and goods transported to the city – legal and illegal. And it was the Timian Monks, who worshipped Sadrak and other lesser gods, who made up most of the council. Lara remembered one of them, Gan, who had been sent to tutor Ferros on that first voyage to Corinthium after the revelation of his immortality. The tall, black monk had been gentle, smiling, but had said almost nothing to her, and she'd been too young and foolish to ask him anything of his world.

I need to learn it now, she thought, sipping juice.

In the middle of the day, Arak left her to rest for the hottest part of it at the camp they'd made in the shade of the date palms, in the furthest oasis. In the late afternoon, when it was meant to be a little cooler, he collected her again and took her to the fields.

He'd been right. The work there was harder. Lara didn't feel any diminishment of the heat that gripped the land, held it in its furnace hand. Squeezed her breath, so that she felt she was inhaling flame. The worst of the sun was kept off her with fabric stretched over a wicker frame, held above her on a pole by an old man who was himself protected only by a wide-brimmed hat. From his toothless mouth, unintelligible words tumbled continuously, and he only looked above the ground to check that she was still shaded.

They stood on a cliff above land gouged and broken by steep-sided gulleys. The kefa vines lined the gulleys, sprawling over the ground in a thick tangle out into the far distance. Through it men slipped and scrambled, trimming, cutting, digging. Attempting to impose an order that Arak said the plant required to thrive. 'Otherwise it would grow too long and stringy, the leaves would be too big, and poor in quality,' he added.

'Does it not need water?'

'It must. We can't find any here, but the plant's roots go so deep into the ground we have never been able to reach their ends.' He pointed into the earth. 'There must be water down there.'

But none up here, Lara thought, sweat running down her spine, staring again at the men moving among the plants. Even as she looked, one of them collapsed, falling silently to the ground. She took a step forward, wondering in a mad moment if it could be her father. But others rushed to him, pulled off his hat, revealing the sunburned face of a youth. Water was brought in a large stone jar. He was carried into a gulley and a patch of shade, was made to drink. He revived enough to sit up, so they left him there, with the water jug and some dates to eat, as supervisors yelled at the man's rescuers to return to their work.

'Are slaves treated so well?' Arak asked, his expression sour. Her remark earlier had obviously rankled him. 'Have you seen enough?'

'I would like to see where these people live,' she said.

'Why?'

'Graco will want to know,' she said, without explaining.

He shrugged, and led her back along the cliffs. They came to a descent and in the valley below she could see the sprawl of a small town. Red-walled houses were crammed together forming narrow, twisting streets with no order to them. Heat haze made the town shimmer, as if it was unreal, a vision. But it did look exactly like another vision she'd had, and, for a moment, her heated breath caught with hope.

'How many people live here?'

'All those who fled the coast. Perhaps ten thousand?'

She took a short, hot breath. 'But there cannot be more than a ... a thousand houses there.'

He curled a lip. 'So?'

She looked back. There was no point in provoking him further. She needed this man to take her back across the Sarphardi desert to Balbek. With her family, she hoped. 'Thank you for your guidance today,' she said. 'Graco will be very pleased. As am I. But I can go on alone now.'

He raised an eyebrow. 'Those streets are not safe,' he said.

'I will manage.'

He shrugged. 'Then may Sadrak protect you,' he said, fingers fluttering before his face. 'Do you wish to keep the shade?'

He gestured to the mumbling old man, still holding the

stretched fabric above her. 'I will manage without him also,' she said.

'Very well. Then I will see you at our camp. We leave at dawn the day after tomorrow.'

With that, he turned, and walked back the way they'd come. The old man did not move. 'Thank you for your kindness. You may leave me,' she said. He muttered something without looking at her, then followed Arak, catching up, sheltering him again.

Lara turned back to the dismal view. Her people lived crammed together on the very edge of Xan, placed there to work the kefa fields. Beyond those ...

She sheltered her eyes, and looked south. Her vision was distorted by haze but there was little to see anyway. Only endless desert sweeping on and on ... to what, no one knew and few had ever tried to find out, for the Great Wastelands made the Sarphardi desert look like a scrap of sandy beach on a shore.

She stared, shivered despite the heat, then started down the faint track that led to the town.

It was worse than her vision. In that, there'd been fewer people, and wider streets. Here, narrow paths cluttered with rubbish wove between the rough walls of houses made of bound red earth, the fronts of which gave directly onto the streets. Hard-eyed women stared at her from steps as she passed, or through gaps cut into walls as crude windows. Skinny children, with filthy faces, flies clustered about their eyes, their hands on the prominent ribs of dogs panting at their feet, aped their mothers' dull regard. A few old men lay about, eyes staring, cheeks bulging with kefa.

She'd have felt threatened, if everyone hadn't looked so exhausted, so drained by heat and hunger. And though she was dressed in newer clothes, she wore as little as them, enough only to keep off the sun, and carried nothing.

She asked three times if any knew of Fruka or Brankos. She

got no reply in words from the women, just the slighest shake of their heads before they looked away. She stopped asking, just wandered, increasingly doubtful. She had seen a vision given by a drug that was meant to make people happy. She had seen what she wanted to see. A family she'd lost, alive.

And then she squeezed out between two walls into a wider space. There was a well at its centre, and a line of women with big stone jars waiting their turn at it.

The fifth in line was her sister, Aisha.

She looked like the girl from her vision. Not at all like the child she'd left behind when she followed Ferros sixteen years before. Then her sister's cheeks had been stained with tears at the farewell. Now they were drawn by suffering. She was only twenty-five but looked twice that.

Lara's first urge was to run to her, take her sister in her arms. But she held herself back. It was doubtful that Aisha would even remember her; besides, her sister being alive did not mean their parents were. Also, a reunion, needing to explain, was something that had to be done in private. Lara had no idea how the Exiles' society worked. Someone coming from outside, even a family member, might be seen as a threat. Even if they all were still alive, she would want to get them away quietly, without drawing any attention.

Get them away to where though, she wondered, watching as women drew the bucket up from the well, filled their jars, staggered away with them, Aisha moving closer to the front. The news she'd heard in that Balbek tavern was of an army assembling there. Not a place of safety.

Aisha filled her two large jars, then bent to slip the yoke over her shoulders. She breathed deep, took the weight, stood. Her first few steps were jittery but then she got the balance and rhythm. She moved down the wider street the well was in, and Lara followed.

The ways got narrower, her sister needing to turn sideways to let people pass. Finally she emerged into a kind of square, three-storey houses on all sides. Children played in the dust, old men and women found what shade they could, their backs to the red-mud walls. She crossed, to the house straight ahead where strings of beads hung in a doorless opening. 'Mother, I come,' Aisha called. There was a shuffling, the beads parted, and a woman stepped out.

Lara, watching from the entrance to the last alley, felt the tears start into her eyes. Her sister looked old for her years. Her mother looked ancient. She'd been a woman of curves and substance, forever claiming with a laugh how much weight she'd put on. There were no curves on the woman who stood there, just sharp angles, and the only extra flesh was at the neck, where dried folds hung like empty pouches. Her hair, that had once fallen on her shoulders in thick brown waves, was now a few strands, tied back. The skin, light brown and shiny before, was the dark of aliantha wood. Lara knew she could have passed this woman in the street and not recognised her. Unless she'd spoken – as she did now – because her voice had not truly changed, and still rang with the sounds of Balbek port and the fisherman's family she was raised in.

'Aisha, wonderful daughter of light and life!' she called. 'Put the jars there and let's wait till a dozen young men fight to help you carry them into the house.'

It had the slighty tired ring of something often said. Aisha groaned, partly from the relief of obeying, putting down the jars, slipping the yoke off her shoulders. 'None will come, Mother,' she said, bent over. 'None ever have.'

'That can change in a day,' her mother trilled. 'But if they do not, I will come.'

She placed a hand on the side of the door opening, took a

step forward. But Lara could see by the way she moved that there was something else greatly altered about her.

Her mother was blind.

'No, no. Do not move. I come. I come,' Aisha called, bending to the stone jar to her left.

Wiping the tears from her eyes, Lara crossed the square. 'May I help?' she asked.

Her sister squinted up. Her voice, when it came, was harsh. 'Why would you?' she asked. 'Just leave us be.'

'I knew it, I knew it. A young man!' Fruka was moving her head, using senses other than her lost sight. 'Let him help, daughter. Let him come in.'

Perhaps Aisha couldn't see Lara fully, with the sun behind her. Perhaps she was simply exhausted. But she just shrugged and picked up the one jar. Lara shouldered the other, and together they went up the three steps to the entrance. Fruka shuffled back and let them in.

Lara looked about her. The room was not dissimilar to the one from her vision. But there were five cots turned on their sides and leaning against the inner walls, not three. There was a crude hearth, cooking pots over it on a metal frame, but no other furniture. There were two clay cups though. Fruka had swept her hands about the floor, and found two cups. 'Give the kind young man some water, Aisha. We still understand about hospitality in this house.' Fruka held out one cup. 'Please, young sir, help yourself.'

Lara had felt her throat contract the moment she stepped into the impoverished room; when she could see her mother properly, close to, see what time and hardship had done to her. So she struggled to form words. Could only squeeze one out. 'Mother,' she whispered.

'Yes, yes.' Fruka beamed. 'I am Aisha's mother.'

Lara swallowed. 'As you are mine,' she whispered.

Fruka smiled. 'I will be yours too, child,' she said, reaching out a hand, moving it in the air. 'Everyone needs a mother.'

Lara caught the hand, kissed it, brought it to her face. 'It is me, Mother. It is Lara.'

Aisha gasped. Fruka's bony hand traced the face before her. 'L-Lara?' she whispered.

The reunion was different in reality than it had been in her vision. Aisha did not walk away in fury but clung to them, as they both clung to her, all three slipping to the ground as Fruka's legs gave. There were tears, many tears, of course. But there was laughter as well, and questions which mostly went unanswered in the noisy joy. Until Lara remembered who was missing and asked the question to which she dreaded, but needed, the answer. 'Father? Is ... is he still—?'

'He is well.' Fruka wiped tears from her face with one hand, her other clutching Lara's. 'He is at the meeting of the men. They talk of taking Balbek back.'

Aisha snorted. 'Men! Talk is all they do. And have for years.'

Fruka laid a hand on her face too. 'It is good for them to dream. To believe that one day—' She broke off, sighed. 'Otherwise how could they rise each day to do their labour?'

Lara thought back to what she'd seen in the kefa fields, in the warehouses. 'Is there no other work for our people? I'd heard that the Timian Monks who rule this place were kind. Why would they turn us into slaves?'

'They are kind, child. They took us in, and everyone that came after. But they are not a wealthy people, with barely enough to feed their own.' She squeezed Lara's hand. 'Kefa provided an answer of a kind. What had been a trade for a few who tended the plants, became an industry for many.'

Aisha laughed. 'It is said the monks believe that if more and more people learn to love kefa in Corinthium, the less likely they are to interfere with those in Xan.'

'Though it is not Corinthium any more, child. The Four Tribes rule there now.'

Lara thought it was not the time to share the latest news she'd heard in the Balbek tavern.

'True, Mother,' Aisha said. 'But the rumours of the One worry the monks here more than the old empire ever did. Corinthium largely left them alone, as long as they sent taxes and provided some tutors and soldiers.' She nodded. 'They fear that once every other part of the world is fully conquered, the Four Tribes will come here and all Xan's independence will be gone.'

'Do they?' Lara frowned. 'And how do you know this?'

'I know.' Beneath her dark skin, Aisha blushed. 'I have a … friend who studies to be a monk. She tells me.'

Lara thought, 'She?' but didn't ask. Grateful that, amidst all the sorrows, her sister's blush told her that she had found some joy. Besides, her mind was racing elsewhere. All she'd seen of her family's – her people's – suffering had made her furious. This was all the fault of the Four Tribes, their plan to impose the belief of the One on the whole world. They were close to succeeding. Now the other news she'd heard in that Balbek tavern echoed again for her. How an army was assembling there to go off and finish the rebels in Corinthium once and for all …

… leaving Balbek largely undefended.

'Do you know where this meeting of the men is?' she asked. 'Can you take me there?'

Aisha looked up. 'I know. I could. But they listen to no women there.' She looked Lara up and down. 'Even if you pass as a man for now.'

'No more. My father will know me. Besides,' Lara smiled, 'It is about time they began to listen to women.' She began to strip off her men's garments. 'Aisha, can you lend me some clothes.'

*

Like his wife, Brankos had shrunk in flesh. But nothing else in her father had diminished. He was still a firebrand.

'And I say the time *is* now, Havlos!' He pointed down at the man who'd argued with him. 'Did you yourself not faint in the fields today? Did three men not die in them last week alone?' He looked up, his gaze now taking in all three hundred men who stood before him on the sand. He was on an outcrop in the cliff face about twice as wide as himself, and a man's height from the ground. Lined up beside him on that were five men, waiting their turn to speak. 'We cannot keep losing men to the hottest part of the day,' Brankos continued. 'All we ask is that they allow us to rest for three hours, make up the work at dawn and dusk—'

'We have already asked the monks that and they have said no.' It was the same man, Havlos, arguing again.

'Which is why we need to take further action,' Brankos shouted. 'Refuse to go into the fields at all until—'

'They will cut off our food. Deny us access to the wells!'

'Which is why we do it now, before the caravan leaves for the coast. They need two more days' supplies of raw kefa to make up a full load. Deny them that—'

Uproar, for and against his position, drowned out her father's further words. It is time, Lara thought, and began to push her way in from the back. She wore a kaliyah, the heavy wool garment her mother had given her against the chill of the night. Some men saw within her hood and gasped before stepping aside. Others, with a curse, tried to block her. With a dip of the shoulder and a smile, she shoved past them. By the time she reached the front, and the queue of men waiting to speak, the murmur of the word 'woman' had grown to a roar.

She halted, looked up. On his rock platform, Brankos looked down. He jabbed his arm at her. 'You must not be here,' he shouted.

'I think I must.' She threw back the hood. 'Because a good daughter must always return to her father.'

Brankos started, stared. Then he swayed and she was frightened he was going to fall. But he grabbed at the rock wall beside him, steadied. 'Lara?' he said, all the fury and force gone from his voice.

'It does not matter that she is your daughter.' It was the same man, Havlos, who spoke, who stepped forward and grabbed her by her upper arm. 'Get out,' he yelled, thrusting his face close.

One of the first men she'd ever possessed, a sailor, had been an expert knife fighter, and she had retained his skill as herself. Another, more recently, was gifted in all ways of fighting without a weapon so it was his gift she used now. Taking the man's hand at the wrist, she bent it sharply against its inclination. One moment he was beside her, the next he was crying out, and staring up at her from somewhere around her waist. Then he was on the ground, and she was on the platform beside her father.

It had happened so fast, for a moment no one made a noise. Then everyone did, at once. But it was her father she heard, his stunned words in her ear. 'Lara! How is this possible? Where have you—? How have you—?'

'Later for all that, Father. Let me speak to the men here.'

'It is forbidden.'

'I know. But the world has changed so much, Father, and so has the idea of what is allowed and not allowed.' She squeezed his arm. 'Trust me, they will want to hear what I have to say. For I bring news from Balbek – and hope.'

He stared at her a long moment, then turned back to the shouting crowd. His raised arms, his own silence, finally brought theirs. Into it, he spoke. 'This is my child, lost to me for sixteen years. Gone with her immortal ... *husband*,' he faltered a little on the word-lie, then continued, 'to Corinthium.' He glanced at her, before adding, 'Despite our rules, listen to her for a moment. If what she says does not please, we will send her away.'

There were mutterings still, like the twittering of small birds. But Lara had long since lost any shyness. She knew they wouldn't give her long. Yet she had seen over the years – on the grass plains of the Assani, in the streets of the great city, in the forests of the Wattenwold – the way that men could be roused: by giving them what they wanted, which was hope. So she took a step forward to the edge of the platform and, with her voice centred and low, said, 'Brothers and fathers! I bring you news. The Four Tribes are leaving Balbek and Tarfona. So I have come to help you take your cities back.'

The roar, a mix of hope and doubt and fear and fury, made her sway. Her father's arm steadied her and when the noise slackened, she added, 'This is how it will be done.'

Later, when the thrumming crowd had dispersed to begin making preparations for the return, Aisha and her father led her back through the streets towards their home. She answered his questions as best she could; they came so fast, she scarce had time to respond before another overtook her words. Yet they had not gone very far before three figures stepped out and blocked their path. All three of them reached for the comfort of a knife at their waist. But the tall men just stood there, and the little light from the two moons shone in their dark brown eyes.

'What do you want with us?' asked Brankos.

'She is to come with us,' the man in the middle replied. 'The Monks' Council would see her.'

'She is not going anywhere—'

Lara gripped her father's arm, halting the slip of dagger from sheath. 'It is all right. If we are to go, we will need the monks' help to do so.'

'Very well.' Brankos shoved the blade fully back in. 'But you do not go alone.'

They followed the three men – monks themselves, their skins as black as midnight – through the tight alleys and out onto the wider paths that led to the oases. They were led to the centre of the central, largest one, past the market where Lara had drunk frothy juices with Arak earlier that day, on through the gates of the large, white-walled palace and down corridors lined with aliantha panels, emerging eventually into a large dome-roofed chamber.

It reminded her of the Pantheon which she had seen once in Corinthium, where the elites of the city met and debated. Though in that, rising rows of benches faced each other over an open space. Here, individual chairs radiated out from a central point, like spokes on a wagon wheel. Monks stood before every chair, all dressed the same, in hooded white robes with a single purple stripe about a hand's breadth wide running from shoulder to ankle. Their bare feet were in sandals and every man had black skin.

At the hub sat one man. 'Welcome, Lara,' he said, his voice deep and rich. 'It is good to see you again.'

She peered. Before she came to Xan, she had only ever met one man from the city: the tutor who accompanied them on the sea voyage to Corinthium to begin Ferros's training in the ways of the immortals.

The same man who stood before her now. 'Gan?' she said. 'Is it you?'

A ripple of murmurs came from the monks along the spokes as they all sat. They didn't sound pleased. But Gan just smiled as he pulled down his hood. 'It is.'

He gestured to the corners of the room. Immediately, men came from them, bringing chairs, placing them so she, Aisha and Brankos could sit near him at the centre. Her father leaned in to her as he took his seat, his whisper incredulous. 'You know the Grand Monk?'

'A little.'

'No one calls him by his name. He is the master here. He—'

It was all he could hiss because the Grand Monk had himself sat and was speaking again.

'It is both good and interesting to see you again,' he said. 'When I was out in the world performing my *katan* – our time of sacred wandering – my duties were to educate new immortals. I know that you and I did not speak much. The soldier you were with needed so much attention. But in the times I observed you, I noted that there was something different about you. That you were marked for a role in the movements of the world. Tell me – has it proved so?'

Lara wondered if it was the time and place to reveal that she was immortal too. She decided not. For one, her family did not know it. For another, since the Four Tribes had taken over the whole of Corinthium's empire, they were the ultimate overlords here. Immortals might be criminals here too. Besides, the true power of an immortal – possession – was only useful if you were not known to have it. And she was pretty sure that even if the other monks did not know of that power, Gan, educator of immortals, would. I may need it later, she thought, so replied merely, 'I have travelled far. When I have seen evil in the world, I have tried to oppose it.'

'A wise … and a cautious answer.' Gan steepled his fingers, putting their tips to his lips. 'Is there an evil that you have found yourself opposing more than any other?'

Lara looked around again. At least fifty pairs of eyes stared hard at her. She suddenly fervently wished that she had had a better education, that she knew how Xan, and its ruling Timian Monks, regarded the world. Then she remembered something Arak, the caravan guide, had said in one of the night camps they had made. That though Xan was part of the empire, and sent tribute goods and people to work within it, they also had laws and systems of governance that applied only in their own lands. Corinthium, benefiting as it did from what it received, had not thought to change them too much. But Arak had feared, from all he'd observed of the Four Tribes, that one day they might.

Everything she'd done lately had been a risk. She didn't see how she could stop now. 'I came to believe that the empire was corrupt, and its rulers especially so. Its *immortal* rulers,' she added. 'Corruption is harmful and unfair – yet it is different from coercion. Which, I believe, is the evil that is facing the world now, with the Four Tribes.'

Her father drew in a sharp breath. There was another ripple down the spokes from the sitting monks. Ahead, Gan lowered his hands. 'Yet it is reported that just now you have urged your people to return with you to their world. To return and to confront this evil. Given the strength of these Four Tribes, does that not seem ... most dangerous?'

Lara looked around again. News evidently moved quickly here. But since she was not being shouted at, or seized as a traitor, she thought that she'd hit upon the right way forward. 'Of course. But given what is happening in the empire right now, this appears to be a chance for my people to go home.'

'What is happening?' Gan leaned forward. 'You speak of the Tribes gathering to go and finish off Corinthium?'

'I do. Though I believe that the city will not be so easy to "finish". Now Corinthium allies with the Wattenwolden. Also they have ... capable people leading them.'

Gan picked up on her slight hesitation. 'Capable? I notice that you did not say good.'

She smiled. 'That is because I do not think they *are* good.' She shrugged. 'But what they will do is either defeat the Four Tribes or weaken them so much that my people, and all the people of the coast, will have a chance to take back their towns and cities.'

'And hold them?'

'That we will have to learn.'

'Hmm. You call it a chance.' Gan shifted his gaze. 'Do you believe in this chance, Brankos?'

Her father looked at her for a moment, then nodded. 'What I think, Grand Master, is that it is a better chance than staying here to drag out our lives in your kefa fields.' He bobbed his head. 'No offence offered.'

'None taken.' Gan shook his own head. 'It was never our intention to make you work there. But our choice was to do that, or turn you away, back into the deserts where you would die. Increasing the kefa trade paid for you to live. If you had stayed without it, without the money some in the empire were willing to pay for it, Xan would be no more.' Brankos began to speak again, but Gan interrupted him. 'It does not matter now. Your complaints. Your conditions. When you go, we will cease the trade entirely.' He looked at Lara again. 'So I was right about you, Lara. You were destined for greater things. If what you say is true, should the Four Tribes triumph it will be only a matter of time before they bring their ... *coercion*, was that the word you used? ... here. And all we've known will be at an end.' He sat back, and looked each way at the other monks. 'We will be dead. And the people we have shepherded for five hundred years will be worshipping the One.'

'Perhaps. Perhaps not.' She swallowed. 'For I have met the One.'

Where the others present had sometimes given vent to their surprise or emotions, Gan had been unshakeable. But he, along with everyone else in the room, gasped at that. 'How ... how is that possible? The One is an idea, not a person.'

'The power of the One is in an idea, that is true,' she replied.

'But I have met the person, though he ... she ... *they* were only a baby at the time. They will have sixteen summers now. They disappeared – but the last rumour I heard is that they have been found. And found in the company of a man who has fought the Four Tribes from the very beginning. A good man. If he lives, I know he will be finding ways to fight them still.'

That silenced Gan, and he stared, until the whispering her statements had brought finally ceased. When it did, he lifted his hands level with his shoulders, palms upwards. 'We of the Council of Timian have always known this day would come. When we would be forced to fight to save our way of life. We thought it might be a war fought in the deserts which we know well, and we have prepared and trained our warriors for that. Then we thought that, at the last, and if all else failed, we should choose to die in the oases we love.' He looked around, swallowed. 'However, you have brought us another choice here, Lara of Balbek. To go and fight with all the others that oppose the Four Tribes. To strike together, not wait to be dealt with separately.' He nodded, stood. 'So we will join with you, and the peoples of the coast. We will journey with you, and fight the Four Tribes there.'

She did not see how the other monks agreed. She just knew they had when all stood too, and bowed.

She rose and turned. 'Pack everything you need, Father,' she said. 'We are going home.'

II

Father and Child

In the tiny cubicle that passed for the only cabin on the ship, Luck and Poum faced each other on the small bunk where they took turns to sleep. Though they were both small of stature, even they were cramped upon it, their heads scraping the low roof. More so because of the glass globe which lay between them.

'Are you ready?'

'I am ready, Father.'

'And no tricks this time. We journey only to speak, not to—' Luck hesitated. He knew that to do more than travel was what they both desired. To escape, for a while, the dreary confines of the ship, the endless days and nights of wave and wind which, after the excitement of some initial storms in the first week of the voyage, just blew them steadily, drearily south. Three weeks of it, with barely a change except in the temperature, passing from colder climes into a steadily growing heat. It would be lovely, Luck thought, still hesitating, to go to a temperate world, to have ground beneath him that did not move. To visit Atisha, and their home. Even if the touch of her hand in his hair would only be a vision, such was the power of Sirene that it would feel as real ... as the real thing.

Yet he knew he must not. He'd been told by Anazat before

his very first voyage with her that Sirene could not truly be controlled. It had proved true for Luck – but it was also one of many lies. For the black-eyed monk had found a way to control her, at least partially. Enough to lure Poum and himself into the trap at Askaug from which they'd barely escaped. Had only escaped because Poum had revealed a power they alone, in all the world, had – the ability to possess both man *and* beast. Looking at them now, their eager face over the smoke-filled globe, Luck knew that the greatest reason of all why they must not escape so, were the unknown powers still latent within the being opposite him.

Poum's eyes went wider as Luck's hesitation lengthened. 'Yes, yes! No tricks.' They raised their hands beside their head in all innocence. 'But let us go and see what this Corinthian proposes.'

The Corinthian. Ferros. Glimpsed that very first time Luck had journeyed in the smoke. Met later at the Keep when Luck had helped him and his woman escape. Finally, and briefly, that time three weeks before in Askaug whence this course had been decided. Each time he had felt something in the man, a determination to do what was right.

Luck nodded. 'Let us,' he said, and carefully tipped three drops onto the glass. They both leaned in, breathed the vapour that rose. He saw Poum's hand rise, as if they would again play the trick and tip Luck's elbow as they had before, to dive deep. But the hand lowered, and they pressed their backs into the wood, both regarding the man who immediately appeared. It was another strangeness of the experience that they both, equally, saw him face on in the globe.

'Where are you, Ferros?'

The Corinthian raised a hand above his head, and they heard the sound of tapped wood. 'The same place as you. Aboard ship.'

'How long have you been so?'

'Fourteen days. If the winds hold, we are about a week from Malpak, the gathering place, a port which is two hours' steady ride west of Balbek. You?'

'If my calculations of our wind speed are correct, we will make landfall on the western coast in three days.' Luck scratched his head. 'But while the water charts I stole from the Keep appear accurate – at least judging by how they mapped Midgarth – I failed to take one that shows the western approach from the coast to Malpak. Perhaps no one ever thought they might sail here this way.'

'No one thought of so many of the things that have happened. But I once rode from Malpak to the bay where you are to drop anchor, chasing cattle thieves. It took a day.' Ferros smiled. 'It was a chase on horseback and so at speed. You'll be walking. But if you have calculated correctly?' Ferros scratched his head. 'It will take you three, perhaps four days? So you could reach Malpak at much the same time as us.'

'Do you know yet how many of the Four Tribes rally in Balbek?'

'No. The last report was the day before we sailed from Corinthium. And that was ten days old then.' Ferros sighed. 'But it will be many. Anazat will not risk failing again. He knows that the city and the Wattenwolden are allied. He will wait till he has an army five times our size so he can be certain to storm the city and crush us.'

'Are you not frightened of those numbers?' It was Poum who asked.

Ferros shook his head. 'Why would I be? Because we will not be in the city, waiting like cattle by a butcher's block. We will be shoving swords up their arses in their tents outside Balbek.'

Luck smiled. There was the confidence he remembered, that he'd always seen.

Then Ferros continued, his gaze shifting, 'Besides, we have

you, Poum. Their whole reason for fighting. You are more powerful for us than five thousand more swords.'

'I see.' Poum swallowed. 'And, uh, how exactly will I use that power?'

'The gods will decide. Wait! No, there are no gods, unless they're us.' Ferros smiled again. 'So we decide, when the time is right.'

The smoke began to fray. At the same time, from the deck, Luck heard shouting. There was concern in it. 'Ferros, I will not use Sirene again. All that needs to be said, has been.'

'True. So let us speak next in Malpak, in person, in about seven days.'

The smoke swirled again and he was gone. As Luck tucked the globe into its sack, someone started to shout from the deck above. 'Let us go and see what is going on,' he said.

Ulrich greeted them at the door to the deck. 'I was coming to get you. We have company.'

He gestured and they crossed to the starboard side of the vessel, looking out to the open sea. At first Luck could not see anything. Then he squinted along Ulrich's pointing arm – and made out, three shapes on the horizon.

'Who would they be?'

'I assume Seafarers. Though they could be pirates, which is one and the same.'

'Neither one do we want to meet.' Luck looked up at the huge smith. 'They will have seen us?'

'We have to believe they have.'

'Can we outrun them?'

'The same wind that fills our sails fills theirs.' Ulrich ran his hand over his beard. 'So it will depend if theirs are bigger.'

Luck cursed under his breath. How, in this huge sea, had they encountered anyone? 'It is your business, Ulrich. But I would suggest every sail that's possible.'

The smith gestured up, where canvas bellied. 'We have done all that we can. Now we just have to see.'

'Will we catch them?' Besema asked. She was near the forward rail of the raised afterdeck, leaning on her stick. Intitepe was in his customary place at the wheel.

He spun it, the vessel turning just a little, just enough to catch some extra push of wind. It was already moving fast, and surged a little faster. The wind filled sail and lifted the cloak he wore, made from the rich plumage of seabirds. It glittered in emerald green and sun yellow. 'We will,' he replied.

'And why will we? Do you seek battle? Plunder?'

He laughed. 'I know you think me many cruel things, Besema. But I am not a pirat. Did I not get rid of all of those?'

'You did. By chaining them to benches below.' She glanced to the other vessels, one either side of them, just behind, keeping pace. 'On all your ships.'

'Yes. I had learned all I needed from them years ago. Once I was sure that my native crews had as well, were as well trained, as good, I realised I didn't need pirats any more. Except to row, when the wind drops.'

'But those below weren't pirats, were they? They are men of the Four Tribes.'

Intitepe shrugged. 'All pirats to me. Except these seemed to think I should obey their commands.'

'Foolish of them.'

'Very.' Intitepe shouted an order. It was in the language they both spoke, using words she did not understand. Something to do with masts, sails, braces.

'So why do we chase this ship? For sport?'

'For news. The last I had was when we sailed from Ometepe. If that munke had not jumped off the ship with his globe, we would not need to chase. Except for fun!'

He spun the wheel again, shouted something else incomprehensible to her. She turned back, stared again at the vessel ahead which, even in the little time they had been talking, appeared closer. Though she had swiftly grown used to the motion of the sea, she had still not become accustomed to being with the Fire King. She had loved him once, for twelve years, long ago. She had fought him, hated him, for nearly six times that span of years. Yet here they were, together again, crossing the sea to a world whose size she was still unable to comprehend, to do … what? He claimed that it was about his … child. Said he no longer feared the prophecy of his doom because if Poum was not quite a daughter they were also not fully the son fated to kill the father. Instead of death, he saw destiny. That vast world ruled by the two of them.

So one thing has not changed with him in all those years, she thought. *It has only come more to the surface. His madness.* She sighed. *And yet if he is mad, what of me?*

She thought she'd known clearly why she'd come: to save her people from massacre at the City of Women by accepting his offer. Now, three weeks into the voyage, she was not so clear. Was it Atisha she came to look for? Was it Poum? Did she believe in the promise of the One almost as much as the men chained to the benches below? A world at peace?

She looked up again. Even in the time of her thoughts they had gained on their quarry. Her eyesight was still keen, despite her years. She could make out figures on the other deck now. It would not be long.

Perhaps news is what I need most too, she thought. *Anything to make some sense of the madness.*

'They will overhaul us soon. What do you wish to do?'

Luck, wiping the raindrops from his eyes, looked from the fast approaching vessels to the smith. 'Can we fight them?'

'I am not sure how. Those are the same vessels we fought at Askaug. Like the one Bjorn and Stromvar captured on that raid. They will have those giant, what were they called? They shot huge arrows?'

'Bows of Mavros.'

'Those. Yet even if they try to board us we have, what, ten fighting men?' He blew out his lips. 'No, I think we're fucked.'

'Indeed.' Luck turned back to gaze, then glanced at the two cages on the deck. Each contained a hawk, ready for possession. To be used in desperate times by him or Poum. Yet was this the time? They'd come far out to sea seeking faster winds. They'd found them. Now they were too far from land to risk a flight. They could lose possession halfway there and plummet into the sea. They might not die, being immortal. But weeks in water, carried where the tides chose? Never mind the discomfort, all the plans they'd made would be finished.

He looked again. Then looked closer. 'Those sailors? They don't look like Seafarers to me.'

'They don't. They look …' Ulrich leaned a little further off the side of the vessel. 'They look like those bastards who sacked Askaug. From that island, whatsisname?'

'Ometepe.' Luck flushed cold. 'By all the gods, I wonder …' He looked up, yelled, 'Poum?'

They were in the crow's nest, their favourite place on the ship, alone on top of the little wooden world. 'Yes?' they answered.

'Are all on those ships from Ometepe?'

'Those I can see, yes.'

'Come down,' Luck called, and looked back. He could see the other vessel clearly now. See who was at its wheel. It was still too far to make out a face, but the cloak made from the feathers of a dozen different glittering birds revealed him.

'Intitepe,' he breathed.

He did not know how this was possible. He just knew what

was. So when Poum joined him on the deck, he took their arm, led them to the side. 'Your father steers that boat,' he said.

Colour fled their face. 'How is that possible?'

'It is the question I asked myself. The answer doesn't matter. All that does is that you must hide.'

'Hide? Where? This boat is so small, there's no place—'

'You know where.'

Poum's eyes went wide. 'But these are our friends. How can I—'

'They are. And they know how important you are.' He turned, called, 'Tiny Elric?'

The smith's huge son looked round. Like everyone else aboard, now that every sail had been hoisted and trimmed and the vessel was going as fast as it could, which was still not fast enough, he was at the railing watching their pursuers get closer, closer. 'What is it, Luck?'

'May we ... *borrow* you for a moment?'

Though Tiny Elric had agreed to what Luck proposed, once it was explained that it would not harm him, it did not mean the smith's son was calm within the possession. His life ... roiled, the way he saw the world, his skills and memories, all playing before and within, churning Poum. It was only the second time they had possessed another person. The first, of course, had been Anazat and the monk had somehow been both lost and aware of what had happened, and had fought it from the beginning. Poum, inexperienced, had not been able to keep within him for long. They were not sure how long they would be able to hide within Elric. Long enough, they hoped. Long enough for ... ?

They did not know what Luck's plans were. Their father's strengths were in his mind. Yet it is my other father, father of my flesh, who comes now, on this boat fast approaching. And Intitepe has different ... strengths.

Poum-as-Elric, along with the rest of the crew, just stared. The Seafarer vessel, twice the size of their own, was perhaps two hundred paces away now. They could see its details, its crew. Most wore only a loincloth and a turban, protection against the hot sun. Their skins were a light brown, like Poum's. Their faces, even at this distance, were like Poum's too. The only other they'd ever seen who was the same was Atisha, their mother. Dark hair, almond-shaped eyes. Everyone else, even their little brother and sister who were a blend, was different.

Poum was looking at their people. One especially, who stood near the only woman they could see, both on the raised aft deck.

Intitepe. The father who they'd heard so much about. Who'd tried to kill them almost from their birth. Who was spinning the wheel now, swooping ever closer, closer, close enough already for his shout to be heard. The first shock, the sound of his voice – so like Atisha's, low in pitch. The second shock, that the words shouted were not in Bunami, the main language of Ometepe, but in Midgarthian.

'Lower your sails,' Intitepe called, 'and prepare to receive your lord.'

It did not need the Bow of Mavros, clearly pointed at their midships. Luck had already decided with Ulrich that to fight was futile. Whatever was to be their fate – all their fates – would be determined by words.

Ulrich called out a command. Not all sails were taken down, for the ship would have wallowed, but most were, and they slowed. Intitepe shouted orders to match the lowering, the speed. He was skilled, and the two vessels were soon running parallel, and a short bowshot apart. Within moments, three smaller boats were lowered from davits on the deck. Men descended, armed men. Last to climb down the rope webs was Intitepe, moving very slowly because he was helping another behind him to place her feet in the woven rungs – the old woman Poum had seen standing with him on the deck. As soon as they were sitting, the three boats set off, powered by oars. One made for the bow of the Midgarthian vessel, one for the aft. The third, carrying Intitepe, let them precede, grapple, disgorge their men. Only when these had surrounded and disarmed Ulrich's crew, all gathered on the *caraca*'s maindeck, did Intitepe's boat draw alongside.

The Fire King climbed up the wooden ladder built into the vessel amidships. A door set in the wall was already swung open. He stepped through, then reached back and down, offering an arm. A gnarled hand gripped his, and he helped the woman climb up onto the deck. She was very old, judging by her wrinkled skin and the whiteness of her hair. But that was still thick, and though she leaned on a stick, she was upright and looked strong.

All his men on the deck fell to both knees and touched their heads to the deck. Following Luck's lead, Poum-within-Elric and everyone else did the same. 'Good, good,' Intitepe said, in Bunami.

Poum looked up, the only one to do so. Couldn't help it. Couldn't help studying their father. Atisha had described him, when Poum nagged. Always with an edge to her voice, anger there, hurt. Described the lighter shade of brown skin, the black hair that had some grey dusted through it. Once she had talked of his eyes, how they were grey too, a thing almost unknown in Ometepe. When she'd talked of them, her anger left for a moment, replaced by a deep sadness, a well of loss.

Eyes that met Poum's now. They held each other's for a moment, before Poum looked down.

'Good, good,' Intitepe said again, then called some names, spoke some commands, still in his native tongue. The men addressed obeyed, and went off to search the ship. 'Now,' Intitepe continued, switching to Midgarthian, 'who commands here?'

'I do.' Ulrich stood, stepped forward. It had been decided before that, if possible, Luck and Poum would be concealed. And it was not a complete lie.

'Why are you sailing this way?' Intitepe crossed the deck to stand before the smith. 'From all that I have studied of the land that I rule – for Midgarth, as you know, is mine – your ships have never sailed this far south.'

'As you will know, lord, we of Midgarth are mighty sailors. Once we discovered that we could sail this way, we had to.'

'To trade?'

'Perhaps. We have some goods to—'

'Or to raid?' Intitepe interrupted. 'My studies also tell me that you are great thieves and raiders.'

'Sometimes, indeed, lord. But we are too few to raid. We seek—'

The Fire King raised a hand, and Ulrich stopped talking immediately. 'I wish for news,' Intitepe continued. 'Tell me of the world.'

'I . . . I know little of it. I am but a trader from a small town, lord.'

'Which town?'

'Askaug, lord.'

'Askaug.' Intitepe hummed the word, his gaze passing over the still-kneeling men. All kept their eyes down. 'I know this town. It is the place of your most famous gods.'

'Gods are from everywhere, lord.' Ulrich broke off, coughed, as Intitepe's eyes swivelled back to him, impatience in them at the contradiction. 'But yes, lord, some famous gods are from there.'

'I know them. After our great victory at the place you call Galahur, I wanted to learn of those I had killed.' He began to walk around the smith, his eyes gleaming. 'I killed your greatest warrior god, Bjorn Swiftsword, did you know?'

'No, lord. I mean, yes, lord, yes. They sing of your victory still.'

'Ha! Do they? Who do? Few were pleased at my coming there. The people who sought to conquer you before me. The Four Tribes.' He stopped behind Ulrich's left shoulder, and whispered, 'Tell me of them.'

'I know, uh, little, lord. They ruled us through one of us.'

'Peki Asarko. He was another not pleased at my coming. His crimes would—' He broke off, eyes narrowing. 'You said *ruled*. Ruled in the past.'

'No, lord, a slip of the tongue. Rule, they rule us.'

'Liar!' Intitepe screamed. He seized Ulrich's left hand, bent the fingers and the wrist, hard. Now it was the Fire King looking down, the smith up. 'Tell me what you know!'

'I am a simple trader, lord, I—'

Intitepe looked up, past him. 'Ha! The proof of your lie. Because a simple trader does not carry one of these.'

Poum looked, all looked – at the man who'd just emerged from the cabin below, holding the seeing globe. He and Luck had hidden it as well as they could in the time they had. Not well enough.

The Fire King kept bending the smith's wrist, until Ulrich sat quite suddenly on the deck. Then he released him, and took the globe he was proffered. 'Now, you tell me what you see in this, of the world,' he said softly, 'or you start to die, right now, but very slowly.'

There was silence for a long moment. Until another man raised his eyes, spoke.

'He cannot tell you anything. But I can.'

Intitepe looked at the speaker. 'Who are you?'

'My name is Luck.'

'Ha! I have heard of you.'

'And I of you.'

'Which means this is not a trading voyage. Am I not right?'

'You are.'

'Then would you like to tell me what it is? Or rather,' he tapped the globe, 'would you like to show me? For I can see by the darkness in your eyes, like the darkness in a munke's eyes, that you are a traveller with Sirene.'

Luck rose from his knees. 'I am. And I will tell you everything you wish to know. As long as you harm no one on this vessel.'

Intitepe stared for a moment, then laughed. 'One thing I have heard of you, Luck of Askaug, is that you are a master of bargaining. But why should I bargain, when I can get you to tell me what I want by killing your people – slowly – one after the other in front of you.'

'One thing I have heard of you, Fire Lord,' Luck replied, 'is that you have not lived for five hundred years without learning that information freely given is better than information forced.'

'You are right. It is one of the things we immortals learn, is it not?' He nodded. 'None of your people will suffer. As long as you tell me, freely, what I wish to hear.'

'I will. And will you also tell me what I wish to hear, lord?'

Intitepe's almond eyes narrowed. 'Bargaining still? Interesting. Tell me then. What is it that you wish to hear?'

'Why you have sailed across the world.'

'That's easy to answer.' Intitepe nodded. 'I have come to find my child.'

Poum, watching and listening hard, could not help the slight gasp they gave. But neither god heard, so focused were they on each other.

'All that way to slay your son?'

'No, Luck. Because he is not a son. She is not a daughter. They are both, and neither. And I know now, believe now that they are born to unite the world. My child!' His eyes glowed. 'Mine! So I have realised that it is our destiny, ours, to rule that world together.'

Poum's next, louder gasp was lost in the many, as Intitepe continued, 'So you will tell me of that world now. Tell me where I shall find my child. For I know something else about you, Luck of Askaug. That you are he who stole both mother and child.' He was the taller of the two by a little and bent now so he could look closely into the Midgarthian's eyes. 'Tell me where they are.'

'Far from here.' Luck took a breath. 'If I do, how do I know you will not kill them?'

'I have already told you what I plan to do when I find them. Both of them.'

'But can I believe that? Since you have spent so much of your life wishing to kill them.'

'You think I lie?' There was no anger in his voice, only amusement. 'Five hundred years of life has taught me that I never have to. They have also taught me to tell when people are lying to me.' He leaned in closer, so close that his eyes danced between Luck's. 'Like you just did when you said "far from here".' He nodded. 'Yet I can understand why you would not believe me. Perhaps you will believe … someone else.' He stood straight again, then called over his shoulder, 'Besema.'

The old woman came forward, her stick tapping on the wooden deck. 'Intitepe?'

He switched to Bunami. 'Tell this man – this god – if you believe I lie to them when I tell them my plans for Atisha and Poum. I will turn your words into theirs.'

She took a deep breath, let it go slowly. 'I believe what you told me. I believe that you do not wish to harm mother or child. I—'

Intitepe started to translate her words but Luck held up his hand. 'I speak some Bunami, lord,' he said, in that tongue. 'And I suspect, having lived as long, that I am as good at telling a lie from the truth as you are.' He turned to the woman, spoke. 'You are Besema. The rebel. The leader. Atisha's friend.'

'I am all those things. Now tell me,' she continued, eagerly, 'do they both live?'

'They do, and they have had a happy life.'

'I praise the gods for it. The gods above, that is,' she added, glancing at Intitepe.

It made Luck smile, the touch of fierceness in the woman. He believed her, and so believed him. 'I will tell you everything,' he said, looking back at Intitepe. 'But may I tell you in my own way? Tell you first why they are where they are before I tell you the place? May I show you in the glass?'

'You may. Though I wish to tell my men whether to keep sailing south or whether we are turning north.'

'You can give that command within an hour. Is that acceptable?'

Intitepe thought for a moment. 'It is. What would make it more acceptable is if you show me while we drink some beer.' Over the sudden surprised inhalations he continued, 'We ran out of the munke's brew a week ago. And I have developed a taste for it ever since a pirat called Sekantor the Savage first gave it to me.' He shook his head. 'He had his head ripped off by a giant bear at that same battle you call "the Coming of the Dark". It is the first time I ever saw this "possession" that occurs in your northlands among your gods. It is not a sight I will ever forget.' He shuddered, then turned to Ulrich, who was still clutching his wrist. 'You northmen always have some, yes?'

'Yes, lord,' he mumbled. 'Kroken ale, the finest in the world.'

'I will be the judge of that,' Intitepe said. Then he looked up, into a sky which had started to spatter down rain again. 'I assume you keep it in the hold below. Let us go to it, then, and get out of this.'

Ulrich stepped over to the hold cover, began unfastening it.

Intitepe went to his captain and spoke rapidly. Luck bent his head to Poum, still kneeling. 'Keep out of sight,' he whispered, then went to help Ulrich with the fastenings.

Poum began to shake but it wasn't because Elric was roiling within, even though the younger smith was getting more agitated, caught in what he would think of as a dream. Poum could have held him, kept him, had they chosen to. They did not. They realised they wanted something else.

It was Intitepe. The man whose terrible crimes they'd listened to all their life. The immortal who had killed all Poum's brothers over the centuries, swum them in lava because of an ancient prophecy. Who had wanted to kill Poum themselves – until he'd accepted what all did, what a world had been changed completely because of – that Poum was neither man nor woman.

The man was a monster. The man was their father. Poum could see it in the way he held himself; in the colours of his voice, in the steel of his eyes. And they would not be shoved aside while their other father tried to quiet and soothe the monster with Kroken ale and a version of the story Luck thought he would want to hear.

So instead of answering Ulrich's call – a third father aboard, calling to his son to come away – he followed Luck, and Intitepe, and the old woman who they helped down the steep steps into the hold. Luck turned, saw. 'Elric,' he warned, 'go see to your duties.'

'They are here,' Poum said, 'for is not a child's first duty to listen to their father?'

And with that, he released Elric, stepped away from the smith's tumbling body, stepped up to Intitepe and said, 'You wished to see me ... Father!'

There was a silence, the kind that screamed. Until the true screams came, as Besema cried out, as Intitepe gasped, as Luck yelled and stepped forward too late to block the punch Poum threw which reached their father's jaw, and dropped him suddenly to the ground beside Tiny Elric.

And then the tiny hold, crowded already, was filled, as men came from the deck above, with knives in hand, knives soon at the throats of all there – groggy Elric, Luck, Poum, even Besema. The only man who did not have a blade against his skin was Intitepe, who shook off the man holding him, grabbed his knife, stood, swayed, at last focused his eyes. Stared at Poum, disbelieving, took a step towards them, all he needed in that small space.

'No!' screamed Luck, pressing his neck against the blade at his throat till the blood ran. But an iron grip held him, he could do nothing, as father and child stared at each other, and a dagger rose between them.

And then Intitepe said, 'It was not a bad punch. For a girl. But if you are also going to be a man, I will have to teach you to punch better.' He changed his grip on the knife to overhand, then drove it suddenly down into the top of the beer barrel. The scent of malt overcame the scent of fear, as Intitepe stepped close to Poum, took them by the shoulders, and pulled them into his chest.

'My child,' he murmured, 'oh, my immortal child.'

And Poum wept.

Night had fully fallen when Luck sought out Ulrich and Tiny Elric. Father and son were on the aft deck, each with one hand upon the wheel. The wind was full in their sails again, and neither had to pull much to keep the vessel steady. Luck looked beyond, to the other three ships, surging forward.

'Poum?' Ulrich asked.

'Below. They have made a nest in the hold. And by they I mean Besema, father and child.'

'Poum cannot have forgiven him,' Elric said. 'Intitepe tried to murder him.'

'They have not forgiven. But they seek to understand.' Luck scratched at the stubble on his face. 'Besides, even if they wished to fight him, now is not the time. For now, Intitepe does what Poum, what we all wish him to do.'

'Sail south with us? Fight the Four Tribes with us?' Ulrich shook himself. 'I'd rather make an alliance with a serpent.'

'Nevertheless,' Luck sighed. 'This world has made for strange alliances before, forged from former hatreds. The Horse Lords, Seafarers, Huntresses and monks all joining. The Wattenwolden siding with Corinthium. Why not Midgarth and Ometepe united?'

'It is what he thinks anyway,' grunted Tiny Elric. 'That both those kingdoms are his.'

'Well, let them be, for now. Until the greater enemy is defeated.'

'Those who fight for the One … fighting the One?'

'Why not?' said Luck. 'It is no stranger than anything else. Besides, the strangeness will not last long,' he put his hand on the wheel between the other two, and stared forward into the night, 'because all will be decided at Balbek.'

12
War Plans

On the parade ground beside the fortress, the family – father, mother, two children – jerked their last. Their strangled groans were stilled, and they swayed, silhouetted against the setting sun.

Anazat waited a few moments, then walked from the edge of the scaffold to its centre. With death as his backdrop, he looked down at the sea of faces. Five thousand men and women looked back, some of Balbek, some of the Four Tribes. 'Thus die all traitors,' he cried. 'Thus die all who turn away from the One.'

'Praise her! Praise him! Praise the One!'

Anazat turned from the gathering, and looked to the water. The harbour was crammed with vessels of all sizes and types. The largest fleet ever assembled, to move the largest army ever gathered. He would take no more chances. As soon as the wind veered to blow off the land, not from the sea – a change the locals told him might happen even this night – then, with overwhelming force he would sail to the Great City and crush its resistance. March on, and burn every village in the Wattenwold, killing everyone who did not surrender. Which would be most of that savage people. When that was done, he would bring part of the army back, march with it across the deserts and subdue Xan. It had been allowed its partial independence too long.

Within a year, with all the wealth of the conquered lands, and all the new recruits for his army – who would fight or starve – he would lead a fleet across the ocean and conquer Ometepe.

He felt suddenly tired, with all he still had to do. Swayed, and reached up to steady himself on what swung nearby – a child's foot. He looked up, at the girl's contorted face. She, daughter of a rebel father, who'd worked in Balbek to overthrow its conquerors, along with her mother and brother? They had served their purpose. Served as an example to all.

Anazat looked down to the boards of the platform. The brownish red stains there were memories of other examples, other traitors who had had their heads chopped off there. It was a different approach to the same problem: how to unite a people behind the cause. Before, he had tried to do it with the promise of love that belief in the One offered. But he had learned, in a sudden, sharp lesson, that before love must come hate. Before life, death. Previously enemies had been dealt with quietly in the dark of night. Now all had to be witnessed in the clear light of the day.

That lesson had come – suddenly, sharply – when he'd been possessed by Poum in Askaug.

Poum. He could no longer think of them as the One. Before, the child had been an idea, the subject of a prophecy, a way to bring peace first to the Four Tribes, eventually to the wide world. But that idea ended when the child had gone *inside* him. Makron had told him that the possessed never remembered the possession, except perhaps as a dream. Anazat remembered *everything*. And hated every memory.

It was like when he'd been a child himself. Born of a Huntress, and so given away because of his sex, to be raised as a monk. At seven, an older monk had raped him, doing so for the two years it took Anazat to learn, from the same monk, which plants cured and which plants killed, and to put one that killed into the man's hot wine. But terrible though it had been, he had always been able to keep a part of himself removed, a part that his abuser could never touch.

Poum had touched all of him. Penetrated everything. All his memories, all his hopes, all his dreams.

He'd concluded that Poum had been able to possess him so completely and yet leave him aware because he'd travelled so often with Sirene; that his mind was thus more open, more sensitive. It was like that dream where a monster came for him, one he could not describe, a force more than a body, taking him as he lay incapable of moving, of resisting. Yet the strangest thing had been that it wasn't just Poum taking him. He had *experienced* Poum as well. Felt, not the god he'd worshipped ever since he'd heard the saving prophecy, but … a person, a human, subject to everything that beset a person: hope, hunger, desire, even lust. Love and hatred. All overlaid with this terrible uncertainty. Poum did not embrace the very thing that made them a god, sent to save the whole world. They loathed it. They loathed being *they*. And it was the realisation of that, his part possession of the possessor, that made him certain now that Poum was not what was needed. That indeed Poum was the problem. That Poum must die, just as the monk who'd abused him had needed to die. Die as an example, a little like the family that swayed above him now. Die … so that the One could live for ever.

Someone coughed. He looked up, and saw Toparak, who assisted him. There was concern in the older monk's eyes. Anazat realised he was still holding the hanged child's foot, and let it go.

'I did not wish to disturb you, master. But the people—'

He gestured, and Anazat turned. On the parade ground, warriors and townsfolk stared back. On the faces of those nearest him, he could see unease. He didn't know how long he'd been standing there. These reveries had become a more common thing since the possession. But the lesson had been given, the message reinforced: believe only in the One. Those who don't will die. As the One will die, he thought, but said, 'Dismiss them.'

Toparak turned, clapped his hands. Three trumpeters who'd stood by in readiness raised their horns and blew. Immediately, with relief, the crowd began to disperse.

'Is all else arranged?' Anazat asked.

'All, master. The leaders of the Four Tribes will meet in the fortress as soon as the two moons rise on each horizon.'

'Good. Then I have time to pray.'

'The monks are beginning the chant of the setting sun. Will you join us?'

It had been a while. He'd been too busy. But it would be good to lose himself for a time in raised, harmonising voices. 'I will.'

Toparak smiled. 'We shall pray all the better with you with us, lord. For the winds that will blow us to our victory at Corinthium.' He glanced up, and a shadow came into his eyes as he looked at the swaying bodies. 'For the ending of all sorrows.' His eyes cleared. 'For the return of the One.'

'Yes, Toparak,' Anazat answered. 'We will chant especially for that.'

They'd been standing near the back of the crowd so they could get away more quickly. They'd stabled their horses by Balbek's western gate, and the crowd thinned as they got closer to it. Still, they kept the silence they'd mostly maintained for their day scouting the city. They would have long enough on the ride back to Malpak to share observations, and develop their plans.

Yet, with the stables in sight, busy with people, Roxanna took Ferros's arm and drew him into the shelter of a closed tavern's awning. Pulled him to her, pressing her body tightly against his. 'Are you all right?' he asked, concerned, because she was not given to displaying affection in public.

'I am. Give me a moment. It is this baby.'

'Ha!' He placed one hand on her face. 'It – you – are well?'

'Yes. Both are fine.' She took the hand, laid it on her belly. 'See? No, it is what it does to me. It makes me ... sentimental. I have never known this ... this type of feeling before.' She closed her eyes. 'Those children. On the scaffold.'

'I know. We have dealt in death, you and I, for most of our lives. But now,' he pressed his hand into her belly, 'now perhaps we think more on life.' Ferros pulled her even closer. 'So now I ask again what I asked yesterday and will tomorrow: will you remain behind when we go to the fight?'

She opened her eyes. 'And I will answer the same now as yesterday and as I will tomorrow. I will not.' She laid her hand on his face, matching his. 'Why do you fear so? I am immortal, like you.'

'But it is unlikely the child will be. Do you know an immortal child born to an immortal?'

'Other than myself, daughter of Lucan? No.'

'So then. Do not go to war.'

She pushed him away, stood straight. 'You know I must, Ferros. The squadrons of Corinthium – half our army – follow only me. They still think of you as Wattenwolden, and their recent enemy.'

Ferros ran his hand over his naked chin, his shaved head. 'Even now I am hairless?'

'Even now.' She reached up, ran fingers down his jawline. 'But will the Wattenwolden follow you into battle now you are?'

'I am the Spear and Shield, bearded or not.' He smiled. 'Besides, I will be riding into battle beside Malvolen, and him they would follow into the fires of Karatha themselves.'

'They may need to.' Roxanna stepped out from under the awning, and started walking again towards the stables. 'For you counted their numbers as well as I did.'

'Aye. They have at least five times ours. Perhaps a little more. That is why we will use my famous stratagem.'

'Which is?'

'I will tell you just as soon as I think of it.'

They'd reached the door of the stables. Though the owner was harassed by many customers, he stopped to attend to them as soon as he saw them. They had paid him double to do so. Gold stolen from the seizing of Malpak the night before was easily spent.

It was a two-hour ride back down the coast, the road well lit by the fading sun and then by the two moons' rise. They encountered no one riding the other way, would have been shocked if they had. The orders had been clear: no inhabitant of the small port was allowed to leave it. The garrison could not, for the simple reason that they were all dead.

They did not discuss what they'd seen. The odds were as clear as they were poor. But Balbek was Ferros's town and he knew its strengths and its weaknesses. As he rode he considered the famous stratagem he had yet to devise. Its main strength was the same as the one he'd employed the night before at Malpak. Sudden surprise. All he knew for certain was that, before the two moons set this night, he would be riding down this road again at the head of a small army.

On the outskirts of the town they were challenged, recognised, passed. They then rode on to the centre through the horse yards. Those had been the main reason for seizing this town above any other – for Malpak had been where the army of Corinthium bred its mounts. The conquering Horse Lords, cavalrymen too, had recognised a good set-up when they saw it, and continued it there. It had been the way he'd finally persuaded Malvolen to join the fight. Sailing across the Great Sea, far from their forests, to fight a numerically larger enemy – on foot! – was not the Wattenwolden way. But the promise of horses had been enough. Besides, the old warlord accepted that this was the best chance both to avenge the betrayal at the Tribute feast, and to defeat foes who would otherwise come for them in numbers that would be impossible to counter.

The man himself was at the entrance to his pavilion, pitched between the horse yards and the town centre. Malvolen and some others were throwing javelins, breaking off when Ferros and Roxanna rode up. 'Well?' he said, as they dismounted and turned their horses over to grooms. 'Did you learn all you needed to?'

'We did. And we will tell you shortly.' Ferros lifted the wineskin he was offered, squirted liquid into his mouth. 'But tell me first – have the Northmen come?'

'No. I have riders out further west, reporting back. No one has been sighted.' He sniffed. 'Do we need them?'

'Need? No. They will not be coming in numbers. But I would have liked that man Luck at my side in what is to come.' He shrugged. 'Never mind. Shall we gather in your pavilion, lord, and plan?'

'I need a little time, Ferros,' Roxanna said. 'I must go and see the City Guard.'

'Bring back their commander, when,' he squinted up, 'when Horned Saipha hangs off the port's watch tower.'

'I will.'

She turned, walked away. The two men watched her go. 'I can see why you would risk your life for her, Arcturien,' Malvolen said, using Ferros's Wattenwolden name. 'But do you really trust her? She was our enemy until most recently. And that traitor Barallingen screamed before the flames took him that she had seduced him. That it was she who organised the betrayal at the Tribute feast, not her husband, Makron.'

Ferros considered again. He had hated her far longer than he had loved her. Knew the levels of deceit she could sink to. But now? 'I do trust her, lord. I have my … reasons.'

Mavolen looked into his eyes a moment longer before nodding and glancing down – at his Balbekian clothes. 'Go and change your gear, Arcturien. Because if you are going to persuade my warriors of your great plan you are going to need to look like the Spear and Shield of our tribe to do it.'

'I will,' Ferros replied, and headed for his own tent. There he worked with ink and a stencil on two cured sheepskins, on which had already been drawn maps of Balbek. When he was done, he stripped, poured a bucket of water over himself, then slowly began to dress in his fine Wattenwolden armour, thinking all the time. He could do nothing now about his lack of hair. But in some ways, perhaps, that was for the best. For if he could be both the clean-shaven soldier of Corinthium he'd always been, and the scale-coated forest warrior he'd chosen to become, perhaps he could lead this small, divided army, made up of enemies who had fought each other for centuries until recently, to victory against a great foe. He donned his City helmet and his Wattenwolden long sword; both made him realise that in their divisions also lay a kind of strength. By the time he picked up his case of maps, he had his plan.

As Horned Saipha touched the tower, he walked up to Malvolen's pavilion. The chief had had a table brought from the town and placed before the tent, the inside of which, even at night, was too hot to be comfortable. Around one end of the table were the leaders of the twelve tribes of the Wattenwolden, with Malvolen the only one sitting. Roxanna was at the other end. She too had changed, into her customary body-clinging leather, but wore on top of it the breastplate of Corinthium, embossed with the state's twin eagles, over which was draped the city's purple sash. Beside her, dressed in an officer's tunic and armour, stood Speros, a confident young man recently appointed to lead the five squadrons of the City Guard. Six of those stood behind him at attention, holding pikes.

The former enemies looked uneasily at each other down the length of the table. No one spoke, but the silence was loud with ancient animosities.

Their separation is my plan, Ferros thought and went straight to the middle of the table. He looked slowly to both ends, the man who was of both Corinthium and the Wattenwold, the link between the two.

He took off his Corinthian helmet, drew and laid down the Wattenwolden sword, then opened the case, pulled out the two sheepskins and spread them over the table. One was a wider map of the area with Balbek at its centre. The other showed the town in more detail: its defences, and where each of the Four Tribes and their native allies were gathered. He cleared his throat, and spoke.

'Our enemies are getting restless, as they wait for the wind to change. It is at this time of year, near midsummer, that the cooler wind from the north, the rodun, that brought us to this coast, yields to the hot desert wind from the south, the kana, also known as the Breath of Sadrak.'

'Hotter than this?' Malvolen who, like all Wattenwolden, was used to the cool northern forests, was dabbing his face with a cloth.

'Much hotter, lord. You will know the change immediately.' Ferros looked up, at the platter-sized leaves of the giant alian-tha stirring in the breeze. Small birds swooped, perched and squabbled over the insects that moved through the branches. 'It may be even as soon as tonight.'

'And as soon as it does they will sail?'

'Within a day or two, yes, lord. So many crammed into a

small, hot town is causing tensions, even if they are all believers in the One. They will want to be aboard as soon as they can be.'

'So we attack tonight.'

'We do.' He looked left and right, at Corinthians and Wattenwolden. 'And though we are united in a cause, and fight the same enemy, we will fight separately, in separate tasks.'

There was a sound, a clear sigh moving around the table. 'Come closer all, and let me show you what the Lady Roxanna and I learned. Of their dispositions and how we can defeat them.' All gathered and he took out his bestrel, a carved stick the length of a forearm that officers carried more to denote their rank than for any practical purpose. Though it could be useful for disciplining a disobedient soldier; or, as in this case, for pointing.

Ferros began on the wider chart, tapping: 'Here we are at Malpak. We took two hours to return, without tiring our horses. We will leave at midnight so as to arrive an hour before the dawn.'

'That's four hours later. Why twice the time, Arcturien?'

'Again, so as not to tire the horses. As most will be carrying a double load.'

'How so?'

'Seven hundred Wattenwolden warriors will each bear a member of the City Guard.'

Again the words stirred the men at the table, not as contentedly. 'I thought you said we would fight separately?' It was a chieftain who asked, one whom Ferros had never liked: Trosten, younger brother of the executed traitor Barallingen. 'Our horses are not meant to be asses for burden.'

'No, Trosten. But it would take the City Guard nine or ten hours to march to Balbek. They would then arrive long past dawn, and too exhausted to join a fight that will already be over.'

The chieftain jutted out his jaw. 'And why would it be?'

'Because although we Wattenwolden are the greatest fighters in the world, even seven hundred of us cannot alone defeat near five thousand of this enemy.'

'*We?*' Trosten began. 'When were you—'

'Silence, Trosten, and let Arcturien speak,' Malvolen interrupted.

'Thank you, lord.' Ferros placed the tip of his bestrel on the skin again. 'Here, on the western edge of the town, is where the Horse Lords are camped. It is where their horses are tethered too. At dawn, on a trumpet, the Lady Roxanna will lead one hundred Wattenwolden to drive off all their horses at the edge of their camp. Then they will have to fight on foot, surprised and unarmoured, against our guards,' he nodded at their young officer who smiled, 'who will slaughter them.'

'The Lady Roxanna leading Wattenwolden?' Malvolen growled, mutters coming from all around.

'Guiding them, I meant. Not leading, of course. But she knows exactly where the horse lines run.' He glanced across at Roxanna who nodded. 'Then she will return and lead her own troops, the City Guard.'

'So I will lead my men?'

'You … *could*, my lord, if you so choose. Though having scouted the land, I had hoped to use your special skills for another purpose.'

'What skills?'

'Those of hunting. For is it not said that Malvolen can stalk through a forest without making a sound and shoot a sparrow from a tree in the dark at fifty paces?'

'You have learned the tricks of Corinthium with your flatteries, boy,' the old chief grunted, then shrugged. 'Though it is true, there's never been a hunter to match me in the tribe. I could pluck you one of these off a branch right now if someone would bring me my bow.' He glanced up at the birds flitting in the foliage then around at his men to see if any would make an argument. None did. He looked back at Ferros. 'Do you wish me to kill sparrows, Arcturien?'

'No, lord. Huntresses.' He slid his stick to the eastern side of Balbek. 'In these woods, the Huntresses have made their camp. They like to be as far away from the men of the other tribes as they can. They are here, in two great pavilions.' He lifted, tapped. 'I fear them almost above all their other warriors. They might even be able to rival you with a bow, lord. So if they were to come swiftly to the Horse Lords' aid, they would kill many of our guards. Can you delay them? Even stop them?' He slid his stick in a half circle past the town, 'You ride around here, kill their sentries silently and, when you hear the trumpets of attack, attack yourself. Fire arrows for the pavilions, bone and steel for the enemy, then—'

'You don't need to advise me on my work,' Malvolen growled, though there was more amusement than irritation in his voice now. Indeed, he laughed. 'No, wait, that is your job, isn't it, as my Spear and Shield?' He scratched his beard, peering at the inked skins. 'How many Huntresses are there?'

'We calculate four hundred.'

'And how many men do I take?'

'One hundred.'

'One hundred?' His bushy eyebrows went up. 'If she's led a hundred in to drive off the horses, where will the other six hundred be?'

Ferros brought the stick down again. 'With me. Here. Slaughtering Seafarers.'

'The port?'

'Yes. Perhaps the biggest part of their force is those Seafarers. Three thousand men between the ships and the docks.'

'Three thousand? That's a lot for six hundred to take.'

'Yes. But at dawn half will be aboard ship, and half still sleeping off all the wine they've guzzled in the brothels and taverns of the docks.'

'We seem to be killing a lot of dozy people right now, Arcturien.' Malvolen sat back in his chair. 'It all sounds so easy. Will it be?'

Ferros paused. He wanted everyone to believe they could win. And Malvolen was right, he had learned some flatteries in the Sanctum on the Hill. But these were experienced warriors he was speaking to here. They knew this was a gamble. How they were outnumbered. And that what sounded easy beneath an aliantha tree on a warm evening in Malpak would be quite different in a cool dawn in Balbek. 'It will not be easy, lord. These men – and women – have conquered most of the world. They are excellent fighters. But with this plan,' he shrugged, 'we have a chance.'

'That is all a warrior can ask,' the old chief said softly then leaned in again, peered. 'But what is this on your map? This black square on the edge of the port? Why have you drawn ... is that a skull above it?'

'I did not draw it. The first map-maker, who is from the city, did. But it is apt.' Ferros took a deep breath and let it out slowly. 'It is the fortress of Balbek. It is their special place of torture and execution. But it is also where the Warrior Monks live. Perhaps close to two hundred of them. I would like to take it fast, almost above everything else. Anazat is there, the leader of them all. And if you cut off the head, the body may die.' A sudden flash of Makron's head tumbling onto the platform back in the city came to him, and he looked up, catching Roxanna's eye again. 'But the monks barely sleep, they are always up and chanting, so we cannot take them by surprise. And they are perhaps the greatest fighters of all the enemy.' He shrugged. 'My hope, since we cannot take the fortress by stealth, or force, is that we kill almost everyone else before the monks can respond.'

An uneasy silence came as all stared down, contemplating the extent of what they must do. Ferros searched for some way to break it, to rouse them again to the fight. And then … something fell onto his head.

He reached up, brought his hand down, saw … bird shit. Yellow and white, it was running down his face. He let out a curse – and one by one everyone began to laugh. It was so absurd. All had been considering their likely deaths at dawn – but the birds in the tree didn't care.

The laughter grew, as Ferros cursed and wiped. Then, as it started to fade, another voice came, unheard to that point. Speaking not Wattenwolden but the language of Corinthium.

'I am so sorry. My, uh, control is not what it was.'

Everyone leaped back, startled. All reached for weapons. All looked up – at the man now sitting on a tree branch above them.

'Ai!' Luck called, peering down. 'It's a bit of a drop. Could one of you fetch a ladder?'

Despite the bird shit on his face, Ferros laughed. 'Welcome, Luck,' he said.

Though he had been delighted to find Ferros again, Luck had chosen not to reveal himself straight away. He did not know who these others were, though he recognised them from those early voyages he'd taken with Sirene when Anazat had shown him the world. But why the young Corinthian warrior was now allied with the fierce Wattenwolden he did not understand. More, why was the woman – Roxanna was her name – there? When Luck had last heard of her she was ruling the empire for the Four Tribes. Yet there she was, helping to plot their defeat.

Listening answered some of the questions, but not all. What he established was what he'd hoped to learn – that the Four

Tribes would be attacked in the morning. They had arrived in time, but only just. And though they did not arrive in numbers – a storm had scattered Intitepe's small fleet, so he had only one hundred warriors still with him – they did have some useful skills and weapons to add to the fight. Things that Luck was keen to discuss.

A ladder was brought. Luck climbed down, then gazed up at all the tall warriors standing round the table. Though he had seen them, he imagined most of them had never seen a Northman. Since, only sixteen years before, the worlds of Midgarth and Corinthium had been separate and unknown to each other, he was sure he was a curiosity. This at least he knew – nearly every Wattenwolden warrior had served some time fighting as a mercenary in Corinthium's army. And since he had spent part of his time in the steading teaching himself languages, he spoke to them again in the language of the city now.

'I may have a solution for you, Ferros,' Luck said, as he crossed to the table, and tapped the skull at the centre of the map, 'for how you can take this fortress.'

He sometimes forgot that other people were not as relaxed about his sudden appearances as he was. Shock had held those at the table. Now, oaths broke out, warriors drew swords, and the men of the Guard lowered their spears. 'It is all right,' Ferros called loudly, stepping forward, arms raised. 'This is the man I have been waiting for. An ally in the fight.'

'By the gods, Arcturien, but where did he come from? How did he—?' Malvolen glanced up into the canopy then down at Luck. 'He does not look shaped for climbing.'

Luck opened his mouth to answer – but Ferros intervened. 'Later for that perhaps, lord, since time moves against us.' He looked at the Northman. 'You say you have a solution to our problem?'

'Perhaps. It's risky. But no riskier than everything else you discussed.'

'So how will we take the fortress?'

Luck smiled. 'I'll fly to it.'

It was later, in Ferros's tent, after Malvolen had allowed his Spear and Shield to go and examine the newcomer alone while he prepared his forces for the fight, that Luck explained how. Both Roxanna, who'd also come, and Ferros were incredulous to begin with, and hard to persuade. It seemed impossible. But then Luck reminded them that since the whole plan was close to impossible, why not just one more thing?

When Luck returned to his own camp on a hill overlooking the harbour of Malpak, Poum, Intitepe and Besema were all still awake and by a fire, despite the heat of the night. Necessary for the cauldron that swung over it, filled with heated ale, which was the Fire King's favourite way of drinking it. Accepting a goblet, Luck sipped, then looked at them each in turn. Each had a burning question in the flames reflected in their eyes.

They are so different from those I have just come from, he thought, with their brown faces, their dark, almond-shaped eyes. Small, like me. But fierce as any Wattenwolden. And as complicated in relationship as Ferros and Roxanna: love existing so long within hate. It still played there in their eyes, along with the questions.

Besema. Lover of a king, seventy years before. Hating him for those seventy years since. Now … *allied* with him at least, putting aside hatred for the cause that stood beside her.

For Poum. Child of her friend – Luck's wife – Atisha. Child embodying a prophecy – of the doom of one world, the rising of another. The death of a king, the man – the immortal – beside them.

Intitepe. The Fire King. Tyrant, murderer, of men and of

children – and father. Of all the complexities, was that not the greatest? For the father who had tried to kill the son and failed. For his child, neither son nor daughter and both, now seen by him not as threat but as destiny? And did Poum accept that destiny now? Accept the father who'd tried to kill them? Who they'd been raised all their life to hate?

Luck shook his head. Such love, such hate. Even for a four-hundred-year-old immortal it was too much to deal with, especially now. Ferros, in the conversation they'd just had in his tent, had quoted the soldier's first rule of battle to him: forget everything else. Deal with what is in front of you. This enemy. This blow.

It was all they could do now. All the questions in their eyes must remain unanswered – except one: what they would do come the dawn. That had an answer that would please them all.

'We fight,' he said, and unfurled the map Ferros had given him. 'And this is how.'

13
The Battle for Balbek

The sweat drop ran down and, finding the trail of all the others, vanished into the valley between her breasts.

Roxanna wondered again why she'd chosen to fight swathed in leather. Especially on a night like this. Ferros had said that the southern wind might come this very day. He'd been right. The Breath of Sadrak he'd called it, named for a dragon-headed god worshipped by the people across the desert, in the land of Xan.

The people there were black-skinned like her and she'd often thought to travel there someday, to see if there were more similarities than colour and height. Just like her grandfather, a Timian monk whom she'd never known, who had journeyed all the way to Corinthium, sired a child with a local woman, fair-skinned: a daughter who was her father Lucan's consort for a time, and died even as Roxanna was born – three hundred years before.

She shook her head. Dark, the doubling of the heat in a few moments, together with what lay ahead, made her mind move in strange ways. For she knew why she dressed thus. Firstly it was easy to move in leather; to kill in it. Secondly, sometimes in the middle of a fight it was useful to provoke a man's lust; either to open him to a killing thrust when his eyes went, albeit briefly, to her breasts. Or to persuade one of her own to get her away, if necessary at the cost of his life.

She looked to one side, then to the other, to the men within her sight. Wattenwolden all, none of them looking at her, though they had looked before, some in desire, most in disgust that a woman was leading them. A woman from their ancient foes, no less. All looking ahead, through the trees, to the torches that flared in the horse lines of their enemies.

As she did again now. She had described the gulley that led from this wood into those lines, how it split into three closer to them. It was easy to miss the junction which was why she … *guided*. She smiled at Ferros's rationale. She would *guide* these Wattenwolden to this first vital part of his battle plan. Then she would return to the squadrons from the city, seven hundred men she'd helped train. There would be no question of who led *them* into the attack.

She sat, and sweated, and wished that the sun would begin to trouble the treetops. Only at the first hint of dawn could she be assured that the whole force was in position for their various tasks. Only then would Ferros give the whistle he said he'd striven so hard to master. The one that would pierce the morning stillness. The one that would send them all into the battle for Balbek.

Birds began to call. None were him but they sensed the coming of the light before any human could.

And then it came. Though he was five hundred paces away, outside the western gate of the city, the sound was clear. Three notes: high, lower, high.

Down the line, every man stirred and drew a javelin from the sheath that rested on his mount's flank. There were six men on foot directly behind her, and they did now what had been commanded – opened a cauldron that contained burning logs, blew the smoulder into flame, then dipped the cloth heads of torches into it. A dozen caught, and the men ran with them each way down the line.

She looked each way too, saw the flaring in the woods. Those ahead would see it soon enough, and much closer to.

The first man back dipped a last torch, came and handed it to her. She held it in her left hand, drew her own javelin with her right. After nearly three centuries' experience, she did not need to grasp the reins of Shadowfire, the stallion she'd ridden for twenty years. He danced a little, as keen to be gone as she. She looked down at the torch-giver. 'Go bring the Guard,' she said. Then, as he ran off, she waved her torch to either side and led the Wattenwolden at a canter out from the treeline.

The first gulley they entered was wide enough for four to ride abreast. When they reached the junction, the two to each side were narrower. She felt, rather than saw, the men behind her split. They each had their tasks, their destinations. Hers was ahead, in the only place in the lines where Horse Lords were gathered.

They burst from the gulley, following her flaming brand. She rode straight at the tent in the clearing. A man stepped out who must have heard the drumming of their hooves. Putting her javelin into his open mouth as he began to scream, she drew her sword.

Ferros lowered the fingers from his mouth and began to run. A group of six Wattenwolden ran either side of him, carrying ladders. The guards in the tower above the western gate spotted them, but neither man made the alarm bell they ran for, because at least two of the fifty arrows that flew in between the roof and the wall found them.

Ladders slapped into the crenels. Ferros was at the top of the one to the left of the tower in three heartbeats while Domen, who had followed at his heels like a hound ever since the fight after the Tribute feast, was as fast up the other. There were no further guards on the walls. As soon as the Breath of Sadrak had started to blow, an hour before, most had left to prepare for their departure.

Ferros and Domen met at the inner side of the gate. They put their shoulders under the crossbar, bent, and lifted it away. Other men came and heaved open the tall, heavy gates. Once again, Ferros put fingers to his lips and blew, a different call – a single note, but sliding up and down in pitch.

It was the signal for five hundred Wattenwolden to come galloping through the gate. They looked like a comet flaming through the sky for many had torches and their flames streamed backwards.

On the open square just within the walls, they reined in. Fifty men dismounted, tethered their horses, and ran up into the tower or into windows that overlooked the space, clutching bows and sheaves of arrows. They had been selected by lot, to cover the retreat if one became necessary. All had grumbled but accepted the command.

As they took their positions, the last one hundred soldiers rode in. They had followed more slowly, for each carried a double load – behind them on the horse's rump and clinging to their backs were other, very different warriors. These wore wood-slat armour, and helms that were carved of hardwood, not forged in metal. The warriors from Ometepe.

Ferros shook his head. It was a late, mad addition to his plan. But Luck had insisted.

Horses were brought to the men who'd taken the gates. When all were mounted, Ferros seized the torch handed him, drew his sword, cried, 'With me!' and kicked his mount into motion.

It had been strange to walk disguised through the streets where he'd grown up. It was doubly strange to be riding down them leading half a thousand Wattenwolden and a hundred men from across the ocean, with the only sounds their hoof-falls on the packed sand, and the occasional shriek of a startled citizen, which vanished fast behind. Usually they rode screaming into battle, calling upon their gods and ancestors, cursing their enemies. Not this time though. The port was a ten-minute canter from the western gate, and Ferros had impressed upon them that they must give as little warning as possible of their coming.

Someone must have heard something – at least the man who was standing in the centre of the last street they turned onto, that led straight to the port. He screamed, one word, in the Horse Lord tongue. Ferros didn't waste a javelin on him, just rode him down.

That last street was lined each side by rooming houses, brothels and taverns. Several men rose on porches from where their carousing had left them; stared in silent disbelief, died from a flung spear or shot arrow. At the end of the street, Ferros reined in before the port's closed and slatted gates. Through those he could see the raised platform. The family's bodies still dangled from ropes above it. His fellow Balbekians, slain by this enemy. At the far end of the port square sat the squat black tower of Balbek's fortress.

He looked from it up into a sky that was already lightening. And there it was. Sent a swift, whispered prayer for success to Luck then turned to look at his command. The warriors from Ometepe had dismounted and had already unbarred the gate to the port. Their leader, a fierce, quiet, older man with grey eyes and a name Ferros found hard to pronounce, studied him, impatiently awaiting the signal.

All along the road, his Wattenwolden had halted, every second man dismounting and swivelling to face a different side of the street. Ferros dismounted too. There was no need for silence now. 'For the Wattenwold! Gods and Soil!' he yelled, stooped, and pitched his torch straight through the front window of the building before him. Beside him, six men did the same, as others did all down the street. Then drawing his sword, he charged into the flames.

His men cried, 'For the Wattenwold! Gods and Soil!' and charged too. Behind him, he heard the screech of gate hinges as the men from Ometepe ran through.

At first Anazat thought it was only another monk's voice. Not all of them were blessed with a good one, the ability to harmonise, even to hold a line. Mostly the poor singers whispered along, so as not to take away from the glory of the chant raised for the One. But this voice jarred, and Anazat paused his own chanting to listen for the offender, to rebuke with a hiss, to halt him. As he listened, the voice came a little clearer; voices, he realised, more than one. Many more, and growing in number. Some were raised in screams. It was not the first time he'd heard screaming in the night, for the Seafarers were celebrating their departure in their customary way – any way they pleased. Now, though, there was no accompanying drunken laughter, no foul-worded songs.

Those are screams of terror, he thought, and grabbed Toparak who was still chanting next to him. 'Go and see who is making that noise and why,' he commanded.

The monk nodded, rose, exited. The opening door let in more noise. Anazat had feared one thing this night – that even though the native allies, drawn from the various tribes of Sarphardi and Assani, had been confined to their camps, with whores and beer sent to them, some would decide to visit the street of sin anyway. It had happened before, the various tribes remembering that they had fought each other for centuries and had only recently been united under the One. Drink and lust confused them further and they'd quarrel, violently. Over the years, Anazat had been forced to hang many troublemakers to set an example. He hoped it was not the case here. On the eve of invasion he wanted – needed – unity.

The door opened again, bringing much more noise. Toparak crossed swiftly to him. Even in the candlelight, Anazat could see fear in the man's eyes. 'It is a raid, master,' he said.

'What? Who is here to raid?' Anazat grabbed the man by the collar of his robe and pulled himself up from his knees.

'I only glimpsed, master. But,' Toparak swallowed, 'it looks like Wattenwolden.'

'Watt— What are Wattenwolden doing in Balbek? Who could—' He broke off, black eyes shooting wide. 'Ferros!' he cried. Then he breathed deep, settled himself. He had one of the largest armies the Four Tribes had ever raised. Twice as big as that sent to invade Corinthium the first time. No *raid* could stop them. 'Come! To the roof. I must see.' He left the room, began running up the stairs, calling over his shoulder. 'Have the fastest men ready to run to the camps of the Horse Lords and the Huntresses with the orders I shall give them.'

It was three flights of stairs to the roof. Panting heavily, he burst through the door, ran to the low walls. Across the port yard, through the gates, he could see the street of sin. Part of it anyway – and the part he could see was on fire. Nearer to, he could see some Seafarers fighting ... whom he could not tell. He rubbed his eyes, cursed his age-diminshed eyeight, swivelled, looked towards the harbour. The railings of most of the ships were crowded with men who'd been denied a last night ashore in order to keep the boats ready for the turning of the wind – which, Anazat realised as soon as he thought of it, had already happened. 'Send a messenger to the ships. All crews to arm and come ashore. Criminals are in the port. They must be driven out.'

He expected the instant, 'Yes, master,' that was Toparak's usual response. When no answer came, Anazat turned – to find that the old monk was not even looking at him. He was staring over his head, into the sky. 'What are you doing?' he snapped. 'Send the messengers!'

Toparak didn't reply – in words. Just raised an arm and pointed above Anazat's head.

'What?' he grunted, swivelling back. At first he couldn't see anything. Then he did. But because it was something he'd never seen before, his eyes could make no sense of it.

It was moving slowly towards him through the air, at three times the height of the fortress. It reminded him of the globe he used with Sirene. And even though this one had no glass, there was smoke around it, from flames that appeared to rise up within some kind of basket tethered below the globe. In that he saw ... heads, of people, at least ten. Which changed his perspective on the globe: it was enormous. As it drew closer, he suddenly was overcome with something he had not felt in decades: terror.

Followed by his monks, Anazat fled the roof of the fortress as Besema's air globe completed its descent.

Luck shaped the bird's wings, bending them to the wind. At his wingtip, Poum did the same. The rope around their feathered chests tightened, then eased, as the globe followed the slight change of direction. Besema had assured him that they would not be pulling so much as guiding, and it had proved to be true. Though she said that she had discovered some ways to steer her globes in her years of experimentation, it was still hard to reach a single place accurately. Luck, with his god's powers, had suggested a way of doing just that.

Yet she was guiding too, releasing gas from the globe, carefully judging the descent, calling out to Luck and Poum to adjust when she needed. Between them all, they brought the globe over the squat black tower at the edge of Balbek's port.

The bird he'd possessed – one unknown in Midgarth and the biggest he'd ever seen – had a huge wingspan, perfect for gliding upon the hot air rising from the local deserts but not for hovering in place. So as soon as they were over the roof, and the air globe began a sharp direct descent, he dropped ahead of it, perched, transformed, shook off the tying rope. Beside him, Poum did the same, and they both only just got out of the way in time before the basket hit, slid, then tipped. Immediately, the first of its occupants tumbled out.

Five men seized the dangling ropes to hold the globe in place, Besema still giving orders from the basket. 'Did you see them, Father?' Poum called. 'The men who fled?'

'I did. Monks.' He thought back to all those he'd known at the Keep. One especially. 'They are not the kind to be frightened for long. We only have a little time.' He ran to the edge of the roof, looked towards the town, saw the flames, heard the screams and the clash of steel. Between him and it, there was a body of men, who stepped away from bodies on the ground and began running fast towards them. They wore wood-slat armour. 'Come, let us go and let your other father in.'

He knew that every part of Ferros's plan was mad, and his own refinements only more so. Such madness demanded but one thing: no hesitation. Luck looked up at Besema, who was adjusting the flames within the basket. Keeping it from flying away, while five men secured their ropes, then joined Luck, Poum and the other five at the door.

Swivelling, Luck led his men off the roof. Immediately he heard shouts, commands; somewhere within a bell was jangling harshly.

He plunged down the dark stairwell. The first two flights they encountered no one. On the next landing, though, black-robed monks were gathering, turning startled towards the men in gold-rimmed armour suddenly in their midst. Luck stepped aside, pulling Poum with him, and let the elite warriors of Ometepe obey one of only two orders their king had given them: kill everyone who gets in your way.

They did so rapidly, efficiently; the monks were both surprised and unarmed. With the landing swept clear, the warriors charged on, Luck and Poum following.

The main floor had many more people in it, at least one hundred, and many of these, Luck saw in a swift glance from the last landing, were arming. He'd seen the monks at the Keep practising with a variety of weapons, but they were most deadly with a type of long spear that also had a cutting axe blade at one end, and a hook. Some here had such spears in their hands, but like the men on the landing above they were so shocked by the warriors running down the stairs that for a moment, none moved.

The monks were between them and their objective, the door. So Luck and Poum each pulled out one of their particular weapons, a glana bag – filled with oil, and lit from a small brand Poum carried – and hurled them at the beams above the monks' heads.

The bags burst, flamed. Molten fire rained down. Leaving the gods behind, the men from Ometepe embraced the mayhem and ran down the last flight of stairs and through the mob, cutting and slicing, not pausing, in order to obey the second order they'd been given – unbolt and throw open the door to their king.

'Intitepe!' The man – the immortal – screamed his own name and led his hundred men into the fight.

Poum had insisted that *they* would not be left behind, despite all arguments against their going. Had only finally been accepted when they said they would possess a beast and come anyway. Then, given that they had never trained as a fighter, there seemed to be but one place where they would be useful – guiding the air globe, with Luck.

They and their one father had stayed on the landing from which they'd thrown their glana. Now Poum watched their other father fighting, with a skill they envied, desired.

A monk had run at him, his strange spear circling through the air, at last dropping from on high, the axe blade aimed to split Intitepe in half from crown to toe. But the blade found air, not bone and flesh, as the Fire King lunged under it, into the monk, right hand on his sword grip, left placed against the blade's back, blunt edge, opening the monk's neck as he passed by, moving on to duck low beneath the next man's swung blow and pass his sword through his leg. All the while his wedge of warriors was cutting through the black robes, making for the stairs where Poum and Luck waited.

A noise behind them. Four survivors of the first assault above were coming down the stairs to join the fight. Luck turned, and used the only other weapon he'd ever been gifted with – the slingshot. Stone fitted, rope whirling in an instant above his head, almost the next he released and the stone flew true, straight into the forehead of the leading monk. He fell without a sound, bar the crash of his spear-axe as it dropped onto the stairs and slid downwards, forcing Poum to jump over it or lose a foot.

They looked up, at Luck drawing his short axe. He was so small, compared to the three men now starting again down the stairs. And Poum knew this father at least was no fighter.

But *they* were.

As soon as they touched the spear at their feet they knew it. Luck had told them before, how you gained from each possession. Some skill, some insight, though what a man could retain and use from an animal was small indeed.

Not so when you have possessed a man. Everything they'd taken in their time within Anazat was still there. Including how to use the weapon they now grasped and spun through the air, rushing past Luck into the attack.

The first monk, taken off guard by the speed of the cut, died surprised. The second, with a yell, jabbed the point of his spear hard at Poum's face. They swivelled, as they'd seen their father swivel below and, just like him, placed one hand at the back of their weapon and stepped in fast, the axe blade opening their opponent's chest, the man's body falling away.

A yell behind. Poum turned to see Luck disarmed, his hatchet knocked aside. Desperately, the god hurled himself forward to grab the monk around his knees. The man swayed, and Poum swung, feeling the weapon's heft, its perfect balance, using both to take the man's head.

As the monk fell, body and head separately, Luck looked up, amazed. 'Where did you learn to fight like that?' he gasped. Then Poum saw the answer to his own question come into his father's eyes. 'Of course,' he said, 'Anazat.'

Poum raised the spear – kazana, he recalled suddenly, that was its name – and gazed into the fight below. Many more monks lay dead than men from Ometepe. Their other father was still in the middle of it, dealing death. With a surging, savage joy they knew that they would join him, to deal more.

Then they became aware of someone behind them again on the stairs. They whirled, spear rising – and Sayel, Besema's assistant, screamed and raised her hands.

'What is it?' said Luck, taking her arm. 'Why are you not with your mistress?'

Sayel looked past him, her eyes wide, terror in them, as she looked at the fight, the dead and dying. Luck snapped his fingers. 'What, girl?'

Her eyes focused on him. 'She said you must come. That there is danger.'

'She is attacked?'

'No.' She tugged his arm. 'She says you must come and see.'

Poum saw Luck hesitate. 'Go, Father.' They turned back to the fight. 'I will stay here.'

They smiled as they said it.

Luck nodded, turned and, stopping only to pick up his axe, followed Sayel back up the stairs as fast as his limp could carry him.

When Luck reached the roof he looked first towards the globe. It appeared to be fine, not straining too much against its tethers. But Besema was at one edge of the basket, staring out to the water. 'What is it?' he called.

She didn't reply, simply pointed. Luck looked.

It was hard to tell at first, because he'd only glanced at the harbour before, and the ships waiting ready for the army to embark. It had been known, and discussed, that some Seafarers would have been left aboard, and that they might come to the aid of their brothers on the shore. Everyone hoped they would be too few to make a difference.

But then he looked beyond the anchored ships, which had their sails furled and their oars stored, to the mouth of the harbour and the vessels there which had their sails furled but their oars in the water. Twenty of them at least, coming into port.

He lurched fast to the basket. 'Pass me my trumpet,' he said to Besema.

She handed it down. It was a habit born in the years of raid and counter-raid in Midgarth, to always have one near, to warn of a sudden attack. He remembered the last time he had needed it, all those years before, when Stromvar Dragon Lord had come to conquer Askaug, and Luck had been the first to see his ships from the cliffs. He'd blown then, and he blew now, though this time he blew the notes Ferros had taught him, the ones used in the Wattenwold to order the retreat.

He sounded the warning three times. 'Get ready,' he shouted. 'We need to leave'"

They may have been drunk, sleepy, sated with lust, but the Seafarers and Horse Lords were still fine warriors and although a lot of them had died, the ones who remained had rallied and were fighting back.

Ferros had gone through three houses, killing all he encountered. Now he was back in the street. A lookout had found him, told him what he'd expected: that men were coming from the anchored ships – not many, about a hundred, but enough that they must be dealt with. He'd rallied a hundred of his men, met the new enemy at the gate. In the bloody fight that followed, they'd killed all the reinforcements. But he'd lost half his men too.

As the last Seafarer fell, he leaned on his sword, breathing hard, as tired as he'd ever been. Knowing that the fight was only half over, that much more needed to be achieved. Wondering how it was going in the other areas. It made him look to the tower. Almost immediately he heard the trumpet sound there. At first he heard what he wanted to hear, the clarion call of triumph that meant the tower was taken. Joy lasted a moment till he understood what he was hearing, what was being urged – the retreat. For some reason, he looked towards the water – and saw all the new ships, rowing for the docks.

He knew what it meant on the instant. Knew what he must do.

He turned to the trumpeter he kept always near him, a man who only fought if attacked, a man saved for this function alone. 'Blow the retreat,' he said. 'Do not cease.'

Then he ran back into the street of sin to make sure that his men, those that had survived, followed him out.

For men who had never fought before, her City Guard had fought well. First blooding themselves in the slaughter at the Horse Lords' camp, then in the battle which followed as more Horse Lords rallied and came onto the attack. These had courage, even fanaticism, but they did not have their horses. So they ran, screaming, at her pikemen and died, still screaming, on their pikes. While the few who managed to regain their mounts met the hundred Wattenwolden she had *guided* to the camp, and were swiftly cut down.

The enemy, recognising where courage was leading, had drawn off, were regrouping. Still fewer in number than her command. Roxanna smiled. If all goes as well elsewhere, we might just win this day, she thought. She called her bugler to her. 'On my signal, blow me an advance,' she said, lifting her hand.

She didn't let it fall. Because another bugle sounded, distant and clear and from the direction of the port. It was not blowing an advance but the clear three blasts of the retreat. Yet even as it began again, on the second blast it was cut off, as if in a cough.

Ferros had told her – if she heard that signal, she should regroup and withdraw immediately to the small valley he'd shown her where the desert swept closest to the sea. On one side, a hill studded with aliantha trees. On the other, a sand dune. They were to rally under the canopy.

She looked across at the milling Horse Lords. If she ordered a last attack before withdrawing, she could kill many more. Every enemy slaughtered now was one less to harry them on the road back to Malpak, and their ships. This was still a victory that would delay the invasion of Corinthium till the autumn at least. By then … they would have thought of something else. Especially since they had the One with them.

But Ferros had been very clear. He would only order a retreat if absolutely necessary. To save lives for another fight. She did not doubt that her lover had had a similar success at the port. Also it was not just her she needed to protect. In the woods ahead of her, beyond the reach of Ferros's bugle, Malvolen would still be holding off the Huntresses. If they weren't given the command to withdraw now, when the rest did, their one hundred would be cut off and killed. 'Change of order,' she said. 'Sound the retreat.'

As her bugler played, she turned to Speros. Covered head to toe in enemy blood, with cuts on his arm and thigh adding to it, the young commander of the Guard had fought as well as any of them, as a leader. 'March away in squadron order, Fifth down to Second,' she said.

'And the First?'

'Stay to cover. We'll summon them when we are safe.'

He looked at her. Both knew that few of a rearguard ever survived. 'I'll stay with the First,' he said.

'No, Speros. The other squadrons will need you in what will be a fighting retreat.' She laid a hand on his arm. 'As I will need you back in Corinthium.'

The young man shook his head. 'The City? That's a long retreat.'

'It is. And do not fear for the First. They will have help. Be about it.' As Speros moved away, shouting orders, she turned, and called Trosten over. He was leader of that group of Wattenwolden; in fact, all the fighters there were of his tribe.

'We withdraw, lady?' he asked, as he drew close. While looking down. Like his dead brother, her former lover Barallingen, he was unable to keep his eyes from her breasts.

She kept the distaste from her voice as she recalled the obese man she'd seduced when making very different plans. She needed his brother to do what she wished. 'We do, lord. But slowly. Can you stay and command half your force to harry any who would follow? The First City Squadron stays to do that task too.'

'I can.' Curiosity made him raise his eyes at last. 'Where will the other half be?'

'With me, if you will spare them.' She bent, leaned closer, watched his eyeline fall again, touched his arm, letting her voice drop to a purr. 'I would go and help your brothers withdraw from the town.'

'You think they will need help?'

'More than us, perhaps.' She was thinking of that last interrupted, cracked blast of trumpet. It seemed to her a warning of sorts.

'Very well,' Trosten said, tapping his horse's flanks to ride over to his tribe. They gathered round him, and grunted agreement to all he said. By what means he divided them so swiftly she could not know, but even as the Fifth Squadron formed a column and marched away, Trosten was leading some fifty Wattenwolden in a charge at the regrouping Horse Lords while fifty were moving to join her.

She glanced around one more time. The ground was covered with bodies. Some were from her forces but most were the enemy. They had done the task assigned them. The Fourth was now mustering, Speros's cries getting them into swift order. She had done what a good general should do – killed the enemy in numbers. Saved most of her own fighters.

Now it was time to look to herself, and her love. To the father of the child that even now stirred within her.

She stood up in her stirrups. 'With me!' she cried, and led the tribesmen away from the battlefield and towards the town.

It was the decision of a moment. He had to get his men out. But in the next moment he'd remembered the other men who were fighting for their cause. And that if he simply fled back the way they'd come, those men were dead.

The Seafarers who were trapped still in houses didn't seem keen to follow the Wattenwolden as they answered the trumpet's call and rallied in the street. In moments, all were again in their saddles. The trumpeter was dead, an arrow taking him even as he blew the retreat. But despite the noise, Ferros knew that he still could be heard. Putting fingers to his lips he blew – but not the retreat. Ferros blew the charge.

His men looked at their Spear and Shield. Shrugged and followed him as he rode the other way. Not out of the town, but deeper into it.

He just hoped that Luck was watching, and understood.

Luck saw the Wattenwolden ride through the broken port gates and charge towards the fortress. He looked to the docks, where the first of the new ships was tying up, noted the men aboard making ready to disembark and attack. Shortly, there would be too many to fight and hope to live. So he guessed why Ferros was coming. Now he just had to tell Intitepe and Poum.

'Fly, Besema,' he called up, and Sayel began to immediately throw off the tethers.

'Will you come? I could use your bird again.' For someone who'd never seen it before, the old woman had been remarkably calm about Luck's transformation.

'I cannot. Can you escape without me?'

She looked up, at the way her globe was already leaning. 'Perhaps,' she replied. 'The winds do not yet fully blow one way or the other. I will see if I can find one that takes us your way. But if I don't, and I don't see you again, give this to Atisha when next you meet.'

She leaned out, kissed her hand and threw the kiss to him. Just as, with a cry, Sayel threw off the last of the tethers and, with a small scream, leaped into the already rising basket.

Atisha, Luck thought, had a vision of her the way he'd seen her last, her farewell wave. No, not farewell. Return soon. He would. But he could not return without Poum. Setting his jaw, he limped to the stairs and down again into the darkness.

He was in light again quite quickly, for the glana Luck and Poum had thrown had set much on fire, hangings and furniture – and, by the sick smell of it, people. On the landing where the men from the globe had slain the first monks, things moved near their heads, and Luck leaped back, uttering a disgusted cry. Because the fight was all below now, the rats had already come out to feed.

He hurried around the corner, down the next flight, to the last landing. Smoke funnelled up the stairwell, making him cough, and flames danced over the living and the dead, the many dead. From there he could look down on something that would not shame a badly run butcher's shop. Bodies, and body parts, were everywhere.

He coughed, peered through the smoke and the mayhem, at the surging crowd, some black-robed, some wearing wood-slat armour, all united by the same bright red. It was hard to tell, and he was no expert in war, but it seemed to him that though most of the dead were monks, most of the living were too. And that the remaining men of Ometepe were trapped between two groups of them, formed in a rough circle, three quarters of the way across the room towards the door, which had been closed and bolted again, sealing the trap.

He may have been no expert – but he could see that this fight was almost over. More monks were coming from the side rooms, most wielding their deadly spears. He saw one using the hook on the rear to pull down a warrior's shield, opening the exposed man to the killing thrust that came from the monk beside him.

It would not be long. And in the middle of the crumbling circle, through the drifting smoke, he saw Intitepe and Poum fighting.

Luck looked again at the door. He couldn't reach it – as himself. So he turned and ran back up the stairs.

The rats were so bold now, so glutted, they didn't even stir when he appeared again. 'Heh,' he called, stepping forward. The biggest rat there reared up and hissed at him. It was harder to possess a beast so soon after he'd possessed another. Fortunately for him, he'd only been very briefly within the bird. He was in the rat in two heartbeats.

He ran back down and started across the room below. From his new height he couldn't see much except feet slipping on blood, and fallen bodies: the ones already lying there, and the ones cut down in front of him. He wove, leaped, darted into gaps. Was nearly crushed by an armoured man falling. Had his tail stamped upon, held under a boot. Squealing, he jerked it clear, lunged forward. Somehow he made it through, and was standing at the door.

He assumed the monks in front of it were meant to be guarding it. But they were standing away from it, screaming with the rest. So Luck was able to shift back unnoticed into his human form – though it felt as if he'd had the toe of a boot up his arse. Grimacing, he bent and pulled back the bottom bolt. Luckily the top one hadn't been slid shut for he'd never have reached it. All he needed to do now, was turn the key.

Even as he did so, the door flew inwards. He was knocked to the side, wedged between it and the wall, as three Wattenwolden holding a bench they'd obviously used as a ram fell in and onto the floor, surprised by the door's easy opening.

Luck glimpsed Ferros leading more of his men in. Saw the Warrior Monks panic at this influx and as one turn and flee. But Ferros shouted loud over the roar of triumph the men of

Ometepe gave. 'With me!' he cried. 'Rally and retreat. Rally and retreat.'

It was Poum who spoke both languages – Luck had made sure of that. 'Rally and retreat,' they cried in Bunami. 'Rally and retreat.' They and Intitepe led the way out to the warriors waiting on their horses.

As Ferros stepped back, the last to leave, Luck emerged from behind the door. 'Have you a horse for me?' he asked.

'Luck!' Ferros roared. And then, without another word and seemingly without effort he lifted the Midgarthian, ran him forward, and flung him over the rear of a horse. Luck had no time to protest. Ferros was in his saddle a moment later and kicking hard and Luck was too occupied trying not to fall off to say anything else.

Looking back the way he'd come Ferros saw that, even in the short time of the ride and rescue, several boats had landed, and enemies were pouring from them onto the docks. In a swift glimpse he could see members of all the Tribes – Seafarers, Huntresses, even Horse Lords, though not mounted. Beyond them, on the street of sin, the survivors of the attack were stumbling from houses. His men had slaughtered hundreds but, if these joined with the new arrivals, there would be too many of them. Their way out would be blocked. For the briefest of moments he wondered if he should ride north, away from the sea. Dismissed it, even as he thought it. His army, which had split to tackle their separate tasks, would be hopelessly scattered. With these reinforcements, the enemy would muster and pursue each scattered section, and their great numbers would mean a slow massacre. United again, he and his allies had some hope. Retreat to the hill beyond the town, as arranged. Stand there.

All these thoughts in a moment, hesitation death on a

battlefield. Standing tall in his saddle he bellowed, 'Javelins! With me!' Bending to snatch out the last of his projectiles, he kicked his horse and, with Luck clinging hard to him, charged back the way they'd come, towards the street of sin.

The first of the enemy's reinforcements had made the road. Arrows flew and men fell. But there was not a better horse warrior in the world than a Wattenwolden at full charge. Even though many of them were double loaded, they still were able, just as Ferros was able, to lean away and, using the mount's momentum, fling their javelins. Huntresses, Seafarers and Horse Lords died, as they swept through.

The enemy had tried to close the port gates, to pen them in the killing ground. But the bodies on the ground had impeded them, and the Wattenwolden, swords drawn, followed Ferros though the narrowing gap. Reining in, he waited until the last of his men had made it through. He looked back. He'd lost a few, not many. The enemy now had possession of the road to the Tower. The Horse Lords who had emerged from the houses on the street of sin scurried back into them. Some few arrows flew from them.

Luck leaped from behind him, onto a riderless horse. He couldn't reach the stirrups but Ferros could see that the Midgarthian knew how to ride, controlling the animal with rein and heels.

'To the western gate!' Ferros called, and his men obeyed, preceding and following him.

The first streets they passed along were empty, even quiet, the only noise the drumming of their mounts' hooves. Then Ferros became aware of louder noise up ahead. Rounding a final corner he saw what made it.

The men he'd left at the gate were defending it against an attack from beyond the walls.

Ferros dismounted, ran to the stair and up to the tower.

Arrows whizzed and clattered off wood and slate. He snatched a glance amid the storm. The one was enough to tell him before he ducked down again: though many of them were without their mounts, a large party of Horse Lords had rallied before the gates and were assaulting them.

He had no doubt that more would be joining them soon. Just as, looking back, he had no doubt that the newly landed and fresh fighters would be coming from the town before long. Once more, he and his men would be trapped, and this time there would be no escape.

He raised his head again, studied longer, despite the flying steel. There were a lot of them out there, and more joining. Many of his men would die when they charged. All would, if they stayed.

He ran back down to the street. Saw amidst all the tall Wattenwolden two smaller men: Luck and the Fire King Intitepe. Beside them, standing back and also dismounted another, neither man nor woman and, in so many ways, the reason for all the death this day.

He crossed to them. Luck spoke before he did. 'We're breaking out.'

It was not a question. 'We are. But we'll have more chance if we are not double mounted.'

Luck turned to Intitepe and spoke rapidly. The Fire King listened, laughed, spoke himself. Luck turned back. 'He says they came here to fight, not be carried about. What is it you wish?'

Ferros outlined the plan, making it as he spoke it. It took only a short time, and not much longer to spread the word. At his signal, the gates were flung open – and Intitepe led his men out at the charge.

The Horse Lords were expecting cavalry, not a solid body of men with shields. Most of their arrows bounced off the shields, few finding a gap, and, when the Ometepe warriors reached the rough line they'd set up the enemy were swept away. Ferros and his cavalry poured out, riding down men who could not run as fast as horses.

Ferros reined in, his sword unbloodied. He sheathed it. He was tired of killing men who fled like rabbits, though he knew he should kill as many as he could so as to weaken the pursuit he knew was coming. But then he looked ahead down the road and cursed. More horsemen were charging their way. He could not see them in the dust they raised. Horse Lords, almost certainly. Sighing, he put fingers to his lips, found spit, and whistled the rally.

Others had seen them too. The men of Ometepe snapped into a shield wedge, spears bristling at all angles. Ferros was about to whistle again, sound the counter charge, when the first warrior emerged from the cloud. No Horse Lord chieftain. A woman. His love. Roxanna.

She reined in beside him. Joy danced in her eyes, though the words that came were calm. 'You live, Ferros. It is good to see you.'

'As it is to see you.' His words were as calm though he wanted to seize her, hold her, kiss her. Gods help him, he had a sudden urge to lay her down there and then, lose himself in love, not in death. It made him smile, more than he already was. 'Did you do good work?' he asked.

'We did.' She glanced behind him, to exhausted men. 'We would have done more but … you blew the recall. Why?'

'Another fleet came. Too many to fight.'

'Yet we must fight more, mustn't we?'

'Yes.' He looked back. Smoke rose from all over Balbek. 'But not here, and I hope not this day.'

'So all will muster at the hill we chose?' At his nod, she

continued, 'The City Guard will be halfway there by now. Lead the rest there, Ferros. My men will cover the retreat.'

'Your men? The Wattenwolden have accepted your command?'

'Did you ever doubt that they would? Now go.'

Each went to their commands. Men mustered, marched or rode off. The wounded doubled up on horses. Ferros sat his at the side of the road and watched them go. When the last man went past him, he looked back at the city of his birth.

Balbek burned. They had achieved much, killed many. But he knew that, no matter the triumph, it was still not a full victory. Sooner rather than later – and he feared sooner – the enemy would pursue, and in great numbers. And unless a miracle happened, he was not sure there was a way to stop them.

Turning his mount's head, he followed his retreating army.

On the roof of the slaughterhouse that Balbek's fortress had become, with the stench of the dead in their nostrils, the moans of the wounded and the dying in their ears, Anazat raged at the leaders of the other Four Tribes.

'I do not care for your people's great losses, Baromolak. Nor yours, nor yours.' He jabbed a finger at Karania of the Huntresses, then at Framilor, high admiral of the Seafarers. 'I have close to fifty of my brothers dead or dying on the floors below us now. But even those most grievously wounded will pick up their spears and follow me because they must! They must!' he shouted.

'Yes, in a day or two, lord—'

'No! Today, I say. Within hours. Do you not understand what I have told you? They were all here, all our principal enemies. If we catch them we end it. We end all wars! But above all else, this.' He looked at each in turn. 'The One is with them.'

'Praise her. Praise—'

'Silence!' The others had all begun to mutter the stock response to the mention of their god but Anazat cut them off with his hiss. 'You praise them, but you do not understand. When I say with them, I mean fighting on their side. Against us, their chosen people.' Over the leaders' gasps he went on in a lower voice. 'Our enemy must have forced the One to this. Corrupted them somehow. So it is vital we get them back. Today. Today! Or our entire cause is lost. Baromolak,' he turned to the Horse Lords' king 'what reports do you have of them?'

'They are making a fighting retreat, so reports are hard to come by—' He hurried on, over the monk's impatient grunt, 'But there is a valley a few leagues from the town. Where a tongue of the desert slides in and meets the coastal forest strip. We believe they have halted there. For now.'

'Believe? For now?' Anazat's echoes were furious. 'We need to know. Find out! And meantime at least this we do know. Whether they are going on or they stop, we must catch them. Because it ends today.' He leaned in, black eyes gleaming. 'Today!'

14
To Die Upon a Hill

From the top of the hill, from the highest branch of the tallest tree on which they sat – as themself, not as any creature – Poum could see along the road, almost as far as Balbek. The city itself was lost to heat haze and smoke. The Breath of Sadrak had fully come now, its forge heat gripping the land, and fires still raged within the walls, making a great brown cloud that smothered it.

Yet they were not sitting there to watch the city burn but to give notice when something came from it. Poum had volunteered for the task partly because they were young and had always had the long sight. Partly because it was a chance to consider the fight they had just been in, the terror of it, the fierce delight in finding that they were so good at something so terrible. Mainly because they needed to get away – from everyone, but especially from their father.

Not the one they called Father, the one who had brought them up. They were as comfortable with Luck as they ever were – which was sometimes uncomfortable too, in the way of sons and fathers. No, it was the other they were trying to avoid. Him and his … expectations. This man Poum had been raised to fear, even to hate, who had sought their death as soon as they'd come to life, now wishing the opposite. Wishing them to be the god all called them. Yet not to be worshipped by the Four

Tribes. Intitepe had accepted swiftly which side he should fight on, and why. Knew that Anazat and the others had used him, and would keep doing so until he was no longer useful. So he had battled hard in the port, and would again on this hill. Yet Poum also knew that, whether this day saw victory or defeat, Intitepe's ambitions would not end. For he was the father of the One and, to him, their linked destinies were clear.

Together they would rule the whole world.

It was the last thing Poum wanted. They had seen that whole world, both in their travels as themselves, and with Sirene. It was too vast, too complicated. To rule it you would need to be ceaselessly moving with a vision you wanted to impose. Others had such a vision and had tried to impose it in the name of the One. But the One had only one ambition – to find out entirely what *they* were. What the mystery at the very centre of their body meant. That was the only cause they wished to live for.

They took a deep breath. It would be resolved, one way or another, this day. The way the commanders were talking – away from the soldiers – their chances were not great. But Poum knew this: rather than fall into the hands of Anazat again, rather than be used for his cause, *his* vision, they would rather end it all. They knew from talking to their two fathers how hard it was for immortals to die. Hard, but not impossible. Luck's family had managed it, at the Coming of the Dark. They would manage it, somehow, if it became necessary. If the fight truly was lost.

The fight that begins even now, they thought, peering again. The scene this side of the city had changed. Instead of empty road, there were now gleams from thousands of points of light. Poum knew what it was: sunlight on steel. So they descended the tree.

Tiny Elric, who he'd briefly inhabited aboard the ship, had felt a kinship and a protectiveness ever since. He followed Poum about, a little like a huge puppy. Now he was sitting beneath the tree in the dwindling shade of late morning. He'd helped boost them onto the lowest branch which had been too high for Poum to climb to. Now he reached up and helped them down from it. 'Seen enough?' he asked.

'Seen what I needed to.' Poum bent and brushed tree mould off their leggings and tunic. 'Seen that they are coming.'

Elric nodded. He looked neither pleased not concerned. Just, like everyone in the army, exhausted. 'We better go tell our fathers then,' he said.

'Yes,' Poum replied, then added, under their breath, 'all three of them.'

Luck listened, nodded, then sent Elric to fetch the other leaders. They gathered under the tree. The other immortals – Ferros, Roxanna, Intitepe – together with the mortal leaders, Speros of the Guard, Malvolen of the Wattenwolden, and Ulrich the smith. They sat cross-legged in a circle on the pine-needled ground. Poum, looking as if they would be elsewhere, sat beside Intitepe and translated for him the common language of the empire.

Though Poum had been the lookout to give the first warning, other men had been left near the town to shadow the enemy as they emerged. The first of these scouts reported back to Ferros as he was walking up the hill to the meeting.

'Their count is four thousand, more or less. Close to four times what we have.'

'And many of those will be fresh, newly arrived from the ships. While we have many wounded.' Malvolen winced as he said this, lifting his arm to make the point, having taken an arrow through it in his fight with the Huntresses. 'Do we know how their army is made up?'

'I have more riders out,' Ferros answered. 'But the first says that at least half are colourfully dressed – so, Seafarers from the ships.'

'That is good,' said Roxanna. 'They prefer swift assaults on the open sea, ship to ship. A land battle would not be their choice. Do we know how many are mounted?'

'Perhaps five hundred?' He smiled. 'You did a good job of driving off their horses, lady.'

'The Wattenwolden did that,' she replied, smiling in turn at Malvolen.

It was one of her special smiles, and the old chief puffed out his chest at it. 'Which means we have nearly as many cavalry as they do. That will help us.'

Poum, who'd been whispering the words into Intitepe's ear, now spoke. 'The Fire King wishes to know. If they have so few mounted men to pursue us, why do we not keep retreating ahead of them to the port, and our ships?'

Luck, having translated the gist of it all for Ulrich, now looked at Ferros. They and Roxanna had discussed this briefly earlier, and had agreed on what he said now. 'Because most of our army is on foot, with many wounded, and all exhausted. They would be caught on the road and slaughtered. The Wattenwolden might make the port but even if they did—' Luck scratched his beard. 'The Four Tribes will know by now where we came from. And their leaders are no fools. My guess is that a fleet will have sailed for Malpak and retaken that town.' He shrugged. 'There is nowhere to retreat to.'

Intitepe said something else, and Poum translated. 'My … father says he is happy. He says, fighting is good. Though winning is better.' They looked at Ferros directly. 'So I ask for him and for myself: can we win?'

Ferros looked back. He hadn't spent much time with Poum. Saw a young man, as that was how they dressed, and carried themselves, though he knew that they were *they*, and both. He had seen that child first as a baby in the Keep, when Luck freed him and Lara. The child born to change the world. Who *had* changed the world, utterly. What happened on this day would change it again, perhaps finally.

As a soldier, he knew the odds were poor. They were an exhausted army, outnumbered four to one. But all there knew that, so as a leader he knew he did not need to speak any hard truths, only needed to speak what he himself believed – that there were many ways of turning odds in one's favour. They started with a leader showing certainty.

'We can – and we will,' he said, setting the tip of his bestrel on the dry earth, and tracing a first line. 'This is how.'

Ferros took a last look down the eastern edge of Eagle Ridge, the side that faced Balbek. The land rose steeply here from the valley, in dry gulleys that were filled with scrubby pines and bush. Hard terrain to climb up, and a natural defence. He'd placed a few of the less seriously wounded there, armed with bows. They had also gathered rocks to hurl down. He doubted they would need them. The enemy would not attack here. It was not a flank that could easily be turned. Neither would they come from the rear, where near vertical slopes fell to the sea.

He tapped his heels, turned his horse away and cantered down the treeline. His force was tucked just inside it, sitting under the gnarled pine trees that grew along this coast and which largely followed the line of the ridge. They provided some shade from a terrible sun. More importantly they prevented arrows falling from above. Negated what would be the Four Tribes' biggest advantage in an open field – the Huntresses' skill in dropping arrows into his ranks. A few had tried to do that here, but soon realised the waste. Indeed, his own archers had a much better time, for their targets stood exposed, ranks packed tight and sweating under that furnace sun. Though Ferros's orders had been strict – a few arrows only, shot to keep the men and women below ever agitated, fearful of random death falling from the sky. Not enough to significantly deplete his stock, already low following the raid on Balbek the night before. They would need them later.

The men in the thin front line along the ridge were mainly drawn from the squadrons of the City Guard. He passed along them to the two places only that were different – in the centre, where half the Wattenwolden were dismounted, and at the far end, where the fifty survivors of Ometepe were gathered about their leader. The Fire King looked up at his approach and grinned. Ferros knew that, in terms of battle experience, the five-hundred-year-old immortal had much more than him. But this was a different battle, in a very different terrain than the highlands or jungles of his homeland, and he had been content to cede Ferros the command. Only in one thing had he objected and won the argument. For his experience told him that the western flank, which unlike the east fell here in gentle sandy grass to the sea, was where the greatest danger could lie. So he demanded that he and his men fought there.

He was right. Ferros knew it was the weak point of his whole position. Which was why the Wattenwolden cavalry, were also positioned close by. Ferros turned to look at them. Malvolen was watching him, and raised a fist. Ferros nodded, and looked once more from west to east. It had taken him less than fifty heartbeats to canter the length of the ridge. That was the extent and the limit of his forces.

Having contemplated them, he turned his attention again to his enemy.

He looked for weakness; saw only strength. Much stronger than they'd been when he'd fought them before on another, very different ridge at the far end of the Great Sea, in the grasslands of the Assani, outside Tarfona. Though he'd been outnumbered nearly two to one, most of the enemy force that day had consisted of tribesmen. Here there were only a handful of Assani, and only a few more of the local tribe, the Sarphardi – men Ferros had fought both against and alongside throughout his youth. Here, the enemy was mostly made up of the hardened warriors of the Four Tribes who had been fighting each other for centuries, and then had united to conquer the empire of Corinthium, and the northlands of Midgarth. And here, finally, they had at least five times his own forces.

His spies had underestimated.

Ferros raised his eyes and stared above the enemy, to the hill that rose behind them. Sand, not scrub, and treeless, the first of the great dunes. Behind it, the desert that swept through Sarphardi lands, went all the way to Xan. How often had he and Lara raced each other across that desert floor, exhilarated by the chase, and by each other.

Lara, he thought longingly, for just a moment. Longing not only for her. For what they'd been – young, in love and mortal.

Then another spoke behind him – old, in love, immortal. 'I was thinking, Ferros, how this is the second time we have fought together upon a ridge. Outside Tarfona I think you hated me. What do you feel here?'

He turned in his saddle. There she was – Roxanna, with that secret smile, those dark, questioning eyes. 'I never hated you. No, perhaps I did. But I never stopped desiring you even while I did.'

'And now? Here?'

He moved his horse until its head was at her mount's tail, so he could reach across and take her hand. 'You know how I feel.'

'I think I do. But even after three hundred years of life, I never tire of hearing it said.'

'I love you,' he said, raising her hand, kissing it.

He went to pull his hand back, but she held him. 'You know, if all . . . fails here today, you and I can still get away?'

'I know. And I have thought hard on that. On you. On what we've made.' He looked down at her belly, swathed in leather. 'But I have decided this: I would not be the father I wish to be, if I carried with me the knowledge that I left the men who follow me to die without me. This day, life ends. Or it begins. Destiny will decide that.' He raised her hand again, brought it to his chest, held it over his heart. 'But if all does fail, you will know it, and must go.'

She stared at him a long moment before she laughed. 'Really, Ferros, you have so much yet to learn about me. I am going to give you that chance. Once we triumph this day.'

'And if we do not?'

'If we do not, I will not be the mother of a child whose father I left to die without me.' She squeezed his hand. 'Trust me on that.'

They stared at each other, held each other – then heard it, first in a rustle that swept along the treeline as of birds on branches, followed by the voices that cried it out, finally in the enemy's trumpet blast.

'They come!'

'To your post, lady,' he said, squeezed her hand, released it. She rode away without another word or backward glance and he turned to look at the valley below and watch the enemy, as one huge body, begin to advance up the hill. It was both his fear and his hope, that they would all charge at once. Fear, because they did outnumber the defenders five to one, Hope, because they would all come when those defenders were at their freshest. It was not what he would have done, were he them. With a sudden lurch of joy, he realised that this was their best chance.

Joy dashed the next instant. Because most of the enemy

suddenly halted, fifty paces up the slope. But not all. From their midst ran out a screaming group of men – and women, he realised from the cries.

The ascrami were coming.

He had been an ascrami himself, when hiding in the army of the Four Tribes with Lara to get to Corinthium before it fell. He knew why they were being sent in – and he had to stop his people's natural response to enemies running at them.

Putting his fingers to his mouth and his heels to his horse's flank, he set out at a gallop along the ranks, blowing a loud, four-note whistle.

It was the order to hold, to take no action. Shoot no arrows, throw no spears. It was a Wattenwolden commmand, but it was one of three he'd made sure the City Guard also learned on their voyage across the sea. Most obeyed, and the ascrami, meeting few projectiles, kept charging up the hill.

Ferros rode to the mounted tribesmen. 'Why, Arcturien?' Malvolen called, his own bow drawn and an arrow notched.

'These are ascrami. Expendables, probably dragged from their houses in Balbek this morning, and a rusted sword shoved into their hands.' He heard a sound he recognised. 'Hear that crack! Those are Horse Lords at the rear, driving them on with steel-tipped whips. They want us to waste our arrows and our strength on them.'

Malvolen eased the pull on his bowstring. 'So what do we do when they reach us? Let them through?'

'No. Drive them away.' He pointed. 'A hundred of your men, out and angled across the hill.' He looked past his chief. 'Flats of swords! They are not fighters. Drive them to the side!'

It took but moments. Malvolen summoned his own tribe, who were grouped around him anyway. The guards' ranks parted and the horsemen rode through, when the ascrami were still fifty paces from the crest. Ferros wanted to ride with them.

Couldn't. It was the worst part of being the commander this day. Sixteen years before he wouldn't have thought of it, had fought on that ridge near Tarfona shoulder to shoulder with his men. Here he had to stay aloof from the fight. Had to be clear of the fray, ready to react immediately to whatever the enemy tried next.

Malvolen didn't need him. He led his tribe out, cutting down and across the hill. The men and women of Balbek screamed, dropped their weapons, ran to the side, or back down the hill. There was nothing the men with whips could do about it, except stay and die, which a few of them did. And if not every tribesman used the flat of his blade, by the time they passed over it there were few dead ascrami on the hill, and only two Wattenwolden, plucked from their saddles by Huntresses' arrows.

More of those were flying thicker as the tribe rode back and the ranks of the City Guard closed behind them. Ferros sat his horse behind by Speros, the Guard's youthful commander, and looked over his shoulder. More ascrami lay dead before the enemy's ranks than at his own front line. He also saw that the ones driven to the side were already fleeing back to distant Balbek.

He turned his attention back to the main body of the enemy that had spread the length of the hill. The front two ranks were all Seafarers, their clothing gaudy and bright. They were armed as they usually were, with weapons better suited to a sea fight than a land battle: short cleaver-like swords, small round shields. The two ranks behind them were all Horse Lords, but on foot. They wore their lamulin armour, their visored helms, carried spear and shield. Again, without their horses, they were not fighting in their best way.

The dark core behind them would not have that problem – the black-robed Warrior Monks carried their strange axe-spear-hook weapons, that Luck said were called kazana, with which they were so deadly. But there were no more than a hundred of them. The final rank was all Huntresses, at least a thousand of them. Their targets' staying in the shelter of the pines had frustrated them of their best weapon, the bow and arrow. Many had therefore swapped yew and ash for armour and blade, and Ferros knew they'd be doughty fighters with those too.

At the very rear, on mounts they had managed to recapture, around five hundred Horse Lords sat in their saddles.

A near silence had taken the battlefield since the last whip crack, the last ascrami scream. The Breath of Sadrak blew hot through the pine boughs above them, and snapped the enemy's banners, the Eye of the One under which they fought appearing, disappearing, reappearing, like a game to amuse a baby. The silence was ended by a single voice roaring the name of their god. Their god, who, as most there did not know, was standing on the hill with their foes.

Ferros was certain he recognised the voice. That it was Anazat who shouted it out. The man who'd held him and Lara prisoner all those years before in the Keep; who'd starved and abused them. The man Ferros had promised himself he would meet on this day, on this ground, with a sword in his hand.

The voice hung in the air alone only for a moment, and then was lost in the roar of five thousand. 'One!' screamed its army, and began to run up the hill.

'Shoot!' Ferros yelled, though many had not waited for the command. Arrows flew down. Arrows flew up, for Huntresses were advancing behind the Seafarers and Horse Lords, so many shooting that the trees could not shelter them all. And then the arrow storm ceased, from both sides, because swords, axes and spears were needed now as the waves of Seafarers crashed the length of the ridge against the City Guard, against the Wattenwolden, the men of Ometepe, the few men and women of Midgarth. While Ferros still held himself aloof, even as he saw his love laying about her with a long sword, in the heart of the Corinthian Guard. Even when he saw Luck charged down by three Seafarers, felling one with a slung stone before being knocked down by the other two, only to spring up again when Poum stepped in and killed them both, using one of the monks' bladed spears. Even when he saw Domen, who had followed at his heels ever since the fight at the Tribute feast, fall to the blades of three Horse Lords, killing one even as he died.

He was the leader. He had to lead. He was also the Spear and Shield of Malvolen and it was by him he sat his horse, with the only reserve he had – five hundred mounted Wattenwolden.

He heard before he saw it. The cry from the right flank, the weak flank, above the gentler slope. Saw the men of Ometepe reeling back, charged by mounted Horse Lords who had outflanked them.

Now there was no question. It was the moment he'd waited for. With his sword in one hand, his lance in the other, he cried, 'Wattenwold!' as he and his lord led their men in the charge.

The Horse Lords were distracted by the men in wood-slat armour still fighting fiercely among them. So they were stationary, stabbing down, unprepared for the horsemen who swept in. Ferros charged straight at the One banner, Malvolen a pace behind. He couched his lance, drove it into the bannerman's armpit. The weapon entered him, knocked him from his horse, snapped. Malvolen parried a cut meant to take Ferros's head, let the Horse Lord's curved blade slide down his own. Off balance the man exposed his side – and Ferros put his straight blade into it.

Elsewhere, his men must have had the same success. Trumpets screamed – enemy ones. Those of the Horse Lords who could, fled. Many tried and failed, for the men from Ometepe leaped onto the backs of the horses, daggers in hand, blades to throats.

'Hold here, lord!' Ferros gasped, turned his horse, aware again of the strangeness of giving orders to the man he followed. But Malvolen had ceded him the command without a murmur. 'Your fight, Arcturien,' he'd said, 'your ways.'

Ferros turned and cantered the length of the ridge again. Dead lay both below the brow of the hill and behind it. The wounded of both sides were everywhere, crying out, the only difference between them being that those of the Four Tribes quickly ceased crying.

The enemy had retreated to the base of the hill. There were fewer of them.

Yet there were a lot less of his own forces too. Death lay all around, wearing different uniforms. Corinthian Guards, Wattenwolden, those from the far north, the far west. Battlefield calculations were always hard to make. But Ferros reckoned he had lost perhaps one third of his force, dead or incapacitated. He had perhaps seven hundred men, and a few women, left.

One of those women strode up to him now. Roxanna smiled, through a mask of blood. 'Do you think that will stop them, Ferros?' she called.

'Would it stop you?'

He looked behind her, down the hill. The forces there were rallying again, into their different groupings. And they parted in the middle to let the soldiers who had not yet fought come through – one hundred Warrior Monks, armed with their deadly kazana. Three hundred mounted Horse Lords moved ahead of them.

He looked back at his own reserve. Perhaps half that number of Wattenwolden remained.

It was over. He knew this. Every chamber of his soldier heart told the truth of that. Yet his heart also told him this. That he would strive to the last breath to make that truth a lie.

'Wattenwolden! With me!' he called.

They rode to the treeline. He would meet the enemy head on.

They did not have the numbers but they had the slope. Perhaps it would be enough.

The two forces stared at each other for a long moment. From the enemy's centre a monk's hand went up.

Yet the cry that broke the silence did not come from the army in the valley but from somewhere else, somewhere further away. Sound got distorted on a battlefield. Yet it seemed to Ferros that the cry came from the crest of the far ridge. The top of the sand dune, beyond which the Great Desert began. So it was to that he looked ... and saw an army march over its brow.

Lara had been watching for a while, as the people who'd followed her across the Great Desert assembled below the crest of the dune. She'd seen the ascrami charge, remembered with a shudder her time as one on the rocks beneath the Twins, the guardian statues at Corinthium's harbour. Watched the main assault go in and be driven back, noted the piles of the dead on both sides. Yes, the Four Tribes had lost three times what the defenders had. But they could afford to. Even as she watched now, she saw them adjust their positions, so that the mounted Horse Lords came to the centre. Behind them were the black-robed monks. Around them, she could see the rest, readying. They would all charge as one and soon, and sheer numbers would sweep the defenders away.

'Are we too late?'

She turned at the question: Gan had joined her on the ridgeline without her noticing, moving silently as ever. She looked at the crevassed black face, knew in a glance its troughs and valleys, the azure eyes all the brighter in their dark setting. Had studied it more closely one night the week before when, halfway across the desert and camped in an oasis, they had become lovers. She'd been surprised when he approached her thus, for she knew that the Warrior Monks of the Four Tribes lived without women. He'd smiled as he told her it was not a burden the Timian Monks were asked to carry, before he took her face in his gentle hands.

'No. In fact I think we have arrived just in time.'

'It is the gift of Sadrak whose breath has blown us here.' He nodded. 'What order shall I give?'

Unlike many men she'd known, Gan had made no argument when she had taken the decisions necessary for an army on the move. He'd accepted the fact that she was immortal, and had gained skills in soldiering while possessing soldiers, with that same gentle smile. He was a fighter, for the white-robed monks trained in the martial arts in the southern desert just as much as their black-robed counterparts did in the northern mountains. But he knew nothing of the tactics of war, and deferred to her.

Lara studied the valley again. The forces of the One were still moving into position. It would not be long now. Then she looked back the other way, at her own force. Both men and women in equal numbers; three thousand had come on this first return. None of them were really soldiers, though the hundred monks who'd joined them had tried to teach them some skills in the nights when they rested on the journey. They were armed, after a fashion. Some with hunting bows, and slingshots; most with spears, the simplest weapon to use. But these men and women had been driven from this coast, their families slaughtered, their sons and daughters raped, their houses burned and their possessions stolen fifteen years before by those who were preparing to attack in the valley below. When she looked at them now – saw her own father and sister looking back – she saw determination in their eyes, in all their eyes.

Once again, Lara stared down into the valley. She had possessed soldiers, it was true, had learned from them the tactics of battle, of feints and manoeuvres. None of those skills were required now. There was only one choice here.

Lara drew a sword in one hand, a dagger in the other. Raised them high. 'Balbek!' she cried.

'Balbek!' came the echo from three thousand throats, as the Exiles followed Lara over the ridgeline and down the slope of the dune.

Ferros saw them charge. There was no time to consider who they were. All that mattered was that they had come to fight.

Battles were won or lost in the decisions of a moment. He made his. As he saw the enemy below see and hear what was coming from behind them, as some began to shift to face it, he whistled once again, each way, a new command, another he'd drilled into them all. And each man and woman who could do so, obeyed. Unslung bows, notched arrows and sent them in high parabola down into the mass of men below. Three times they shot, and it was like poking a stick into a hive, as the mass shifted and surged. Another whistle, a different command. Bows were dropped, swords, spears, axes raised.

Ferros looked both ways along the line. There was a whistle command for this too. But he decided his voice could be heard.

'Charge!' he yelled and, at his cry, his entire army charged down the hill.

Anazat had been with his monks, urging them to a final glory, when the yelling began on the dune behind him. He'd looked, but his eyes were no longer good for distance, could only see a flowing mass, dark against the sand. It was those around him who told him what it was.

'More enemies! They come! They come!'

'Who could they be?' he snarled but got no answer as arrows began to fall and men cried out in terror, holding useless arms up to the skies. He yelled at the other leaders of the Four Tribes – Baromolak trying to control his horse, Framilor swirling his short sword above his head and bellowing commands to his Seafarers, Karania raising her own bow, notching an arrow to shoot it up at the hill, like spitting into the rain. They could not hear him for all the screaming and he began to push and dodge through the falling, flailing bodies to reach them. But then yelps of warning came from behind him too, and he turned back. This was close enough even for his eyes to see – the force his forces were about to overwhelm charging down from the forest above. And right in their centre, making straight for him, Wattenwolden cavalry, bellowing their war cry.

There was no reply of defiance around him. Only one word, that spread faster than a plague, shouted by one, then ten, then a thousand voices.

'Trapped!'

And on the word, his army dissolved into a mob. They ran into each other. Tried to dodge the hooves and falling steel that entered. A few men fought. Most tried to run. But there was nowhere to run to.

Someone grabbed him by the back of his collar, yanked him from the path of a charging horse. 'Here, master, here!' the man yelled, pulling him harder, further back. Spluttering, half-choked, Anazat jerked himself free, looked up. It was Toparak who'd saved him, pulling him into a tight group of monks, a still centre in the chaos. He saw that they all faced outwards, their kazana raised, a steel barrier. Wattenwolden flowed around it, cutting down with swords, but for the moment they could not break through that circle of steel.

Anazat pulled himself upright on Toparak's arm. 'Raise the banner of the One. Find a trumpeter. Rally on us.'

'No, master, this battle is over.'

'No! Obey me—'

'Over.' Toparak grimaced. 'I may be a monk now, but I was a

Horse Lord once, and trust me, this fight is done. We must get you out, to fight another day.'

Anazat sagged. Suddenly he felt exhausted. 'Out where?' he croaked.

'To the port. Our ships there.'

'I cannot … I cannot run to the port.'

'I know. I will—' Toparak was looking away, out into the fight. A bellowing Wattenwolden charged hard at the circle. The monk shoved Anazat one way, lunged the other then, as the horseman came level, jabbed his kazana up. He didn't use the spear point, or the axe blade, he used the hook on the reverse, snagged one edge of the warrior's breastplate, dropped all his weight hard down, and hooked the man from the saddle.

Other monks finished him on the ground. With the leap of a man half his age, Toparak was up and in the saddle. 'Come, master,' he said, reaching an arm down. 'The port.'

Anazat felt his energy return. How many setbacks had he faced in his life? As soon as he'd heard the word of the One, he knew he'd found his cause. All trials had always been a test of faith. This was but another on the road to triumph.

He caught the arm, pulled himself up and behind the Horse Lord turned monk. Toparak put his heels to the horse's flanks and started to weave through the dissolving mob.

Poum fought, in the way they knew, the way they'd absorbed from their time within Anazat. With a kazana. Killed once with its blade, once with its spear point, a Seafarer, a Huntress. But when they used the hook to lower the guard of a Horse Lord by snagging his sword arm, dropping it, laying the man's neck open to the finishing cut, they paused, looked into the man's eyes. Saw the terror in them, in a youth no older than themself. Changing their grip, they swept the shaft around, struck him in the head. The youth's eyes slammed shut and he fell. Poum had their duty, to those they fought beside. This boy must not be free to kill. But neither would Poum kill. They knew, in that moment of eyes, that they never would again. Stepping over the unconscious body, they started to search though the chaos for their father.

They had started the day at Intitepe's side, had charged down the hill with him. The Fire King had not gone far. As Poum had realised, you did not have to go far to find someone else to slaughter.

They heard him before they saw him. His joyous voice rose clear.

'Mine!' Intitepe yelled, then soon again, 'Mine!'

Poum knew what that was. Their mother had told them, when describing the savagery of war in Ometepe. When a warrior took another's life, he took the force of that life too, absorbed it into himself in the moment of death. Claimed it with a word.

Intitepe had claimed a lot, Poum saw as soon as they stepped between two warriors in wood-slat armour. Two of a small circle facing outwards, defending their king, their god. Doing more than that – keeping a space clear for him to keep killing.

'Mine!' their father yelled again, just as they stepped through – as another body fell to join the heap of those who lay around him. There were at least a dozen, and six more of the enemy were standing in front of him, four men and two women, who had swords half raised, but had no will to use them. 'Please,' one of the women begged, dropping her sword, raising her hands, 'Spare us.'

But Intitepe didn't speak the language of the Huntress – nor the language of surrender. Poum saw that he didn't know any language but the dealing of death as he laughed, stepped forward, raising his sword high. 'Stop, Father!' Poum yelled, and his father did, keeping the sword raised but turning, his face a sheen of blood. Grey eyes gleamed in the red when he saw who called. 'My son!' he cried. 'My daughter! My child! Let me show you how a warrior of our land gains glory. A last one for me, and then you may have the rest.'

'No!' Poum yelled again, and again their father held the blow, as the weeping young woman sank to her knees before him. Poum came forward. 'We have won, Father. The killing must stop.'

The grey eyes narrowed, the smile went. His voice, when it came again was softer, harsher. 'The killing never stops,' he said. 'You will learn that lesson again and again, my child, before we rule the whole world.'

It was there, in what their father spoke. All of it. Everything they'd been born to, everything prophesied for them. All they did not want. All coming together in those few words. Hearing them, they realised something else. After they'd spared the young Horse Lord's life, they'd thought that they would never kill again. Now they knew they must. One last time.

'Leave her!' they cried, and leaped forward, swirling the kazana.

Intitepe had been fighting for five hundred years, Poum for five hours. The Fire King dropped into a guard, confident as ever. But then . . .

Then he looked into his child's eyes.

And recognised something there, something he hadn't noticed before. How Poum's eyes were exactly like his own father's. The immortal he'd slain to take the throne. How they were also like the eyes of each of his seven sons, all of whom he'd slain to keep that throne. Recalled finally the eyes of another. Not blood kin, but another immortal, the last other immortal of Ometepe: Saroc, priest and prophet, keeping those eyes open to the last as he sank into the lava of Toluc, staring at Intitepe, repeating in those eyes his last prophecy. 'Just as you killed your father and all your sons, so a son of yours shall kill you.'

He had lived all his life since with that prophecy, those words. Hearing them again in his head, seeing the eyes of his father and all the sons he'd killed, Intitepe lowered his own eyes, lowered his sword.

But Poum was already striking as he did. They expected a block, then a counterstrike. None came. The axe blade passed cleanly, easily through their father's neck. Head and body reached the ground at the same time but Poum did not see it. Heard but did not see how the men of Ometepe turned and kneeled before them. Heard but did not see the prisoners flee. Tears blocked their vision, constricted their throat. So the word they spoke, when it came, came on a choked whisper.

'Mine,' they said, and wept.

Luck had not followed the others into battle. It was not fear that held him back. He just knew he was no good at fighting. He could be killed, even if he could not die, and he could not spare the time required to be reborn. So he sat on the riderless horse he'd captured, and watched the army of his enemies destroyed.

Then he noticed one horse breaking clear of the fray, two men upon it, galloping towards the town. Both riders were black-robed, and Luck knew instantly who one of them had to be. Tapping in his heels, he followed.

The distinct and awful sounds of battle faded fast; became a distant roar, like sea surge on a pebbled beach. The drumming of hooves took over. His horse's and, quite soon, the mount of the men he pursued, as he caught up to them.

The rider had looked back once, then put spurs to flank, hoping a burst of speed might put off the pursuit. But as Luck got closer, the man knew he could not escape and slowed, then stopped. Luck halted his own horse thirty paces away and watched as the rider slipped from the saddle. The man snatched a javelin from the sheath that hung from the horn, and began to walk back towards Luck … who recognised him.

'Toparak,' he called, and the monk stopped, peered. 'It is Luck,' he added.

The monk's face creased in wonder. 'Luck?'

When Luck had been a prisoner all those years before at the Keep, this man had been his only friend. A man tortured by a past of killing, seeking forgiveness for his sins in following the One. While taking pleasure in what he and Luck found they shared – a love of riding. 'Luck,' he said again, softly, lowering the javelin. Then the man still on the horse hissed something, and he raised it again, brandished it. 'Go back, Luck,' he called. 'Let us be.'

'No, Toparak. I must talk with Anazat.'

Another harsh whisper from the saddle. Toparak listened then swallowed. 'You cannot. We have to go, before more come from the battlefield.'

'I must. Stand aside, my friend.' As he spoke, he already knew what the answer would be. Which was why he'd already reached up to the rope around his neck. Toparak ran at him, javelin arm going back for the throw. But Luck was ready to do one of the few things he was gifted at – take the slingshot from around his neck, fit it with a stone from his pouch, stand in the stirrups and whirl the weapon over his head. When Toparak was fifteen paces away, had leaned back to throw the javelin, Luck threw the rock. He aimed for the man's chest, not his head. There was a chance then that his friend might survive.

Toparak flew, as if jerked backwards on invisible ropes. He didn't make a sound, just crumpled to the roadway, lay still.

Luck stared at the body. 'I am sorry for this,' he said. 'Are you sorry for this, Anazat?'

When the monk made no reply, Luck clicked his tongue and his horse moved forward. He halted her by the man on the ground, dismounted, bent to check. Toparak was still breathing, though blood bubbled at his lips. Luck rolled him onto his side, so he would not drown in it, then looked up. 'Are you sorry for all the men and women who died for you this day, or who are yet to die for you this day?'

'Why should I be sorry?' Anazat said. 'They did not die for me but for their god.'

'So you will not be sorry when *you* die?'

'I will not.' Anazat threw back his cowl. Sunlight glowed on his shaven head. 'But is today that day? And will it be by your hand, Luck of Askaug?'

Luck studied the man. Though the thin circlet of hair about his head was now entirely white, his eyes were as black as they had ever been. They reminded him of something he needed to know, that perhaps only this man of any man alive could answer. So instead of replying, he spoke to his own question. 'When you first introduced me to Sirene, the day I came to the Keep, you told me that she was not controllable. That she would only do what she willed.' His horse shook herself, head moving from side to side. Luck rose, patted her neck, calmed her, continued. 'Yet you controlled her, did you not? When you met Poum and myself in the smoke? When you became Gytta, and Peki Asarko became Kipé and you lured us to the ambush at Askaug?'

Anazat's gaze went beyond him, to the distant noise of battle. 'Why this now, Luck? Do you think it the appropriate time?'

'I think it may be the only time.' He ran his tongue over his lips. 'Come, you tell me what I do not know about her and I'll tell you what you do not.'

'Something I do not know of Sirene? I doubt that. Do you not see my eyes?' When Luck didn't reply, he grunted, then said, 'I did not control her. I know how to use her … illusions. Once I knew what you craved, and suspected what Poum would crave, it was not hard to … lure you both for a time.'

'But you did not control her?'

'No. Why do you ask this?'

'Because someone, some … *thing* does control her. Some force beyond this world.'

'Impossible.' The monk's eyes narrowed. Yet there was doubt in his voice. 'Why would you say that?'

'Because I asked her what you never had. I asked her not who she was, but *why* she was.'

Anazat stiffened. 'And her reply?'

'That she watched, for others. Whom she called gods. More, that these gods gave us the gifts that some called curses. Immortality. The immortals' gift of possession. Finally, the gift of hope, given to you in prophecy. In the coming of the One.'

'Gave us these gifts?' Anazat frowned. 'What for?'

'It was my first question.'

'And the reply?'

'To see what we would do with them.'

'Do with them?' Anazat echoed, and looked up into the bright sky. 'You mean they are … *using us*?'

'Which was my second question.'

'And the answer?'

'The answer … was yes.' Luck nodded. 'Yes. So I demanded to see these gods. She told me I wasn't ready.' He leaned forward. 'But I'm ready now.'

Anazat stared back for a long moment. His breath was coming faster. 'But if this is true … if this is true … then you and I have a journey to take.' His mount was catching his excitement, his agitation, starting to move in circles. Anazat, no horseman, could not control her. 'Come with me. Let us journey together with Sirene once again. To challenge these … so-called gods.'

'And the One? What of the god of here?'

Luck was studying Anazat carefully, looking deep into those black eyes. It was so hard to see anything within them. Yet now he saw light come, brought by words. 'The One was always better as an idea than as a fact,' the monk replied. 'A fact is … uncontrollable.' The eyes widened, with the mouth's smile. 'So let us replace it with a better idea. Let us go, you and I, and find the gods.'

'Which … is what I thought you would say.' Luck nodded then picked up Toparak's javelin, stood, and put it through Anazat's chest. He was not a warrior, never had been. But a god who'd lived over four hundred years picked up a few skills and the monk was only fifteen paces away.

As the body tumbled off her back, Anazat's horse whinnied and fled. Luck went and checked the body where it had fallen. There was blood at Anazat's lips too, though unlike with Toparak, this blood didn't bubble. Still, Luck kneeled by him for a little while, fingers on the neck where the pulse would be if the man was alive. Or rather if the man was also a god. It would seem unlikely.

He was not.

Luck's own mount had not run off. He grabbed her reins, led her back to Toparak. After three attempts he managed to get the man lifted and across the horse's neck. He climbed back into the saddle, making sure his friend was secure in front of him, then rode back towards the sea-surge of battle.

Even though she was in the heart of it, Lara could sense the battle was over. Enemies were trying to flee, not fight. Defending themselves, but seeking some way out.

There was none. And though she'd grown weary of the killing, she had no hope of halting her people's savagery. For those who'd been driven from their homes, robbed and abused, forced to live like slaves in exile, this was their chance for vengeance – and the men and women of Balbek took it. If any tried to surrender, Horse Lord or Seafarer or Huntress, throwing down their swords, raising their hands, spears would be shoved through their bodies, or knives slashed across their throats. There were trumpets blowing from somewhere beyond and, as a soldier's girl, she recognised the calls to regroup, to rally, to cease fighting. Someone was attempting to stop the slaughter. They may as well try to halt the waves, she thought.

Yet she could also sense that the slaughter *was* slowing. Not from lack of blood lust. From exhaustion. She'd fought in battle before, as herself, as others, and she was feeling hardly able to lift her sword. Those who'd followed her across the Great Desert were not soldiers, this was their first battle, and, though they felt the urge to keep killing, the mechanics of it were harder – the thrust, the slash. More and more she could see the townsfolk leaning on their weapons in front of their kneeling, begging enemies, trying to summon the breath and the will to kill again.

There was fighting still, though. She could hear it, as she, too, leaned on her sword, its tip to the ground, taking shuddering breaths. It was like the approach of some huge wagon, driving closer, closer to where she stood. Then she could see it, as if someone was approaching through a field of tall wheat, the stalks made up of enemies, rippling as they were scythed.

It was when she saw the scyther that she realised she did have the strength for one more kill, and lifted her sword from the ground.

It was Roxanna. The uncrowned queen of Corinthium was having no scruples about killing. Indeed, Lara could see she revelled in it still, dispatching those who stood before her whether they fought or tried to surrender with equal skill and no pity.

Men followed her – City Guard, Wattenwolden. But even they had ceased fighting. Everyone had ceased, suddenly, as if by collective will. Only Roxanna still fought, a Horse Lord facing her now, offering his curved sword in defiance or in surrender – Lara could not tell which and it did not matter, since Roxanna opened him from belly to neck.

It was only when she stepped over his body, when no one else appeared in his place, that her eyes focused on something other than dealing death. Focused on the woman standing ahead of her, the flat of her long sword on her shoulder.

Lara saw the recognition come, in the second before she moved, crossed the five paces between them in a heartbeat. Roxanna's shorter sword rose but too slowly, too late as, with a rising blow, Lara struck it from her hand. Dipping her shoulder, Lara charged into Roxanna, knocking her to the ground. She tried to get to her feet, got as far as her knees, when Lara's blade, pressed against her neck, stopped her.

'Twice you have killed me,' Lara said softly. 'But I vowed I would kill you at the last.'

Roxanna looked at her and said nothing.

Though Ferros had killed, and killed again, he was done with it. Once he knew that victory was certain, and the day theirs, he had tried to stop the massacre of men and women who wanted only to surrender. He hadn't been very successful at first. But gradually trumpets, shouts and, truly, exhaustion had slowed the slaughter.

Only just ahead of him now did the fight continue. He followed the sound, tracked it along what was almost a pathway marked in bodies and blood through the battlefield. He had an idea who had cut the path.

Then he saw her. Not armed, not killing. Kneeling before a slight woman so covered in blood it took him a long moment to recognise her too.

'Lara,' he cried.

She did not raise her eyes. 'Fifteen years ago, on the day

Corinthium fell, you found us fighting in a stable, Ferros,' she said. 'You called, like you call me now. I looked up – and she killed me. Not a final death, but the second she'd given me. I'd vowed before, I vowed after, that it would be me that made that final kill.' She ran her tongue over her cracked, bloodied lips. 'Now here we are. Here we all are again.'

Ferros could see that it would be the matter of a moment for Lara to do what she had vowed. He could not get across in time to stop her. And though he knew that many watched them, within the circle of the dead, the wounded, the victors, the defeated, now there was somehow only him, Lara and Roxanna.

He spoke slowly, clearly. 'I beg you not to do this, Lara.'

'Beg?' An eyebrow lifted, but her eyes did not rise, staring still into Roxanna's, who stared back. 'It is not a word I have ever heard you use, Ferros. Do you love her that much?'

Ferros breathed, thought. Took a chance, a last battlefield chance. 'I love her as much as I once loved you,' he said. 'Here, beneath the dunes where I taught you to ride, here where we made love under the stars.' He swallowed. 'But you do not love me like that any more. You have not loved me, truly loved me, for many years. I know why. I betrayed you, with the woman you now would kill. There is no excuse for it, and I am sorry for it, so sorry. Yet I was only obsessed with her then. I love her now. And so I beg you to spare her life.'

Lara was so still she could have been a statue in the Sanctum on the Hill. Only her robes moved a little, lifted by Sadrak's hot breath. Finally she spoke. 'I do not think it enough, Ferros. You know what she is – or does love blind you to her nature? She has lived three hundred years, and how many has she killed? How many more will she kill?' She lifted the sword just a little from the neck, and the blade made a small sucking sound as it came away from Roxanna's hot skin. 'Do I not save them, all of them, by ending her life now?'

It was the last thing he could say. He wasn't sure if it would make any difference. But the lifting blade left him no choice. 'By killing her now, you also kill the child she carries. My child.'

Lara swayed at that, and Roxanna lifted her hands just a little. But the blade dropped fast to rest again against the neck, and Lara's eyes still did not rise. 'Your child,' she murmured. 'The one we did not have.'

'The one you chose not to have, Lara,' Ferros whispered.

Again a silence, disturbed only by the moans of the wounded, by some distant cries of agony and terror. Beyond them, far beyond. And then another voice came, gentle, deep.

'Leave her, my love,' it said. 'The time for killing has passed.'

Ferros looked at the one who'd spoken. A tall black man, in the white robes of a Timian Monk, though these were much streaked with blood. He looked familiar; but it took Lara's next words to bring him the name.

'Are you sure of that, Gan?'

'What you have done this day may make it certain.' Gan was moving slowly towards her now. 'Yet if you take this woman's life, and the life within her, I think it will be a sign that the killing must go on.' He reached her, and stretched out his own empty hands. 'Let it end. Show the world that it can end.'

That silence again. Even the moans stilled, as if that whole world, and everyone in it, held its breath, waiting on her reply. Which she gave, simply, without words, by lifting the sword from Roxanna's neck, and placing it in Gan's outstretched, gentle hands.

15
Storming Heaven

Closing the door behind him, Luck leaned against it, and shut his eyes. Though he was no warrior, there had been innumerable times in the last three months when he'd craved the simplicities of war. Peace – not merely a truce, a pause of war, but something that actually had a chance of lasting – was so much more complicated.

Yet they'd made one, at last. He could feel it, through hands pressed to the wood of the door, down the stone of stairs, all the way to the debating chamber. They *vibrated*, not only with the celebrations that were beginning, the music being played, the voices raised, the toasts pledged. It was more than that. As if peace were a tangible thing, in the air they breathed, the ground they stood on, in their very flesh. Like energy made by a lightning strike, or a wave crashing onto a promontory. That energy filled him now and, exhausted though he was, he also felt more alive than he had in most of his four hundred years of existence.

'Is it over?'

Luck opened his eyes. Poum was across the room, sitting where they always sat – in the alcove of a window, looking down into the main courtyard. As usual they were surrounded by books. They devoured them, hungry for the knowledge that had been accumulated over the centuries in the library of the Sanctum. They were learning of this world, this whole, complex world of which they were a part – but in which they were no longer a god. *The* God. Poum had accepted their new state joyfully; the chance to be who they were, not what everyone expected them to be. Though it was difficult to decide what that was, given all that they *had* been. So, while the representatives debated in the chamber below what a newly godless world should look like, Poum sought for their own truth – in books.

Luck shook his head, remembering again some of the earliest debates. It had been harder for those who believed in the One to accept the renunciation of the title than it had been for the One themself. Yet once the leaders of the Four Tribes *had* accepted it – the new leaders, for the old ones had all been killed at the Battle of the Hill – it brought a new energy to the talks. If things would no longer be decided with reference to a god, any god, that left the choice to Man.

And Woman of course. Luck smiled now as he remembered some of the points that Besema and Roxanna had made and rigorously pursued. If before the Corinthian had seemed made for her twin battlefields of war and sex, wearing her tight leather clothes that had allowed her to triumph in both, her new state, growing more visible each day under the flowing dresses she now wore, made her triumphant on this battlefield too. She fought as hard for the cause of peace as she had ever fought in war. Often everyone else, himself included, just stood back wordless and watched her go.

He realised that he'd been lost again to the place he'd just left. That Poum had asked a question. 'It is over,' he replied, going to the table with its jug of ale. He held the jug up, raised an eyebrow at Poum, who shrugged a 'no'. Luck poured a mugful, drank. 'As you can hear,' he said, 'the celebrations are starting.'

Poum closed the book on their lap, slid out of the alcove. 'But what do they celebrate, Father?'

'The hard-fought peace.'

'A contradiction, surely?'

'It is. One I believe has a good chance of being resolved.'

'Why?'

'Because in the end, it is simple. Most people want – need – simplicity.' He took another sip. 'Instead of war, we have chosen peace. Instead of gods,' he indicated both of them, 'we have given them … themselves.'

Poum stared above him for a moment. 'What will they do with themselves, do you think?'

'Rule their own lands, in their own ways. Trade the riches of those lands with each other. Meet every five years here, and discuss any issues that have arisen. Celebrate what joins us, not exploit what divides.'

Poum lifted the book they held. 'It talks of such things in this. An ideal state, where the majority prosper, not just the few.' He shook his head. 'It also tells of how hard that is to achieve and, once achieved, maintain. Ambition keeps getting in the way.'

'It always does. What we have striven for, what scribes are now setting into words, will *not* be easy to maintain. But it is what we have begun this day. There is hope again.' He pointed back with his head, to the noises that had grown even louder below. 'Which is what they have begun to celebrate.'

Poum laid the book down on the pile. 'Do we join these celebrations?'

'No. Because you and I have something else to do. A final task. Something that is as important as anything that was made beyond this door. Something only you and I, in all the world, can do.'

Poum grinned. 'Sounds ominous. What must we do, Father?'

'For one last time,' Luck replied, 'we must travel with Sirene.'

'Ha!' Poum slid out of the alcove. 'To lose ourselves again in smoke in the glass?'

'No. To find these so-called gods,' Luck put down the mug, still half full, 'and get them to leave us alone.'

There were no half measures. To storm heaven, Luck knew they would need the full dose.

They inhaled – and were both gone on the instant, their bodies slumped in chairs, their minds, their spirits free, and together . . .

. . . in darkness. No garden path, no birdsong, no trees dripping blossom. Just a void, in which they knew the other also existed, but nothing else.

Until there was light. A little, and only on her face. Her shrouded face. Under the veil of her hood, Sirene's lips shaped some first words, adding sound to emptiness.

'You have come again, Luck, God of Midgarth. You and the One.'

'Me . . . and Poum.' As he spoke, light showed both his face, and Poum's beside him. 'We are neither of us gods any more. But you will take us now to those who claim they are.'

'You would command me? You know, you have always known, that I cannot be controlled.'

'I also know that you show seekers what they wish most to see.' Luck leaned forward, and the light expanded, haloing his head and shoulders now as well. 'We wish to see them.'

'See?' The smile returned, to lips, to voice. 'That will be difficult, since they have no form. Since they exist mainly as thought.'

'Yet they set you to watch us, did they not? They gave us their . . . interferences, is that what you called them? Gave some few immortality, and those immortals the gift of possession.

Gave a prophecy to another people, a child to fulfil that prophecy.' Luck stepped out of the dark, and Poum followed. Both of them were now covered in light. 'If they can choose to do all that, they can choose a form that we can talk to.'

'You are right,' Sirene replied, moving from her dark … which was gone on the movement, was also made now of light. There was nothing to stand on, yet Luck and Poum stood. As did Sirene.

As did the one who came.

She wore a long gown, deep scarlet in colour and of a style similar to those that Roxanna now wore in Corinthium. She had white hair woven into tresses, with one long one reaching down the length of her back, and a smooth-skinned face. That was unwrinkled, yet also ancient.

'Who are you?' Luck called.

'I am …' She looked down, at her dress, and sighed. 'I have had so many names. So many lives.' She lifted a hand, studied it. 'Melgayne,' she said. 'This one was Melgayne.'

'Melgayne. I am Luck of Midgarth. This is Poum of Ometepe.'

She looked from her hand to them. 'I know who you are. Where you are from.'

'Of course you do. Since you made us.'

'We did not … make *you*.' Her gaze moved from him, to Poum. 'Only them.'

Poum flinched. Silent till then, their voice rasped as it came. 'You made me?'

'Yes. And no. Your parents made you. We … *shaped* you.' She smiled. 'To be using words again is so strange.' She looked at Sirene, silently standing by. 'Do you not find them strange? They mean so many different things. Would it not be easier … ?'

Luck felt it, a shifting in his mind, as if something – someone – sought to open it, let herself in. 'No!' he said firmly. 'We need words. To fix things. As we have just done in our world.'

The feeling, whatever it was, withdrew. Melgayne smiled again. 'Fix? An example there. Do you mean repair or settle?'

'Both.' Luck glanced at Poum, who was still glaring at Melgayne. 'Sirene told me that you interfered on our planet many years ago.'

'She did?' Her grey eyes moved briefly to the shrouded, silent figure. 'She should not have.'

'Because experimenting on creatures that know it damages the experiment?' Poum asked, their voice steeped in venom.

The grey gaze went to them. But before she could answer, Luck continued, 'And ever since she did, though there were many . . . problems we needed to deal with, I have realised something: that all of those problems arose *from* these interferences.'

'Problems? These amazing gifts?'

'They were not gifts!' Poum spat. 'Gifts are given for love. Yours have poisoned our entire world.'

Her voice did not match theirs in anger. Instead, it filled with wonder. 'You, Luck? You would not have chosen to live so long? You would rather not have run as beasts, flown as birds, swum—'

'I would not,' Luck interrupted, 'despite losing the pleasures, because in the end I would not be a plaything.' He thought back, to something he'd seen for the first time, and only recently, in Corinthium. The Timian Monks, to explain their land, their culture, and so what they required from any peace, had put on a performance. They used figures carved from wood, images, with jointed arms, legs, heads, and moved their shadows on a sunlit wall to tell of their lives. These figures – they called them *ashranak* – and the stories they told with them were the core of who they were; their faith, their reason for being. 'No,' Luck continued, 'I would not be your ashranak for four hundred more years of life, and every beast upon the earth.'

It was clear that Melgayne knew the term. 'I remember

another word from one of the worlds I once inhabited, when I still had form. Ingratitude.' She looked straight at Luck and her voice, when it came again, was colder. 'What is it you seek here?'

Luck breathed deep before he spoke. 'To be rid of all interference. The removal of what you call gifts. If that is not done, the peace we have just settled between us will not hold.' He glanced at Poum. 'Another Intitepe will come. Another Peki Asarko. And they will use their powers to enslave others, just as you have enslaved us.'

She stared a moment, then spoke. 'You know that this would mean an end to what you are.'

'Yes.'

'And do all others like you *feel* like you?'

Luck thought. He had not asked any of them. The ones he knew well: he was certain what *their* answer would be. As to those he did not know: he was confident it would be the same, once they knew all. For no one wanted to be ashranak. 'All.'

Melgayne shook her head. 'I disagree. This one's father,' she turned to Poum, 'would have wanted to have lived much longer. To have ruled the whole world for ever. To have possessed beasts, if we had given him that gift as well. We did not – for with that gift and his ambition he would have conquered your world much sooner.' She looked back at Luck. 'And I suspect there are people in your world of Midgarth who would feel very differently from someone like you, who has already had his four hundred years of life.' She tipped her head. 'What of those who are dying even as we speak here? Dying of wounds, of disease. A child drowns. A young mother has her guts eaten away. Do you think they would not thrill in rebirth? Why should we take away that possibility? Also I know of one there who revels in his powers – Peki Asarko. I do not think he would agree with you.' She smiled though there was no humour in it, only a cruel delight. 'I could do what you ask. It is as easy as thought. But why would I? When we have so much more to learn from you ... ashranak?' She turned to Sirene. 'These creatures amused me for a time. Now they bore me. Never trouble me with them again.'

Within her shroud, Sirene frowned. 'I watch for you. But I cannot be controlled – by them, or by you.'

'It does not matter. They are gone. It is as easy as thought.'

Luck, aware that there was nothing he could do, braced for a return to his body. He had failed. He had no power here. Yet even so he was watching Melgayne very closely, so he saw the thought of his dismissal come into her eyes ... then saw the crease appear between them, the puzzlement in that.

'What?' she asked, but of herself.

'I said, I do not think so.'

It was a different voice that spoke, one Luck recognised instantly. He had heard it for most of his long life though he had not thought to hear it ever again, since the speaker was dead. Yet there she was. 'Hello, Freya,' he said.

'Hello, Luck,' Freya replied.

She did not look much different. No older certainly. Death had not aged her at all, nor diminished her beauty. Her fair hair *was* different, cut shorter. She also wore clothes that shone, as if woven through with metal threads, and fitted tight to her body.

'Are you a ghost, Freya?'

'It is a hard question to answer. In this case, words might not help us. Besides,' she turned to Melgayne, who was staring at her, a mix of shock and fury on her face, 'this one needs all my attention. Indeed, I am going to need some help to hold her.'

'I am always here to help you, my love.'

He appeared as he spoke. 'Hovard!' Luck cried.

'Yes, brother, and excuse me.' He stepped beside his wife, both now staring hard at Melgayne.

The shock had left her face. Only that sneer ruled it now. 'You think you can hold me? You lesser gods? You ashranak? Two of you?'

'Maybe not. But do you think three might do it?'

Luck was not shocked by the new appearance. In fact he'd been expecting him.

Bjorn Swift-Sword, like the other two, was dressed in clothes that clung, and shone. Unlike them, he'd kept his hair long. Unlike them, he carried a weapon – Sever-Life, his sword, as ever in the sheath on his back. 'Hail, Luck!' he said, though he did not look at him, only at Melgayne, writhing now under the three gods' invisible grip.

Freya called, but not aloud. In his head, the ability which was the gift she'd given him when they made love the night before he left Askaug to journey to Saghaz-a. *Luck,* she said, *we need your help too.*

He didn't know what he was supposed to do. Assumed that – just like with so much of the knowledge he'd acquired in his life – it would come. So he took a step towards his fellow immortals, bent his mind to the place where they bent theirs.

Yet he did not step, nor bend, alone: Poum moved in beside him.

Luck felt it was like a bout of stararnen – a game his people would play at the midsummer festival all over Midgarth. A game of strength and some cunning. A thick rope would be held by two teams of men and women, each trying to pull it from the other team's grasp. Here the rope was invisible, a line of power running between the five on one side, the ancient god on the other. Each pulled, tried to wrest control from the other's grip.

He did not know how long it lasted. Did not know if time meant anything where – when – they were. Just felt it eventually, a weakening on their side; a giving, a slackening. Felt his fellows redouble their efforts; knew it was in vain. The struggle showed on their faces, in sweat running, in creases forming. In Melgayne's face relaxing.

Failed, Luck thought, even as he strove on, as they all strove on.

Then Melgayne's smile went. Just as Luck knew, as they all must have known, that a new power was surging again from their side.

He could not look to its source, not yet. But he knew it anyway. Because out of the corner of his eye, he saw the flowing white shrouds of Sirene as she stepped in beside them.

With a cry, Melgayne fell forward, as if jerked on the rope. They all staggered but held on, keeping the bind on their opponent. On her knees now, looking up at them in wonder. 'You,' she said, her voice quaking, raising a hand, one finger, to point at Sirene. 'You betray me?'

'There is no you to betray. I am Sirene. And there is only the task you set me. The experiment, which is over.'

As she spoke, she threw back her shroud, and for the first time Luck saw her face – neither man nor woman, old nor young. A human shape and features. Not human.

'Then it is done.' Melgayne rose to her feet. She frowned again, and Luck felt something shift within him. Where there was presence, now there was absence. As if once there'd been liquid, now there was only vapour, and soon not even that.

'I leave you then, to your puny lives,' she said. 'I blink and yours will be over.' She looked at Freya, Hovard and Bjorn in turn. 'Though we three shall meet again. Trust me.'

It was Bjorn who answered with a grin and a tap of Sever-Life on his back. 'Looking forward to it, Melgayne.'

The threat delayed her a moment – which was when Poum spoke.

'One last thing.' They stepped forward. 'If all interferences end, that must include mine.'

'Yours?' Her eyebrows rose. 'But you are already … you.'

'No. I am *them*. And I would not remain so.' They looked at Luck. 'I would be one, not both.'

She stared for a moment, nodded once, and was gone.

Everyone except for Sirene collapsed onto the ground. For a time the only noises that came were heaved gasps. Until Hovard chuckled. 'That was interesting,' he said, turning to Bjorn and Freya. 'We've never tried that before.'

'Very interesting, brother.' Bjorn sat up, rotated his neck. 'Stromvar will be furious he missed it.'

'Stromvar?' Luck got to his feet, then put out a hand to help Freya rise. 'So he is alive too? Where is he?'

'Where? Impossible to describe. When? Also hard to say. Doing what? Now that's easy!' Bjorn grinned. 'He's fighting.'

Luck frowned. 'So there's fighting?'

'Brother,' said Hovard, rising too, 'there's … *everything*.' He put one arm around Freya, one around Luck. 'Come and see.'

'See … *everything*?' Luck grinned. 'But that's all I've ever wanted.'

'So that's settled.' Bjorn, who'd stayed lying on the ground, now sprang up in one easy movement from his knees. 'What are we waiting for?'

He turned – but Luck's voice halted him. 'I cannot.'

'Brother …'

'Cannot.' Luck turned to Poum. His child was smiling at him. They looked … different somehow. 'I have a promise to keep.' He turned back. 'And it won't be too long, will it? I only have the one life to live out, after all.'

'But …'

'Hush, Bjorn.' Freya laid her hand on Luck's arm, squeezed. 'Go keep your promise. We will see you soon enough.'

'We will,' Hovard said, 'and when we do we'll show you,' he

laughed, and stretched his arms wide, 'what immortality truly means.'

They were gone on his words. There were only the three of them again, in the white void. Yet as he looked at Sirene, shrouded once more, Luck saw that her edges were dissolving. 'If all interferences are finished, does that mean you are too, Sirene?' he asked.

'There is still one person in your world who travels with me.'

'Peki Asarko.'

'Yes.'

Luck felt his body flush with heat, with fury, as he thought of the Lord of the Lake of Souls. 'He is the first person I will deal with when I return to Midgarth.'

'You will not need to.' She was nearly gone, edges merging into light. 'For he seeks to travel with me one more time. I plan to show him something ... special.'

Luck stepped towards what was now only a disturbance in the air. 'Stop. You should let us Midgarthians serve justice on our own.'

'Should?' Just a voice now, a whisper on the wind. 'Oh Luck, do you not remember what Anazat told you the first time you journeyed with me? I cannot be controlled. I will do what I will do.' Her voice now came as if from far off. 'Though remember, Luck of Midgarth. The plant I live in remains. So you will always be able to find me, if you need me ... in smoke in the glass.'

All gone. Sirene. Her void. They were back in the Sanctum, sprawled in chairs. In the globe between them, smoke still swirled.

Luck sat up. 'Are you all right?'

Poum sat up too, stretched, arms rising to the ceiling. 'Never better.'

'You know what I want to do now? More than anything?'

'I know. Because it will be the same as me.' A smile came. 'You want to keep your promise.'

In his longhouse, Peki Asarko walked among his creations.

So beautiful, he thought, running fingers along embalmed skin, pushing them through hair he'd cut from his slaves, the tribe that he ruled on the Lake of Souls.

Here was the black-eyed assassin his people had so badly wounded. Had marred with spear and knife. Restored to his youth, his health, by the wonders of their lord's art. Here the young hunter Rukka of Askaug, Bjorn Swift-Sword's friend, who'd strayed to the lake and been caught.

Extra special, he thought, because I took his face and wore it like a mask for a while.

He stroked it now. He'd restored it eventually to the hunter's body, a masterpiece of repair. Now he looked around at all the men and women of the lake, young and old, who'd given themselves, sacrificed themselves to his knives and potions.

He giggled as he touched them. He always did when he thought of how he'd shared his gift of immortality. Though perhaps they might not know it, still they would stare out from the glass eyes he'd fashioned for them ... for ever.

He reached the end of his exhibits, the place where the two longhouses had been joined together. In this one, his art. In the next, where he lived. Before his raised throne on its dais was a table. On that a globe, swirling with smoke. Beside that, a vial.

He frowned. It was time. He moved to the table, sat. No face had appeared in the glass for three months. He'd several times now used a couple of drops, enough to call Anazat. But the black-eyed monk had not come. He looked again at the vial. So little left.

He scratched the back of his hand, mumbling. He could not waste any more. He had to learn what had happened in the world. With Anazat silent, he'd sent spies out. None had come back. So now he would use all the drug he had left and journey himself. First, with Sirene here. Later, in person. He would have to find more of her. He could not live without her.

He looked at his hand. He couldn't understand why the rash there had grown so large, a fiery patch of reddened skin. Yes, he'd scratched at it. But the healing powers of a god meant that it should have gone away overnight. This hadn't. It had grown. Tormented his sleep, and his days.

Another question I will answer, he thought. Picking up the vial, he did not hesitate. Just poured all its contents onto the glass, leaned in, breathed deep.

He couldn't understand it. There was no motion. No falling, no dark void, leading to eventual light. No … delight. All the other times he'd gone to places and times where he could do things, *be* things, he could not do and be even on the Lake of Souls, where he could do almost anything to the slave-people who worshipped him. But this time? He had not even left his longhouse. In the glass, smoke still swirled.

Where was Sirene? She should be there to guide him!

'Where are you?' he called.

'I am here.'

The low voice came from behind him. He jumped, turned.

There she was, standing in the middle of his creations, her white robes swirling among the silent, frozen bodies.

He rose. 'Why are we still here?' he whined. 'Come, take me. We must journey. There are things I must know.'

'This is the journey, Peki Asarko. All you need to learn is here as well.'

Peki felt pain, looked down. He'd scratched his skin even harder. The rash had erupted and bled. He raised it to his lips, sucked at it, then looked again for Sirene.

She had moved, gone deeper into the crowd of preserved

bodies. But they ... they had moved too. All had been turned to face him. No, he suddenly realised, they had not been turned. They had turned themselves.

He cried out, lurched back, stumbling into his chair. But then he remembered: this was Sirene's doing. Sometimes his journeys with her had begun in just such strange ways. In something like a nightmare, for the drug worked on who he was ... and he had seen terrible things in his three hundred years of life. Done terrible things. But nightmare always – *always* – gave way to joy.

That was it! Now he even smiled. 'Take me,' he said, closing his eyes, stretching out his arms.

'I will not,' Sirene replied, 'but they surely will.'

Peki opened his eyes. His creations had moved again. *Were* moving. Leading them was Rukka the Handsome, light glimmering in eyes made of coloured glass. Beside him walked the assassin, his own black orbs gleaming, lit by inner fire. Behind them came the others. Silent. Staring.

Alive.

It was a dream, nothing more. It was Sirene. He knew it, yet still he cried out, and turned to flee. Lurched to a halt.

The doors of the longhouse had been flung wide. In the entrance stood a crowd of tribesmen. Men and women, with their children before them. The children who he loved. Who loved him. Except now he did not see love in their eyes. He saw its opposite. While in the hands of their parents he saw ... rope, blade, flame.

'No!' he yelled, staggering back.

A hand gripped his shoulder, turned him around.

More eyes there. Green, blue, black. Made of glass.

Filled with hate.

As he was forced to his knees, as the first blade cut him,

he cried out to her who would end the horror. 'Help me!' he screamed.

But Sirene was no longer there.

Epilogue

It was a beautiful day on the mountain, the warmth of the short summer still there, with not even a cool finger in the breeze blowing over the peak, come from the mountains of Midgarth, to remind Atisha that it would be over all too soon.

She'd prepared a basket of treats – pastries and sweetmeats – and taken Bjorn and Freya to the stream. Ufda's puppies had followed of course and the young ones, human and dog, splashed in the shallows while she lay on the bank, enjoying the sun, staring up into the cloudless sky, and the peak they called Hawk's Crag.

She could not help it, but every time she looked there, at the trail that led over it, she saw Luck, felt his last kiss on her lips. Saw her child moving away from her, not looking back. She went over it again, yet again. Tried to change it, that past. Refuse to be left behind, insist on going, helping, fighting at her child and her husband's side. When the past would not change, she imagined a future. Saw them walking back over the crest; saw movement there each time, born of hope; that hope dissolving as she recognised a mountain sheep moving, or cloud shadow changing shape.

Then the reasons she hadn't gone were before her, both of them, complaining about some childhood unfairness the other had worked against them. She soothed it away with honeyed cake, the sweetness of berry cream. When they'd eaten, all grumbles forgotten, and run off again to rejoin the dogs, she lay back, looked once again to the peak …

… and watched an air globe fly over it.

She'd seen so many things that were not there over the months they'd been gone she wasn't certain at first that what she saw was real. Until the young ones confirmed it, children shrieking and running, puppies barking and chasing them.

She rose, tried to keep all her hopes and all her fears down, as she walked into the valley where the ground was level and onto which the air globe was descending.

It was low enough, soon enough, for her to see Luck's face, and her happiness in that equalled her fear because she knew he would not have returned alone unless … and then she saw the other face – *their* face – so she could breathe again.

Then it was all one joy, as the basket landed, bounced, almost tipped, settled. The joy of faces. The wrinkled one of Besema, grinning as she closed off her furnace valves. The ecstatic one of Luck, coming close fast, kissing her three times and hard before he was pulled to the ground by screaming children and smothered on the instant by puppies. Finally, at last, rising from the anchors where they'd tethered down the globe, her child, her Poum. *Her* One, no one else's.

She took the face she loved in both her hands. Did not kiss it, could not trust anything but her eyes and her fingers. Poum had changed. The child was gone completely now. There was something else though. Something even stronger in the face. Some certainty, that had never been there before.

The question was in her eyes. Poum answered it. 'Yes, Mother. I am not *them* any more. I am *I*.'

'Who?' she croaked, coughed, found her voice. 'Who are you?'

Poum smiled. 'I am ...'

THE END

So ends *The Wars of Gods and Men*,
Book Three of the Immortals' Blood Trilogy.

Author's Note

If, as I believe, every novel is a journey … what a long, strange and fascinating one these three have been.

The idea for the Immortal's Blood Trilogy began four years ago with a hint from my then agent, Mike Bryan, that 'fantasy is a strong market right now' and then continued with the writing of a single word in the centre of a blank sheet of paper.

Immortality.

Don't know why, but the idea of it intrigued me. I riffed on it on that page, drawing word association bubbles. From blankness came something, enough to begin to form a plot of sorts. From a word, to a single page to a fifteen page treatment, those bubbles now expanding largely in my head. Mike drew in an editor – Marcus Gipps of Gollancz. Marcus asked questions, asked for more … bubbles. I ended up writing six chapters. He gave me a commission for three books.

The thing was that though I had written more than I usually would to land the deal, and had a good idea of some central characters and their plotlines, I still didn't truly know where I was going. It is the way I write – the story tells me the story, the characters ask me their questions, I follow the leads I am given. Sometimes they lead me up blind alleys. Sometimes they blind me with their light.

I coined a phrase once: Writing is Writing. It is in the act of the writing that things happen, things you could not really plan. It does not mean that I never plot ahead, or consider character traits and arcs. But I keep them very loose. I like to be surprised – and sometimes appalled – by the way my mind works.

There were many cases in these books where things didn't work out as half-planned, but worked out way better. I really thought when setting out that Lara would be sacrificed early, to free Ferros to pursue his destiny with Roxanna. I believed that almost up to the moment when she has her throat cut in the suicides' ceremony – then halted the falling blade and wondered what it would be like if she lived. What would Ferros be like when pulled between old and new loves. Lara became one of my absolute favourite characters to write, her journey so far-reaching. I'd also planned on killing off Intitepe in Book One. Again, he demanded that he stay. As the plot became more complex, as the world grew larger and more peopled, the Fire King became one of its prime movers.

It was also fascinating to me to bring in Poum – a character who had driven so much of the plot and yet couldn't affect it till they came of age in Book Three. I wondered what it would be like to be the focus of destiny, to be seen as a saviour and unifier of worlds yet to have no control over their own life. I admit I was daunted when I began the final book – so many strong characters demanded their page time, how could I do justice to another one? Yet I feel I did, that 'they' were indeed essential to bring all the complex plotlines together. (I suppose it helped that I gave myself some room by killing off three main characters in *The Coming of the Dark*).

There were two other main aspects of the book that started peripherally and became central: Sirene, and the idea of the 'over' gods. To have a drug that was personified I just thought was a really cool idea. That she could affect the plot never occurred to me. I also was going to run the Over Gods as a kind of chorus, commenting on everything, bringing us up to date at the beginning and end of books. It was very late on when I decided that it would be huge fun to challenge them, and actually storm heaven.

Ah me! There is so much more I could talk about. Every character presented challenges, demanded 'page time', had to fulfil their destinies within the confines of what became a hugely labyrinthine plot. Now I am at the end of the journey though, I think I'll leave them to speak for themselves. Though I suspect – and hope – you will all let me know if you disagree and need some further explanations.

For now though, let me conclude with a thank you to all who helped me in this journey.

Mike Bryan was the agent who suggested the new direction and then both he and his business (and life) partner, the wonderful Heather Adams, suggested great ways to proceed. The Gollancz team were also terrific. Paul Stark sorted out the audiobooks wonderfully. Brendan Durkin organized everything superbly well. Elizabeth Dobson was my strict and super smart copy editor for all three books – and saved me much grief from basic grammatical errors and loss of timeline details. Above all there was Marcus Gipps who brought me aboard and made such great suggestions throughout the long process.

So here we are at the end of the journey ... or are we? Just as I am never entirely sure if a character I intend to kill off will actually die, so I am sure that most endings, like most beginnings, are fairly arbitrary. I like to leave some loose ends, just in case. And in this case ... what's with Freya, Hovard and Bjorn and those shiny suits?

Maybe I need to write the words 'science fiction' in the centre of another blank piece of paper.

Chris Humphreys
Salt Spring Island, BC, Canada
25 August 2021

Glossary

Corinthium:

Sevrapol – the fourth hill. Entertainment district of the city
Asprodon – Assani God of Mayhem and Lust. Also, underground sin city
Kristun – famous historical victory over the Wattenwolden
Lamulin – a type of armour
Danari, Wobelani, Mishrani – Cuerdocian border tribes
Perilonos – sixth hill.
Serang – venomous snake
Omersh – island with pirates
Torba – stringed instrument
Centano – coinage
Mavros – God of War
Simbala – goddess
Timian Monks of Xan
Sadrak – supreme god of Xan
Breath of Sadrak – hot wind from south, also known as kana
aliantha – a type of wood, often used in carving
manala, robara – Xanian plants
katan – Timian Monks' time of sacred wandering
rodun – wind from north
bestrel – a baton

kazana – Monk's spear/axe
ashranak – Xanian puppets

Saghaz-a (Land of the Four Tribes):
Saghaz-a-akana – literally, 'The Little Land of Joy'. What they now call Corinthium
taramazak – Horse Lords' name for themselves. Literally, 'those who hunt from the horse'
azama-klosh – a type of bison
pazamor-ash – pirates; literally, 'the devils of the flood'
paza – little doe
Billandah – Northern port
tolanpa-sen – the common tongue of Saghaz-a; literally, 'the only word'
ascrami – 'mad fighters' or expendables. The first wave of attack
Sirkesami's breath – poisonous mist

Midgarth:
stringen – plant, a purgative
Inge-gerd – goddess of all waters
Raina – goddess of fertility
sorghan – a fish, a type of lake perch
Palur – Northern forests
Havfor – their name for the Blue Moon
stararnen – tug of war

Ometepe:
munke – a kind of basket
bura – luck
aztapi – the Blue Moon
marana – a type of harem
Palaga – northern region

Volpaio – southern region
Bunami – common language of Ometepe

Wattenwolden:
aurens – giant wild ox
Varinger – father god
Karatha – the Afterworld

Credits

Chris Humphreys and Gollancz would like to thank everyone at Orion who worked on the publication of *The Wars of Gods and Men* in the UK.

Editorial
Marcus Gipps
Claire Ormsby-Potter

Copy editor
Elizabeth Dobson

Proof reader
Gabriella Nemeth

Audio
Paul Stark

Contracts
Anne Goddard
Paul Bulos
Jake Alderson

Design
Lucie Stericker
Joanna Ridley
Nick May

Editorial Management
Charlie Panayiotou
Jane Hughes
Alice Davis

Finance
Jennifer Muchan
Jasdip Nandra
Afeera Ahmed
Elizabeth Beaumont
Sue Baker

Marketing
Lucy Cameron

Production
Paul Hussey

Publicity
Will O'Mullane

Sales
Jen Wilson
Esther Waters
Victoria Laws
Rachael Hum
Ellie Kyrke-Smith
Frances Doyle
Georgina Cutler

Operations
Jo Jacobs
Sharon Willis
Lisa Pryde
Lucy Brem